A
Stirri...

THE STEEPWOOD
Scandals

VOLUME EIGHT

When the debauched Marquis of Sywell won Steepwood
Abbey years ago at cards, it led to the death of the Earl
of Yardley. Now he's caused scandal again by marrying
a girl out of his class – and young enough to be his
granddaughter! After being married only a short time,
the Marchioness has disappeared, leaving no trace of her
whereabouts. There is every expectation that yet more
scandals will emerge, though no one yet knows just
how shocking they will be.

The four villages surrounding the Steepwood Abbey
estate are in turmoil, not only with the dire goings-on at
the Abbey, but also with their own affairs. Each of the
eight volumes in THE STEEPWOOD SCANDALS
contains two full novels that follow the mystery behind
the disappearance of the young woman, and the
individual romances of lovers connected in some way
with the intrigue.

THE STEEPWOOD
Scandals

*Regency drama, intrigue, mischief...
and marriage*

THE STEEPWOOD
Scandals

Volume 8

Sylvia Andrew & Paula Marshall

*M&B™ and M&B™ with the Rose Device
are trademarks of the publisher.*

*Harlequin Mills & Boon Limited, Eton House,
18-24 Paradise Road, Richmond, Surrey TW9 1SR*

First published in Great Britain in 2002

THE STEEPWOOD SCANDALS © Harlequin Books S.A. 2007

An Inescapable Match © Harlequin Books S.A. 2002
The Missing Marchioness © Harlequin Books S.A. 2002

*Special thanks and acknowledgement are given to Sylvia Andrew
and Paula Marshall for their contribution to
The Steepwood Scandals series*

ISBN: 978 0 263 85502 9

052-0607

*Printed and bound in Spain
by Litografía Rosés S.A., Barcelona*

An Inescapable Match

by

Sylvia Andrew

Sylvia Andrew taught modern languages for a number of years, ultimately becoming Vice-Principal of a sixth-form college. She lives in Somerset with two cats, a dog, and a husband who has a very necessary sense of humour and a stern approach to punctuation. Sylvia has one daughter living in London and they share a lively interest in the theatre. She describes herself as an 'unrepentant romantic'.

Chapter One

July 1812

The curricle hardly slowed down at all as it swept off the main London highway into the narrow road leading to Abbot Quincey. But the driver judged to a nicety the difficult angle of the turn, controlling his two spirited horses with confident hands. Though it was obvious that he knew the road well, it was nevertheless an impressive demonstration of skill and strength. It was an attractive picture, too—a pair of perfectly matched bays, the tall blond young driver, and behind him his groom sitting stiffly upright—all in a verdant countryside under a cobalt blue sky. Hugo Perceval, heir to Sir James Perceval of Perceval Hall, was on his way back to the village of Abbot Quincey after a morning visit to Northampton.

Timothy Potts, the groom, allowed himself a rare nod of approval at the expert negotiation of the turn. Then, as the road straightened out ahead, empty except for a tiny figure in the distance, he relaxed and allowed his thoughts to wander… He was very fortunate in his master. The guv'nor was a nonpareil, no doubt about that! Whether in the town or in the country he always seemed to know what he was about. Of course, some would say he had been luckier than most, Nature having been very generous in her gifts. A fine, strong, handsome young fellow, he was, and good at everything he did. A proper gentleman and a very fair master. No showy exhibitions, no excesses, no sudden starts or tantrums. Always reasonable, but he wouldn't stand any nonsense, not from anyone! Though he seldom raised his voice, when the guv'nor spoke in a certain tone they all jumped to it…

Timothy Potts's musings were brought to a sudden halt when Hugo gave an exclamation and drew the horses up level with the slight figure of a girl, who stood by the milestone on the verge waiting for them to pass. Her face was pale, and dominated by a pointed chin and huge, shadowed eyes. She wore a white muslin dress which was creased and dirty, and a straw hat one side of which was badly tattered. But what made the ensemble really remarkable was the presence of a tall cage covered in a duster on the ground at her side, and a large animal, something like a dog, which was at the end of a piece of rope she was holding in her hand.

With a quick command to the groom to go to the horses' heads, Hugo jumped down from the curricle. 'Deborah? Deborah Staunton? What the *devil* are you doing here?' The dog, taking exception to Hugo's tone, growled ominously. 'And what in the name of heaven is that ill-tempered animal?'

Miss Staunton eyed him resentfully. Fate was really very unkind. She was tired, dirty and hot. The dog had chewed her best straw hat, and her arms and fingers were sore from carrying that wretched cage. The ill-luck that had dogged her for the past week didn't seem to have changed. When she had last seen Hugo Perceval he had been expressing—forcibly—his desire never to have anything more to do with her, and he didn't appear to have changed his mind. She had hoped to encounter some kindly soul, a farmer or one of the villagers, who would help her on the road to Abbot Quincey, but this was the first vehicle she had seen. Why did it have to belong to the last man in Northamptonshire she wanted to meet like this?

'Well?' said Hugo impatiently.

Miss Staunton straightened her shoulders and rallied. Four years had passed since Hugo's harsh words to her—four years in which she had learned that life was seldom fair, and that the weak usually went to the wall. She was no longer a tender-hearted sixteen-year-old, and she wasn't about to let Hugo Perceval treat her in his usual high-handed fashion!

'Really, Hugo! It's a dog, of course! And Autolycus isn't at all ill-tempered—he just didn't like the way you spoke to me. To tell the truth, nor did I!'

The groom turned and regarded her with astonishment. Not many people—least of all little dabs of females—spoke to the guv'nor in this manner!

Hugo took a breath, then said carefully, 'I'm sorry. It was a surprise. I didn't know you were in the district.'

'I haven't been. I'm just arriving.'

'And this is your luggage?' Hugo said with an expressive glance at the cage and the dog. 'All of it?'

Miss Staunton bit her lip. 'N…not all of it. I had to leave the rest in the inn at the crossroads. Nanny Humble stayed with it. I was hoping that Aunt Elizabeth would send someone to collect her.'

A look of foreboding crossed Hugo's face. 'What happened?' he asked.

'I… I'm not sure I want to tell you, Hugo. You'll only lose patience with me. But if you would take a message to the Vicarage I would be very obliged to you.'

He shook his head. 'You're out of luck. There's no one there. Except for me, the whole family is spending the day with the Vernons at Stoke Park.'

Miss Staunton sat down rather suddenly on the milestone. 'Oh dear!' she said.

'Weren't they expecting you?'

'Well…not exactly. Not today. I've come two days early, you see.'

Hugo took a deep breath. 'You'd better tell me,' he said with resignation. 'Just the bare bones.'

Miss Staunton swallowed her resentment and said with dignity, 'I had to come early for reasons which I won't go into here. But Mr Hobson refused to take us further than the crossroads.'

'Who is Mr Hobson?'

'The owner of the dogcart. I paid him to bring us from Maids Moreton.'

'The dogcart? You mean to tell me that you've come twenty miles in a *dogcart*? You must be mad!'

'No, Hugo. Just…just not very rich. But I think I must have miscalculated the distance when making the arrangement with Mr Hobson. When we reached Yardley Gobion he said he'd done the distance we agreed. He wanted more money before he would go any further. It was most unreasonable of him, for what could I have done in Yardley Gobion?'

'What indeed?'

'I finally managed to persuade him to come as far as the crossroads at the end of the road here, but he wouldn't come a yard further unless I paid him some more. And…and I couldn't do that.'

'You didn't have the means?'

Miss Staunton nodded. 'Because of Mrs Dearborne's hat.'

Hugo regarded her with fascination. He said after a pause, 'I'm not going to ask about Mrs Dearborne's hat. It will have to wait. But the situation, as I understand it, is that Mr Hobson and his dogcart have gone off back to Maids Moreton…'

'Buckingham. He comes from Buckingham.'

'Buckingham, leaving your servant and all your worldly goods at the Travellers' Rest. And there they will stay until you can find some way of conveying them to the Vicarage. Meanwhile, *you* have been forced to walk the three miles to Abbot Quincey in the heat of the day, accompanied by a large dog and…what *is* in the cage, anyway?' He twitched the cover away. A sleepy green parrot with a bright blue and yellow head looked at him with irritation and swore picturesquely. Hugo took a step back.

'Good God!'

'Hugo! Look what you've done! He was asleep and now you've woken him up!' Deborah snatched the cloth from Hugo's grasp and rearranged it over the cage. The parrot muttered for a moment then grew silent.

'Deborah Staunton, do you mean to tell me that you're taking that—' Hugo pointed an accusing finger at the cage— 'that parrot to *Aunt Elizabeth*? At the *Vicarage*?' His finger shifted to the dog, now sitting scratching his fleas. 'And the dog, too? What on earth were you thinking of?'

'I couldn't very well leave them behind in Maids Moreton, could I?'

'I don't know. But you must have windmills in your head if you expect Aunt Elizabeth to take them in—especially if the parrot often says the sort of thing I've just heard. And do you mind telling me why you found it necessary to drag them with you along this road? Why on earth didn't you leave them with Nanny Humble at the inn?'

'Er… It wasn't possible.'

Hugo looked at Miss Staunton's companions and nodded. 'I suppose the landlord refused to have them?'

Miss Staunton hung her head. 'The landlord's wife took great offence at something the parrot said to her. And she caught Autolycus stealing… Well, he was very hungry, Hugo! I must say I think it was very foolish of her to leave a whole leg of mutton out on the table.'

Hugo surveyed her grimly. 'You haven't lost your talent for getting into trouble, have you?'

'I do try not to, Hugo.' Miss Staunton sighed. 'Things just seem to happen. And I've had so much to deal with…'

'And now there's no one at the Vicarage today to help you…' Hugo eyed her for a moment, then, with the air of a man facing the inevitable, he said reluctantly, 'Very well, I shall have to take you to the Hall. I haven't room in the curricle for the animals, but we'll tie the dog to that tree over there—he'll be all right in the shade. And the parrot can stay with him. As soon as we get to the Hall we'll send someone to fetch Nanny Humble and the rest of your things. They can pick up these two, as well.'

'Hugo! I wouldn't dream of tying Autolycus to a tree and leaving him behind. Nor will I leave the parrot. Autolycus and the parrot both stay with me.'

'Don't be such a simpleton, Deborah! I can't take you all. There isn't nearly enough room in the curricle.'

'I won't leave them behind!' said Miss Staunton stubbornly. Autolycus, hearing further sounds of disagreement, left his fleas to their own devices, got up bristling, and growled again. He advanced on Hugo.

'*Down*, sir!'

The authority in Hugo's voice stopped the dog in his tracks. He looked uncertainly at Miss Staunton, who took a firmer hold of the rope and said gently, 'Sit, Autolycus dear.' The dog looked again at Hugo.

'*Sit!*'

Autolycus sat. Hugo nodded in satisfaction and then turned to Miss Staunton. 'You will leave the dog and the bird here,' he said, quite pleasantly, 'and I promise that they will be collected within the hour. Come, no more nonsense! Get in, there's a good girl. My horses won't tolerate this heat much longer. Get into the curricle, Deborah.'

'I will not!'

Timothy Potts peered round to gaze again at the creature who had dared to oppose his master's will with such determination. She looked as if a breath of wind would blow her away, but the pointed chin was raised in defiance, and her voice was firm.

'It's no use your trying to bully me, Hugo. My mind is quite made up. The animals and I stay together. So pray continue on your way, and let me continue on mine.' With this she picked up the cage, gave the rope a slight tug and set off towards Abbot Quincey.

'Stop!' She paused without turning round. Hugo ran his hand through his hair and said in exasperation, 'I can't leave you to walk the rest of the way in this heat. Be reasonable, Deborah. Look—the animals would do perfectly well in the shade over there, and it wouldn't be long before they were collected.'

Miss Staunton hesitated, and Hugo pressed his advantage. 'I'll come for them myself, if you insist,' he added with a persuasively charming smile.

'Very well. I'll see if they will stay,' she said, as she coaxed Autolycus over to the tree. Hugo shook his head at such soft-heartedness.

But the animals refused to stay for even two seconds. When Miss Staunton moved away, Autolycus sat down and howled long and mournfully as soon as he found he could not follow. The parrot took exception to this powerful lament and danced on his perch with loud squawks and raucously vulgar cries. It was an impressive duet and the sound echoed far and wide across the peaceful countryside.

'For God's sake!' said Hugo disgustedly. 'I can't bear it. You've won, the three of you. Deborah, you can take that parrot on your knee, and the dog can run alongside. Hold the horses, Potts, while I release that misbegotten hearthrug.' Autolycus who had apparently regarded this last remark as a compliment of no mean order, stood wagging his tail and very ready to oblige. 'Right!' Hugo released the dog and walked to the curricle. 'Now, sir! Come here!' This command was obeyed with such enthusiasm that Hugo staggered under the onslaught. *'Down, sir!'* he roared, brushing his previously immaculate coat. It was evident that cattle had recently sought shade under the tree. Autolycus grovelled with an anxious look up at his new friend. Hugo took the rope and tied it to the side of the curricle. 'That dog needs a few lessons in manners, I don't trust him to behave properly. Let's hope that somewhere in the general medley there's carriage-dog ancestry.'

'He's half Dalmatian,' Deborah informed him. 'And half Irish wolfhound. I think.'

'I suppose that might account for his...unusual appearance,' said Hugo.

Deborah fired up in defence of her pet. 'He's lovely!' she said fiercely. 'And he's been out quite often with Mrs Dearborne's gig.'

'Good! Potts, if the dog starts pulling away, let him loose—understand? He could pull the lot of us over.'

Hugo got into his seat. 'Let them go, Potts!' The curricle moved slowly off, the horses, impatient at the
delay, kept to a moderate pace under Hugo's iron
hand.

All went well, though the sight was now curious,
rather than stylish. The driver was, as before, blond,
tall, handsome and still reasonably immaculate. But
the pace was considerably less dashing. Other than a
tattered straw hat leaning out to the side, nothing
could be seen of his passenger, hidden as she was
behind a large, duster-covered cage. The groom's upright posture in the rumble seat was somewhat spoilt
by his nervous hold on a rope knotted round the rail.
And at the end of the rope was a dog, clearly having
the time of its life, as it loped alongside the curricle,
waving its tail like a banner. It was hard to say what
colour it was, for its coat was half plain, half a patch-
work of white, brindle and fawn with touches of
black. But though so large, it looked amiable enough,
a large black patch over one eye giving it a comically
rakish air.

As the combination approached Abbot Quincey,
the duster slipped off the parrot's cage and the bird
woke up again. It mistook the motion of the carriage
for the movement of a ship and began to cry raucously, 'Belay, there! Avast, you lubbers!' with other
comments of a similar but less polite character. Miss
Staunton had some difficulty in covering the cage
again, and long before she did so half the population
of Abbot Quincey was grinning at Hugo and his load.
It was a relief when they reached the drive up to the
Hall on other side of the village.

'You've done it again, Deborah,' said Hugo grimly as they came to a halt in the courtyard.

'What do you mean?'

'You've made a laughing stock of me. Just as you did in London.'

'Oh no, Hugo! That wasn't nearly as bad as what happened in London. I thought those people in the village were enjoying it in a…a *friendly* kind of way. They like you.' Miss Staunton shuddered. 'That was nothing like what happened in London.' Then after a pause she said wistfully, 'I so hoped you had forgotten that episode. That we could begin again, and be friendly as we were in the old days, when we were children. You didn't seem to mind so much when I got into scrapes then. But you're still angry, aren't you? Even after four years.' When he frowned, she added, 'I was very *young*, Hugo…'

He looked down at her with a reluctant twinkle in his eye. 'It took me a long time to regain credibility with my friends after wading out of that lake.'

'But I didn't *mean* to upset the boat, Hugo!'

'Oh, I know you never *mean* to. But you never seem to learn, either! I've lost count of the times I've been the victim of your not *meaning* to! You were only in London for a month, but I spent a small fortune getting you out of trouble one way or another. And in the process you managed to get me bitten by a dog, set upon by footpads, accused of abduction… I can't remember the rest. Falling into the lake was the last straw. And it was *all* brought about without your meaning to!'

'That last time you were so angry. You said you never wanted to see me again.'

'Did I? Well, if I did, it was probably prompted by an instinct of self-preservation. I didn't like to imagine what you might do next!' He looked at her crestfallen expression. 'But you're right. That's all in the past and should be forgotten. I'm not angry any more, Deborah.'

'I've grown up a lot since then, Hugo.'

Hugo cast an eye over the dog and the parrot. 'Have you? I'm relieved to hear it.'

'I swear I'll be more careful in the future! Are we…are we friends?'

He got down, untied Autolycus, then came round to take the cage from her. 'I suppose so.' He smiled at her. 'I can't be at odds with my little cousin, can I?' His face was on a level with hers.

'I…I'm not your cousin,' she stammered. 'I'm a cousin of your cousins, remember?'

'I've always thought of you as a cousin of mine, too. And now you'll be living with them at the Vicarage, won't you? Come, we must arrange for one of the men to pick Nanny Humble up. Will he need to take some money with him? Have you any other debts?'

Miss Staunton, somewhat out of breath, got down and followed her rescuer through the courtyard, hurrying to keep up with Hugo's long strides.

'It would be a good idea to pay the landlady at the Traveller's Rest something… She was quite upset about Autolycus and the meat. But you must keep a careful account of what you spend. I shall pay it all back.'

Hugo looked down at her with a certain amount of sympathy. The sum was insignificant. But how was Deborah Staunton, who was as near destitute as made no difference, planning to pay back anything at all?

'We'll sort all that out later,' he said. 'Meanwhile I shall put you into the hands of the housekeeper, while I see to things. I propose to put your canine friend in an empty stable. He must be tired and thirsty after that run. He'll probably sleep. Will he want more to eat?'

'Autolycus always wants more to eat. It would help him to settle down if you gave him something.'

Hugo handed Miss Staunton and the parrot over to the housekeeper, then disappeared. Mrs Banks, who had been with the Perceval family since before Hugo was born, accepted without comment the advent of an exotic new pet, saw it settled on a table in the small parlour, then turned her attention to Miss Deborah.

By the time Hugo came into the parlour Miss Staunton was looking a lot more respectable—she had had a wash, her dress had been shaken and pressed and her hair had been brushed and tied up again.

'That's all settled. Autolycus has had a good meal, and is now snoring off his exertions of the day. I've despatched a carriage to collect your nurse and possessions. They should be back within the hour, and we can all go over to the Vicarage when they arrive. Meanwhile I think we would both like some refreshment. It's very hot—would you like to sit outside under the cedar?'

Deborah nodded silently, and Hugo went to give the necessary orders. She wandered into the garden and sat down in the shade. It was four years since she had last seen Hugo, but he was the same as ever— autocratic, decisive, efficient. And underneath it all, very kind. The Vicarage girls all adored him, though they were very much in awe of him. As the eldest of the young generation of Percevals, Hugo had always taken his responsibilities towards them all very seriously. Deborah knew that he had counted her among those responsibilities, even though their actual connection was remote. Her mother's sister, Elizabeth, was married to Hugo's Uncle William, his father's brother, and the vicar of Abbot Quincey.

Deborah's parents' marriage had been a difficult one, and as a child she had often spent months at Abbot Quincey, joining the games and pastimes of her Vicarage cousins and the three Perceval children from the Hall. Herself an only child, at home she had often been lonely, left to her own devices. Those months at the Vicarage had been the happiest times of her young life, and Hugo, who was quite a few years older than the rest of them, had been her hero and chief confidant.

And now Hugo still seemed to regard her as one of his flock. Apparently, even though he had just returned home himself after ten years spent among the very highest London society, the old habit refused to die. It might have wavered four years before after the disasters she had brought about during her short visit to the capital, but the old feeling seemed to have survived, after all.

Deborah was not sure whether she was glad of this or not. It had certainly helped today. She would have been at her wits' end without Hugo's intervention. But though she seldom allowed herself to dwell on the true state of her feelings towards Hugo Perceval, she had never regarded him with the same awe as her cousins did. They were gentle, affectionate, biddable girls and she loved them all dearly. But they would never dream of disagreeing with anything Hugo said. Deborah was by nature more critical, and recent events had forced her to be more independent. Life had not dealt as kindly with her as it had with the young Percevals. Ever since her father's death she had had to be strong enough to make decisions for herself and her mother. She had grown used to it. And she wondered whether she might find Hugo's calm assumption of authority a touch overbearing…

They were so different, too, she and Hugo. He set himself and everyone else a high standard of perfection in dress, conversation, manners…in anything he undertook. Nothing was left to chance in Hugo's scheme of things. In contrast, Deborah's own life had always been chaotic. She had always been inclined to act first and ponder on the consequences afterwards, and, obliged though she was for the many times he had rescued her, she had often found Hugo's calm forethought and assurance irritating… She had frequently had to battle with a desire to shake that complacency.

But when he met her in London, she had been feel-

ing very lost. She had been so grateful for his attempts
to ease her passage into society, but what had she
done in return? She had turned his perfect life upside
down, and made him an object of ridicule to his acquaintances. No wonder he had been so angry with
her...

'That's fixed. Now, Deborah Staunton, I want to
hear your explanation!' Hugo had come back while
she had been dreaming and was sitting on the other
side of the small teatable.

'Where do you want me to begin?'

'With Mrs Dearborne's hat, of course! My guess is
that Autolycus had a hand in it. Or do I mean a paw?'

'You're right, as usual. Autolycus cannot resist a
nice straw hat.'

'So I see,' he said, eyeing the tattered straw on her
own head. 'And did Mrs Dearborne make you pay for
another?'

'I had to offer—and she accepted! It was new, of
course. One of those big ones with lots of ribbon
and...and feathers. It was very expensive, Hugo.' She
started to chuckle. 'It was almost worth it just to see
Autolycus running off with feathers streaming out of
his mouth and Mrs Dearborne in full pursuit. She
is...is quite a portly lady, and was soon out of breath.
But when I caught him in the end, the hat was ruined.
I must say that I think Mrs Dearborne was very severe. After all, I *had* taken the parrot off her hands!
And—'

'One moment. Why did you take the parrot?'

'Well, someone had to! Mrs Dearborne didn't want it any more and no one else would have it.'

'And how did Mrs Dearborne, whom I am growing to dislike, come to have a parrot with such an exotic vocabulary?'

'Her lodger, who had been a sailor, passed it on to her before he left. She thought it would be company. But then she discovered its...its...er...social disadvantages. The ladies of Maids Moreton were quite shocked by some of the things it said.'

'I can well imagine it. Carry on.'

'Well, even though I had helped her out with the parrot, Mrs Dearborne was very angry with Autolycus... So I paid. And that meant I didn't have quite enough for the journey.'

'Where was your aunt while this excitement was going on? Your father's sister, I mean. I thought she was looking after you?'

Deborah paused for a moment. Then she said awkwardly, 'She left. She went back to Ireland the day before yesterday.'

'What? Leaving you to look after yourself?' Hugo was shocked. 'I can't believe it!'

'She went very suddenly. Of course, she had arranged to go back to Ireland soon, anyway. She always knew that I would eventually make my home with Aunt Elizabeth after Mama died. But why she left Maids Moreton with so little warning, I don't know. It was very awkward. After she'd gone there was hardly any money, and I wasn't sure if Aunt Elizabeth would be back from London after Robina's come-out.' Then with a lightning change of mood

which was typical she said, 'Oh, Hugo, I quite forgot
to ask! Do tell me! How did Robina do? Was her
début a success?'

'You could say so. From what I observed, Cousin
Robina is going to make a very good match. She's in
Brighton with the Dowager Lady Exmouth at the mo-
ment.'

'You mean she might marry Lord Exmouth?...
How wonderful! But she deserves it! She's so pretty,
and good. And I'm sure she would behave beautifully...' For a moment Deborah looked wistful. Then
she laughed and said, 'Aunt Elizabeth will be delighted—her eldest daughter so suitably engaged!
Perhaps she will let me keep Autolycus at the
Vicarage, after all?'

Hugo smiled. 'Perhaps. But I wouldn't bet a groat
on her toleration of the parrot.' He watched Deborah's
face with amusement as her look of dismay was replaced with an expression of hopeful pleading. 'All
right! I might be able to help you. In fact I've thought
of someone who might, just might, enjoy the parrot's
company.'

'That would be such a relief! It's not that I don't
like it, exactly. But I quite realise that it is not a suitable inhabitant of a Vicarage. I wouldn't have brought
it, except that I didn't know what else to do with it.
Do you really know someone, Hugo?'

'I think so—but I won't say any more at the moment in case it doesn't work. Leave it with me,
Deborah. I promise to find a home for it somewhere.'

'Oh, Hugo! Thank you!'

Hugo had forgotten how Deborah Staunton's face

could light up in a way he hadn't seen in anyone else. She was not conventionally beautiful, and certainly did not possess the sort of looks he particularly admired. His preference was for pretty blondes, with regular features, and gentle manners. Even when Deborah was looking her best—which was not the case at the moment—the combination of a mane of black hair, pale cheeks and eyes of such a dark indigo that they looked black was too dramatic for his more conventional taste. Among her cousins she was like a young falcon set down in a dovecote, with much the same unexpected consequences. Judging from his experience in the past, life with Deborah would always consist of a succession of crises, a far cry from his own calm, well-judged existence. But all the same, without feeling himself in the slightest danger, he found the manner in which her face could light up with joy very appealing.

They had been sitting with their backs to the house, taking advantage of the splendid view, but turned when they heard voices behind them.

'Deborah! What a surprise! Where did you find her, Hugo?'

The visitors to Stoke Park had returned. Lady Perceval was hurrying over the lawn to greet her unexpected guest, closely followed by Lady Elizabeth and the rest of the family. There followed a series of huggings and kissings and exclamations as Deborah was passed from one to the other. The Perceval girls in particular greeted their cousin with the greatest possible affection. Deborah held a special place in their hearts, and though she was by no means the

youngest of them they had all always regarded her as
someone in need of special care and protection. It was
some time since they had seen her and they exclaimed
at the change in her appearance.

'Girls, girls, be quiet!' said Lady Elizabeth. 'I am
sure you mean well, but I think you forget your manners! Deborah has had a trying time these past years,
but it cannot be pleasant for her to hear your tactless
comments.'

'But she's so pale and thin, Mama!' cried
Henrietta, the youngest and liveliest of the Vicar's
four daughters.

'That is quite enough, Henrietta!' Lady Elizabeth
took Deborah's hands in hers. 'My dear, as you can
see, we are all delighted that you've come at last. But
surely you were not due for another two days? I
would never have accepted the Vernons' invitation if
I had known you were coming today. You must have
thought us very remiss. How did you come? And
what have you done with all your possessions?'

'I...I'm sorry, Aunt. I...I...'

Hugo came to Deborah's aid. 'Deborah has been
well taken care of, I assure you, Aunt Elizabeth. And
Nanny Humble is looking after the rest of their goods
and chattels. They should all be here at any moment.'

As if on cue, a servant came out to tell Lady
Perceval that the carriage with Mrs Humble and a
number of goods had arrived in the courtyard.
Deborah excused herself and hurried off ahead of the
others. She wished to make sure that Nanny Humble
did not reveal the facts behind her unconventional
arrival in Abbot Quincey before she had had time to

prepare her aunt for it. Hugo had divined her purpose and she was grateful to see that he was delaying her aunt and Lady Perceval with questions about the Vernons.

Chapter Two

Nanny Humble was not in the most cooperative of moods. She was too old, she said, to be traipsing about the countryside in a dogcart, then left to while her time away in an ill-kept inn with a landlord who couldn't wait to get rid of her, while Miss Deborah went off into the blue with that dratted dog and that heathen-tongued bird, leaving her to wonder whether she'd ever see her young mistress again... If Miss Deborah knew how much... Deborah recognised the anxiety behind the angry words, and dealt gently with her old servant. She managed to cut the tirade short without causing further offence, begging Nanny Humble to leave complaints and explanations till later.

'I'm sorry our journey was so uncomfortable, Nanny dear. But we're nearly at the Vicarage now, and we'll soon be in our old rooms.'

'Her ladyship is very kind, Miss Deborah. But it's different now. I'm sure I don't know what's to become of us...' Nanny Humble's voice wavered and Deborah put her arms round her.

'We'll be safe here in Abbot Quincey. Try not to worry. Look, here comes Lady Elizabeth. Remember, not a word to her of our recent difficulties—you must leave it to me to tell her about them later. Not now.'

Lady Elizabeth greeted Deborah's old servant and asked how she was. Then, turning to her sister-in-law, she suggested that Mrs Humble should wait in the servants' quarters while they finished their talk with Deborah. Lady Perceval readily agreed.

'I think a drink of something cool would be welcome on such a hot day, would it not, Mrs Humble? My housekeeper will take care of you until Miss Deborah is ready to go to the Vicarage. Shall we say an hour? Come, Deborah! I cannot wait to hear your adventures.'

More chairs and cushions were brought out and the two families settled once again in the shade of the cedar. Frederica and Edwina each took one of Deborah's hands and towed her gently to one of the benches. Here they sat her down between them, expressing in their soft voices their delight at seeing her, and showing their loving concern for her. She felt herself relax. Here at Abbot Quincey she felt…cherished. She looked at them all. The Percevals were a tall, blond race with a remarkable family resemblance. Sir James and his wife, the owners of Perceval Hall, were on a garden seat opposite her, enjoying the cool shade of the cedar. Hugo, their elder son, stood behind them, leaning against the trunk of the tree. Hester, their only daughter, so like Hugo in appearance, was perched on the arm of her parents' seat. It was quite normal for Hester to seem quiet and withdrawn in company, but today she looked pale and preoccupied, and kept casting anxious glances in the direction of the drive. Deborah wondered what was wrong. She made a note to ask Hugo later. On another bench to the right sat Sir James's brother, the Reverend William Perceval and his wife, the Lady Elizabeth, Deborah's aunt. Aunt Elizabeth, the elder daughter of the Duke of Inglesham, was always the same—narrow, aristocratic face, upright posture, dressed plainly but with exquisite neatness. Today her normally somewhat severe expression was softened. Though she was a strict parent, with impossibly high standards of behaviour, Lady Elizabeth had a loving, caring heart. She had invited Deborah to make her home at the Vicarage some time ago, and was now obviously happy to see her niece in Abbot Quincey at last. Deborah smiled. For the first time in many months she felt secure.

She was trying to decide how best to present the story of her arrival in Abbot Quincey when she was forestalled. Lowell Perceval came bounding across the lawn, closely followed by the youngest of the Vicarage girls, Deborah's cousin Henrietta.

'I say, Deborah! Whose is the parrot? And where's the dog?'

Deborah wondered, not for the first time, why Hugo's younger brother was so unlike him. Lowell was rather like Autolycus. Enthusiastic, reckless, he never seemed to consider the consequences of his actions, but plunged in, scattering all before him. She was still wrestling with what to say when Hugo once again came to her rescue.

'The parrot is mine. And the dog is asleep in the stables, not to be disturbed.' When Hugo spoke in that tone of voice even Lowell subsided. He sat down on the lawn and looked at his brother with eager curiosity, reminding Deborah even more of her dog.

'You have a parrot, Hugo?' Lady Perceval asked, turning in amazement towards her son. 'Did you buy it in Northampton? It must have been on impulse, surely. You didn't mention it before you went.'

Deborah directed a pleading glance at Hugo and said, 'I… I brought the parrot with me, Lady Perceval. I… I gave it to Hugo.'

'How nice,' said Lady Perceval, a touch faintly.

'It's a beautiful bird,' said Lowell. 'And it talks. But—'

'Yes, quite!' said Hugo, directing another quelling glance at Lowell. 'I have no intention of leaving it where it is, Mama. It is merely on its way to someone who will appreciate it, I think. Deborah, perhaps we should explain to Aunt Elizabeth that an unfortunate accident prevented your carrier from bringing you all the way to Abbot Quincey.' He turned to his aunt. 'Deborah would have been in some difficulty if I had not chanced upon her at the beginning of the Abbot Quincey road.'

'An accident? Was anyone hurt?'

'No,' said Deborah, picking the story up. 'But I was forced to leave Nanny Humble and the bulk of our things at the inn at the crossroads.' She paused and Hugo spoke once again.

'I despatched a carriage for them as soon as we got here.'

'But how did the animals get here? The…the parrot and the dog?' said Lady Perceval. 'They weren't with Mrs Humble.'

'I thought I ought not to leave them with Nanny Humble, so Hugo kindly brought them with us,' Deborah replied, not looking at Hugo.

'That dog and the parrot? In the curricle?' asked Lowell in disbelieving accents.

'Of course.'

'I wish I'd been there to see it,' said Lowell with a grin.

'Half of Abbot Quincey did.' Hugo's tone was grim.

'So you have a dog with you, Deborah. I had a pug once—he was a dear little thing and very affectionate,' said Lady Elizabeth. 'I think I still have his basket. I must look it out.'

'Er… I don't think Autolycus would fit into a pug's basket,' said Hugo.

'Autolycus? What a strange name for a dog! Deborah, why have you called your dog Autolycus?' Henrietta's question was a welcome diversion, and Deborah turned to her with relief.

'He was a character in Shakespeare.'

'A rogue and a thief,' added Hugo. 'I'm sorry to say that the name reflects on the dog's moral character. The original Autolycus was a "picker up of unconsidered trifles". At a guess I'd say it's a good name for the animal.'

Henrietta laughed. 'He sounds a real character. Who chose the name? You, Deborah?'

'My father named him,' said Deborah with reserve. 'Just before he died.'

There was an awkward silence, and several members of the family threw an anxious glance at Lady Elizabeth. It did not please Deborah's aunt to hear any mention of Edmund Staunton. Her father, the late Duke of Inglesham, had cast her sister Frances off for marrying Mr Staunton against his commands. He had ignored Lady Frances's further existence till the day he died, and had ordered the rest of the family to do the same. Lady Elizabeth had not found this possible. She had remained in touch with the Stauntons in defiance of her father's wishes, and had now offered their daughter a home. But she had never approved of the man for whom her sister had sacrificed so much. Lady Frances and her husband were now both dead, but Elizabeth Perceval's Christian conscience was still wrestling with the problem of forgiveness for the man who had run off with her sister and reduced her to penury. With an obvious effort at brightness she said, 'Well, are we to see this dog of yours, Deborah?'

Hugo gave his brother a speaking look. It was Lowell's fault that Autolycus was to be sprung on the family without careful preparation for the blow.

'I think he's asleep, as Hugo said,' protested Deborah weakly.

'Then we shall all go to the stables to visit him,' announced Lady Perceval with a smile. 'I'm beginning to think you're ashamed of him, Deborah.'

'Oh no! I love him dearly. It's just…'

'Come along then!' The party got up and made for the stables.

Autolycus was lying where Hugo had left him, snoring gently. He had the supremely contented air of a dog well exercised, well fed and now comfortably settled. When he heard Deborah's voice he raised his head, wagged a sleepy tail and flopped down once again.

'He's very big,' said Lady Elizabeth slowly.

'He doesn't expect to live indoors, Aunt Elizabeth! He's well used to being kept in a stable or one of the outhouses.' Deborah was perhaps unaware of the desperation in her voice. But Hugo heard it.

'It's time you had another guard dog, Aunt Elizabeth. You still haven't replaced old Beavis, have you?'

'But—' Deborah began, but Hugo interrupted her. His frown told her plainly that this was no time to be expressing foolish doubts about Autolycus's qualifications as a guard dog.

'The dog is amiable enough,' he said firmly, 'but he can growl quite terrifyingly. And his size would put most ruffians off.'

'I suppose you're right,' said Lady Elizabeth. 'We'll see what your Uncle William has to say.'

The tension eased visibly. Everyone knew that, except in matters connected with his ministry, the Vicar would do whatever his wife suggested.

'Well, I suppose we must gather ourselves together and set off for home. It has been a most eventful day,' said Lady Elizabeth. 'First the Vernons, then finding dearest Deborah here waiting for us, then the dog...'

Her voice trailed away as she glanced doubtfully back at the stable.

The Reverend William and his wife drove off to the Vicarage in the carriage, followed by Nanny Humble and Deborah's possessions in the gig. With the exception of Hester, who returned to her attic, the young people had elected to walk to the Vicarage, collecting Autolycus as they went. Deborah took the opportunity of a moment alone with Hugo to ask what was wrong with Hester.

'Is she ill?'

'No, she's in love.'

'In love! Hester? But...'

'Yes, I know. My sister has always sworn she would never marry. And now she's in love, and she doesn't know what to do. It's an absurd situation!'

'Poor Hester! If her affection isn't returned what *can* she do?'

'That's what makes it all so ridiculous! The man she loves is Robert Dungarran, one of my best friends—the most sensible, reasonable chap you could wish to meet. In all the years I've known him he has never shown the slightest sign of idiocy. But now he is in as desperate a case as Hester. He adores her! He writes notes to her which she tears up, he calls to see her every day—even though she absolutely refuses to receive him. That's why she went up to her attic when we left—in case he calls.'

Deborah looked bewildered. 'But if she is in love with him, and he with her...?'

'Exactly! They are both mad! I tell you, Deborah,

passionate love is a plague to be avoided. There is neither sense nor reason in it. To be honest, I am surprised and a little disappointed in Dungarran. I would not have thought his present behaviour at all his style. When I choose a wife I promise you I shan't have all this drama. I shall find a pretty, well-behaved girl who, like myself, has little taste for such extravagances. We shall, I hope, live in amicable harmony, but I want no passionate scenes, no tantrums, no dramatic encounters. I give you leave to push me into the nearest duckpond, Deborah, if you ever see signs of such madness in me.'

Deborah looked at Hugo in silence. She was not surprised at his words, though they chilled her. He had always disliked scenes and avoided them whenever possible, taking pride in keeping calm whatever the provocation. She could count on the fingers of one hand the number of times she had seen Hugo lose his temper. When he did, the resulting explosion was spectacular, as she knew only too well. It was a sad fact that she appeared to be one of the few people in the world who could provoke Hugo into a rage—usually quite inadvertently.

Theirs had always been a strange friendship. In the past she had looked up to him along with all the other children, though never with the same awe. And in spite of the ten years' difference in age between them he had always talked to her more freely than to the others. Perhaps it was because she had been the outsider, the cuckoo in the nest. Perhaps it had started because he had been sorry for her. But for whatever reason, Hugo had always confided in her, used her as

a sounding board for his views. She sighed, then said,
'What will happen to Hester, do you suppose?'

'I'm sure I haven't the slightest idea. She can be
extremely pig-headed. But on the other hand
Dungarran can be very determined. We shall no doubt
see eventually, but meanwhile I hardly like to watch
them both making such fools of themselves.'

It was as well that Lady Elizabeth did not observe
the walking party. Autolycus, refreshed by his nap
and encouraged by the astonished admiration of
Lowell and Henrietta, was in tearing spirits. But Hugo
had only to snap his fingers for the dog to come to
him. And on the one occasion when Hugo was forced
to address him severely, Autolycus grovelled in pit-
eous abasement.

The twins, who had till now been slightly nervous
of such a large dog, laughed delightedly and bent over
to comfort him.

'He's lovely, Deborah!'

'He's so sweet!'

'He's a confidence trickster!' said Hugo in disgust.
'Look at him! One minute after chasing one of my
pheasants with evil intent, he's doing his best to look
as if he'd never harm a fly in his life.' He was right.
Autolycus was now standing between the twins, gazing from one to the other with gentle submission. It
was impossible not to admire the picture they presented—Edwina and Frederica in their delicate muslins and shady hats, Autolycus standing waist high
between them, gently waving his fearsome tail. A
Beast and not one, but two Beauties.

Hugo regarded his cousins with a connoisseur's eye. They had grown up during his years in London, and he was of the opinion that they were now the prettiest of all the Perceval girls. Robina, the eldest Vicarage daughter, and Henrietta, the youngest, were dark like their mother, but the twins were true Percevals, tall, blue-eyed blondes with rose-petal skins and regular features, gentle in manner and graceful in movement. Lady Elizabeth was a woman of strong principles, and all four of her daughters had been reared with a sound knowledge of Christian duty, and a clear sense of proper behaviour. Robina had just come through a very successful Season and was now well on the way to becoming the wife of one of society's most distinguished aristocrats. Henrietta, still only seventeen, seemed to be developing a penchant for his brother Lowell. But Frederica and Edwina were, as far as he knew, still unattached. They were now nineteen—time to be thinking of marriage. Either one of them would make some man an excellent wife…

Deborah noticed Hugo's admiring appraisal of his cousins, and her heart gave a little lurch, then sank. She had always known that he would one day find the sort of girl he admired and marry her. And now that his thirtieth birthday was so close, he was bound to be looking more energetically for a wife. Either of her cousins would fulfil Hugo's requirements to perfection. Edwina was livelier than Frederica, but they were both gentle, affectionate, biddable girls. Neither of them would ever argue or create a scene—scenes distressed them. With the right husband they would lead tranquil, loving lives, dispensing their own brand of affection and encouragement to the world around them. But she could not believe that Hugo would be the right husband for either of them. He would be kind, there was no question of that, but he would take it for granted that his wife would acquiesce in all his wishes. Neither of the twins, already so much in awe of him, would ever argue with him. Hugo would become a benevolent despot, and his wife's personality would be stifled. The twins deserved better. And such a marriage would do Hugo no good either.

She gave an impatient sigh. If Hugo did set his heart on one of them, what could she do to prevent it? What influence could Deborah Staunton have—a pale, dark-haired little dab of a thing, dependent on her aunt for a roof over her head, a scatterbrain, frequently guilty of acting before she thought—in short, the opposite of everything Hugo admired in a woman... It was sometimes all she could do to keep him on friendly terms with her! If only she didn't have this unfortunate propensity for getting into trouble!

When they arrived at the Vicarage they found the gig with Deborah's possessions waiting for them in the courtyard. Nanny Humble had already gone into the house.

Hugo watched as the servants carried in a couple of old valises, one or two parcels tied with string, some boxes of books and music—all that was left of Deborah Staunton's family home. It brought home to him how bereft she was, how slender her resources.

One had to admire her courage, her gaiety, in the face of what must be a difficult future.

'Stop! Oh, please handle that more carefully! Give it to me—I'll carry it!'

Deborah's urgent cry roused Hugo's curiosity. What was she so concerned about? He saw that she now had a rosewood box in her arms, about eighteen inches by twelve and six or seven inches deep. She hugged it close, though it was clearly awkward to carry.

'Let me,' he said, taking the box from her. He could now see that the top was beautifully worked marquetry of variously coloured woods surrounding a small silver oval with *'Frances'* written on it. Deborah's eyes followed the box anxiously as he carried it in for her.

'I shan't drop it, nor shall I run away with it,' he said with amusement. 'Where shall I put it down?'

'It will go in my room. Thank you, Hugo—you could put it there until I take it upstairs.'

'Nonsense, I shall carry it for you. What is it? It looks like a writing-box. Was it your mother's?'

'Yes. It's almost the only possession of hers that I've managed to keep. But I refused to let it go…'

'Why should you?'

She looked at him sombrely. 'You don't understand.'

They were interrupted by Lady Elizabeth. 'What on earth are you doing on the stairs, Hugo? Surely the servants can carry Deborah's things to her room? What have you there? Oh!' There was unusual delight in Lady Elizabeth's face. 'It's Frances's writing-box!

I have one just the same! Come and see!' She took
them into her little parlour at the back. On a table to
one side of the window was a twin of the box in
Hugo's arms. It had the same marquetry top, but this
one had *'Elizabeth'* on the silver name plate. 'My
father had them made for us. He presented them to
us as soon as we were able to write a full page of
perfect copybook writing.' She smiled fondly.
'Frances had a hard time getting hers. She was always
too hasty, and there was usually a blot before she had
finished. But she managed in the end. What do you
keep in it, Deborah? I keep recipes in mine!'

'I... I have some letters. Letters from my mother,
and correspondence between my mother and my...my
father.'

The pleasure faded from Lady Elizabeth's face. 'I
see. Of course. Well, give it to one of the servants to
take upstairs.'

'I have it now, Aunt Elizabeth. I'll take it,' said
Hugo. 'Is Deborah using her old room?'

'Of course. You'll find Mrs Humble up there.
Come down straight away again, Hugo. You're no
longer children, and it isn't fitting for you to be in
Deborah's room.'

Hugo burst out laughing. 'Aunt Elizabeth! Set your
mind at rest. Deborah would never be in the slightest
danger from me!'

'I know that, of course. But the rest of the world
may not.'

Somewhat depressed, Deborah followed Hugo up
the wide oak staircase. The precious box was depos-
ited on a chest of drawers in Deborah's room. Aunt

Elizabeth was very fond of her niece and had always done all she could to make her feel at home. The Vicarage was large, and Deborah's room had been given to her when she had first come as a child to Abbot Quincey. It was the same size as those of her cousins, and furnished in the same simple, but pretty way, with plenty of room for small treasures.

Just as Hugo was turning to go, Edwina came in with a vase of flowers in her hand.

'We didn't expect you for another two days, Deborah. Otherwise these roses would have been in your room when you arrived. Why did you come so unexpectedly?'

Deborah hesitated and colour rose in her cheeks. 'I… I was lonely. I couldn't wait any longer to be with you. But I should have thought it out more carefully, I see that now. I'm sorry if I've put you all out.'

While Edwina protested strongly at this and hugged her cousin to prove it, Hugo went slowly downstairs looking thoughtful. Deborah Staunton had always been a poor liar. There was more to her hasty disappearance from her former home than she had so far admitted. He must have the truth from her before very long, and see if she needed help.

After Deborah came downstairs again he took her to see the stable where Autolycus had been housed. The dog was already asleep again.

'I hope you haven't been rash in recommending him as a guard dog,' said Deborah, eyeing Autolycus doubtfully. 'He's not really very brave. But thank you for thinking of it. And…and for the rest of your help today.'

'It was nothing,' he said. 'It was quite like the old days. But some time soon I intend to hear the real reason for your sudden departure from Maids Moreton.'

Deborah looked up at him, eyes wide in shock, then she looked away. 'W-what do you mean?'

'You mustn't thank me one minute, then treat me like a simpleton the next, Deborah, my dear,' he said pleasantly. 'I am not as gullible as the twins. If you had waited another forty-eight hours you and Nanny Humble would have travelled at your ease in a carriage sent by Uncle William. As it was you came in a dogcart—not the most comfortable of vehicles. Moreover, the dogcart had been hired in Buckingham—two miles away from your old home. It's natural to wonder why. Also, you hired it, even though you knew you didn't have enough money to pay the full charge. Such desperation doesn't arise from loneliness or a simple lack of patience, my friend.' He looked at her gravely, but she remained silent. He went on, 'And then there is the matter of your aunt's equally hurried return to Ireland. Is it all connected?'

She looked at him in dismay. 'I... I can't tell you, Hugo.'

'Not now, I agree. But you'll confide in me before long. Good night, Deborah. Try to keep out of trouble for the next week. We shall all be busy with preparations for the fête.'

'The annual fête! I'd forgotten all about it. We used to have such fun at the fête... I'll do my best to be good, Hugo.' She made a face. 'Though my best doesn't always seem to work… I'll certainly be extra careful, I promise—and the twins are very good to me—they'll help.' She sighed. 'They don't know how lucky they are—they seem to know how to behave without even trying!'

Hugo nodded, smiling fondly. 'They certainly do. As well as being pretty… Very pretty. The two of them together are indeed a striking sight. They would cast a number of accredited society beauties quite in the shade.'

Deborah's heart sank. Hugo really was becoming serious. She said hopefully, 'Perhaps Robina will introduce them to the Ton after she is married? I'm sure they would be a success.'

He frowned. 'Perhaps… Though I'm not sure it's at all necessary. They are so unspoilt, it would be a pity if… Well, we shall see, we shall see. They may well find suitable partners here in Northamptonshire.'

When Hugo wasn't being the kindest man she knew, thought Deborah in exasperation, he was far too lordly! It was obvious to her that he had now decided that one of his cousins would make a suitable wife and assumed that all he had to do was to decide which one. Such arrogance! It would serve him right if neither would accept him—but she couldn't imagine that would happen. She suddenly felt weary beyond measure.

'Good night, Hugo,' she said and turned to go. Then, to her astonishment, Hugo put his hands on her shoulders and pulled her nearer. He kissed her on the cheek.

'Don't lose heart,' he said. 'Things will be better for you now. We are here to look after you.'

'Thank you.' Deborah could not have said anything more. Hugo's nearness was playing havoc with her emotions. Delight, despair, an almost irresistible impulse to reach up and bring his head round so that his lips could meet hers… She stiffened and withdrew. Such wanton behaviour would shock him to the core. What was worse, he would be embarrassed and uncomfortable, too. She knew how he thought of her, and it was not as a man thinks of a possible wife. 'Deborah would never be in the slightest danger from me!' he had said to Aunt Elizabeth, laughing at the very idea. It had hurt, but it had not surprised her.

'Good night, and thank you once again.' She turned and went into the house.

Hugo slowly walked back to the Hall. He was puzzled. The impulse to kiss Deborah Staunton had taken him by surprise, but he supposed it had been a natural one. She had looked so forlorn, and he had frequently comforted her in the past. But what astonished him was that once she was in his arms the simple desire to comfort had changed into something much more dangerous. The feel of her fragile bones beneath his hands, the look of helplessness in those dark, indigo eyes, had been unexpectedly seductive. He had been within a hair's breadth of kissing her in real earnest. Kissing little, penniless, hopelessly disorganised Deborah Staunton! And then she had, quite understandably, stiffened and pulled away and the moment had passed... He shook his head. Midsummer madness! It would not be repeated.

He firmly dismissed the incident and turned to contemplating his own future. Now that he was based more or less permanently in Northamptonshire, was he going to find the life of a country gentleman intolerably dull? For the last ten years he had lived in the fashionable world, and though he had never outrun his budget he had managed to enjoy most of the delights London had to offer. He was aware that he was known in society as a man of taste and judgement. He had always been a keen sportsman, and through practice and, yes, luck, he had achieved success in most of the activities admired by his London acquaintances. They had been good years...

But he had promised his parents he would settle down when he reached thirty, and that time had now come. He had returned to Abbot Quincey with the fixed intention of marrying, and it seemed to him that either of his twin cousins would make a very suitable wife. The Percevals were a good sound stock—there could be no objection to marriage between cousins. The problem would be which one to choose! He was fond of them both, and they both seemed to like him. Yes, he could do a lot worse. Life with either one of them would be very pleasant...

Might it be dull, perhaps? Possibly, but he would be kept fully occupied with the responsibilities to his family and to the estate he would one day inherit. He and Frederica—or Edwina—would have a sound relationship based on friendship, love for their children and their separate duties. That would be enough.

Quite enough. Indeed, excessive feeling of any kind was in rather poor taste—he had usually managed to avoid it. Yes—marriage to someone like Edwina—or Frederica—would suit him very well. Either of them would make an excellent future Lady Perceval. Unlike poor Deborah Staunton... She would lead a man a pretty dance indeed! He would never know what she might do next!

Chapter Three

Deborah had the promised talk with her aunt the next morning, and was so shocked by what she heard that she collected Autolycus and set out to find solitude and peace in the woods surrounding the Hall. She walked along the familiar paths, lost in her own thoughts, until she was roused by excited barks and yelps from the dog. Hugo was walking towards her, Autolycus leaping up at his adopted new master.

'That *damned* dog! Down, sir! Why the devil don't you keep him on the leash until he knows how to behave?' Hugo said testily. 'Ill-disciplined dogs are a menace to all! I said *down*!' Autolycus flattened himself in his usual posture of abject apology whenever Hugo addressed him thus, and lay quiet. 'I've been looking for you. Edwina told me you had come this way.' He took a look at her dazed expression. 'You've been crying! What's wrong?'

Deborah threw up her head and said angrily, 'I haven't been crying! I never cry. If my eyes are red it's because…it's because I had a fly in one of them.'

'Let me see.'

'It's gone now.'

'Deborah, tell me why you are upset.'

'I'm not upset, I tell you! I'm very pleased!' Deborah took a breath and said more calmly, 'I've just learned that I'm not poor! Not at all! I have an income of a hundred pounds a year!'

'My poor girl, that won't go far!'

'It's riches, Hugo! I thought I had nothing.'

Hugo fell into step beside her and they walked along the shady path together. 'Tell me,' he said. 'Where has this wealth come from?'

'Grandmother Inglesham.'

'The Duchess? I thought that the Ingleshams had cut you all off?'

'They had. But when she died my grandmother left some money with Aunt Elizabeth to provide an allowance for my mother. One hundred pounds a year. But not before my father was dead. The Duchess of Inglesham was determined not to let Edmund Staunton benefit in any possible way.'

'So she still loved her daughter, though she couldn't forgive Staunton!'

'Loved!' Her scorn was devastating. 'It's not my idea of love, Hugo.'

'Oh come, Deborah! She did leave her the money…'

'Money? It's not the question of money! My mother didn't care about the money! It was a word from her own mother that she wanted. What sort of love denies any contact with someone who loves you? Sends money through someone else, refuses to meet a daughter who is aching to see you, to have your forgiveness? My poor mother hoped for a reconciliation till the day the Duchess died!'

'Perhaps your grandmother was afraid of what the old Duke would say?'

'Pshaw! Real love doesn't count that sort of cost, Hugo! If I loved someone I wouldn't let anything or anyone stop me! I would fight to be with them, help them, show them how much I loved them. That's what I would call love.' Unaccustomed colour was in her cheeks and her indigo eyes were flashing blue fire. Hugo was fascinated. He could well believe what she said. Deborah Staunton would fling herself into the fray with passion, with no thought for her own good. He wondered what it would be like to love or be loved like that. For a fleeting moment the vision of such devotion was extraordinarily appealing. But then his customary dislike of excessive emotion reasserted itself. He nodded and said calmly, 'All the same, a hundred pounds a year is not a fortune, Deborah.'

She looked at him with a strange smile in her eyes. Then she said wryly, 'I know the Percevals do not consider themselves rich. Compared with what they were in the past they might even think they are poor. But you've never known what it is to be really poor, Hugo. I don't suppose it occurred to you when you saw me in London four years ago that I was living on a shoestring.'

'Then why on earth did your mother send you?'

'She was worried about my future and hoped that I would find a husband. If I had been able to make a good match it would have solved the chief of her worries. When Mrs Young offered to have me with her for the Season, Mama was delighted. Poor Mama! She was so sure that some gentleman or other would be glad to marry the granddaughter of a Duke. So she sold everything she had left that was of any value and sent me off to London.'

'It was mad to do such a thing!'

'It wasn't very sensible, I agree. It meant that later, when times were hard, she had nothing to fall back on. But Mama was like that. She took the risk because she loved me. She knew that the Inglesham family were to be in London that year for the season, so she wrote to them. I think she hoped that…that they would take an interest in me, once I was there in front of them, so to speak. But they refused even to acknowledge me. And the rest of the Ton followed suit.' When Hugo gave a muffled exclamation Deborah said fiercely, 'I didn't mind! I could see as soon as I arrived that I wouldn't "take", as they say—even if I'd had twice as many dresses and jewels and introductions. And the Ingleshams were just the sort of people I disliked most. I disliked London, too. I sometimes thought that you were the only creature in the capital who cared anything at all about me.'

Hugo walked on in silence for a moment, frowning. Then he said brusquely, 'Why didn't you tell me this before? After you had tipped us both into the lake I was pardonable angry. It was the last in a whole series of mishaps and I had had enough. But you let me drag you back to Mrs Young's, ranting all the while, swearing never to see you again and you didn't say a word—not a word—of all these difficulties! Do you

think I'd have rejected you quite so comprehensively
if I'd known?'

'I didn't want your pity!' flashed Deborah. Then
she gave him a fleeting grin. 'Besides, as I remember
it, Hugo, you didn't give me a chance to say anything
at all! You're very fluent when you're in a rage.
Anyway, there was little enough you could have done.
I'm not sure whether you knew or not, but the morning after that awful episode news came that Papa was
ill, and I left London for good.'

'All the same...' Hugo was seriously upset, and
Deborah tried to comfort him.

'I didn't blame you, Hugo. Really, I didn't. After
all your kindness to me I'd disgraced you again. You
called it the curse of the Stauntons, and you were
right.'

There was silence for a moment, then Hugo said,
'Are you going to tell me why Miss Staunton left for
Ireland so unexpectedly—leaving you to fend for
yourself?'

'I can tell what you are thinking, and once again
you're right!' Deborah's tone was bitter. 'The
Stauntons are not at all good Ton. I'm surprised you
even bother to talk to one.'

'Don't be so stupid, Deborah!'

'It's not stupidity,' she cried. 'It's shame! The real
reason my aunt left was because she had taken money
that wasn't hers.'

'*What?* What money?'

'Mine! As I learned this morning from Aunt
Elizabeth. I thought that the Inglesham allowance had
finished when my mother died, but it hadn't. It was

transferred to me—though no one told me at the time.' Deborah's voice trembled and she stopped for a moment. Then she went on, 'For eight or nine months my aunt regularly collected my allowance from the lawyer in Buckingham and said nothing at all about it. I suppose she simply pocketed the money.'

'So that is why she left so suddenly? You started to suspect her?'

'Far from it! I might have been puzzled when she packed and left within twenty-four hours, but I kissed her fondly and wished her a safe journey. I was a gullible fool. But she *was* in some kind of trouble, and I think she was running away from something— or someone. There was a man who called the day before she left. They had a furious argument—I don't know what it was about, but I heard money mentioned. He left in the end saying that he would be back. She packed her things and departed early the next morning.'

'With no thought for you?'

'Well, before she went she did advise me to leave Maids Moreton as soon as possible. And I did.'

'Did you see this man again?'

'No. And I didn't want to. He was dressed like a gentleman, but he didn't behave like one. He frightened me.'

'Have you told Aunt Elizabeth about this man?'

'No! And I'm not going to!' She clutched his arm. 'Hugo, you mustn't mention it either. It's not as if I'm not in any danger, and…and the whole shameful episode is better forgotten.'

'There's no need to ruffle your feathers and stare at me so fiercely. I think you're right. There's no reason to upset Aunt Elizabeth. This man, whoever he is, is unlikely to come here. And I don't suppose your Aunt Staunton will want to show her face again, either.' At the touch of contempt in Hugo's tone Deborah turned her head away in shame. She gave a sob. He swore under his breath and pulled her into his arms.

'Don't let it hurt you so, Deborah. Your aunt's deceit must have been a blow, but you must forget her now and be happy here.'

'But we all tr-trusted her, Hugo! She…she was f-family—my father's s-sister. My m-mother l-loved her.'

Hugo held her tight, her face against his chest, while she wept away a hopeless mixture of feelings— sorrow, outrage, shame, a bitter sense of betrayal and, perhaps more than anything, a sense of relief after months of tension and deprivation which had followed her mother's death—deprivation which she would have been spared, if only her aunt had been honest. It was all perfectly understandable, but Hugo had never seen Deborah give way so completely, and it twisted his heart.

'My poor girl! What a time you've had!' He let her cry for a moment and when she grew calmer he said, 'But think of your inheritance! I see I must be prepared to fight off the fortune-hunters, now that you're a woman of substance.' A watery chuckle told him that his nonsense had succeeded in diverting her. She pulled away and looked up at him, her face beginning to dissolve into laughter. Sunshine always followed swiftly after cloud with Deborah. He was filled with admiration at her courage, at her refusal to be daunted for long by the blows that life had dealt her. It seemed very natural that he should hold her like this, and his arms tightened round her. So often in the past he had held her so—after a fall from the apple tree, a slip on the stepping-stones over the stream, the death of some little animal she had befriended. Deborah had always come to him for comfort. And he had always found it surprisingly easy to talk to her.

After a short moment Deborah released herself. 'Thank you, Hugo,' she said, mopping her eyes. 'You are very good to tolerate such a watering pot. I'm sorry I gave way quite so completely—it suddenly seemed just too much. I feel better now.'

They walked on in a companionable silence. Summer was at its height, and the oaks and elms, the ash trees and alders were in full foliage. Autolycus ran to and fro, rummaging in the undergrowth, leaping back with a startled yelp when a rabbit popped up out of its hole and as quickly disappeared again, chasing a squirrel with enthusiasm, only to bark with frustration when it sought refuge in a tall tree. Deborah occasionally made a short foray to gather some flowers, leaves and seed-heads, and when Hugo asked about them he was told of their properties.

'I am surprised that you have to ask, Hugo! I suppose in London you merely called in the pharmacist when you had various aches and pains. Here in the country we make our own, and the woods and hedgerows are full of all kinds of remedies.'

'I don't remember that I ever had to call anyone in.'

'Oh? So you've never had sprains and bruises during all those gentlemanly pursuits? You've been fortunate!'

He laughed. 'Of course I have, you little shrew. What would you have done for me? Given me one of those?'

'No, I'd use comfrey for any sprains and that doesn't grow here. I'd have to go to the other side of the village for it. Agrimony is found there, too—that's good for gout.'

'Thank you, but I am not a victim yet. What do you have there to help me?'

'This is burdock, which is good for burns, betony to help your digestion, bugle to cure dementia after drinking...'

'How useful!' Hugo interposed drily. 'That yellow one is weaselsnout, isn't it?'

Deborah pulled a face at him. 'Hugo! Is that what you call it? It has a much prettier name—and a wonderful reputation.'

'Oh?'

'It's called yellow archangel, and the herbalists claim that it "makes the heart merry, drives away melancholy and quickens the spirits". What else could one ask for?'

'What indeed? Perhaps I should call you weaselsnout, Deborah. You often have the same effect.'

'Hugo!' Deborah protested laughing, not sure whether she was flattered at his compliment or not too pleased about the name.

'Do you know all the plants?'

'On the contrary. I am an ignoramus compared with Lavender Brabant!'

'What? The Admiral's daughter? Lives in Hewly Manor? I don't think I've exchanged more than two words with her in my life.'

'Years ago, when I stayed with Aunt Elizabeth, I sometimes met Lavender in the woods. She taught me the little I know—I think she can recognise every plant that grows round here. I'm not surprised you haven't spoken to her—she's somewhat elusive. A recluse, like Hester.'

'Ah yes. Hester…' He walked on in silence for a moment.

'You're worried about her, aren't you, Hugo? What do you think she will do? About Lord Dungarran, I mean.'

'My sister is famous for her stubbornness, but I think… I hope she might eventually give in. Dungarran can be very persuasive. He was saying something last night about taking extreme measures. I don't know what they can be, but I hope he doesn't intend to carry her off. I don't see him as a latterday Lochinvar, and only extreme youth could excuse such dramatic behaviour. Oh, it's all rather ridiculous. What a pair of fools they are!'

'No, Hugo. Love is never ridiculous. You watch— Hester will see reason in the end. I know she will.'

'Reason? Reason has absolutely nothing to do with it. But Robert Dungarran would be a splendid match for her. He is extremely eligible, and an excellent fellow besides. I admit that I should like to see Hester settled, especially before...' He hesitated.

'Yes?'

'Before I settle down with a wife myself. I've been talking to my father. As you know, he is anxious to see me married.'

'Yes, I know.' Deborah's voice was muffled as she bent her head, ostensibly to avoid some overhanging branches. 'And?'

'I mentioned the twins to him. He would be well pleased if I offered for one of them and he believes that my Uncle William would be delighted to give his consent.'

'Really?'

'Finding husbands for four daughters is a heavy burden. It looks as if Robina's future is now secure, but my poor uncle still has three more dowries to find. As you well know, sending a daughter to London for the Season is an expensive business—and for the twins he would have to find enough for two!'

'But surely Robina would help!'

'She isn't married yet, Deborah. The twins are past their nineteenth birthday already.'

'Oh come, Hugo! There's still plenty of time! Robina will certainly be married before next year's Season starts. She would be delighted to sponsor the twins in London. I am sure. Indeed, she will enjoy it. The twins are certain to be a huge success! Two of them, identically pretty, identically charming... Society will be hugely impressed. How can you have any doubts?'

Hugo went on almost as if he had not heard her.

'And either of them would be perfect as the next chatelaine of Perceval Hall.'

There was a pause. Then Deborah said quietly, 'What about you, Hugo? Which one would be perfect for you?'

He shook his head. 'That's the trouble! I would find it very difficult to make up my mind between them!'

She looked at him with astonished disapproval. 'You mean you don't *know*? Hugo, you can't, you *mustn't* contemplate marriage with either of my cousins until you know which one you love!'

'How can I do that? They are both equally lovable!'

'I agree. But they are not...not interchangeable. Frederica is a person in her own right, and so is Edwina. Each one of them has her own quite distinct personality.'

'Aren't you being a little absurd, Deborah? Of course I know they are different. Edwina is livelier, Frederica has more forethought. Edwina has the better seat on a horse, Frederica is the more graceful dancer. They both play the harp well, though you have always been the truly musical member of the family...'

'Stop! Stop!' cried Deborah. 'I don't wish to hear any more of this...this soulless catalogue of my cousins' talents. How can you possibly choose a wife by such superficial criteria?'

Hugo was offended. 'I don't understand you,' he said coldly. 'What do you propose I should do? Disappoint both families by looking elsewhere?'

'By no means. But I do think you ought to get to know both Edwina and Frederica a great deal better before you contemplate marrying either of them. I love them both dearly, and any man who won the affection of either of them would be very lucky. But without strong and lasting affection—equally strong on both sides—marriage is a dangerous enterprise.'

'How you exaggerate, Deborah!'

'Hugo, I know what I am talking about, believe me!'

'I assure you that I haven't the slightest intention of making my marriage a dangerous enterprise. I have always maintained that two reasonable people, with similar interests and good will on both sides, can make a success of any partnership—marriage included. Romantic extravagance poses the greatest danger to such a partnership, and neither of the twins would ever indulge in that!'

Deborah shook her head, but saw it was useless to argue. She changed her ground. 'What about Edwina and Frederica? Do you know how they would regard an offer from you?'

'Whichever one I approached would naturally consider it very seriously.'

Deborah gave a most unladylike snort. 'Naturally!'

Hugo wasn't offended by this. He said in quite a matter-of-fact way, 'You mustn't think me a coxcomb, Deborah. My cousins are reasonably sensible girls. They must know that marriage to me would enhance their position in the world. My wife would eventually be mistress of a very handsome estate, with an assured place in society. That must be worth something. And I am not, as far as I am aware, a monster.'

He looked at her with a touch of anxiety. 'I think

they like me enough. Don't they? Don't they, Deborah?'

'They are certainly fond of you, Hugo—we all are. But...enough to marry? That's something you would have to ask the lady of your choice yourself. Even if I knew, I wouldn't tell you.' She hesitated, then said, 'May I say something? Something you might not like?'

'Do,' said Hugo. 'You don't usually hesitate.'

'I... I think that, if you were to ask one of my cousins to marry you, she might accept you without questioning her own feelings in the matter. They both admire you so much. And, of course, they are both aware of how much it would please the family.'

'Is that so very wrong? Admiration is not a bad basis for a loving relationship. And in the absence of any previous attachment, what is wrong with pleasing one's family?'

'But what if their affections *are* already engaged elsewhere, however tentatively? I suspect that they would still defer to their parents' wishes.'

'You might give me some credit for better feelings,' said Hugo a touch impatiently. 'If I knew that to be the case, I should not approach them, of course. I should look for someone else.'

Deborah commented somewhat acidly that she was pleased to see that Hugo could be so philosophical. That, whatever else, his heart did not seem to be very passionately involved in this choosing of a partner for life.

'Deborah, I think you are in danger of falling into the same trap as poor Robert Dungarran. Passionate love is a hindrance to good understanding. It leads one into all sorts of foolishness, and I will have no part of it.'

Hugo was becoming exasperated. He decided to end the discussion. Deborah Staunton's views were just as he would have expected—all feeling and no sense, and he would not heed them. Ignoring the slight doubt she had raised in his mind, he said, 'Now, where is that wretched dog? He seems to have disappeared!'

They had been so absorbed in their discussion that they had forgotten the dog. When they looked round they saw that they had reached the edge of the wood, and were passing one of the estate cottages. There was no sign of Autolycus in any of the fields round about, and Deborah was just about to see if he had slipped into Mrs Bember's cottage in his perennial search for food, when pandemonium broke out inside the large chicken-house at the end of the garden. There was a crash as the side of the building collapsed and Autolycus scrambled out, closely pursued by a furious cockerel and a stream of hens. He leapt over the hedge on which Mrs Bember had spread some clothes to dry, and raced away over the field, clearly in fear of his life, with his ears flapping and a large petticoat trailing behind him like the tail of a comet.

It was such an absurdly comic sight that they both burst out laughing, but they soon stopped in dismay when old Mrs Bember came hurrying out shouting, 'Come back! Come back here! Oh dearie me, what shall I do? Come back here, you dratted creatures!' She stopped short when she saw Hugo. 'Oh, whatever can I do, Mr Hugo? Some dog has broken down my hen-house and let out all the chickens. They're such silly creatures, I'll never get 'm back! What'll happen to all my egg money? And my petticoat's gone! My best one, too.' She peered shortsightedly at Hugo's companion. 'Why, it's Miss Deborah! Oh, excuse me, ma'am, I was just that upset I didn't see you. I didn't know you was back, y'see. But Miss Deborah, you're here at a bad moment, I can tell you. I'm in such a pickle! That animal has chased away all the chickens. What am I to do, Miss Deborah? They'll never come back—and I can't go chasing about after 'm the way I used to. I've lost 'm! And my best flannel petticoat, too.'

Deborah went up to the old lady and led her gently back towards the cottage. 'Mrs Bember, I'm so sorry! But you really needn't be so worried. We'll sort it out. Look, why don't I make you something to drink, while Mr Hugo sees what he can do.' As she said this, she threw an appealing glance at Hugo.

Hugo smiled at Mrs Bember. 'Leave things to me. I'll get some of the men to put things right for you, Mrs B. Your chickens will be in a new home by nightfall, I promise. I can't answer for your... er...petticoat, though.'

'Oh, it's ruined anyway, sir! I don't want 'm back. Tes a pity, though. A real handsome one, it were. Yer blessed mother gave it to me when it was so cold last winter. "Wear this, Mrs Bember," she said, "it'll keep you warm." And it did, too. Can you really get me chickens back, sir?'

'Every one! Or we'll find others to take their place.

Don't worry. Miss Deborah will stay here with you until you feel more the thing.' Hugo went out with another encouraging smile for Mrs Bember and a departing look at Deborah which boded ill for her and her dog.

'And I'll buy you a new petticoat, Mrs Bember,' said Deborah. 'Now you must sit down here and stop worrying!'

'Thank you, Miss Deborah. You're very kind. I do wonder where that dog come from, though. I never see'd um before.'

Deborah made a face, and took a breath. 'I'm sorry to tell you that the dog is mine, Mrs B. He…he's not very well-behaved, I'm afraid. Mr Hugo said I ought to keep him on a leash, and he was right!'

'You should get rid of 'm, Miss Deborah! Afore he does some real damage. Not but what a real dog, one that knew its job, wouldn't be a comfort to an old woman like me living on her own. Especially nowadays. But there—what would I feed 'm on?'

Resisting the urge to claim that Autolycus was a perfectly 'real' dog, Deborah asked Mrs Bember what she meant by 'especially nowadays'.

'Why, Miss Deborah, anyone'll tell you! We're not safe in our beds any more! Things have been bad since his lordship was murdered.'

'Lord Sywell? I thought they were worse when he was alive, Mrs Bember?'

'And so they were! Especially for the poor creatures who lived on the Abbey lands. It wasn't so bad for Abbot Quincey folk—the Percevals have always looked after their own. But the Marquis of Sywell was a bad master and a worse landlord. You wouldn't 'ardly believe some of the stories we've 'eard. And now he's been and got himself murdered. Found lying in a great pool of his own blood, I've been told...' Mrs Bember said, not without a certain relish.

'Don't they know who did it?'

'There's some as say it was Solomon Burneck. He's a miserable enough creature, but I'm not so sure he could do a thing like that. And now they've got an interfering busybody with a nose like a billhook going round asking all sorts of questions. Jackson, 'e calls 'imself. Says 'e's a Broad Street Runner, whatever that may signify.'

'Don't you mean a Bow Street Runner, Mrs B.?'

'That would be it. But Bow or Broad, there's no call for 'im to come round disturbing honest folk, that's what I say!'

'But perhaps he will succeed in finding out who killed his lordship? Surely that would be a good thing? You'd feel safer then, wouldn't you?'

'Safer or not, Miss Deborah, you won't find many folk round here willing to talk. Not to anyone. Not even if the Prince Regent hisself wants to know!'

'The Prince Regent? What has he to do with it?'

'This Jackson says the Prince wants the murderer found. Well, I'm as loyal a subject of King George, God bless 'im, as anyone else round 'ere, and if it were anything else I'd please his Royal Highness with all my heart. But not with this! Sywell was a wicked man and 'e deserved to die. If some poor soul 'as been driven to murder by that villain's sinful acts then I'm not the one to betray 'im. My lips are sealed.'

She paused. 'Not that I know anything, mind. It's just a way of talking. But we all feel the same way, Miss Deborah. This Broad Street Runner can ask all 'e likes. He won't get much satisfaction from anyone round 'ere.'

Deborah abandoned any attempt to convince Mrs Bember. In fact, she was secretly in agreement with the people of the four villages. The Marquis had done enough harm in his lifetime, without the destruction of yet another victim. It was better to let the matter rest.

Hugo returned after an hour with Mrs Bember's niece, and a lad from the farm. 'We've rounded up most of the chickens, including the rooster. They weren't far away. They're at the farm waiting for Seth to repair your hen-house—and I've told him it's to be better than the old one. So you should be all right, Mrs B.'

'Thank you kindly, Mr Hugo! It was a good day for Abbot Quincey when you came back after all these years! And Miss Deborah, too! Thank you for all your help.'

'It was the least we could do! Er…has Miss Deborah told you that the villainous dog was ours?'

'Yes, sir. I don't rightly know what to say…'

'I do. But I'll say it later. And in the right quarters. Now, let your niece look after things while you rest for a bit. Here.' Hugo pressed something into Mrs Bember's hand, took Deborah's arm and took his leave. Deborah was firmly walked out of the cottage and through the garden gate on to the path.

'Now! Now, Deborah, we shall have a talk.'

'If you insist. But first of all, I must find Autolycus—or have you found him already?'

'He's back in his stable, feeling very sorry for himself.'

'Was he hurt?'

'Not before I found him. He didn't enjoy his thrashing, though.'

'*Thrashing!* You *thrashed* my dog? How…how dare you!'

Hugo looked at her in amazement. 'You're lucky some farmer or other didn't shoot him! When I caught him he was racing round the ten-acre field causing havoc among the sheep there. Deborah, I don't think you appreciate what a liability an undisciplined dog is in the country. If Autolycus is to survive here, he *has* to be taught how to behave.'

'And I don't think you appreciate the fact that you have no right—no right whatsoever—to beat my dog!' replied Deborah hotly.

'Don't be such a sentimental simpleton!' Hugo took a deep breath and made himself speak calmly. 'Autolycus has a great character, and I would be sorry if we had to get rid of him. But go he must if he cannot learn discipline. That is why I thrashed him today. And why I would thrash him again if he did the same tomorrow. But it won't be necessary. He won't.'

'I refuse to let you break my dog's spirit!' stormed Deborah.

'You really are the most annoying creature of my whole acquaintance! How can you have known me all this time without realising that I would never knowingly break any creature's spirit. But animals have to be taught to obey.'

'With kindness!'

'With kindness, yes. But not indulgence. Autolycus must learn that when he disobeys me—or you—he is punished.'

Deborah looked at him coldly. 'If I see you raising a whip to my dog I will make you sorry, Hugo. I mean it.'

'You're being excessively childish, Deborah! What is more, you are very much mistaken if you think such a silly threat will stop me. I refuse to see an animal I like ruined for want of a little discipline. Anyway, how do you suppose Mrs Bember felt when she saw what your dog had done? Do you not think he deserved a little punishment for causing her such distress?'

Deborah was silenced. She finally said with reluctance, 'You put it all right for her. I have to thank you for that.'

'Well then…'

'Oh, I suppose I shall have to forgive you. But please don't punish Autolycus like that again, Hugo, *please*!'

Hugo made no reply to this but said, 'What are we to do about Mrs Bember's petticoat? Shall I consult my mother?'

'I've already said I shall get a new one for her. I'll talk to the twins—they'll know where. I don't especially wish to involve anyone else, Hugo. Your mother is bound to say something to Aunt Elizabeth.

And though she is very kind I... I'm not sure Aunt Elizabeth would approve of this morning's work.'

'I am quite sure she wouldn't! But if you are not to use up your inheritance before the year is out we had better teach Autolycus some manners, don't you agree?'

The next week was comparatively peaceful. Deborah spent time with her aunt and her cousins, settling in to what was to be her permanent home. The easy relationship she had always enjoyed with the twins was quickly renewed, and their old habit of protecting Deborah from their mother's censure was soon in force. They were very happy to arrange for a new petticoat to be made for Mrs Bember, and were in full agreement with Deborah that the less Lady Elizabeth knew about Autolycus's misdemeanours the better. Though they were still nervous of the dog in his more boisterous moods, they had quickly grown fond of him. In return, Autolycus seemed to know by instinct that though Edwina and Frederica were his friends, they liked him best when he was in a quieter mood, and when he was left with them his manners were usually impeccably gentle.

Hugo was now busy, along with other members of the family at the Hall, on preparations for the fête. But he took time to visit his cousins at the Vicarage, and to oversee Autolycus's schooling. Since Hugo had as yet confided his intentions to no one but his father and Deborah, the twins were slightly puzzled at Hugo's regular appearances but accepted his visits with their usual placid good humour. The dog was equally puzzled, but, as ever, very willing to learn whatever Hugo wished to teach him. Deborah, who knew what lay behind Hugo's visits, was grateful to him for his efforts with Autolycus, and tried not to mind when he spent time doing what she had suggested—improving his acquaintance with her cousins.

Chapter Four

Preparations for the fête now took precedence over everything else. It was a traditional occasion, and the same events and amusements were offered year after year. No one wanted it different. As usual, wandering acrobats, magicians, fire-eaters, fortune-tellers and showmen of every variety had by their own mysterious means found out the date, and were beginning to arrive in the neighbourhood. One or two of them needed a close eye kept on them, but most were hard-working and reasonably honest, and added a touch of the exotic to the scene. The local people as usual produced a team of Morris Dancers and a couple of bands, together with a number of stalls which offered refreshments or wares for sale. And then there were the traditional competitions—the tug o' war for teams from the four villages, the archery competition, and other, less energetic diversions such as guessing the weight of the pig, the cake, the number of beans in a bottle...

The weather on the day of the fête itself was clear and fine with a faint breeze—just enough to moderate the heat of the sun and set the bunting and the flags on the stalls fluttering. It was a lively scene. Stalls and booths had been laid out round the edges of the south lawn, benches and tables in the shade of the cedar, while in the centre was a large space for spectacles such as the dancers or the tug o' war. In one corner of the lawn was a board presided over by Farmer Buller, Steep Abbot's spare-time blacksmith, which read in uneven lettering, 'TRY YOUR STRENGTH!' The young men of the district, muscles bulging, sweat gleaming on their brows, swung the hammer valiantly, sending the cannon ball shooting away up the pole to ring the bell at the top. Then they put on their shirts again, and, with a touch of a swagger, or a sheepish glance, turned to face the laughing admiration of the village maidens, before walking off with them. The farmers' wives and sisters gathered round the produce stalls, while the farmers themselves wandered off to the field nearby where they could watch the sheepdog trials or view the horses on offer there.

On the grass at the foot of the steps in front of the house itself was a low platform under a brightly coloured awning. Here Lady Perceval stood to open the fête, and here was where all the prizes would be awarded. This year they would be presented by Hugo, in honour of his return to Northamptonshire.

The party from the Vicarage arrived in good time, and joined the rest of the invited guests on the terrace immediately in front of the house. Though Deborah recognised most of them—Lady Perceval's sister, Mrs

Rushford, and her family, the Vernons from Stoke Park and others—there were one or two new faces. When she asked Hugo who they were he drew her over to be introduced.

'Lady Martindale, may I present my cousin, Deborah Staunton?' Then he turned to a dark-haired, rather serious-looking man beside the lady. 'This is Lady Martindale's nephew, Deborah. Lord Dungarran.' While Hugo chatted with his friends, Deborah looked with interest at the man who had managed to capture Hester's heart, if not yet her agreement to marry him. Handsome, assured, with a pleasantly easy air and a charming smile, he didn't look like a man hopelessly in love. Then Hester Perceval appeared on the terrace, and Robert Dungarran went to join her. There was no obvious display, no extravagant gesture as he greeted her, but there was something about his whole manner to her which declared that he was unmistakeably, truly, deeply in love. But not hopelessly, Deborah decided, looking at Hester. Hester looked quite different from the pale recluse of a week before. Her eyes were sparkling and the faint colour in her cheeks as she looked shyly up at Dungarran was most becoming. Deborah smiled to herself. It looked as if the 'idiocy' was about to be most happily resolved. If Hester Perceval had not already succumbed to her lover's charm, she soon would.

'I hope Autolycus was not too disappointed at being left behind.' Deborah jumped as Hugo came up behind her.

'I... I didn't leave him behind,' she stammered.

Hugo frowned and she went on, 'He was so miserable, Hugo! I just couldn't abandon him. Lowell has found an empty stable for me, and Autolycus is securely locked up in it. I wanted to have him near enough for me to slip away occasionally and talk to him. He'll be safe, I promise you.'

'You'd better make certain he is! I'm not sure his training would stand all the temptations to cause chaos which are offered today. What do you suppose Autolycus would do if he was let loose on the sheep trials in the next field...'

'Not to mention the pigs, ducks, hens, chicks and rabbits at the stalls here round the lawn,' said Lowell, joining them. 'Don't worry, Hugo. He's tied up quite securely, I promise you. I saw to it myself.'

'He had better be! Don't, whatever you do, let him out!'

'Oh, I won't Hugo, I won't!' said Deborah with conviction. 'What do you take me for?'

By late afternoon the prevailing mood was one of happy contentment. The sun had shone without a break, the stalls had done a roaring trade, the entertainers were busy counting their pennies, the tug o' war had been won, as usual, by the team from the Angel at Abbot Quincey. The crowds had gathered on the south lawn for the last excitement of the day— the presentation of the prizes. When Hugo appeared on the low dais there were quite genuine cheers and applause, and Deborah was impressed with the obvious pleasure the local people felt at his return. He made a short straightforward speech which was very well received, and then turned to the business of the awards. There were quite a lot, and the list was only halfway through when Deborah felt a tug on her sleeve. It was Frederica.

'Deborah, I think you should have a look at Autolycus. I was walking past the stable just now and he was howling quite dreadfully. I didn't like to go in myself. You know how he would leap up, and I am not sure I would be strong enough to hold him. Has Lowell tied him up too tightly, do you suppose?'

The two girls squeezed through the crowds and made their way to the stable where Autolycus was confined. The howls had stopped, and the silence worried Deborah so much that she ran the last few yards to see what was wrong...

It was clear what had happened. Lowell had in fact given the dog quite a lot of freedom with a rope which was several yards long. But in his frantic efforts to join the party Autolycus had tangled himself up, and he was now lying on the ground with the rope wrapped round his neck... With an exclamation of horror, Deborah threw open the stable door and ran forward to release him. What she had not observed was that the enterprising dog had been silently gnawing through the rope nearest the bar to which he was tied. As soon as she approached him, Autolycus gave a yelp of ecstasy, broke free from his restraint and leapt on her, frantically licking her with great sweeps of his tongue. Deborah staggered back, but made a valiant effort to grab him. She managed to snatch a piece of the frayed rope, but it was too little to restrain Autolycus in his exuberant state.

'Frederica! Help! Help me to get a better hold! Quickly!'

When he saw another friend outside the stable door Autolycus yelped again, then, barking joyfully, made a rush for Frederica.

'Autolycus! No! Don't! Frederica—don't run away! That's the worst thing—' It was too late. Deborah's cries were in vain. Frederica was running for dear life out of the stable yard towards the house. Autolycus, delighted at this prospect of a game, tore out of Deborah's grasp and set off in enthusiastic pursuit. After hours of confinement with only brief visits from his mistress to console him, Autolycus was full of spirits, oblivious to anything but the feeling of freedom, and the joy of movement. He caught up with Frederica as she reached the edge of the lawn, whereupon she gave a little scream and climbed on to a nearby haywain. The dog stopped in frustration at the bottom of the wain and Deborah almost caught him again... But not quite.

Hugo was making the last presentation—a sucking pig to Farmer Gantry of Abbot Giles—when he caught sight of Frederica on top of the haywain staring down at Autolycus. He stopped. 'That damned dog! Autolycus!' he roared.

Autolycus turned and saw his idol. Unmindful of the threat in Hugo's voice, he gave a deep bay and raced across the lawn, scattering anything and anyone in his way. When he reached the platform he crashed into Farmer Gantry's legs with such force that the sturdy farmer's knees buckled and, clutching in vain

at the nearest post, he fell over. The post groaned and
swayed, then toppled after him, bringing the rest of
the structure with it. Hugo, Farmer Gantry and the
piglet were suddenly a heaving mass on the ground
covered in a gaily striped awning…

It was not a silent mass. Hugo was swearing and
uttering the direst threats against Autolycus, Deborah
and anyone else he could think of. Farmer Gantry was
blowing and wheezing in his efforts to escape, and
the pig squealed incessantly as it wriggled out and
scampered away through the crowds. There was no
real danger. Willing hands lifted the awning up for
the two men to crawl out unharmed, while numbers
of others chased after the piglet. After the first appalled moment, there was a lot of laughter and ribald
comment—even among the visitors on the terrace.
Henrietta could hardly speak for laughing, Lady
Martindale was holding a discreet handkerchief to her
mouth, and once Hugo's parents were sure he was
unharmed they, too, joined in the mirth. It was too
much. Hugo shook himself like a dog, straightened
his cravat, and passed a hand through his hair. Then,
with a hasty word to the farmer, he strode off in
search of the culprit.

Deborah had watched the scene with unbelieving
horror. Her personal evil demon had struck again! But
this time there would surely be no reprieve, no forgiveness. Both she and her dog would be anathema.
Autolycus, terrified at the damage he had caused, had
made off, tail between his legs, as quickly as he had
come—this time in the direction of his own stable at
the Vicarage. Once Deborah had seen Hugo emerge

safely, she circled discreetly round the back of the lawn, and then hurried off to join her dog in his retreat...

It took some time for Hugo to find them. He had gone first to the stables at Perceval Hall, only to find them deserted. Then he had accosted Lowell, who was not only unable to help, but had also found it impossible to hide his glee at Hugo's recent loss of dignity. Hugo's command of himself was severely taxed, too, by solicitous enquiries from neighbours, tenants and friends, all of whom had found the situation highly entertaining. Apparently it was the presence of the pig which had added the finishing touch. 'Better nor all o' them sideshows put together!' was a typical reaction. Hugo assured everybody he was quite unhurt, laughed with them, agreed that something should be done about the dog, and continued with his search. He finally decided that both Deborah and her dog had left for home. On his way out of the grounds he came across Frederica.

'Oh, Hugo! I'm so glad to have found you! Have you recovered from your mishap?'

'Yes, of course. Shaken in dignity, but in nothing else,' he said with a wry smile. 'But what about you?'

'I'm perfectly all right. I know Autolycus didn't mean any harm, really. I just got in a stupid panic. You won't punish him, will you? It really wasn't his fault.'

'I expect Deborah was to blame—she usually is,' said Hugo grimly.

'No, no! It wasn't Deborah, either. It was as much

my fault as hers. You look so angry—please don't be hard on them, Hugo!'

'Frederica, you're a dear girl with a very soft heart. It's like you to want to defend Deborah and her wretched dog. But it won't do! Now, tell me where I may find them.'

'I shan't tell you if you are going to be horrid to them!' said Frederica with unwonted defiance.

'Frederica!' said Hugo, much surprised. But after he had regarded her sternly for a moment she gave in.

'I… I expect they're at the V-Vicarage,' she stammered. 'I saw Autolycus running in that direction a few minutes ago. But it really was an accident! I heard Autolycus howling and I came to fetch Deborah—'

'Thank you. I expect your mother will be looking for you—the fête is coming to an end, thank God, and they will want as much help as they can find. Hester and Dungarran seem to have disappeared, and I'm not available at the moment—not until I've dealt with Deborah Staunton and the dog. Be a good girl, and go back to the Hall. I'll join you later. No, no more! I won't listen to you. Go back to the Hall!'

Frederica turned disconsolately and walked back over the lawn. Hugo watched her go, then set off for the Vicarage.

He found Deborah huddled in a corner of the stable with Autolycus's head on her lap. She didn't look up as he arrived but bent over and put her arms protectively round the dog's neck.

'Let the dog go!' said Hugo evenly. She shook her head without looking at him.

'I said, let the dog go, Deborah!'

'I won't! I know what you mean to do and I shan't let you!'

'I'm in no mood for games,' Hugo said, removing his coat. 'Get up, Autolycus! Stand, sir!'

Autolycus gave Deborah an apologetic glance and got up. He looked up at Hugo ingratiatingly and gave a slight wag of his tail. When this overture failed, his tail drooped and his huge head hung down. He was the picture of abject misery.

Hugo picked up a whip which was hanging on the wall and took hold of Autolycus's collar. He raised the whip and gave the dog a whack across his hindquarters. It was comparatively mild—meant to punish, not to hurt—but Autolycus yelped and pulled frantically against Hugo's iron grasp. Hugo raised his arm again...

'Stop it! Stop!' Deborah leapt up and snatched the whip out of Hugo's hand. When he would have taken it back she backed away out of his reach. 'I told you, Hugo! I won't let you hit Autolycus!'

Deborah's defiance was the last straw. Hugo, who had to this moment, under the severest provocation, kept his temper, now lost it. 'Give me that whip, Deborah! By God, if I have to force it from you it won't be the dog who is punished!'

'You'd better not come any nearer!'

Hugo ignored her warning and started towards her. Deborah raised her arm and let fly. The tip of the whip grazed Hugo's cheek. With a roar of surprised fury Hugo covered the remaining distance in one bound and twisted the whip out of her hand, not very gently. His hold on her wrist was painful and she gave a cry of fright. This incensed Hugo more than ever. He threw the whip down, grabbed her by the shoulders and shook her hard. Then he lifted her up till her feet were off the ground and kissed her roughly, paying no heed to her muffled cries and frantic kicks. The intimate warmth of Deborah's body through her thin summer garments inflamed Hugo even more and though the kiss lost some of its ferocity it grew even more intense. Deborah's protests gradually died away, and the two figures were locked together in a passionate embrace...

Till this moment Autolycus had been unable to decide where his loyalties lay. But he suddenly made up his mind and launched himself on Hugo with a deep growl. Deborah was freed as Hugo turned to defend himself. Autolycus had his teeth on Hugo's shirt sleeve... Deborah had almost fallen when she was released, but now she darted forward again and shouted in fright, 'No, Autolycus, no! Down! Down!'

Autolycus reluctantly let go and, still bristling, every sense alert, lay down, ready to leap again if required.

For a moment the stable was quiet, except for the dog's panting, and the rapid breathing of the two humans. Hugo picked up his coat and put it on. Then he walked to the doors, dabbing at his cheek with his handkerchief, while Deborah went over to the dog and tried to calm him. It wasn't easy, for the dog sensed the tension and hostility still filling the stable.

'You deserved it!' said Hugo harshly, staring out through the open doors.

Deborah swallowed, but said nothing.

'But I shouldn't have done it,' he went on. 'I don't know why I did.'

'You were angry,' said Deborah forlornly. 'You…you did say that you wanted to punish me. And you did.' She shook her head and put her fingers to her lips. 'It's strange. I thought a kiss was an expression of love, not…not a desire to hurt.' He gave her a quick look, then turned away again. There was another pause. Deborah busied herself putting her clothing in order while she fought to regain control of her chaotic emotions. At last she spoke. 'What are you going to do now? About Autolycus?'

Hugo kept his back to her as he said, 'Oh, you needn't be concerned. I'm not going to use the whip on him again. I have never yet hit an animal when I was as angry as I am at this moment.'

Deborah got up and took a step towards him. 'Hugo…' She lifted her hands, but dropped them in despair at his lack of response. She said, 'Are you…are you going to persuade Aunt Elizabeth to get rid of him? I can't stop you. And she would very probably listen to you. But…but Hugo… Oh, I know I'm in no position to ask favours of you at the moment! But I wish you wouldn't.' She waited a moment, but when there was still no reaction she went back to her dog and sank down beside him.

Hugo turned at last and looked sombrely at the girl and the dog, huddled together once again on the floor of the stable. 'I don't know. It wouldn't be easy to find another home for him. But I wouldn't want him destroyed. Basically he's a good dog.'

'Destroyed!' Deborah scrambled to her feet. 'He's not vicious, Hugo! He didn't mean it when he attacked you…'

'Oh, he meant it all right! But I don't blame him for that. He was protecting you, as he saw it. And…and I regret to say that you were in need of protection.' He suddenly turned away and looked out of the doors again.

Deborah regarded Hugo's back. He was a proud man. And he was ashamed. She drew a deep breath. 'I can forget that you kissed me as you did. You were provoked. I should never have attacked you with the whip. That was…was very wrong of me. We…we both behaved badly. I know it won't be easy, but can we…can we put the past half hour out of our minds? Except for the m-matter of Autolycus's f-future?'

There was another pause. Then Hugo turned round. 'I'll try.' He was still grim-faced, but was at least making an effort to speak normally. 'Nothing much can be done anyway. I shall be away for the next few days. I'm to fetch my grandmother home.'

Deborah followed his lead. 'The Dowager? I wondered why she wasn't at the fête.'

'She says she's too old to enjoy the fuss. She stayed with some old friends in Derbyshire while we were all in London this spring, and the Broughtons invited her to wait till after the fête before she came back.'

'I was always afraid of her. And she terrified the twins.'

'She can be intimidating.' Hugo was still not giving

much away. 'Deborah, I need to think. I'll use the next few days to decide about the dog.'

Deborah nodded without saying anything. What she wanted to know, and dared not ask, was what Hugo would do about her. She rather feared that she was once again, and this time perhaps permanently, out of his favour. It was quite possible that he would never forgive her for provoking him into such disgraceful behaviour. Behaviour which was so far removed from his own high standards.

How Hugo explained the cut on his cheek and the rip in the sleeve of his shirt Deborah never knew. By the time she got up the next morning he was already on his way to Derbyshire. He was to spend a couple of nights with the Broughtons, and since the Dowager Lady Perceval believed in travelling in comfort and very slowly, he would not be back before the end of the week.

While Hugo was away Deborah deliberately kept herself as busy as possible. She wanted no time to think. At the time, she had suppressed the shock of what had happened in the stable, concentrating on Autolycus and his fate instead. It had seemed the best course. But as time went on she found herself less and less able to bury the truth. That savage kiss had devastated her, had knocked down years of careful defences. She had loved Hugo for almost as long as she had known him, but he had always been merely a good friend. Knowing that her case was hopeless, she had never permitted herself to think of him in any other way. When he had lost his temper in London he had treated her like an elder brother handling a naughty child. That was how he had always regarded her... Till now.

But when he had lost his temper in the stable Hugo had for the first time treated her as a woman. He had meant to punish and had succeeded—that kiss had been painfully humiliating. But if she were to be completely honest with herself she must acknowledge that it had raised a previously unknown demon of desire inside her... Hugo may have kissed her in anger, but it had still been a kiss and there had been passion behind it... Deborah told herself again and again that it had meant nothing to him, must mean nothing to her. During the day she made sure that her hours were filled with activity, giving her no time to think. But at night she lay awake, a prey to the new and disturbing emotions which had been roused by that kiss—remembering how her initial fright had given way to a passion which had equalled Hugo's, how the feel of his hands on her body had excited her... But with determination she applied all her considerable strength of character to forgetting it. She must. If she were not to spend the rest of her life in useless repining, the demon must be put back in its bottle, and Deborah Staunton must regard Hugo Perceval as nothing more than a good friend—if that were still possible.

There was plenty to occupy her. Much to the delight of everyone in the family, Hester and Lord Dungarran had announced their engagement on the evening of the fête. Plans for the wedding were already under discussion, and there was to be a joint

celebration of their betrothal and Hugo's thirtieth
birthday after Hugo and his grandmother were back.
Lady Perceval, knowing Deborah's gifts, had asked
her to prepare a small concert to entertain the guests.
Edwina and Frederica would sing a couple of duets
and play the harp. Henrietta and Lowell said they had
a dramatic dialogue to offer, and Deborah herself
would of course play as usual, and sing one or two
solos. Practising these and rehearsing the twins in
their pieces took a great deal of energy and time.
Persuading Henrietta and Lowell to treat the occasion
seriously took even more.

Deborah also made a point of renewing her old
acquaintances in the neighbourhood. These were a
surprising collection, not to be found among the gentry, some of them not even among the deserving poor.
As a child she had the gift of making friends with the
lonely, the outcasts, those who had been rejected by
society, or had themselves rejected it. They lived in
isolated cottages, or primitive huts in the woods
scraping a living from the land. They were often sus-
picious of others, and it had taken patience and understanding to gain their confidence. But Deborah had
a fellow feeling for their loneliness, had taken pains
with them, and had been rewarded in the past with
their trust.

Driven now by her own unhappiness, Deborah
spent time finding her old friends and assuring them
once again of her good faith. She took Autolycus with
her, for some of the paths were lonely, but she kept
a very close watch on him. At the slightest sign of
excitement or high spirits she would call him back

and put him on the leash. He seemed to accept the discipline willingly enough. It almost looked as if Hugo's patient training of the dog, coupled with the punishment for disobedience, had worked, after all. But Deborah's heart was heavy as she wondered what Hugo would decide to do about him. Though Autolycus might belong to her, it was her Aunt Elizabeth who had the final say in whether the dog could be kept at the Vicarage, and Aunt Elizabeth would listen to what Hugo said. Deborah could not bear the thought of losing the dog. In the absence of anyone she could confide in, his simple, uncomplicated devotion was a solace to her bruised heart.

Hester's betrothal and the plans for her marriage in September were the chief topics of conversation among the young ladies at the Vicarage. All four were to be bridesmaids, and when they were not actually rehearsing for Lady Perceval's party, much time was spent in discussing muslins, silks, laces, ribbons and flowers. And the exchange of confidences.

'I am so pleased for Hester,' said Edwina one day when she and Deborah were walking back to the Vicarage. 'We thought she would never marry, you know.'

'Not all women wish to, Edwina,' said Deborah with a wry smile. 'Hester always seemed to me to be quite happy with her books in the attic. But I hear that she and Lord Dungarran got to know each other while working together on some important state documents?'

'Yes! They are said to have saved the Duke of

Wellington's life between them. Isn't it romantic? At least… I suppose it is. Lord Dungarran is quite old.'

'Old! He's the same age as Hugo!'

'That's what I mean. And Lord Dungarran is usually rather serious, as well. Not what I would have called at all romantic.'

'Oh come, Edwina! Have you *seen* the way he looks at Hester? I only wish that I would one day mean as much to someone as Hester clearly means to him. And he isn't serious all the time. Yesterday he and Hester were laughing about his love letters—apparently they have a secret way of writing them, and she was teasing him about having *blackmailed* her into meeting him again! I wonder how he did it? Oh, he's romantic, no doubt about that!'

'You're probably right. I suppose it's because I… I prefer younger men. Ones that are not perhaps as clever as Hugo and Lord Dungarran.'

'What did you mean when you called Hugo old?'

'Well, he is. He's very nearly thirty. And he always seems to know exactly what he's doing, and what he wants us to do.'

'That's certainly true,' said Deborah with feeling. 'But you don't necessarily have to do as he says.'

'Oh but I do! I would never dream of arguing with him. I… I do hope…'

'What? What is it, Edwina, dear?' Edwina was very nervous. The handkerchief she held in her hand was twisted into a tight ball.

'Well, I know it's absurd to think he would, but…but I hope that Hugo won't ask me to marry him! I should never have the courage to refuse.'

'What makes you think he might?'

'Oh, nothing he has said! But Frederica and I were talking about him the other night. It's well known that he always promised to marry when he was thirty. And he doesn't appear to have found anyone yet. We thought that perhaps he might ask *you*—but you and he are always falling out, aren't you? And Hugo hates arguments or scenes.'

'Quite true. I can't imagine anything less likely.'

'Nor can I, really,' said Edwina, quite unaware of the pain she was causing. 'But you see, Deborah, it is quite likely that Mama would be happy to see one of us marry Hugo. I know she no longer has Robina to worry over, but there are still three of us left. She has to think of things like dowries and suchlike, and there has never been very much money. If Uncle James suggested it, and Hugo agreed, I am sure Papa would be pleased to give his consent.'

Deborah put aside her own feelings. Since Hugo would never dream of asking her to marry him they were irrelevant. But she was in a real dilemma, all the same. Knowing of Hugo's intentions towards the twins tied her hands. If he decided that Edwina was his choice, it would be very wrong of her to encourage the girl in an entirely uncharacteristic rebellion against authority. Especially as there was no good reason for either of her cousins to refuse such an extremely favourable offer. Deborah was carefully objective in her reply. 'Hugo would make a kind husband,' she said slowly.

'Oh yes! He's very kind! You mustn't think I don't like him!' said Edwina swiftly. 'But I think I would be happier with someone who is…is more patient with me. Who gives me time to make up my own mind, rather than telling me all the time what he thinks I should do. I'm not terribly clever, I know, but I'm not an *idiot*, Deborah!'

'Do you really think Hugo treats you like an idiot?'

'Not exactly. But he doesn't listen to what I have to say.'

Deborah sighed. It was as she had feared. But there was not very much she could do. Except for the twins, she had very little influence with anyone. She was wondering whether she dared consult Hester when Edwina spoke again.

'I think I would like to marry someone who is more my own age, and…and more like me. Someone like Richard Vernon, for example. He's very nice.'

'Richard Vernon? Of Stoke Park?'

'Yes. He…he has said he likes me, too.'

Deborah stared at Edwina. She knew Richard Vernon. He was indeed very nice. A charming boy, for all his twenty-three years. How could anyone prefer such a…nonentity to Hugo…? But when she considered it, she saw that young Vernon would be a perfect match for her cousin Edwina. He appeared to be kind and generous, and he was certainly eligible enough—the eldest son of a very respectable family, he would eventually inherit a modest but comfortable estate not far from Abbot Quincey. Edwina would remain within reach of her family and all her friends. The two had shared interests—she was a keen horse-woman, and he was mad on horses. Richard's manners were unexceptionable and though his humour was a touch juvenile it was never cruel. Yes, Richard Vernon would make an ideal partner for her cousin. Hugo mustn't be allowed to spoil that.

Deborah made up her mind. Edwina must be persuaded to take her mother into her confidence. Aunt Elizabeth was strict, but if she knew that Edwina was in love with someone else—a perfectly eligible friend of the family—she would see to it that Hugo did not make the girl an offer. And Hugo…would have to look to Frederica, or outside the family altogether for a bride. The thought came before Deborah could suppress it—if only he would consider her! But Edwina was right. Whatever that kiss had meant, Hugo would never ever think of Deborah Staunton as a suitable bride. The sooner she shut the door on that particular dream, and threw away the key, the better for her peace of mind. If only she could forget what had happened in the stable…!

Had Deborah only known it, the incident in the stable had had an equally devastating effect on Hugo. His journey to Derbyshire was far from comfortable…

Chapter Five

Hugo Perceval was a man who took pride in behaving as he ought. Though he usually managed to have his own way in most matters, he maintained a high standard of manners and a genuine concern for the feelings of others. Since reaching manhood he had hardly ever acted on impulse or without due thought for the consequences. Indeed, in London society he had been respected and popular—an amusing companion, whose taste and behaviour were always impeccable.

So Hugo was every bit as shaken as Deborah as he journeyed to Derbyshire. The memory of his actions in that accursed stable tormented him! He told himself in vain that he had been provoked beyond endurance. Deborah Staunton was an untamed gypsy who would never pay any attention to the things he cared most about. She was like that damned dog of hers—unpredictable, immoderate, with neither sense nor decorum. She had made him look a fool in the eyes of the whole neighbourhood, she had challenged his perfectly proper right to chastise the dog, and then to top it all she had...she had actually attacked him with a whip!

All of which was undeniably true. But it didn't help. He was ashamed of himself. God knew, he had kissed many a woman in his time, but never before in such a fury. Nor with so much uncontrolled passion. He did not like to contemplate what would have happened if he had not been brought to his senses by the dog's attack. He had been so beside himself—and not only with anger, either—that he might have done far worse than just kiss Deborah Staunton. What *had* come over him? Why was it, in heaven's name, that this girl had the power to bring out the very worst in him? With everyone else in the world he could keep in control, make his wishes known without even raising his voice! But not with that...that witch!

He swore at a sudden, uncontrollable vision of black hair flying round a pale face, of darkest blue eyes, eyes that were almost black, sparking flame at him... He had been outraged at the sudden pain as the end of the whip had caught his cheek, and had leapt forward with the intention of taking it from her. The shaking he had given her after that was hardly his style, but, given the provocation, it had been within reason. But what followed...

Why? Why the devil *had* he kissed her? Her cry of pain when he had wrenched the whip from her haunted him. Why had it added fuel to his rage? He could not banish the memory of the delicate bones beneath his hands as he shook her, of the ease with which he had lifted her against him before kissing her so brutally... It was impossible to forget the way she had struggled against him, her cries… All these thoughts gave Hugo Perceval sleepless nights while he was collecting his grandmother and bringing her back to Abbot Quincey. On the way to Derbyshire he was at least left to his own thoughts, unpleasant though they were. But the return journey was much worse—his grandmother's gimlet eye saw that something was wrong with her favourite grandchild, and, undeterred by the presence of Gossage, her elderly maid, who was in the carriage with them, she set herself to find out what was troubling him.

'What is it, Hugo? Is life in the country already beginning to pall? Is that it?'

'Not at all.'

'Is it this business with Sywell's murder? From what the Broughtons said they think now that that wretch Burneck murdered his own father! That was a bad business, though Sywell isn't any great loss. But are you and your father having trouble with the Steepwood lot? The Perceval lands aren't affected, are they?'

Hugo smiled in spite of himself. His grandmother's first thought had always been for the estate. When his grandfather, the first Sir Hugo, had inherited the title the Percevals had been very close to ruin. But old Sir Hugo and his wife had worked hard to re-establish the family fortunes—with some success. The lands were once again in good heart, the farms prosperous. The Percevals would never again be as rich as they had once been, but they owed their present moderately comfortable state to the efforts of this redoubtable lady and her husband. Hugo laid his hand on his grandmother's.

'Have no fear, ma'am. My future inheritance is in good heart. We have had some fun and games with the people at Steepwood, I won't deny that. Sywell left a dreadful mess behind him. My father has been doing his best to calm the hotheads and give help where he can. But the trouble has not so far spread to any other properties.'

'Then it must be woman trouble,' said the Dowager, reverting to her former topic. 'Loose ends in London? Mistresses being difficult?'

'Upon my word, ma'am, you're a touch outspoken! I believe you've shocked Gossage.'

'I've never been missish, my boy! I haven't had the time. But I'd be disappointed in you if there was anything like that. The Percevals have usually managed such matters with grace—and generosity. Always excepting Sanford, your late unlamented great-grandfather, of course. He was a disgrace to the Perceval name, besides ruining us all.'

'There isn't anyone in London who has reason to think me either ungraceful or mean. Will that do?'

An end was put to this conversation by their arrival at their lodging for the night, and since the Dowager Lady Perceval retired immediately to her large and comfortable suite of rooms, there to be cosseted by Gossage and put to bed, it was not resumed till the next day.

'Well, Hugo,' Lady Perceval began as they left the inn, 'I've told Gossage to ride on the box this morning, so you can talk quite freely. She grumbled, of course, but it won't do her any harm—it's a beautiful morning and she could do with some air.'

Hugo regarded his grandmother with affectionate amusement. Gossage had been with Lady Perceval for over forty years, and was devoted to her. But their relationship had the character of a running battle. In spite of the respect Gossage always showed in public towards her mistress, she was often critical in private. She watched jealously over the Dowager's health, and was ready to comment unfavourably whenever her mistress showed any inclination to do too much, or to over-indulge her surprisingly good appetite. Lady Perceval was not particularly grateful for this, and was often rude to her maid. Gossage had probably been over-zealous the night before and was now paying for it with dismissal to the box. But the two were very close. Gossage was maidservant, nurse, and companion all in one, and Lady Perceval would have been lost without her.

'Now! You can tell me what is bothering you, Hugo. I intend to know, so you might as well tell me straight away and save us both some time.'

Hugo had known that his grandmother would not let the subject drop, and had had time the night before to decide what he would say and, more important, how much he would conceal. He said calmly, 'It's the question of my marriage.'

'Ah! Yes, of course. You promised your father, didn't you? And now that Hester is off his hands—and very successfully, too, from all accounts—he'll be looking to you to set up your family. So, who is the lucky girl to be?'

'That's just it! I can't make up my mind!'

'What, no heiresses in London willing to marry you?'

'There are never as many heiresses as rumour would have it, Grandmother! Nor is there ever a shortage of men to pursue them.'

'That may be! But I don't believe that a well set-up young fellow like you couldn't have found one if you'd tried. What about Sophia Cleeve, for example?'

'Sophia is a very beautiful girl and I like her enormously. She regards me as a good friend—at least, I hope so—but she has too much spirit for my taste. In any case you're behind with the news. Sophia has got herself engaged to Sharnbrook quite recently. It's a brilliant match for her, of course, and from what I've heard of the man he'll know how to keep her in line, though it won't always be easy.'

'And that's what you're looking for, is it? An easy life? I'm disappointed in you.'

'What on earth do you mean?'

'I always hoped you'd bring a bit of vigour into the family! Oh, don't misunderstand—y'r father and y'r Uncle William are good sons, I'm not denying that. But they're...they're dull! I want a bit of vitality, a bit of amusement in my old age, and I rather hoped you would provide it!'

'My father has put a great deal of energy into improving the estate,' said Hugo somewhat stiffly. 'And Uncle William is very well loved by the parish...'

'Don't poker up in that pompous way with me, my boy! I know my sons' virtues—you don't have to remind me of them! And their wives are good crea-

tures, both of them.' Lady Perceval sighed. 'Very
good. But life isn't only good works and worthy efforts! I was hoping you'd bring a bit of London frivolity back to Northamptonshire.'

'Lowell is the lad for that.'

'Lowell is a lightweight! I'm very fond of him—
he's the only one of you who makes me laugh. But
he's the other side of the coin—all frivolity and no
substance. No, you're the one to liven up Perceval
Hall and do justice to the place at the same time.
What you need is the right wife. What about the rest
of the heiresses?'

'They really wouldn't have done, ma'am. Besides,
I always assumed I would marry someone from the
neighbourhood. Someone who knows the country.'

'Not a bad idea. Not at all a bad idea. So who is
it to be?' She thought for a moment. 'Carrie Vernon
is too old for you—she's thirty, if she's a day. Sophia
Cleeve and the Roade girls have gone... A pity, that.
I always had a soft spot for Beatrice—she has a rare
sense of humour.'

'Olivia Roade is prettier.'

'I suppose you mean she's a blue-eyed blonde. You
always had a weakness for them. Well, I don't believe
I ever met the younger Roade girl to speak to, so I
can't say. But looks ain't everything, my boy. I
should have thought you'd be old enough to have
found that out for yourself. Beatrice Roade has character! Still, she's married now, so we're wasting our
time talking of her! Who else is there...? The
Courtney Hall chit—what's her name? Felicity, that's
it! What about her?'

'She's thirteen, Grandmother. I'm not looking for a child bride. In fact, I had thought…'

'Well, speak up!'

'What would you say to one of the twins?'

'The twins! Edwina and Frederica? Oh no! That wouldn't do at all!'

'You're surely not against marriage between cousins?'

'I don't like it. But there's nothing in the family background to suggest it would be undesirable. No, that's not the reason.'

'Their lack of fortune? I've told you—I'm not looking for an heiress, Grandmother.'

'Don't despise money, young man. It isn't everything, not by any means, but it helps! Your grandfather was glad enough of my dowry when we married. Mind you, it all went into the estate—we didn't have two pence left to rub together for our own use.'

'And we have you and Sir Hugo to thank for our present comparative prosperity, ma'am! I shall never forget it.'

'Never mind that! It's your wife we're talking about.'

'Well then, what is wrong with Edwina—or Frederica?'

'You'd walk all over either of them! Oh no, they would never do! It wouldn't be at all good for you. You'd be even more stuffy than you are.'

'Ma'am!'

'It's no good mincing words, Hugo! You're the best one of your generation, but you are too used to having your own way. You need a wife who will stand up to you, stir you up. Someone like Beatrice Roade, or Sophia Cleeve.' She shook her head. 'It's a real pity that Sophia is already spoken for. She would have been perfect for you—lively, beautiful, *and* rich!'

'I was never in love with Sophia, Grandmother. I've told you why.'

'And you're telling me you're in love with one of your cousins,' Lady Perceval said derisively, 'when you can't even make up your mind which one you would choose? Balderdash!'

'Till now I've thought that liking would be enough—especially when I know them so well. We would be easy in each other's company—'

'There's that word again! Easy! It's excitement you should be looking for, Hugo! You may have left the pleasures of London behind you, but you're not yet middle-aged! Besides, though you might well be easy in the company of the twins, I don't believe they'd be easy in yours! They are far too much in awe of you. Don't misunderstand me—they are dear, good girls with plenty of character in their quiet way. I'm very fond of them, but they need someone less powerful than you to look after them. Put them out of your mind—unless you've already spoken to them?'

'No, of course not. So far I have only discussed it with my father... And...' He stopped short.

'Well? Who else have you discussed it with?'

'No one.' Hugo silenced his conscience. He had not exactly *discussed* marriage to the twins with Deborah. He went on swiftly, 'My father likes the idea.'

'Of course he would!' Lady Perceval's tone implied that she did not think much of her son's good sense. 'He'd like to help his brother. Four girls are a heavy burden, and William is too unworldly to bestir himself.'

'Surely my Aunt Elizabeth makes up for that?'

'Elizabeth?' Lady Perceval shook her head in pity for his obtuseness. 'Your Aunt Elizabeth may be more energetic than William, but she's every bit as unworldly! Have you never asked yourself what the daughter of a Duke was doing in marrying my William? We're an old family—older than the Ingleshams—but it was a step down for her, there's no doubt about that!'

Relieved that his grandmother was distracted, temporarily at least, from discussing his choice of a wife, Hugo asked, 'Why did she, then?'

'She says she respected his character.' A derisive cackle followed. 'You'd never get your aunt to admit that she fell head over ears in love! But that's the truth of the matter. She married for love, Hugo, and if that's not unworldly, then I'm a Dutchman! Talked her family into accepting him, as well, which is more than that wretched sister of hers did. Of course, sister Frances went completely the wrong way about it. She defied her father outright, ran off with Edmund Staunton to Gretna and married him there. That was the end of her. The old Duke was a demon if anyone disobeyed him, and he never forgave her for it.'

'But even if she had behaved differently, surely a Perceval was more acceptable to the Ingleshams than a Staunton! Lady Frances might not have persuaded her family as easily as her sister had.'

'I'm not saying Elizabeth found it easy, either! But she had patience and self-discipline. Frances had neither, and she ruined everything by being too hasty. There was nothing actually wrong with the Stauntons. They were an old family, too. Anglo-Irish. There's a title in it somewhere. An Irish one, of course, and Staunton himself was not in the direct line. And there was no money in his branch of the family, just some run-down estate or other in County Cork. But the family was well enough.'

'What about Edmund Staunton himself?'

'Ah, there was the rub! The Ingleshams had the highest opinion of William's character—that's why they eventually consented to Elizabeth's engagement to him. But they suspected Edmund Staunton of making up to Frances in the hope of a handsome dowry. He was a charming, selfish rogue, but Frances could never see it, of course. Well, she paid for it in the end. And her daughter, Deborah, too. Cast off without a penny, both of them.'

Hugo moved restlessly, and his grandmother gave him a sharp look. She said slyly, 'Now, *Deborah* was a taking little thing—all hair and eyes. Always in trouble, but how she made us laugh! You could never be annoyed with her for long. There was nothing wrong with her courage—or her heart. She was the only one who would stand up to you, though she liked you well enough. In fact, I'd go so far as to say she worshipped you in the old days!'

This was an unwelcome reminder of Hugo's present discomfort. He said, a touch grimly, 'Yes, but she's grown up now. I doubt she has much affection for me at the moment.'

'Oh?' said his grandmother. And waited.

'If you haven't heard already, I might as well tell you myself. The others will be only too glad to tell you the tale before you've gone two steps into the house.'

Hugo went on to recount the story of the fête, and Autolycus's disastrous intervention. Lady Perceval laughed till she cried as he described the collapse of the awning and the antics of the pig.

Somewhat sourly, Hugo said, 'I thought it would amuse you. It amused everyone else, too.'

'And I suppose you gave her a dressing-down and she answered you back. There's nothing wrong with that, Hugo! No, she's the girl you should marry! You'd never have a dull moment with that one. And I would enjoy her company, too.'

'Since she's to stay with Aunt Elizabeth for the forseeable future, you'll be able to enjoy her company without my having to marry her.' His answer had come swiftly, instinctively. His grandmother was too clever. He rather thought she must have already heard something of the events at the fête—one of the twins might have written to her, or Hester when she wrote to tell her grandmother of her engagement. The old lady had quite possibly been working towards this point ever since they had set out from Derbyshire. He must not let her see how powerfully the name of Deborah Staunton affected him, otherwise she would begin to suspect that there was more to the story than anyone had told her. As indeed there was.

But it wasn't easy to stay impassive in the face of his grandmother's bright-eyed curiosity. Not when the scene in the stable was vivid in his mind's eye, and the words she had just spoken were resounding in his brain—*'she's the girl you should marry'*. Marry Deborah Staunton? Ask her to be his wife? The idea had never occurred to him before. Up till the day of the fête he had always regarded her as a sort of younger sister—someone who had often been a sympathetic ear, someone who often seemed in need of protection, who could also be infuriating, outrageous, totally exasperating. But there had been that strange impulse to kiss her soon after she had arrived... And then, of course, that incomprehensible reaction in the stable...

He realised that he had been silent for longer than was wise. His grandmother was regarding him with speculation in her eye. 'I...I...' Dammit, why was he stammering? He took a deep breath and said firmly, 'I don't intend to marry anyone until I am clearer in my own mind. You may be right about the twins, though I would deny that I am as domineering as you say I am.'

The Dowager Lady Perceval looked at him in silence. Then, to his relief, she started to talk of the Broughtons and their family.

Believe me, if all those endearing young charms,
    Which I gaze on so fondly today,
        Were to change by tomorrow and

fleet in my arms,
Like fairy gifts fading away,
Thou wouldst still be adored
as this moment thou art,
Let thy loveliness fade as it will;
And, around the dear ruins, each wish of my heart
Would entwine itself verdantly still!

The voice died away, a last liquid arpeggio ran through the air, then Frederica stilled the humming strings of her harp, and there was silence. Hugo looked round the candlelit room. Its occupants were still held in the enchantment of the music. Robert and Hester were standing close together at the window, Robert holding Hester's hand at his lips in a silent promise of his love. But the song had put a spell on more than the betrothed couple for whom it had been intended. Sir James was sitting on the sofa, his arm along the back, his hand no more than touching his wife's shoulder, but the whole of their happiness together was conveyed in that simple gesture. Nearby, Lady Elizabeth was looking at her husband with the sort of smile which Hugo was ready to swear had rarely, if ever, been seen in public before. And what was young Vernon doing, gazing at his cousin Edwina in such a besotted manner?

As the applause began he looked over to Deborah by the piano. The candles shone on her black hair, and cast a luminous glow over her face. Her eyes were sparkling in the light. She looked for once...beautiful. And strange. What was the magic she exercised? On this night of Hester's betrothal and his own thirtieth birthday they had been given over an hour's royal entertainment with verse, laughter and music. His brother and cousins had never performed better, and, according to his mother, it was all Deborah's doing. And now this song of love that would last... What spell had she put on them all? He had never seen such a demonstration of the abiding love his parents felt for each other, or caught such a glimpse of his Aunt Elizabeth's feeling for her husband... All because of a sentimental Irish ballad! But no, that wasn't it at all! It was the simple, unaffected performance which had enchanted them, Frederica's harp blending with Deborah's pure soprano, creating magic for everyone. He went over to the piano...

But before he reached it Deborah, who had seen him coming, sat down and struck up a lively tune. The moment was lost. Chairs were hastily cleared away and an energetic set of country dances began, which lasted half an hour and at the end of which most people sat down laughing and panting. The evening was hot and the table of cold drinks was soon surrounded by gentlemen fetching glasses of wine or lemonade for their partners.

'Deborah, I've brought you a drink.' Edwina's face was flushed and her eyes were shining. Richard Vernon was in close attendance. 'Frederica and I have been very selfish! One of us should have taken your place at the piano—at least for a while. You haven't danced at all!'

'Nonsense! I like playing. I'm an infinitely better pianist than I am a dancer,' laughed Deborah.

'That is because you lack practice! Come, look, I'm going to sit down at the piano, and when everyone else is ready you shall dance. I'm sure that Richard would ask you.'

'That won't be necessary,' said a voice behind them. 'I shall ask Deborah.'

Deborah choked on her drink. When she recovered she tried to excuse herself.

'No, no! You must go with Hugo if he invites you!' cried Edwina, quite shocked. 'It's his party!'

To Deborah's astonishment Hugo remained adamant, and it was settled that Edwina would play for the next set and Deborah would dance.

'I dare say you're surprised,' said Hugo curtly as he led her out, and started off the dance. It was a slow one, and almost seemed expressly invented to give the couples opportunity for talk. 'It seemed to be the only way I could have a word with you. You seem to have been avoiding my company since I got back from Derbyshire.'

'I...I've been very busy with preparations for this.' Deborah waved a hand over the room.

'They've been worth it. My congratulations. I've seldom been better entertained.'

'Not even in London?' asked Deborah with a smile of polite disbelief.

'Not even there. But that's not what I wanted to talk about.'

'I know,' said Deborah nervously. 'But if you are about to tell me that Autolycus is to go, I warn you that this is neither the time nor the place. I shall probably create a scene.'

'That's not it at all! I may have been angry—'

'Furious. You were furious, Hugo.'

'But I never intended to get rid of the dog.'

Deborah was so astonished that she stopped short. 'Never intended…! Of course you did!'

'Dance!' said Hugo between his teeth. 'For God's sake, don't make another fuss.' He took her arm and led her on. After a pause he said, 'I don't know why it is, Deborah, but you have a talent for making me say more than I mean. I assure you, Autolycus is safe. Now can we forget him and…and come to the question of my conduct?'

'I think that is an even less suitable topic for discussion here,' said Deborah nervously, with a quick look round. The other couples all seemed to be intent on their own partners, with no time for anyone else. She went on, 'But you may be easy, Hugo. I have no intention of telling anyone, nor even…' For a moment Deborah's voice wavered. Then she continued with resolution, 'Of remembering it myself!'

'You always were a poor liar,' said Hugo with a small smile.

The movement of the dance separated them for a few moments, moments in which Deborah wrestled with the riotous feelings roused by the touch of Hugo's hand, the sound of his voice in her ears. She must control herself—she would be so ashamed if he ever suspected their existence! When they were together again he said, 'I do wish to talk to you, but after my behaviour in the stable…I'm not sure…. I don't know whether you will feel secure enough to meet me again in private.'

Deborah wondered briefly if Hugo would feel safe in *her* presence, if he knew how she really felt! Then she smiled wryly. 'We both know that such a thing is most unlikely ever to happen again. You don't…I mean, *we* don't regard each other in that way. It was a momentary aberration. I'll meet you, Hugo.'

After a short silence Hugo said, 'Thank you.' He said no more to the end of the dance, but as they were coming away, Lowell came up to them to say that the Dowager wished to see them.

'She means you, Hugo. I'll join the others,' said Deborah nervously.

'No, she meant you, too, Deborah,' Lowell said. He looked curiously at his brother as he spoke. Hugo seemed uncharacteristically tense. 'I think it's only about the parrot,' he added.

The Dowager was at her most imposing, with a black silk dress and an awesome turban. 'My congratulations, Deborah! A most amusing evening! You have a very pretty voice, too! I hope my grandson has been duly grateful?'

'He has, ma'am. But I did it willingly. I enjoy it. And your other grandchildren all played an important part, too!'

'Yes, yes! I've already spoken to them. Lowell and Henrietta are a graceless pair, but they made me laugh. What's this about a parrot?'

Deborah looked at Hugo. He said smoothly, 'I haven't yet had a chance to introduce you to the parrot, grandmother. He's yours, if you want him. Who told you about him? Lowell?'

'No, Banks told Gossage. She didn't say he was

for me, though. And I'm not sure I want such a pet. I'm told he can be extremely rude.'

Deborah would have pleaded the parrot's case, but Hugo gave her a slight nudge and she was silent. 'Well then, you mustn't have him, of course,' he said with apparent indifference. 'I can arrange another home for him. But perhaps you'd give him a trial? He can be very amusing.'

'Bring him tomorrow at noon.'

'Isn't that too early for you?'

'Don't be absurd! And bring that girl, too!' she said, fixing Deborah with a stare which much resembled that of the parrot. 'I want to talk to her.'

Chapter Six

Years before, when the Percevals' fortunes had been at their lowest ebb, they had sold off the Dower House and its park. As a consequence, Hugo's grandmother had her own suite of rooms in the main house. At noon exactly on the day after the party, Hugo and Deborah presented themselves at the door which separated the Dowager's apartment from the rest of the house. Hugo was carrying the parrot's cage covered in a large cloth, but mutterings from beneath the cloth informed the world that the bird was awake, and not at all happy with his situation.

'I'm not sure her ladyship is fit enough to see you, Master Hugo,' said Gossage when she opened the door. 'She enjoyed the party far too well, I'm sorry to say.'

'Gossage!' The Dowager's voice called imperiously. ''No more nonsense from you! I'm as fit as a fiddle. I've invited my grandson and Miss Staunton to pay me a visit, and you're not to turn them away, you interfering hag. Come in, come in, Hugo!'

Gossage pursed her lips and moved aside to allow

Deborah and Hugo into the Dowager's sitting-room. The long windows were shaded by half-drawn blinds, but the view from them was superb. In the distance could be seen the tower of Abbot Quincey church, and leading to it was a magnificent avenue of chestnuts, their broad-spreading branches creating a shady drive for churchgoers from the great house. To the left, immediately in front of the windows, was a wide lawn broken up with beds of flowers and shrubs, and to the right was the graceful, rose brick curve of one of Perceval Hall's wings.

'Yes, yes, the room has one of the best views in the house,' said the Dowager as Deborah joined her by the window and admired the outlook. 'But I haven't asked you here to discuss the view. Come and sit down, girl.'

Undeterred by her hostess's somewhat unconventional greeting, Deborah curtseyed and sat down in a chair close to her hostess. Hugo put the cage on a small table nearby and came to kiss his grandmother.

'So this is my new house guest?' said the Dowager somewhat sourly, gazing at the cage. 'You'd better unveil it.'

Hugo removed the cloth and the parrot uttered a single, pithy epithet.

'Mercy me!' said Gossage and almost dropped the tray she was bringing in.

'Pull yourself together, Gossage,' the Dowager snapped. 'Don't just stand there! Put the tray down and serve my guests!'

'And where might that be, my lady?' said Gossage, looking significantly at the table now occupied by the cage. Hugo got up, fetched another small table, and put it down by the Dowager's chair. The maid put the tray on it in silent disapproval. On the tray were two delicate old glasses, a decanter of Madeira wine and a plate of thin wafer biscuits. The Dowager frowned.

'You'd better fetch another glass, Gossage! I'll have some wine, too.' It was very evident that Gossage would have argued but for the presence of the two guests. With something perilously close to a flounce, she left the room. The Dowager turned on Hugo.

'So you think this a suitable pet for me, do you?' Her face was a thundercloud.

'You're one of the few people of my acquaintance who is not too mealy-mouthed to be shocked by the bird. I thought you might even enjoy its...somewhat unusual vocabulary.'

'Well, you're wrong! I'm not having that bird any-where near me! You'd better take it somewhere else.' The Dowager sounded so ill-tempered that Hugo abandoned any further effort to persuade her.

'I'll take it with me when we go,' he said calmly.

'Gossage! Where's that glass?' called the Dowager pettishly. 'Where is the dratted woman?' It was clear to both visitors that Gossage was right. The Dowager was indeed feeling liverish after the previous night's celebrations.

'Let me pour you some Madeira,' Hugo said gently. He poured a small quantity into one of the glasses on the tray and handed it to his grandmother.

Then he filled the other and gave it to Deborah with a wry look.

When Gossage came in with the third glass Hugo took it from her and filled it for himself. Gossage gave him a small nod of approval as she noticed the effort he had made to limit his grandmother's drink. Then she turned to leave the room again.

'Gossage!' said the parrot.

'Yes, my lady?' said the maid, turning again.

'Pull yourself together, Gossage!' said the parrot.

The Dowager almost choked on her Madeira. She handed the glass to Hugo and then gave way to a fit of cackling mirth.

'Wonderful!' she said at last. Then she went into another fit of laughter at her maid's expression of outrage. She turned to the parrot. 'Say it again,' she said.

The parrot regarded her gloomily, then closed its eyes.

'Will that be all, my lady?' asked Gossage oppressively.

'Yes, yes. Go away, do. Hugo, give Miss Staunton a wafer biscuit and take one yourself.'

As Gossage went out again, the parrot cried, 'Go away, do! Pull yourself together, Gossage!'

The Dowager's malaise was forgotten. She was enchanted. 'The bird's a genius. I do believe I could teach him anything! We could have such fun with Gossage, couldn't we, my treasure?' she crooned, turning to the cage.

'May I take it that you've changed your mind, then? Or do you still wish me to take the bird away?'

'Don't be absurd, Hugo! Of course I'll keep him!'

'Absurd, absurd, absurd! Pull yourself together, Gossage!' repeated the parrot, who evidently found the Dowager's voice easy to imitate.

'That's settled, then. You must tell me what to feed him with and so on. Gossage will look after him— she will be so annoyed! Now, what were we going to talk about?'

'Hugo! Don't be absurd, Hugo!' called the parrot.

'Yes, yes, but now I want to talk, my precious.' She turned to Deborah. 'How do I make him be quiet?'

Deborah got up and put the cloth over the cage. The parrot fell silent immediately.

'Thank you, my dear. You're a good, kind, clever girl to have found me such an interesting pet!'

'It was Hugo's idea, Lady Perceval. I would never have dared expose you to the parrot's comments.'

'Nonsense! I'm not as prudish as you think, miss! Tell me about that dog of yours.'

Deborah began hesitantly, conscious of Hugo's eye on her. But in response to some clever questioning she quickly lost her reserve and talked with all her old eagerness. The old lady listening so carefully learned a great deal more than the virtues or otherwise of Autolycus. At the end of half an hour's chat Lady Perceval knew more about her young visitor's life and character than Deborah would have thought possible. And she had heard nothing to cause her to change her mind. In her own odd, eccentric way Hugo's grandmother was sure that Deborah Staunton would make her beloved grandson just the wife he needed. The difficulty was to convince everyone else of this—not least, Hugo himself.

The talk turned to matters on the estate. Lady Perceval had been away for some months and was determined to find out how it had fared during her absence. Hugo stood up quite well to some close questioning, but he was eventually forced to say that he had only been back himself for six weeks or so.

'Don't give me that excuse! Five minutes should be enough!' said Lady Perceval.

'But I haven't your stamina, Grandmother—or your…flair.'

'Don't try to cozen me, my boy! Still, I suppose you haven't done too badly. What's this about Ellen Bember's chicken-house? I hear she has a new one. And a new petticoat,' she added with a sly grin at Deborah.

Hugo looked at her in amazement. 'By the Lord Harry! Not three days back and you seem to know everything! Who told you about that?'

'Never you mind! And don't worry, either—I'm not about to tell the rest of them. But Ellen Bember was a good worker in her day and I try to keep an eye on my old servants.'

'Hugo did very well, ma'am,' Deborah said. 'I'm afraid my dog was at fault.'

'What happened?'

Once again the Dowager laughed aloud at the tale of Autolycus and the chickens. 'Well, I'll say this for you, Deborah. Life is not dull when you are with us! And it sounds as if Hugo here is very good at picking up the pieces. I hope you're grateful.'

The silence between her guests was deafening. She looked sharply at each of them in turn but made no comment. She went on, 'It would be a kindness if you visited Ellen again. She has the cottage for her lifetime, but she hasn't any money—she spent what we gave her on that wastrel son of hers. And now he's dead and what she manages to get from selling her eggs is hardly enough to keep body and soul together. Your Aunt Elizabeth is very good—she looks after what she calls her deserving poor—but Ellen means a little more than that to me. Would you take her a few extras from me, Deborah? I gather she knows you quite well.'

Deborah grew pink as she stammered that she had always enjoyed talking to Mrs Bember.

'And a few others, from what I hear. You're a good girl. But you're not to go alone.'

'I would take Autolycus, ma'am.'

'You need more than a half-trained dog. Hugo will go with you.'

'Oh, but I'm...I'm sure that wouldn't be necessary—'

'You'll do as you're told, miss! And so will he. It will do Ellen a world of good to see the young master again. And it won't do him any harm to see how the real world lives.'

'I believe I already know that, grandmother,' said Hugo, a little nettled at this totally unjustified criticism. 'I've spent a good deal of my time in the past six weeks with our people—the prosperous and the poor.'

'Yes, yes, you're a good fellow. I've heard that,

too. But Deborah has a way with her. You'll learn more about ordinary folk in a ten-minute visit in her company than in a week of conscientious calls on your own. You try it.'

'Ma'am, I'm sure that Hugo would rather...'

'Never mind what Hugo would rather! I can see you'd rather not be in each other's company at the moment. You've some fences to mend, you two.' They both stared at her. 'I may be old but I haven't lost my wits! You weren't talking about the weather during the dance last night. Well, it doesn't do any harm to quarrel, but you need to make it up and the walk to Ellen's cottage will give you an opportunity. Off with you both! I'm tired out. Ask Gossage for the things for Ellen on your way out. And Hugo—' Hugo turned. 'Come here a moment!'

Deborah was talking to Gossage as she collected a basket of goods for Mrs Bember, but she heard Lady Perceval say, 'You might remember what I said about Deborah Staunton, Hugo. I am right, I know I am.'

As they came out of the Dowager's apartment Hugo and Deborah were met by Lowell. 'Good!' he said. 'Come and share some of last night's leftovers with us. Hester and Dungarran are with Lady Martindale at Courtney Hall, Henrietta had to stay at the Vicarage, and it's deadly dull here.' He overrode their protests and led them into the small parlour, where a table was laid with meats, pies, jellies and an array of other delicacies. Sir James and Lady Perceval were already helping themselves, and greeted Deborah warmly.

'How did my mother receive the parrot, Hugo? Will you need to find another home for it?'

'Fortunately I don't have to, sir. The parrot had the good sense to amuse her by tricking Gossage, and now has a home for life!'

They all sat down to hear about the visit to the Dowager, and then the talk turned to the party and what a success it had been. The time passed pleasantly, until Hugo said, 'And now Deborah and I have a commission from my grandmother to visit Mrs Bember. We shall have to leave you. Come, Deborah!'

With some difficulty Deborah hid her resentment at Hugo's peremptory tone. 'I must call first at the Vicarage, I'm afraid,' she said coolly. 'Aunt Elizabeth will be wondering what has happened to keep me so long, and I ought to ask her if she needs me this afternoon. And I must change my dress.'

'You look neat enough to me,' said Hugo.

Even his mother could not resist a smile. 'Hugo, Deborah looks very pretty! She is probably wearing her best day dress. I know I would if I had been asked to visit your grandmother. Of course she needs to change—into something *less* ''neat''! Something more sensible. And look at her shoes! They are far too light to wear on a walk through the woods.'

'I understand,' said Hugo. 'Come, Deborah. We'll call at the Vicarage on the way.'

Deborah got up.

'I must say, Deborah, it's not like you to let Hugo order you about like that!' Lowell said. 'Are you really going? Now?'

'Why not? It makes life easier if I do as Hugo says. Especially when I intend to go anyway!'

Everyone laughed as Deborah jammed on her hat and swept out. Even Hugo was grinning as the tiny figure majestically left the room.

But once outside they neither of them found it easy to talk. Deborah looked round as they walked through the courtyard and across the lawn, and remembered her arrival in Hugo's curricle a few weeks before. How kind Hugo had been that day! Life had seemed complicated enough then, disturbed as she was by her Aunt Staunton's defection and the visit from the menacing stranger. Her sudden flight from Maids Moreton had been instinctive, that of a creature sensing danger. Abbot Quincey had appeared to be a safe haven, a place where she would not have to worry any more. Even the news that her Aunt Staunton had cheated her had not upset her for long, and the revelation that she had a small income had added to her feeling of contented security. She had never expected total happiness—that dream had always been out of her reach—but contentment had seemed possible...

Now, such a short time later, life was even harder to deal with than before! Now the danger came from within, and her chief enemy was her own stupid, treacherous heart.

Hugo glanced down at Deborah. She looked pale, remote—far removed from the vivid, magical creature he had seen the night before. From the expression on her face her thoughts were not happy, but now that they were alone he no longer knew how to approach her.

She saved him the trouble. Taking a deep breath she said, 'Did you really mean what you said last night? About Autolycus? You're not going to say anything to Aunt Elizabeth?'

'I've told you. I very rarely lose my temper but when I do, I…I am not always just. I was…was so angry in that stable, Deborah. When I spoke about Autolycus I was not…not reasonable. I certainly don't wish to deprive you of the dog. I had a word with Aunt Elizabeth even before I left for Derbyshire. She was worried about what happened to Frederica.' Deborah looked amazed. 'Did she not say anything to you? No, I see she didn't.'

'I've been so busy with the preparations for your party, I've hardly spoken to her.'

'It's more likely that she was waiting to talk to me again, before she said or did anything. Aunt Elizabeth never acts hastily. We had a talk yesterday. I persuaded her that Frederica was never in the slightest danger, and assured her that Autolycus is trainable.'

Deborah bent her head and her voice wavered as she said, 'Thank you, Hugo.'

Hugo said roughly, 'It was the least—the very least—I could do.' He stopped and turned to face her. 'But I have more important things to say to you. I hurt and humiliated you in that stable, Deborah, and I am sorry for it. Nothing could justify such behaviour. I don't deserve it, but I hope you will forgive me for it. I don't know what came over me. It won't happen again, I promise you. I… I value our friendship, and I was proud of your trust in me. I hope that I haven't destroyed it.'

Deborah shook her head. 'I said so at the time. I provoked you. I don't know what came over *me*, Hugo! Unlike you, I frequently lose my temper, but I have never before hit anyone like that. I certainly didn't mean to hurt you as I did. Shall we…shall we call a truce? Apart from anything else, it would be most awkward to be at odds with each other for long. The family would certainly wonder why.'

'You are generous.'

They walked on in silence for a moment or two. Then Deborah spoke. 'Hugo, what did your grandmother say just before we left? What did she mean when she said she was right about me?'

Hugo hesitated. What his grandmother had meant was the last thing he would be likely to tell her! 'She likes you,' he said at length. 'She thinks you make life interesting.'

A chuckle escaped his companion. 'I suppose I could hardly disagree with that!' she said. 'I daresay you would think I make it too interesting—at least for you!'

'You have your moments. But yes, she is right. Perhaps I was beginning to overvalue ease…' He fell silent. Then, as a figure appeared in the distance, he asked, 'Who's that over there?'

'Where? Oh, I think it's Frederica…yes, it is! She must have been to the church. I wonder why? It can't have been to help Uncle William—he's in Northampton for the day. She seems in a hurry to get back.'

When Frederica saw them she gave a little jump.

'Oh! Oh, you startled me,' she said. 'I...I wasn't expecting to see anyone.'

'You've been to the church?'

'What? The church? Oh... Oh, yes!'

'What were you doing there, Frederica?' Hugo was curious—Frederica was definitely flustered. She gave him a hunted look and bit her lip. 'Well?' Hugo said, a touch impatiently.

Deborah took pity on the girl. 'Did you forget that Uncle William was in Northampton? Were you hoping to sort some more of the registers for him?' She turned to Hugo. 'Frederica volunteered to help her father in putting the church registers in better order— they had become sadly disorganised. What a pity you had a wasted trip! Still, we can all walk to the Vicarage together.'

Frederica was even more tongue-tied than she usually was in Hugo's presence. She responded politely to all his comments, but made no attempt to initiate any conversation. Deborah could sense his growing boredom. It was so unfair! Frederica could be a charming companion, and usually very easy to talk to. In an attempt to get the girl to do herself justice, she said, 'Frederica, I have heard such compliments about your playing last night. It was worth all those hours of practice.'

Frederica went rather pink, but said sweetly, 'It was all due to you, Deborah dear. I enjoy my harp, but I would never have attempted such difficult music if you had not encouraged me. But I think the success of the evening was our love song for Hester and Lord Dungarran. Don't you?'

They came to a stile. Deborah hardly touched Hugo's hand as she landed, but Frederica paused on top to brush a mark off her skirts. Then she eyed the ground below to make sure it was firm and carefully allowed Hugo to help her down. Hugo thought once again how pretty she was. Slender as a wand, pale golden curls escaping from under her chip straw hat, eyes as blue as the summer sky, gracefully careful in movement, her white muslin dress now spotless again—she was everything he had for years regarded as the ideal of female beauty, the perfect choice to succeed his mother as mistress of Perceval Hall. And he was astonished to realise that he was not in the least tempted. Nor did he have the slightest wish to marry her sister Edwina, even if it had not been evident that her affections were already engaged elsewhere. They were sweet, beautiful girls, both of them. But he was now sure that he would soon find their willingness to agree with everything he said, their gentle desire to please, unbearably cloying. It was as well that his two companions were now chattering animatedly about Edwina and the other young people at the party. The shock of his discovery kept Hugo silent till they reached the Vicarage.

They were met by Henrietta. 'Here you are, Frederica! Where have you been? We've been waiting an age for you. Have you seen Mama's box? Or you, Deborah? It has disappeared from Mama's room, and we cannot imagine what has happened to it!'

The three entered the house to find Lady Elizabeth talking to one of the servants. When she saw them she dismissed the girl and greeted Deborah and Hugo, punctiliously asking after the family at the Hall. Hugo replied, then asked, 'What is this about your box, Aunt Elizabeth?'

'Henrietta has told you? It was quite unnecessary. My writing-box was not in its usual place this morning, and we couldn't find it anywhere else, but I think I now know what has happened. The girl says that your Uncle William was carrying a parcel when he left for Northampton. He must have taken my writing-box to be mended—one of the hinges was loose. How kind of him! He knows how much I treasure it. He left rather later than he had intended—I expect that is why he forgot to mention the matter. What a fuss about nothing! So, Hugo, what brings you here? A training session for Deborah's dog?'

Deborah explained their mission, and Lady Elizabeth, somewhat reluctantly, gave her consent. 'I suppose if your grandmother wishes it, then I must bow to her judgement as to what is proper. It would have been better if one of your cousins could have accompanied you, but they have other duties this afternoon. Take your hat, Deborah. And you'd better change your dress and shoes. Where did you get that dirt on your skirt, child? Give the dress to Mrs Humble to be brushed before you put it away. Frederica, there's a mark on your gloves. We must try to remove it before we set off for the Hartnells...'

Hugo walked a little way along the path to wait for Deborah. He was glad of a few minutes alone to think. What had happened? He had been so sure that one of the twins would make him a suitable wife. And now, without really knowing why, he had changed his mind. How had Deborah and his grandmother between them had such an influence on him? They had both advised against it, but he would not normally have allowed that to put him off a plan to which he had given so much thought. His grandmother's suggestion that he should consider Deborah Staunton as a possible bride was of course absurd! Of all possible candidates she was by far the least suitable! He turned to look at her as she came running round the corner, Autolycus leaping and barking up at her. She was clutching the basket of food, her abominable hat was on one side, and her dress already had a mark on the hem.

'I'm sorry to have kept you waiting, Hugo!' she gasped. 'Aunt Elizabeth is such a stickler! I had to change my dress twice before she would let me come.'

'I didn't mind the wait. We have all the afternoon. You should have taken time to do your hair more carefully—it's halfway down your back.' Hugo's voice was calm, but there was a touch of irritation in it. Why couldn't the girl behave with a modicum of care?

Deborah looked guilty. 'I didn't do it at all! Aunt Elizabeth told me to, but in the hurry I forgot! Wait a moment!'

She gave him her hat, the basket of goods and Autolycus's leash to hold, and turned to wind her hair into a knot. Her neck was slender, the mane of hair almost too heavy for it. Hugo felt a totally irrational desire to put his lips to it… He turned away abruptly. What the *devil* was wrong with him?

'There! It's done,' Deborah said cheerfully. 'If Aunt Elizabeth would let me, I would have it cut short. It's the rage in London, they tell me. My hat, please.'

'Shall I buy you a new hat, Deborah?' Hugo said, holding up the tattered straw.

'It would be nice, but there are two things wrong with the idea. One is that Aunt Elizabeth would never allow you to. And the other is that Autolycus would almost certainly reduce it to the state of this one within the month! I do have one hat which I keep for best, but I very seldom wear it. No, if you are looking for neatness and propriety you had much better escort my cousins, Hugo.' She put the hat firmly on her head and took back the leash. 'Shall we let Autolycus free?'

'Try him.' The dog raced round them once, then at Deborah's order came meekly to heel. 'My congratulations. I'm impressed,' said Hugo.

They walked on for a while, then he went on, 'From what I observed last night, Edwina would seem to prefer Richard Vernon's escort to mine.'

'I think she would, yes,' said Deborah carefully. 'I believe she has spoken to her mother about it, too. I'm sorry if it upsets your plans, Hugo, but I think there will be an announcement quite shortly.'

'I'm not upset at all. I've changed my mind about the twins. Both you and my grandmother are in agreement that they would not be happy with me. And who am I to argue with you both?'

'Who indeed? But this isn't at all like you, Hugo. Do you…do you have anyone else in mind?'

'That's the devil of it! It means I shall have to start all over again, and that will involve visits all over the county. It will use time I can hardly afford—there's so much to do on the estate.'

'You'll find someone. There are plenty of girls who would be flattered by an offer from you. You may be high-handed, but you are very presentable.' She gave him a teasing smile, and he felt a sudden lift of his heart.

'I'm glad we are friends again, Deborah,' he said.

She looked away. 'I am, too. Look! We're nearly there. And there's Mrs Bember at the gate.'

During the next half hour Hugo saw what his grandmother had meant. Mrs Bember responded to his enquiries very readily. She was obviously flattered and pleased that he had come to visit her. But she talked to Deborah much more freely. Their conversation was far from gloomy, but for the first time Hugo saw the old lady's loneliness, her longing for company, and watched how Deborah cheered her up and even once or twice made her laugh. After Mrs Bember they went on to visit others—old Gregory, who had once been a gardener at the Great House, the Carters, a former groom and kitchenmaid, and then on to one or two of the working farms. Everywhere they went it was the same. They were both made welcome, but disorganised, scatterbrained Deborah seemed to have the key to the hearts of nearly all of them.

* * *

Hugo had been given much food for thought and on the way back was unusually quiet again. It was getting late—the sun was still up but the light was fading along the woodland path. A sudden rustling in the undergrowth started Autolycus into a fit of barking. They laughed when they saw an elderly goat amble out of the wood.

'That's Sammy Spratton's goat!' exclaimed Deborah. 'Catch it, Hugo!'

It wasn't difficult to capture the animal. The problem was what to do with it after that.

'Sammy won't come near while you're here. He's very shy. You'd better let me take it to him. His hut isn't far—just a little way into the wood.'

'No!' said Hugo very firmly. 'I won't allow you to go into that wood alone.'

'But—'

'No!'

'Well, what do you suggest we do? Sammy will never let himself be seen.'

'Who is this Sammy Spratton?'

'Don't you know? He lives alone in the wood, and scrapes a living wherever he can. He…he can't speak, Hugo, and the villagers don't like him. But he and I are friends, and he's so gentle when you know him. Let me take the goat!'

'I wouldn't even consider it! But—' Hugo turned her round and said softly, 'there's someone in the bushes behind us. I think it might be the man you want. If we tethered the goat to a tree and then walked away he might collect it.'

'I suppose we could come back to make sure he had...' said Deborah doubtfully. 'I couldn't leave the goat tied up all night...'

They had hardly gone fifty yards when they heard sounds which told them that the goat was being collected. They turned and walked on in silence.

'Tell me how you know this Sammy Spratton,' said Hugo finally.

'There are three or four of them in the woods. Outcasts—people who for some reason or other can't live ordinary lives. I've known one or two of them for years. When I was a child I used to come to the woods when I was feeling particularly unhappy. That's when I met them.'

'I can't believe it! Did you never realise the danger?'

'There wasn't any. We understood each other. And now I visit them occasionally. They trust me, you see.'

'Everyone seems to trust you!' Hugo hardly knew what he was saying. He was struggling with a new idea, an idea that was dangerously attractive. Perhaps his grandmother was not as wrong as he had thought. There was no doubt that Deborah Staunton knew a surprising amount about the people on his estates. She would look after the poor and neglected better than anyone. What was more, they all seemed to respect her. What if....

But no! He rejected the thought even before it was fully formed. He simply couldn't see Deborah Staunton as his wife! The thought of the chaos she would bring into his well-ordered life was too awful to contemplate. She was the antithesis of everything he had planned for himself, and he must not let himself be trapped. No! No! And no! He came to a halt, vigorously shaking his head. Until Deborah looked round with a puzzled look he did not realise that he had spoken the last words aloud.

She had stopped by a clearing and the slanting rays of the sun penetrating the leaves surrounded her in a golden light. She had taken off her hat, and her hair had escaped once again. She suddenly seemed... magical. Before he could stop himself he had spoken the fateful words.

'Deborah,' Hugo Perceval said. 'Deborah, will you marry me?'

Chapter Seven

No sooner had these words been uttered than Hugo was filled with horror. What on earth had he been thinking of? He had just condemned himself to a *lifetime* of picking up the pieces after Deborah Staunton had done her worst! He must be a lunatic! There was no escape—he was irretrievably committed. Having asked her he could not now honourably withdraw. And, given her circumstances, it was inconceivable that she would refuse him, whatever her feelings towards him. He waited in trepidation for the axe to fall.

Every bit as shocked as Hugo, Deborah gave way for a short moment—a very short moment—to a wild surge of joy and hope. Then, as he stood there with such a look of surprised dismay on his face, making no effort to touch her or even to meet her eyes, sanity prevailed. 'Forgive me,' she said carefully. 'Would you…could you say that again?'

'I…' Hugo cleared his throat. 'I asked you to marry me.'

Her elation vanished like smoke in the wind. Whatever had led to Hugo's extraordinary proposal, it had not come from the heart. To anyone else, or in any other circumstances, the extreme reserve in his voice would be laughable. But she wasn't able to laugh. In a hundred years, perhaps, but not at the moment.

'Er...why?' she asked.

Hugo looked affronted. 'Why? I should have thought it was obvious! I need a wife, and I...I have now come to realise that you would...would be...'

'Suitable?'

'My grandmother thinks so.'

'So you've asked me because your *grandmother* told you to? I thought you had more spirit than that, Hugo!'

Hugo stiffened. This was not proceeding according to the rules. He had never actually proposed to anyone before, but surely Deborah should have been expressing gratitude and delighted acceptance? Certainly not criticism. 'You misunderstand,' he said rather coldly. 'Though I have a high opinion of my grandmother's judgement, I would not ask you to marry me solely on her recommendation.'

'Why, then?'

'Dammit, we've known each other for a long time, Deborah! You would fit well into the life here. I don't suppose you'll always have such an aptitude for disaster. With a little guidance...'

'And you would do the guiding, of course?'

'Naturally.'

'What about love, Hugo? Do you love me?'

'Of course I do! That is to say, I think highly of

you and once we had settled down I believe we could have a comfortable life together.'

'You mean of course once *I* had settled down. But no…romantic passion? Desperate love?'

'You know what I think of such madness!'

Deborah regarded Hugo with a curious little smile. Then she said, ' I'm sorry. I can't.'

'Can't? Can't what?'

'Marry you!'

Hugo was so taken aback that he was momentarily bereft of speech. Then, after a pause for thought he said, 'If you are worried about what happened after the fête, you need not be. After we are married there will be no repeat of my…my reprehensible behaviour in the stable, I promise you. I am not an animal. When you are my wife I will treat you with the affection and respect due to your position.'

Deborah said, 'I'm not at all afraid you would lose your head again. But I don't think I want to marry you.'

'But *why*? Is there someone else?'

'No.'

Hugo began to get angry. 'I can't believe I'm hearing correctly! Do you mean to say that Deborah Staunton, a penniless, homeless orphan, refuses to marry a man who can offer her both security and comfort? More than that—a position in society which is respected and honoured, and a home which many would envy, in the centre of a loving family.'

'Yes.'

'What does that mean? Yes, you will marry me?'

'No, it means yes, I won't.'

'But what more could you possibly hope for?' he asked, genuinely bewildered.

'I don't think you would understand. It *is* foolish, isn't it? But then I am. Hugo, can't we forget this marriage business? It's very embarrassing to keep having to say no.'

Hugo, who logically speaking should have been relieved at his escape, was baffled and angry. 'You may be assured that I haven't the slightest wish to force unwanted attentions on you,' he said very stiffly indeed. 'But you must allow me to say that I think you are making a serious mistake. I shall not ask you again.'

'You're being very pompous, Hugo. Come, cheer up. You know you don't really want to marry me. It's just that you're thirty and you promised your parents, and the twins are looking elsewhere...'

'Edwina may be, but there's still Frederica!'

After a pause Deborah said, 'Of course! I'd forgotten that. Well, there you are, Hugo. Frederica near to home, and any number of charming, well-bred girls around the county.'

Hugo was unmollified. Very much on his dignity, he said, 'I don't know how we got into this discussion. I find it in very poor taste. It would be better to walk home without saying anything more.'

He set off for the Vicarage at a brisk pace. Deborah would have preferred to seek the shelter of the woods and give way to the anguish she had so far managed to hide, but that was not possible. In spite of his resentment he would come back for her. So she called on her considerable courage, pulled a face and followed him. She refused to run, however, and after a moment he was forced to stop and wait for her to catch him up.

They completed the walk to the Vicarage in silence—and arrived to find the house in confusion. Uncle William had arrived back from Northampton, but he had not, as hoped, taken Lady Elizabeth's box with him. It had undoubtedly been removed by some unauthorised person, probably while the family were all up at Perceval Hall on the evening of Hugo's birthday. Lady Elizabeth was distressed, in spite of her efforts not to show it. More than this, she was puzzled, as was everyone else. Nothing else had been disturbed. And neither the box nor its contents were particularly valuable.

'I kept my recipes in it! I discovered it was missing when I wanted to check how to clean stains from pewter,' said Lady Elizabeth. 'I simply cannot imagine why anyone would wish to take it! Its value lies in its associations. My dear father—' She paused to control her voice. Then she said more calmly, 'My father gave one to each of us when we had mastered how to write. Deborah! Have you looked to see if yours is safe?'

Deborah hurried up the stairs and ran into her room. The writing-box lay, as always, on her chest of drawers. She checked the name on the lid— *'Frances'*—and went downstairs to report.

There seemed nothing more anyone could do. It was late and the light was fading fast. Hugo offered to organise a team of men the next day to search the neighbourhood of the Vicarage in case the thief had abandoned the box. 'Meanwhile I should keep the doors of the Vicarage locked, Uncle William.'

'I should be sorry to do that. They are locked at night, but during the day they are always open to welcome anyone who needs our help. But the loss was Elizabeth's—what do you wish to do, my dear?'

'We shall leave them open, as usual, William. I am not about to let a madman—for so he must be—ruin the reputation for hospitality we have had for years.'

They were not to be dissuaded, and Hugo finally left them to go back to the Hall. He carefully avoided Deborah's eye as he bade them all good night.

During the night, when the house was quiet and the family were asleep, Deborah tossed and turned in her bed, unable to find rest. Now that she was alone she was tormented by doubt, by visions of what she had rejected—a life with Hugo, caring for him, helping him, bearing his children, growing old at his side... The benefits he had listed—position, security and the rest—paled into insignificance beside the simple happiness of spending the rest of her life with him. She would have been glad to marry him whatever his circumstances, if only... *If only!*

Had she been mad to throw it away? He had meant what he said—there would never be another chance. Such desolation swept over her at this thought that she gave way and wept... But her tears gradually dried up as she visualised what life with Hugo would have been in reality. Loving him as she did, with passion and sweet desire, a wild longing to have his love encompass her, to have him kiss her as he had kissed her in the stable, but out of love, not anger or lust…how could she ever have been content in the sort of marriage he had offered her? Hugo did not love her, would never have loved her as deeply, as passionately as she did him. How long would it have been before she demanded so much more than the bloodless affection and respect he had offered her? His proposal may have been made in an uncharacteristically impulsive fashion, but it had been influenced by his promise to his father to marry when he was thirty, and by his grandmother's unexpected approval of Deborah Staunton. He had thought it a mistake almost as soon as he had uttered it…

As she lay there, wide awake, staring into the darkness, remembering her life with her parents, she became ever more convinced that she had been right to refuse Hugo. If she had been foolish enough to marry him, he would before long have turned away from her in distaste, embarrassed by what he saw as an excess of feeling—as her father had turned from her mother. She could not have borne that. Her mother had loved her father in the same all-consuming manner, and he had no more than tolerated her devotion. In the end he had been irritated and bored by her. And though Frances Staunton had been devastated by her husband's early death, it had quite possibly saved her from the shame and humiliation of being a deserted wife. No, no! It was better by far for Frances Staunton's daughter to learn to live alone with an unrequited love, and to keep her self-respect.

* * *

Having fought her battle to an acceptable conclusion, Deborah got up the next morning with a pale face and heavy eyes, but at peace. The only remaining difficulty was that she wondered how she and Hugo would keep up the appearance of friendship for the benefit of the family. They solved it by scarcely ever being in each other's company for long. Autolycus no longer needed training, and Hugo seemed to have given up his interest in the twins.

Though he was very busy about the estate, he found time to make enquiries about his aunt's writing-box, but nothing came of them. The box had completely disappeared, and Lady Elizabeth was forced to resign herself to its loss. The whole affair was a mystery. A second mystery was more easily solved—for Deborah, at least. She had suspected for some time that Frederica's interest in the church registers had more to do with the presence of her father's curate than with a simple desire to help her Papa. Mr Langham was a quiet, unassuming young man with brown hair, brown eyes and a singularly sweet smile. He was related to the owners of a handsome estate on the other side of Northampton, and would in due course take up a prosperous family living there. Meanwhile he worked with the Reverend William, learning from that saintly man the skills of counselling and visiting, and how to deal with the manifold problems of a country parish. He was devoted to his work and his studies, and hardly seemed to notice the Vicar's pretty daughters when he met them at church or came to dinner.

A few days after the momentous conversation with Hugo, Deborah came across her cousin Frederica once again coming from the direction of Abbot Quincey church at a time when the Reverend William was certainly not there—Deborah had seen him setting off for Steep Ride not half an hour before. Frederica was smiling, lost in a dream, and when Deborah came out of the shade of the trees and spoke to her she was startled once again.

'Oh! Oh, it's you, Deborah! Thank goodness! I thought it was Mama.'

'I would have said that was my sort of comment, Frederica, not yours. I'm usually the one who's afraid of being caught out, and you my guardian angel. What have you been up to?'

Frederica hesitated, then spoke in a rush. 'If I don't confide in someone I shall burst! I know you won't tell anyone else. Mr Langham smiled at me today!'

'Heavens! He actually smiled? Frederica, Mr Langham often smiles. He's a very amiable young man. Why shouldn't he smile at you?'

'But this is different! He actually meant it for me! Me! Frederica. I've been trying—in a very discreet way, of course—'

'Of course!'

'You needn't look like that, Deborah—I've been perfectly proper! Anyway, I've been trying to attract his attention for weeks. And today we were in the church porch and he smiled—directly at me!'

'He probably thought you were Edwina,' Deborah teased.

Frederica was quite cast down. 'Do you think so?' Then her face brightened. 'He can't have! He called me Miss Frederica. I never thought of that...Mr Langham can apparently tell us apart. Isn't that strange? I wouldn't have said he had ever looked at us closely enough. Oh, Deborah, isn't that wonderful?'

Deborah hesitated. Frederica was clearly well on the way to being in love. There was nothing wrong with that, of course, but she should not be meeting Mr Langham—whether by accident or design—without her mother's knowledge. 'Why were you worried when you thought I was Aunt Elizabeth?'

'I...I haven't told Mama yet. There's been nothing to tell!' she added in a rush. 'There still isn't. I...I wanted him to get to know me a little better before I said anything. Mama...Mama can be quite formidable, and I think Mr Langham is very shy. It might put him off. Don't tell her! Don't tell anyone! Not yet! Please, Deborah!'

Frederica's lovely face was anxious. Deborah remembered so many occasions in the past when Frederica had helped her to conceal her own misdemeanours from Lady Elizabeth, and said warmly, 'Of course I won't! You're never as foolish as I am, anyway. You'll tell your mother when you're ready—or should I say when Mr Langham is ready?'

'Oh, do you think he will be? Really?'

'My dearest Frederica, if he doesn't fall in love with you he must be blind and stupid. You are beautiful enough to please any man, and if he cannot see what a wonderful parson's wife you will make he is an idiot! And Mr Langham is neither blind nor an idiot... Of course he will.'

'Oh, I do hope so! And I will tell Mama, really I will. In a little while...'

After that Deborah often noticed Frederica discreetly slipping away. But disaster threatened some days later when Lady Elizabeth, who was still occasionally short-tempered after the loss of her writing-box, announced that Frederica had been at the church long enough and she would fetch her.

'I'll go, shall I?' said Deborah hastily. 'It's quite hot outside, Aunt.'

'Thank you, but the air will do me good. I shall take my parasol, and go by way of the tree walk. It's quite cool under the chestnut trees.'

Deborah watched her aunt go out of the house, then slipped round the back, jumped over the stile and ran swiftly to the church. Her aunt would take some minutes—she never hurried, and the path to the church by way of the chestnut drive was by no means direct.

Frederica was just emerging from the church with Mr Langham in attendance. Deborah was slightly out of breath but she spoke lightly. 'Good afternoon, Mr Langham! Isn't it a beautiful day?' Without waiting for an answer she went on, 'I'm so glad I've come across you, Frederica. Aunt Elizabeth was asking where you were. She is just on her way here to look for you.'

'Oh! Is she? Yes,' said Frederica a touch distractedly. 'I must go. Good afternoon, Mr Langham.' She curtseyed and turned to go. In her hurry she dropped a sheaf of pamphlets which she had been carrying, and Mr Langham stooped to pick them up.

Frederica's eyes pleaded with Deborah, who knew what she meant. If Lady Elizabeth found them all here she would demand to know what was happening.

'Frederica, Aunt Elizabeth is in something of a hurry. I'll stay to pick up these papers, shall I, then you can go on to meet her halfway? You'll find her along the chestnut walk.'

'Oh! Thank you! Thank you, Mr Langham. I found our discussion very interesting. Goodbye.' Frederica hurried away and Deborah was left with the young curate, who had forgotten the pamphlets and was gazing after Frederica as her white muslin dress vanished among the trees. He came back to earth with a start and bent to pick up some more pamphlets. His face was flushed—possibly from his exertions, but far more probably from his feelings, thought Deborah.

'Sh-shall I c-carry them for you to the Vicarage, Miss Staunton?'

'Thank you, but it isn't necessary. They aren't heavy…and I'm afraid that Frederica will be out for the rest of the afternoon.' He grew even redder in the face and Deborah smiled to herself. First Edwina and now Frederica. It looked as if her worries about the twins were to be solved most satisfactorily.

The clatter of hooves made them both turn. Hugo was surveying them from outside the church gate. Deborah could feel the colour rising in her cheeks at his cynical expression. He dismounted and came towards them. 'Good day to you. Is the Vicar inside?' he asked.

Mr Langham, brought back again to earth, stammered that the Reverend William was visiting Steep Ride.

'I see,' murmured Hugo, still with that hateful air of cynicism. 'Is he indeed?'

Mr Langham, puzzled, turned with dignity to Deborah and said, 'If you are really sure I cannot help you with the pamphlets, Miss Staunton, I will take my leave. I am already late for another meeting.'

Deborah muttered an incoherent farewell and he went. Hugo and she were alone.

'You think he is more your style, Deborah?' he began unpleasantly. 'Is that it? Milk and water, sermons not arguments, Christian forgiveness instead of retribution? Is that what you want?'

Deborah flushed to the roots of her hair. 'I have no interest in Mr Langham. He and I were merely talking.'

'It did not have the appearance of an innocent meeting.'

'It was, I assure you.' Then she added, 'And if it were not, what is that to you, Hugo?'

'Nothing at all. Except that you told me, I believe, that there was no one else. And I'm not sure I approve of clandestine meetings between my aunt's ward and my uncle's curate. Surely there's no need for such secrecy? But then...' He paused.

'Well?'

'Perhaps you are more like your mother than we thought? Secret assignations appeal to you.'

Deborah's first impulse was to hit that handsome face, smiling so unpleasantly down at her. But perhaps that sort of provocation was what he wanted...

She could tell that underneath his smile Hugo was in a black rage. She remembered what had happened the last time she had attacked an angry Hugo, and resolutely kept her hands to herself.

'You may think what you please about me,' she said coldly. 'But you do yourself no credit by attacking those who are not here to defend themselves. I loved my mother, and would defend her against the world. But it would be a useless exercise as far as you are concerned. You, Hugo, could never *begin* to understand the feelings which drove her into running away with my father. I will not bother to defend her against you. But Mr Langham is a good, honourable, decent man. What on earth has he done to deserve your malicious insinuations?' She looked at him, challenging him. 'Well? I have known you angry before, Hugo, but I have never known you meanly unjust.'

Hugo went white and took a step back, almost as if she *had* hit him. He hesitated, looked as if he was about to say something, staring at her all the while, then turned abruptly and went to the gate. Then he threw himself on to his horse and jerked the animal round. In no time he had disappeared from her sight.

Feeling as if she had just lived through an earthquake, Deborah walked slowly back to the Vicarage.

Frederica was desperate to talk to her, and as soon as they were alone she demanded, 'Did he say anything?'

'Who?' asked Deborah, her mind filled with Hugo's accusations.

'Why, Mr Langham, of course! Did he say anything about me?'

'We didn't have time. Hugo came upon us one minute after you had gone.'

'Oh, thank goodness he didn't arrive earlier!'

'Well, I'm not sure about that. Hugo, my dear girl, now suspects *me* of carrying on an affair with your Mr Langham. In secret.'

Frederica gurgled with laughter. 'What a joke! You didn't tell him, did you?'

'He didn't give me much opportunity. But I wouldn't have, anyway. Apart from not wishing to break your confidence, I don't think Hugo deserves the truth. He's a monster. A heartless, cruel monster!'

'What, *Hugo*? You haven't quarrelled with him again, have you, Deborah? I thought you'd made up.'

'We had. But then we fell out over something else. I…I can't tell you what it was, Frederica, but…but…' Deborah burst into tears, but refused to tell a shocked Frederica what the trouble was. Her cousin gave up after a while and did her best to comfort her. When Deborah had grown quiet again Frederica said, 'You're not in love with Mr Langham yourself, are you, Deborah? If you are I'll…I'll stop meeting him.'

Deborah smiled through her tears. 'I'm not in love with Mr Langham, I promise. And if I were, it wouldn't do me a mite of good, even if you refused ever to see him again. The man is truly in love with you, Frederica, and he's not the sort to change. I think you should talk to your mother about him.'

'I'll try to. Deborah…' Frederica hesitated, gave

Deborah a quick glance, then said in a rush, 'You're not in love with...with Hugo, are you?'

'In love with a monster? How could I be? Really, what an absurd idea!'

Looking not quite convinced by this, Frederica went away. Deborah thought wryly that she was so clever at persuading her cousins to do the right thing. It was really a pity that she seemed unable to manage her own life with equal success.

Life went on in Abbot Quincey. The season was advancing, and high summer was giving way to the first signs of autumn. The day of Hester's marriage was rapidly approaching and Perceval Hall was the scene of much activity. Tradesmen and visitors came and went, extra help in the house was engaged, and rooms which had been out of use for years were opened up, aired, cleaned and rearranged. Outside, the lawns and flower beds were weeded, watered, pruned and raked by a small army of gardeners.

Pleased though she was that her granddaughter, after swearing for years that she would remain a spinster, was to be married to such a delightful man as Robert Dungarran, the noise and disturbance were not always to the Dowager Lady Perceval's liking.

'I can't bear to think of what it is costing! And the noise! It's worse than living in the middle of Northampton! The comings and goings, the never-ending stream of people... I tell you, Hugo, I'm beginning to believe there's something to be said for an elopement after all! Not that you're to take me seriously! It ain't good Ton to elope and there's never

been such a thing in the Perceval family, I'm pleased
to say. But this is the only place in the whole house
that's not bedlam! I daresay you'd like a glass of
wine. Gossage!'

'Gossage,' echoed the parrot. 'Where is the dratted
woman?' The bird was perched on the back of Lady
Perceval's chair, and as the maidservant came in with
a tray he sidled along and looked malevolently at her,
making stabbing motions with his head. Gossage kept
clear, but returned the look with one of equal dislike.

Wine and the tiny wafers the Dowager loved were
served, and Gossage started to leave. As she went to
the door the parrot called, 'Gossage!' Gossage
stopped automatically, started to turn, then sniffed
and walked out. 'Pull yourself together, Gossage!' the
bird called.

The Dowager was chuckling. 'That bird is the best
present you ever gave me, Hugo! Gossage loathes
him, but she looks after him well. He still sometimes
succeeds in fooling her, though she's getting used to
him now, more's the pity. I tell you, I have more
amusement with that bird than with any of my visitors!'

'Thank you, grandmother! It's good to know where
I stand—somewhat lower than the parrot!'

'Rubbish! You are hardly a visitor. No, I meant
these idiots who come day after day to see Hester,
and think they have to pay their respects to me as
well.'

'I can imagine what you would say if they didn't
call on you, ma'am.'

'You may be right. But if I'm crotchety I at least have the excuse of old age. What is yours?'

'I beg your pardon, ma'am?'

'You heard me. Why are you so ill-tempered? Most of the time, so Lowell tells me.'

'Lowell would do better to keep his comments to himself!' said Hugo in an irritated tone.

'That's exactly what they all mean! You are excessively touchy at the moment. What is wrong, my boy? I thought we had everything sorted out. All this fuss over the wedding will soon be over. Or are you getting bored after all with life in the country?'

'You've asked me that before, grandmother, and my answer is still the same. I enjoyed life in London, but I am perfectly happy now to be here in Abbot Quincey.'

'Perfectly happy, are you? You don't look it!'

Hugo got up and walked over to the window. Gazing out, he said moodily, 'I can't be grinning like an ape the whole time. Besides…'

'Tell me!'

His face was in shadow as he turned round and said, 'It's this business of choosing a wife. To tell the truth I seem to have lost my enthusiasm for it. Offering for one of the twins no longer seems to be such a good notion…'

'What about my other notion? What about Deborah Staunton?'

He turned away again and said harshly, 'You can put Deborah Staunton out of your mind, grandmother.'

'Oh? Why?'

'I asked her. I don't know why. I...I found I had done it before I realised it. Isn't that ridiculous?'

'Then why must I forget her?'

'She refused me.'

There was a blank silence. Then the Dowager said incredulously, 'The girl *refused* you? She can't have! It's impossible.'

'I'm glad you rate my attractions so highly. Miss Staunton doesn't, however.' Hugo stopped short, as if he felt he was revealing more of his considerable resentment than he wished. He paused, then came back into the room and sat down by his grandmother. 'She's mad, of course,' he said with an assumption of indifference. 'I cannot imagine any other girl in her situation who would refuse the sort of security and position marriage to me would have given her.'

'To the devil with security and position! The girl is in love with you, Hugo! She's been in love with you for years!'

'You think so, ma'am?' he said with extreme scepticism. 'She has a strange way of showing it.'

'You must have been extraordinarily inept!'

Hugo coloured up. 'Thank you,' he said coldly. 'I may lack practice—it is not, after all, an activity in which one often indulges—but I believe I managed reasonably well.'

'A girl who has loved you for years turns you down and you say you managed reasonably well? You're as much of an idiot as Deborah, Hugo!'

Hugo got up. 'I can't see that this conversation is helping either of us, grandmother. I have other things to do, so if you'll excuse me...'

'Don't take that tone with me, sir! Sit down! Sit down, I say!'

Her grandson sat down again with a shrug. 'I'm not sure what you want to discuss, but I really don't think it will do much good. Even if I were willing to ask Miss Staunton again—which I am not!—the lady is interested in someone else.'

'Who?'

'Mr Langham.'

'Your Uncle William's curate?' A slow smile curled Lady Perceval's lips. 'Really? And what makes you think that?'

'Is this necessary?'

'I wouldn't be wasting my time on a graceless fool if I didn't think so! What makes you think Deborah Staunton is sweet on Mr Langham?'

'I found them together—in the church porch.'

'Did you really? And what were they doing in such a den of iniquity?'

For years Hugo had been able to freeze off what he considered impertinence with a glance, but he was powerless in front of this indomitable old lady.

With a look of distaste he said, 'They were merely talking, of course. But why meet secretly if there isn't something to hide? Uncle William wasn't anywhere near. He was in Steep Ride all afternoon.'

'I see! And you lost your temper?'

'Of course not!' His grandmother looked at him without saying anything. 'Well, I may have been a little harsh to Deborah afterwards. I didn't approve of her deceit.'

'You were jealous!'

Hugo jumped up. 'About *Deborah Staunton*? The idea is absurd! Absolutely absurd! Why should I be jealous about such a thoughtless, irresponsible, harum scarum *dab* of a girl? She's a nitwit!'

'Well, don't ask me! You're the one who knows. And it is quite unnecessary. Mr Langham is in love with Frederica, unless I'm very much mistaken.'

'How do you know that?'

'Your Uncle William isn't as blind as people think. Not about his blessed daughters. He was saying the other day that if Langham didn't speak up soon he would have to have a word with him. But William always hopes that others will do the right thing without prompting from him, and Elizabeth told me just yesterday that Frederica had at last confided in her. So that's that little problem solved. It's not a brilliant match, but Frederica will be happy—she knows what the life is like, and in character she might have been made to be a country parson's wife.'

Hugo was lost in thought. 'When I saw Deborah with Langham...'

'It was, as she said, an innocent meeting.'

'Good God!' Hugo sounded appalled. 'I said such things...'

'Really! I've no patience with either of you!' said the old lady. 'I do my best, but you both seem set on ruining everything between you. Go away, Hugo, pull yourself together and when you are able to control yourself, see if you can persuade Deborah Staunton to listen to you.'

'I'm sorry to have been unjust,' said Hugo. 'But I would be quite mad to risk another refusal.' Seeing the look on his grandmother's face, Hugo added firmly, 'And an acceptance would be even worse! I am still in search of a wife who will add to my comfort, ma'am. I am not in need of any more liabilities.'

Chapter Eight

Hugo left his grandmother's apartment feeling that he needed to go for a brisk walk to clear his mind. He would go through the woods to Ellen Bember's cottage—he hadn't been to see her for the past few days. He set off, still struggling to put his feelings into some sort of order. Uppermost in his mind was annoyance. His grandmother's accusation was totally unfounded. Jealous indeed! Who would be *jealous* about such a small, dark, insignificant little thing as Deborah Staunton? He paused. Not actually insignificant. For such a tiny creature she was remarkably…noticeable. And there was nothing small about her spirit, either. But to accuse him of jealousy! No, he was not jealous, not at all jealous. To be sure, he couldn't understand the attraction of the Langham fellow—he was not particularly handsome…nor was he exactly lively. Deborah had twice the vitality. But he was forgetting! Deborah couldn't have his Uncle William's curate—*Frederica* was the one who was to marry Langham.

Hugo was filled with a warm glow of satisfaction.

He was pleased for his Cousin Frederica—she was a good girl and deserved the best. Langham was a very good chap, after all. Hugo walked on contemplating Frederica's future happiness with a smile. Poor Deborah! He sincerely hoped that she was not unduly upset by the curate's preference for his cousin... However, it wouldn't do her any harm if she suffered a little. She might learn what it was like... At this point he pulled himself up. What was he thinking of? He wasn't *suffering* because Deborah had refused him! He had been highly *relieved*... Annoyed, of course. Any man would have been. But his chief feeling was one of relief that he wouldn't after all have to spend the rest of his life rescuing Deborah Staunton from trouble. Relief, that was it.

Hugo knocked the heads off a few weeds as he walked on. His grandmother was wrong, of course, about Deborah's feelings for him. Perhaps in the old days she had been fond of him, when she was a child. She had looked to him for protection then. It was quite natural. She was a loving little thing, and her home life had been unhappy, he knew... He frowned as he remembered the remarks he had made about her mother, after Langham had gone. He shouldn't have been so unpleasant. He had hurt her. So why had he done it?

Hugo thought for a moment and came to a conclusion which added nothing to his self-esteem. He had badly wanted to make Deborah as angry as he was himself. And she had been. Hurt and angry. She had damn near retaliated by hitting him—he had seen it in her eyes and had welcomed it. And then she had mastered her anger and he had been…disappointed. Disappointed! No wonder he had been ashamed as he had ridden away. How could he hold on to his view of himself as a decent man, who prided himself on his high standards of behaviour? He had deliberately tried to provoke an innocent girl into hitting him! What had been his motive?… The answer to that made him feel even more of a villain.

He swiped viciously at a bramble. Why, oh *why* had the good Lord seen fit to put Deborah Staunton on this earth? What awful sins had Hugo Perceval committed in a previous existence to be punished like this? She must have been designed expressly to provoke him. 'Sir Hugely Perfect'—that's what that wretchedly scandalous book had called him, and it couldn't have been more wrong. Whenever he was within a hundred miles of Deborah Staunton he behaved like a mannerless, heartless, uncontrolled… villain! And she was a witch who caused the change. If he was to hold on to his sanity, he must…*must* avoid her in future like the plague!

It was a pity, therefore, that round the next bend he came upon the witch. And she needed his help.

The first thing Hugo saw was the back of a thick-set, stocky man, who was holding Deborah's arms. Not wishing for another encounter like the one in the church porch, Hugo started to withdraw. He was not about to challenge her again!

Then Autolycus growled and he heard Deborah say, in a clear, firm voice, 'I have not the remotest idea what you're talking about, sir! Please let me loose, or I will tell my dog to attack.'

As Autolycus, ready as ever to oblige, growled again, Hugo turned round. What he saw caused him to make swiftly for the two on the path. Scared back by the dog, the stranger looked up, saw Hugo striding towards them and decided to disappear into the trees. Hugo would have chased after him, but Autolycus, whose discipline had been undermined by his defence of Deborah, greeted Hugo so enthusiastically that he bounced across his path and tripped him up. By the time Hugo had recovered his balance Deborah's attacker was out of sight.

'Are you all right?' Hugo asked.

'Yes. P...perfectly.'

He saw that she was trembling, and put his arm round her shoulders. For a moment she rested her head against his chest, but then she pushed him away.

'Thank you. I...I don't need any more help. It...it was only for the moment.'

Concern for her made him angry. 'Why the *devil* you have to walk unescorted through these woods, I do not know! It really isn't safe!'

'The woods have been safe for years!' she cried. 'And if you...if you scold me again, Hugo, I warn you, I shall burst into tears!'

'Oh, you poor girl,' he said, suddenly tender. 'I'm a fool. Come here!' He pulled her into his arms, held her there and stroked her hair. 'I was angry because I was worried,' he said, resting his cheek on her head.

She nodded, accepting his apology.

'What did he want, Deborah?' He was still holding her close. It felt extraordinarily right.

'I don't know! He was drunk, I think, so he didn't speak very clearly. Something about his dues. He said he wanted "what was due to him". When I asked him what that was, he got angry. He insisted that I knew, that I must have "them" somewhere, or know who had taken "them". I really didn't understand, Hugo. I have no idea what "they" are, but I know the man. He came to Maids Moreton and threatened Aunt Staunton.'

Still holding Deborah, Hugo thought for a minute. 'We know he isn't local. He's taken the trouble to find out where you came when you left Maids Moreton and has come here in pursuit. Whatever it is he wants, he must be serious about it.' He held her away from him and looked earnestly into her face. 'I think he's dangerous, Deborah. You must promise me not to walk unaccompanied in the woods. Not till we know what it all means.'

'But I have to walk Autolycus! And what about Mrs Bember and the others? I can't desert them!'

'We'll arrange something. If I can't come with you, then someone else will. Do as I say in this, Deborah— please!'

'I'm surprised you can tolerate my company,' said Miss Staunton, unwilling to give in so easily. She removed herself from his grasp.

Hugo, who only moments before had decided that, if he wished to stay sane, he must avoid Deborah Staunton like the plague, said, 'Could you forget our differences of the past few weeks, Deborah? All of them?'

'Differences? Is that what you call them? And only of the past few weeks? I'm pleased you can view them so lightly.'

'We've had our disagreements in the past, I grant you that. But we've never before been quite so out of charity with each other. This is something new. It started with...with my absurd behaviour after the fête—'

'Absurd?'

'Oh, it was dishonourable, reprehensible and all the rest, too—I'm not minimising it. I should never have attacked you in that brutish way. Indeed, a gentleman ought never to treat any respectable woman like that, and I still don't know what got into me. But it was absurd as well! Our friendship is not one of passion. And then that stupid, ill-considered proposal made matters even worse...'

Deborah suddenly turned away from him. He couldn't see her face as he went on, 'You were right to reject me—I should never have asked you. I...I know I've hurt and insulted you since then. My vanity was injured by your refusal and I wanted to punish you for it. Not very noble of me, was it? But I'd like you to forgive me, if you would.' Hugo waited a moment, then as Deborah slowly turned round he said, 'It's more than I deserve, but I would very much like to be a friend again. Especially at the moment when I feel you're in some kind of danger.'

Deborah sighed and looked down. 'If only we were

children again, Hugo! Life would be much easier. You were always my friend and protector then.'

'I could still be both.'

'It might work,' she said, almost to herself. 'Being your friend would be better than...'

'Being my wife?'

Deborah nodded her head, but didn't speak. Her expression was still difficult to read.

Hugo was left again with a strange mixture of feelings. There was certainly relief. It looked as if he and Deborah could go back to their old relationship, and for this he was glad, of course. But deep down there was a curious feeling of regret, an elusive sadness, as if he had just let slip something rare and precious...

'Come,' he said. 'We'll visit Mrs Bember together.'

Hester's wedding day was imminent, and the plans for the day relied very much on fair weather. A series of summer storms caused the Perceval family a great deal of anxiety. But to everyone's relief, just two days before the marriage, the skies cleared, the sun shone, the roads and paths dried up again and everything was set fair. In fact, the rains had washed the trees and fields clear of the dust of summer, and the hints of gold in the foliage added touches of colour to a background of clear, fresh green.

On the great day itself the Hall was filled with flowers, and the chestnut drive to the church—a distance of half a mile—was lined with pots of white roses and myrtle. The bride's attendants walked to the church, the twins, as always, looking blondly exquisite in pale green. But today Henrietta and Deborah almost rivalled them, their dresses of pale gold setting off two dark heads, Deborah's hair arranged tidily for once in a becoming knot.

Hester herself had never looked more beautiful. Her white silk dress was embroidered round the hem with threads of gold; her bouquet of golden roses reflected glimpses of the famous Perceval golden-gilt hair which could be seen under her hat and veil. But nothing could rival the glow of happiness which surrounded her. Unconventional as always, she was no nervously blushing bride, but serenely, perfectly composed. It was as if, having made up her mind at last to marry Robert Dungarran, she had no further doubt or hesitation, not about the ceremony itself, nor about the great changes which would follow. She had learned to love and trust her lord, and knew herself to be loved beyond measure in return. And, being Hester, she was not going to pretend an anxiety she did not feel.

After the ceremony a band of local musicians, a pipe, a fiddle and a drum, danced along in front of the bride and groom, leading the large bridal party back along the drive, now lined with a crowd of laughing, chattering people from the farms and villages round about. Bunches of flowers garnered from gardens and hedgerows were pressed on them, and the bridemaids' arms were soon full. Laughing, joking, waving their thanks for the messages of good will being shouted at them, the happy couple made their way through the crowds to Perceval Hall. Once there, the party went inside, relieved to escape from the noise and the glare of the sun.

'It might almost be worth it,' said Hugo as he watched his sister, now Lady Dungarran, smiling radiantly into the face of her husband. Robert Dungarran was a man whose face seldom revealed his thoughts, but today even he was unable to hide his delight in his new wife. As they went round the guests greeting each in turn, his arm was never far from her waist. Hester lost her composed air and blushed at some of the more robust comments made to the newly-married pair, but her husband's laughter was tender as he guided her away from the worst offenders.

'Worth what?' asked Deborah. She and the other bridemaids had disposed of their armfuls of flowers and were now free to enjoy themselves. They wandered among the guests, looking as if they had escaped from Hester's bouquet in their gauzy dresses and their chaplets of green leaves. At the moment she and Hugo were standing in a corner of the beautiful reception room which had been opened for the occasion. They were sipping a cool drink and enjoying the breeze which came through a nearby window. 'What might be worth what, Hugo?'

'The ending. Worth all the drama and distress. Look at them now. I've never seen Hester look happier. Nor Dungarran so relaxed.'

'Dear me! You must beware, Hugo, my friend! Before you know it you'll be insisting that you must fall in love before you marry! And that would never do,' said Deborah lightly.

She and Hugo had achieved a measure of confidence in each other, and on the surface their relationship was as it had been before the disastrous events at the fête and Hugo's subsequent proposal. He had kept his word, and either accompanied her on her walks himself, or saw to it that someone else—Lowell or one of the servants—went with her.

But in reality Deborah could never again be as easy with Hugo as she had once been. Feelings which she had buried deep for years had been brought to the surface by his actions, and would not now go away. Her manner to him might have the appearance of openness. It was achieved, however, by a self-discipline which would have astonished those who regarded her as an impulsive scatterbrain. She talked and smiled and teased and listened with a very good imitation of her former manner to him, and was happy that he appeared not to notice the difference. But at night, once she finally fell asleep, she was haunted by bad dreams and her cheeks were often wet when she woke up...

Life hardly had time to settle down after the excitements of Hester's marriage to Dungarran before another family wedding was in prospect. The Reverend William and Lady Elizabeth were delighted to have a visit from Lord Exmouth, who had come to ask for the hand of their eldest daughter. Hugo had known and liked him in London, of course, and the rest of the family were very impressed with him. The Vicar declared him to be a sensible man, Lady Elizabeth strongly approved of both his manners and his principles and all the others were completely won over by his handsome looks and his charming smile. It was clear that Lord Exmouth was deeply in love with Robina, and eager to marry her as soon as it could be arranged.

The only problem was that, for various reasons, he wanted the ceremony to take place in Kent. But with so much good will on every side, that was quickly agreed and all the details decided. The eldest daughter of the Vicarage would marry Lord Exmouth down in Kent. It was to be a simple affair. Lord Exmouth's wedding to his first wife had been an important social occasion, with a great deal of pomp and ceremony, but she had been killed in a tragic accident not long after. Robina had no desire for a similar fuss to be made about his second marriage, so the wedding was to take place quietly at Lord Exmouth's family home. Her father would perform the ceremony, of course, and her sisters would attend her. Sir James was to give his niece away, and though the guest list was relatively small, the rest of the family was invited.

However, the bride's grandmother, the Dowager Lady Perceval, was in no mood to embark on the long journey south, and announced firmly that she would stay at home. This caused some difficulty, and it looked as if Lady Perceval would have to forgo the ceremony too, since Sir James did not wish to leave his mother alone with just the servants. But the situation was happily resolved when Deborah volunteered to stay behind with the Dowager.

'I should be pleased to do it, ma'am,' she assured Lady Perceval. 'Robina and I are very fond of one another, but, since someone has to stay, I know she would prefer to have you with her on her great day. And so will Sir James! But you must promise to give her my very best love and wishes!'

'Indeed I will, Deborah,' said Lady Perceval. 'I have to confess that I would have been disappointed to be left behind. Sir James must go—he is to give Robina away, as you know. And Hugo will look after me, while his father is performing his duties! I expect you will miss him…?'

'Miss Hugo? I…I don't think so, ma'am.'

'Come, Deborah! Don't pretend that Hugo hasn't been spending a great deal of time with you recently!'

Deborah blushed and stammered, 'Ma'am, you mustn't think… Hugo is not… He has merely been helping me to walk Autolycus!'

'And why should he bother to do that, pray?'

Hugo and Deborah had decided that nothing would be gained by causing anxiety to the rest of the household by telling them of the stranger. Deborah was at a loss. Her hesitation made Lady Perceval laugh.

'Poor child! I am wrong to tease you.' She took Deborah's hand. 'I think Hugo likes you better than he realises. He's blinded by his old prejudice in favour of blonde goddesses, of course. But Edwina and Frederica seem to be looking elsewhere for husbands.'

Deborah regained a little of her spirit. 'You're very kind to confide in me, ma'am. But what makes you think Hugo and I should feel more than friendship for each other?'

'Instinct. Nothing more, I assure you. You have

certainly given no indication that you feel more than friendship for Hugo. But I hope you will before long. Hugo should marry soon, and you and he would seem to be well suited.'

'Suited! Hugo and I? Ma'am, you amaze me! We seem to do nothing but quarrel!'

'Well, that's it. That's just it! Hugo never bothers to quarrel with anyone else! He either simply overrides them, or, with those he respects, such as Sir James, he spends considerable time and effort in persuading them. But he doesn't lose his temper.'

'I would have thought that losing your temper with a lady was not much of a recommendation for choosing her as a wife! But, in any case, I assure you, ma'am, that Hugo does not regard me as a possibility. And he never will.'

'I hope you're wrong, Deborah. Sir James and I are very fond of you. And Hugo's grandmother is forever singing your praises.'

Lady Perceval smiled and went away. Deborah was left not knowing whether she should laugh or cry. Everyone, it seemed, wanted her to marry Hugo, except the man himself! They would be disappointed, as well as incredulous, if they knew she had already refused him! But there was a warm glow at her heart. The Percevals had demonstrated how much they liked and trusted her—a girl who had come to live among them with very little to offer by way of fortune or influence. Deborah knew that she would never be a Perceval by marriage, but it was very comforting to know that she was considered worthy of the honour!

* * *

Deborah enjoyed her stay with the Dowager. The old lady was a pungent raconteuse, and scandalised her visitor with her tales of the local gentry, some of whom Deborah had till now considered of the highest respectability. Deborah sat fascinated for hours, and felt she would never again be able to regard one or two of the neighbours in the same light. They played innumerable games of piquet and whist, and amused themselves by increasing the parrot's repertoire. With time the bird's more lurid phrases had become less frequent, though he still teased Gossage unmercifully. 'Pull yourself together, Gossage!' was a favourite command, and never failed to irritate its target. But after a few days' tuition he was able to say, 'Don't be an idiot, Hugo!' reasonably clearly, and 'Be quiet, Lowell!' almost as well. The two ladies looked forward with agreeable anticipation to the reaction of the two sons of the house to these commands.

For the rest Deborah walked in the grounds, or exercised Autolycus with one of the servants for company. There had been no further sign of the mysterious man, and Deborah was getting restive. With Hugo and Lowell both away, the conversation on her walks was very restricted, and the presence of the servant prevented her from running and playing with Autolycus as she wished. Also, she was becoming worried about Sammy Spratton. Even when she did not enter the wood to visit him, Sammy's company could usually be detected by sundry rustlings along its edge. But for several days she had heard nothing of the sort. He might be ill or injured… Deborah determined to find out. However, it wouldn't do to take the servant with her to visit Sammy...

So when she next set out to visit Mrs Bember, she deliberately left behind a basket of goods. Halfway there she stopped and exclaimed in dismay. 'How stupid of me! I was to collect a basket for Mrs Bember, and I've left it behind! How fortunate that we haven't come very far. Please go back, Tom, and ask Mrs Banks for it. I'll walk on meanwhile to her cottage.' When Tom looked doubtful—he had, after all, his orders from Master Hugo—Deborah said with a touch of impatience, 'Make haste, Tom! I can't wait all afternoon!' Tom went back to Perceval Hall, and as soon as he was out of sight Deborah took a narrow path which led into the thickest part of the wood.

After a short while she came to the ruinous hut which was Sammy's home. She called him, but got no reply. The goat was munching happily a few yards from the hut with no sign of neglect, so Sammy couldn't be too far away. Then she saw him, a wizened little face peering out of bushes some distance away. He became quite agitated as she approached, and suddenly disappeared. Deborah stopped in her tracks, surprised and disappointed. Why was Sammy so frightened of her? She thought she had won his trust. Or had something else happened to scare him off?

'Good afternoon.'

She whirled round. The stranger who had accosted her before in the woods was standing in the doorway of Sammy's hut, smiling at her. He looked even more sinister—he was unshaven and his clothes were creased and grubby. Deborah called Autolycus to her.

'Don't bother calling your dog. I'm not about to attack you,' the stranger said. 'I don't blame you for finding me a touch threatening, but I mean you no harm, Miss Staunton. I have to apologise for my behaviour the last time we met. I'm afraid I had been quenching my thirst too enthusiastically, and my feeling of injustice got the better of me.'

Deborah gave a slight nod, but grasped Autolycus's collar more firmly. 'What do you want, sir?' she asked. 'And why are you apparently living rough in Sammy's hut?'

'Is that his name? I've not been able to get near enough to ask.'

'He is nervous of strangers. You haven't answered my question.'

'You needn't worry about your friend Sammy— I've only been here a day or two, and if I'm lucky I'll be gone by this evening. This is the first opportunity I have had to speak to you alone.'

'If you had called at the Hall and announced yourself in a more conventional manner, I am sure one of the servants would have fetched me.'

'Ah, well. That's the problem, you see. I'm not that fond of being seen in public.' At this Deborah stiffened and Autolycus growled. Eyeing the dog a touch nervously he went on, 'You needn't poker up. I've told you I mean you no harm. But there are certain people who would like to talk to Harry Dodds. However, he doesn't wish to talk to them, if you see what I mean.'

'Dodds? That's your name?'

'At your service, ma'am.'

'Well, Mr Dodds, though I would quite like to know why you wish to speak to me, and what you meant the last time we met, I really haven't the time to linger here. My servant will be looking for me. So if you'll excuse me...'

'No!' Harry Dodds came out of the hut towards her. He stopped short when Autolycus growled again, deep in his throat. A pistol appeared in the man's hand and he levelled it at the dog. 'Tell your dog to be quiet,' he said in a different, more menacing voice.

Deborah stared at the pistol, then said as calmly as she could, 'Sit, Autolycus.' The dog was reluctant but he obeyed. 'I was not lying about my servant,' she said carefully. 'He will come to look for me quite soon.'

'Then the sooner you tell me what you've done with the papers the better.'

'Papers?'

'Yes, papers!' he said impatiently. When she continued to look blank he went on, 'The papers in your box.'

Though Deborah had had a shock she managed to keep it from showing in her face. 'My box?' she said, playing for time.

'Yes, damn you! Don't play with me—you know the box I mean. The one with the secret drawer. I had to take the damned thing to pieces to find that drawer. It took me a while but I did it in the end. She was right—there were papers in it! But not the papers I wanted!'

Deborah's mind was in a whirl. The mysterious theft of her Aunt Elizabeth's box was explained. This man had taken it, mistaking it for the one she had brought with her from Maids Moreton. Except for the names on top they were identical. But what had he meant by a secret drawer? She had never known such a thing existed. 'So it was you who stole...the box!' she said slowly. 'And now it's gone forever! Such a beautiful thing and you've destroyed it! Why are these papers so important to you?'

'Never mind that!' he snarled. 'Come on! You say you haven't much time—neither have I! The sooner you tell me, the sooner I'll be gone. Where are my papers?'

'I don't know.'

He took a step nearer and she said desperately, 'You must believe me, sir! I don't know of any papers of yours. I didn't even know my...my box had a secret drawer!'

He stared hard at her. 'I think you might be telling the truth,' he said at last. 'You really didn't know about that drawer, did you? Strange! It never occurred to me that you wouldn't...' He thought for a moment. 'So you can't have taken them...but in that case, where are they now?'

A vision of her own box, standing so innocently on her chest of drawers rose up before Deborah. She blocked it out of her mind, took a deep breath and said, 'I'm...I'm afraid I can't help you.'

If Hugo had been present he would have known that Deborah was lying, but Harry Dodds was too busy with his own thoughts. 'She definitely said a box,' he muttered. 'She was quite clear that he had talked about hiding them in a secret drawer in the box. Unless she was lying....?' He thought, then made up his mind. 'I'll search the house in Maids Moreton again. And if that fails I'll visit that bitch in Ireland once more. She knows something...'

'Who are you talking about?' asked Deborah hesitantly, half afraid of the answer. 'This ''she'' and ''he''? Who are they?'

'What?' Dodds had forgotten her existence. He looked at her blankly then raised his eyebrows in mock surprise. 'You mean to say you can't guess? My, my! You really *are* an innocent, aren't you? ''She'' is your aunt, now tucked away in Ireland, and ''he'' is Edmund Staunton, your late Papa!'

Deborah went white. 'M...my father?' she stammered.

'Yes! My old friend, Eddy Staunton, the Irish boyo from Dublin. Married the daughter of an English Duke and thought he would make his fortune. Unfortunately it didn't quite turn out like that. So we had to think of something else. And he did. And I helped him to do it. But now he's dead I want my share of the bonds.'

'Bonds?'

'Yes, bonds, Miss Staunton. The so-called ''papers''—bonds for the money I need to get away from this stinking country! But never mind that! That servant of yours might come looking for you at any moment. Perhaps you'd better go.' He regarded her with a smile that chilled her. 'I hope not to have to disturb you again. But...those bonds mean life and liberty to me, Miss Staunton, and I intend to find them. One way or another. And until I do no one is safe.'

Deborah would have asked more, tried to find out what role her father had played in Dodds's games, but she did not dare. She was glad to escape while she could. She had never lied easily—a few more questions and the existence of a second writing-box, together with its present whereabouts, was almost certain to emerge.

She turned and went back to the main path, making a great effort not to run. After a last snarl at Dodds, Autolycus followed her.

The visit to Mrs Bember was unusually short that day. Deborah did her best, but she could not wait to get to the Vicarage to see to her box. She had no doubt that the bonds Dodds had talked about were inside it.

Chapter Nine

Once back at the Vicarage, Deborah ordered the servant to wait outside until she was ready and hurried upstairs to her room. Here she paused. Her mother's box sat so innocently on the chest of drawers, its beautifully crafted woods glowing richly in the sunlight. A thin shaft of light was reflected back into the room from the silver name plate on its lid. Deborah went over and with her finger slowly traced the name there—*"Frances"*. She imagined her mother as a child, the relief she must have felt at passing her stern father's test at last, her delight in this beautiful reward. The box had always meant a lot to Frances Staunton. Though she had sold her jewellery, pictures, and everything else of value, she had always clung to this last remnant of her past. Was it because it had been a link to an innocently happy childhood, a time before she had fallen in love with Edmund Staunton and been cast into the wilderness by her unforgiving parents?

Deborah stirred restlessly and gazed unseeing out of the window. Was Hugo right after all? Passionate, unreasonable love had cost her mother dear. Had it been worth it? Would she have been happier with a more suitable husband chosen by her family, would she have preferred never to experience the heights— or the depths—of her feelings for the man she had married against all opposition? Deborah smiled wryly. Few people had any choice when they fell in love. Once her mother had met Edmund Staunton she was his for the rest of her life, whatever he was, whatever it cost her. And when he died there had been nothing more for her to live for.

But she, Deborah, was not her mother. She had loved Hugo for as long as she could remember—first as a child, grateful for his protective presence and his interest in her small concerns, then later as a girl on the threshold of life, infatuated with the lordly creature who dominated the younger Percevals. He hadn't dominated her, though. Never. She may have adored Hugo, but she had never been blind to his faults, nor been willing to let him rule her as he had ruled the others. And now, she would neither fade away nor pine because Hugo didn't love her as she wished. Life was always interesting, and she would live it as fully as her circumstances permitted.

This last thought reminded her of her present situation, and her face grew troubled. She gazed again at the box. What was the secret it held? And how would it affect the reputation and honour of her family? Dodds had mentioned her Aunt Staunton as well as her father. What had the Stauntons to do with the 'bonds' that meant so much to Dodds? And, more worryingly, where had these bonds come from?

The sound of the servant exchanging pleasantries with Aunt Elizabeth's kitchenmaid reminded her that she had wasted enough time. The Dowager would be awake after her afternoon nap and might well wonder what had happened to her. She had imagined she would carry the box to the Hall to examine it at her leisure but that was impossible. It was too big to disguise and she would not even think of carrying it openly. Harry Dodds might well have taken it into his head to keep her under observation. Swiftly she opened the door of the closet, picked up the box and hid it under some shawls on the floor. She would come back tomorrow to examine its contents—and its structure—more carefully.

The next day Deborah asked the Dowager if she was needed. 'If not, I should like to tidy up some of my things at the Vicarage, ma'am. I was there yesterday afternoon, and was ashamed of the state of my closet.'

'You're not a servant, child! Of course you may spend as long as you like there! You've given so much of your time to me this past week. I've enjoyed them, but you mustn't encourage me to be selfish.'

Deborah smiled and knelt by the Dowager's chair. 'I can't remember when I last had so much amusement, ma'am. You've been very good to me. And I fully intend to challenge you to a game of piquet when I come back later. It's my turn to win, I think?'

'Ha! It's brains, not "turns" that win games! Haven't you learned that yet? Life isn't fair, Deborah. It's the strong who win.'

'I wouldn't exactly describe either of us as strong, ma'am,' said Deborah, puzzled.

'Don't be a fool, girl! I mean strong in spirit, not strong in body. I'm strong—and so are you.'

'*Me?*'

'Oh, you may look as if a puff of wind would blow you away, but you're stronger than any of the rest of them. With the possible exception of Hugo, perhaps. And even he needs to learn a few lessons before he will match you. Don't look so amazed! I'm right, I know I am. Now off with you to clear up your bits and pieces. I shall look forward to our game.'

Deborah was on her way to the door when the Dowager's voice called her. She turned back, to find the parrot sidling up and down on his perch, squawking triumphantly and Lady Perceval cackling with laughter. 'That caught you! You didn't know I'd been teaching him your name, did you? There, my lovely,' she crooned as she gave the parrot a piece of apple. 'You're a clever, clever boy!'

Deborah was smiling as she left the Dowager's room, but she soon sobered. The thought of what was hidden in her mother's box oppressed her. Eager as she was to find the secret drawer, she was haunted by the fear of uncovering yet more shame for her family. Harry Dodds had not impressed her as an honest man, and he had obviously been a friend of her father's. Her aunt, too, was somehow involved. Before Miss Staunton had left for Ireland she had pressed Deborah to sell her the box, been curiously persistent about it, even after Deborah had made it clear that she would

not dream of parting with it. Aunt Staunton had even
tried to claim that her sister-in-law had promised to
leave her the box, something Deborah had refused to
believe. And on the day after Dodds's visit her aunt
had made a strange remark. On being refused the box
yet again, she had shrugged her shoulders and said,
'Be it on your own head then, Deborah, my dear. But
you may well regret not listening to me.' And then
she had gone.

The Vicarage was very quiet. The servants were
about their affairs, and, with the family away, were
working in the back of the house. Deborah went
slowly up the stairs and into her bedchamber. She
opened the door of the closet. The box was still there.
She lifted it up, put it on the bed and started to empty
it. She took out notes from her father, written before
Frances had run away with him, extravagantly affectionate, promising her the world. Then came long letters from her mother written after they were married,
when Edmund Staunton had been in Ireland, or elsewhere, always, always seeking his fortune. A loving
description of their baby daughter was accompanied
by a plea for her husband's early return, an account
of a visit by her sister Elizabeth ended with the bitter
news that the older Ingleshams had finally and absolutely abandoned her. All Frances Staunton's letters
revealed heartbreaking loneliness, together with complete, unquestioning devotion to her husband.
Deborah's eyes were wet and her throat constricted
with pity for her poor, dead mother as she sorted

them. Impulsive, affectionate Frances Staunton had not found much happiness in love.

At last the box was empty. Deborah took it to the light and examined it carefully on every side. In the end, it was a slight interruption in the pattern, the merest hairline split, which showed her where the drawer was. But how to open it? She looked inside again. The box was divided into compartments, the smaller ones fitted with containers for pens and ink. Under the silver-capped ink bottles were small decorative studs to keep the bottles in place. Deborah pressed each of them in turn, but it wasn't until she pushed one of them to the side that, smooth as silk, a drawer in the back of the box slid out and revealed its contents.

Papers. A thick envelope with her father's name on the outside. It was sealed. Deborah took it out and put it on the bed. Underneath was a letter also addressed to her father at their home in Maids Moreton. This had been opened. Deborah hesitated, then unfolded it. The letter was short, the writing scrawled across the page.

Eddy! I hope you still have the bonds safe. Don't try to do anything with them—you'd not succeed. I've been asking about, but there's no safe way of cashing the damned things before the autumn of '12. That's when they mature. After that they're as good as ready money. My situation is not very comfortable at the moment, so I think it might be wiser for me to disappear for a while. But don't try any of your tricks—

I'll be there when it's time to collect my share of the dibs. Meanwhile keep them safe and your mouth shut! HD.

Deborah was puzzled, but not reassured. Whatever Dodds had done to get the bonds, it could hardly have been honest—why else the secrecy? Why hide them in a wooden box when there were bank vaults for such things? With a heavy heart she opened the envelope. Bearer bonds. Five of them, each worth two thousand pounds to be paid to the bearer on or after the last day of October 1812. Deborah sat down suddenly on the bed, and struggled for breath. The shock was too great. In a matter of weeks the contents of this envelope would be worth ten thousand pounds to anyone who presented them for payment!

She had no idea how long she had been sitting there before she heard Nanny Humble's voice outside the room. Hastily stuffing the bonds back inside their envelope, she put both the envelope and Dodds' letter into a bag she had brought for the purpose. Then she pushed the secret drawer back into place and invited the old nurse in.

'They told me you were here, Miss Deborah, so I thought I'd see how you were,' said Nanny Humble as she came into the room. 'Now how many times have I told you not to sit on the bed?' she scolded. 'You were always doing it when your poor mother was sick, God rest her soul, but there's no reason to do it now!' As she came nearer her expression changed. 'Why, Miss Deborah, whatever are they doing to you up at the Hall? You look ill. I should have come with you, I know I should! It was just that I'd got so nicely settled here, and her ladyship said it wasn't necessary...'

'I know, Nanny, I know. There's no need to worry—they look after me very well at the Hall. And I'm not ill, really I'm not. I've...I've been looking through these letters, and I...I've found it upsetting.' Deborah was busy putting the letters back into her box as she spoke.

'That's no occupation for a sunny morning like this! You should be out with that dog of yours!'

'A very good idea! I'll do it.' Deborah got up and carefully placed her box on the chest of drawers. Then she picked up the bag and got up to go.

'Is that bag heavy, Miss Deborah? I'll tell one of the others to carry it for you, shall I?'

'No!' Deborah exclaimed. She went on more calmly, 'The servants have their own work. It isn't heavy. Not heavy at all. I must go.' At the door she paused and said with an apologetic smile, 'I'm sorry I can't stop—but I shall soon be here again to stay. The family will be back from Kent before long. Look after yourself, Nanny, dear!'

'It's you I should be looking after, I should have come with you to the Hall, I know I should...'

Deborah kissed her nurse on the cheek and went down the stairs. The bag was not heavy, but what it contained was a great weight on her mind. However, though the long-term solution was still a problem, the first step was clear. Dodds would be back, of this she was certain. When he failed to find anything at Maids Moreton, he would probably speak to her aunt in

Ireland again. She might well describe Frances
Staunton's box in more detail, and Dodds would return to search the Vicarage again, this time better informed. Deborah dared not risk his finding those
bonds. Until she knew more of their history and to
what extent her father had been involved in it she
must find a safer hiding place for them.

The Dowager made short shrift of Deborah's attempt to win their game of piquet. 'I may have beaten
you, girl, but I take no pride in it. You weren't even
trying. What's the matter?'

Deborah sighed. The temptation to confide, to ask
for advice, was strong, but the Dowager Lady
Perceval was not the right person. For all her indomitable spirit she was too old, too frail to be burdened
with such a problem. She was also too impatient.
Deborah already knew what her reply would be.
Bring it into the open! Tell the truth and shame the
devil! That was the motto the Dowager lived by. And
while Deborah on the whole subscribed to this philosophy herself, she was not at all sure what the truth
was! She wanted to know more of *what* she would
be bringing out into the open before she did anything.

'I suppose I'm suffering from the blue devils,
ma'am,' she said. 'I've been sorting letters from my
parents.'

'Sorting anything is often sad and always tiresome!
Hester was very good—after her grandfather died she
sorted out all his papers for me. Spent years in her
attic working on them, as well as learning about mathematics and inventing ciphers and all the other non-

sense. Unwomanly, that's what it was! But it ended happily enough. The attic was always a dusty hole—have you ever been up there?'

'Yes. I went up once or twice before Hester got engaged to Lord Dungarran. It's not very dusty at all, but it's certainly crammed with papers!'

'She's going to have a wonderful time clearing that lot out when she returns. I wonder if Dungarran will let her take them all to Stancombe?'

'I think Lord Dungarran would do anything to make Hester happy, ma'am. How long do they plan to be away?'

'Another month at least. They were to spend three weeks at Stancombe Court then he was to take her to see the rest of his estates. Since there's more of them than any man deserves, I should be very surprised if we saw them again before October. Now, what about another game? And this time you must concentrate, girl!'

The talk with the Dowager had suggested to Deborah a perfect place to hide the bonds, at least for the moment. Hester's attic would remain undisturbed until Hester herself came to clear it up—or it might even be left as it was for years. Deborah vaguely remembered an old bureau in the corner of the room—her envelope would lie safe there. The next day she slipped away up to the attics, found the bureau and, with a deep sigh of relief laid the envelope inside it, under a folder full of pages of cryptic signs and dashes. Had she only known it, these were Hester's attempts to decipher Robert Dungarran's love letters, including the one which had brought her out of hiding, and finally into his arms. But since they had been written by one expert in ciphers, and translated by another, they were inaccessible to ordinary human beings!

The Percevals returned full of news about Robina and her new family, and ready to give detailed accounts of the wedding. On one matter all were in complete agreement. Robina was as fortunate as Hester in her choice of husband, and as adored by him as Hester was by Dungarran.

'So much has happened in the last twelve months,' said Lady Perceval the day after their return. The family was sitting on the lawn in the shade of the cedar, enjoying the fresh air and tranquillity after days of celebration and journeying. 'There's been a positive rash of betrothals and weddings! Last year Beatrice Roade and dear India, now Sophia Cleeve, Hester and Robina.' Her eyes rested thoughtfully on Hugo. 'I wonder who will be next?'

'It hasn't all been pleasant,' said Sir James. 'Sywell's murder was a bad business.'

'Oh, but Sir James!' exclaimed his wife. 'You cannot say that things have not turned out for the best!' She turned to Deborah. 'Has the news reached the villages? The Steepwood estate has been officially returned to the Cleeves. The Earls of Yardley will live once again in their ancestral home. That must be good news!'

'I doubt the present Earl will ever live there, however,' said Sir James slowly. 'There's a mountain of work to do before the Abbey is habitable. And Yardley has aged a lot in the past year. I can't see him coping with all the fuss.'

'Why should he?' Lowell asked eagerly. 'Surely Marcus could manage the work for him? It's just the sort of challenge he would enjoy.'

'Would someone mind telling me before you say one more word,' said the Dowager icily. 'What you are all talking of? How is it that Lord Yardley is to have the Abbey? Has he bought it? Who from? Does this mean they've found that wretched girl who ran off after less than a year of marriage? And with the Cleeve jewels? Explain, if you please!'

'Forgive me, Mama,' said Sir James. 'We all knew that Sywell was a double-dyed villain, but we didn't know the worst! It has been proved conclusively that Sywell won the Steepwood Abbey estate by deception and murder. Apparently the story he produced about the gaming session when Emmett Cleeve gambled, lost everything and then committed suicide was a complete fabrication.' He paused and shook his head. 'I wish no man dead, but if ever a man deserved his end Sywell did! But at least one major injustice has now been put right. The Abbey and all the estates have been returned to the Cleeve family.'

'What, already?'

'It was quickly done, I agree. But there was every reason not to delay. Steepwood lands urgently need attention, and Sywell's guilt was indisputable.'

'What about the girl? His so-called wife—though I suppose we should now call her his widow. Does this mean she is penniless? If she is alive, that is!'

'No one knows where the Marchioness is,' said Lady Perceval. 'But someone said that Lord Yardley would be prepared to help her if she was ever traced. Perhaps he intends to put some money her way? A dowry perhaps if she should wish to marry again?'

'Hmph! I only hope she deserves it,' said the Dowager grimly. 'So, young Marcus is to run the Abbey, is he?'

'It's too soon to say,' said Sir James. 'But the task will need youth and strength, and his father is short on both of those. Besides, we all know how fond Yardley is of his present home, Jaffrey House. I for one wouldn't be at all surprised if he installed his son in the Abbey. Marcus would be the ideal man to look after its reconstruction.'

The Dowager nodded. 'It will bring plenty of work to those poor creatures who been living on nothing for so long, too. The Cleeves always paid up promptly—and they have the funds to engage as many workmen as they like. I must say, James, that I think this is very good news for all of us! Is young Marcus married?'

'No,' said Lady Perceval. 'But he must be thirty or more. It's time he was.' Her eyes rested on her elder son again. Hugo had taken little part in their conversation, but was watching Deborah with a look of concern on his face. Lady Perceval gave a small smile. 'I wonder who will be next to find a wife? Will it be Marcus? Or…someone else?'

Hugo appeared not to hear. He was listening to Deborah's conversation with Frederica. She had expressed her delight at seeing them all, had asked eager questions about the wedding and was at present talking to Frederica with every sign of animation and interest. Almost feverishly so. Something was wrong. He had known Deborah Staunton too long to be deceived by this airy manner. Underneath it she was as taut as a bowstring. She was surely even paler than before, the shadows under her eyes darker than ever. She had always been tiny, but now her cheekbones were too prominent, the bones in her wrists too marked. Something was very wrong—and before the day was out he would find out what it was.

His chance came quite soon. The talk turned to what had happened in Abbot Quincey during their absence, and Lady Perceval thanked Deborah for keeping her mother-in-law company.

'Has she worn you out?' asked Lowell with a grin.

'Indeed no! I've had a wonderful time. I don't believe there's been a dull moment, but it has never been tiring.' She pulled a face. 'Perhaps I haven't managed to walk Autolycus as much as I would have wanted, but I blame Hugo for that. He gave such strict orders, that no one dared let me go out alone. And I was reluctant to keep the servants away for too long from the house.'

'In that case, I'll show my penitence now, Deborah,' Hugo said, rising from his bench. 'Come! We'll fetch the dog and take him for a walk.'

Before Lady Elizabeth could object, or suggest that one of the twins should go too, Deborah was whisked off. Sir James and Lady Perceval exchanged looks.

'I do so wonder who will be next...' said Lady Perceval with another little smile.

Hugo and Deborah collected Autolycus, waited a while until his raptures at seeing Hugo again had moderated, and then set off along their favourite walk. Hugo was determined to find out what was troubling Deborah, but was not sure quite how to begin. He realised with surprise that he felt more content now, walking along a perfectly ordinary woodland ride with Deborah Staunton, than he had been during any of the days spent celebrating his cousin's marriage to Exmouth. Why was that? All the time he had been away he had felt that something was missing, and here he felt...complete. He glanced at Deborah. She was somehow part of the picture, too. On the way to Kent and back they had called on a couple of friends of his father, both of them with one or two very pretty daughters, and there had been more among Exmouth's neighbours. He was probably being unfair to the poor girls, since the time spent with them had been very short, but he had in fact found all of them really rather boring. He had not the slightest desire to continue the acquaintance with any of them. He stole another glance at Deborah. She was very quiet. He suddenly felt a strong desire to lift whatever burden she was carrying, to see her face light up with joy in the old way, to hear her laugh. Not one of those insipid creatures he had met during his absence had a quarter of her charm! Not one!

Deborah, stealing a glance now and then at Hugo, thought he looked preoccupied. Had he found someone at Robina's wedding who would fit his exacting standards for a wife? The Exmouths were bound to have a wide acquaintance in society. Had there been a beautifully mannered, blonde, blue-eyed daughter among the guests? Or had there been someone among his father's friends who suited him? The thought was painful, and she felt more cast down than ever. Once Hugo married, their comforting relationship, however difficult or odd it had been, would be at an end. She would no longer be able to regard him as someone to confide in, argue with, rely on for help in times of difficulty. And how she needed someone like that, particularly at the moment... But this was not the way to behave! He would ask what the matter with her was if she didn't take care. She rallied and made herself chat gaily about the antics of Autolycus, the difficulty of walking with a servant, Mrs Bember...

'What's wrong, Deborah?'

She looked at him, startled. 'Wrong?' she stammered. 'What makes you think there is something wrong, Hugo?'

'It's obvious. What is it?'

Deborah was in a dilemma. Hugo was undoubtedly the best person to talk to about Harry Dodds and the bonds. He would be annoyed with her for going into the woods to look for Sammy Spratton, of course, but that was nothing compared with the rest of her problems. But what if he decided that he couldn't—or wouldn't—help her in something which might well prove to be a criminal matter? The Percevals were a proud family, highly regarded in the neighbourhood. Hugo might well not wish to risk his family's name. And...and she was ashamed. Aunt Staunton had stolen her allowance, and now her father had possibly been involved in something even worse. How could Hugo think well of a girl with a family like that?

Hugo interrupted her thoughts. 'I intend to find out, Deborah. By the way, did you send Tom back to fetch the basket for Mrs Bember by design?'

Deborah looked at him in amazement. 'How on earth did you find that out so quickly?'

'Well, of course I checked with Tom and the others that you hadn't got into difficulties,' he said impatiently.

'You asked the servants…!' began Deborah furiously.

'I thought the dog might have caused some problems. And I wanted to be sure they had done as I told them. I'm glad to see you a little more like yourself, Deborah, but don't fire up at me like that. I was trying to make sure you were protected while I was away. But it seems you foiled me.'

'It wasn't Tom's fault…'

'He still shouldn't have left you. But I'm willing to wager a considerable sum that you got rid of him deliberately so that you could visit Sammy Spratton.'

'I hadn't seen Sammy for some days—I was worried…'

'And what happened? Was he ill? Or dead, perhaps? Is that why you're so subdued?'

'No. Sammy is quite safe. It was…it was…' Deborah took a deep breath. She was about to risk everything on her belief that Hugo was a true friend, even if she were perhaps about to be disgraced. 'It was that man—Dodds!'

By the end of their walk Hugo had heard the whole story. 'And what do you wish to do?'

'I don't know! I think the only thing I *can* do is to wait until Dodds comes back, and then try to talk to him. He *might* have come by the money honestly. And in any case, I don't believe he is really as violent as he pretends. If he was a friend of my father's he might…'

'Don't say another word! It's out of the question that you should meet Dodds again!'

'But I must! It's the only way! How else would I discover where the bonds came from, whose they really are—and what I can do about them?'

Hugo was silent and Deborah's overburdened nervous system gave way to despair.

'I'll have to go away,' she said dully. 'I can't stay here. You've all been so kind, but I can't involve you in this. I'll go to Ireland, to Aunt Staunton.'

'No! You mustn't go!' Hugo stopped short. Then he said in a calmer tone, 'Of course you mustn't. You're needed here, Deborah!'

'But what am I to *do*?'

The despairing cry twisted Hugo's heart. He was filled with the desire to comfort her, to find a safe place where she would be cherished and protected forever. He opened his mouth to speak, then paused. Was this another disastrous impulse? He would in any case help Deborah to the best of his ability, but if she was married to him he could do so much more. But though the notion now seemed quite natural, not at all absurd or impulsive, he would still take a moment to consider. He must not speak a second time without thinking, say something he would again immediately regret. This time he must be sure he knew and accepted what such a declaration meant *before* he spoke. He looked thoughtfully at his companion. Deborah had turned away from him, he couldn't see her face. It didn't make any difference. He was not at all tempted to change his mind. She needed protection and he would offer the best he could. But the memory of a similar occasion not so very long ago was still vividly in his mind, and he found that he was at a loss for words.

'Deborah,' he began. He looked at her and a wave of tenderness overcame him. He forgot his pride, his reservations. 'Deborah, forgive me if I upset you, but I have a suggestion to make. I…I hope you know how much I value you as a friend, how much I enjoy your company. I could look after you so much better if you would…if you would consider marrying me, after all. No, let me finish! I don't mean to make a nuisance of myself. If you really cannot face the thought of being my wife, then I assure you that I won't take it amiss. I will still remain your good friend and do all I can for you. It's just that as your husband I could do so much more. Will you…will you be my wife?'

Deborah looked up at him. He was perfectly sincere. Her eyes misted over. It was too much! How could she have doubted Hugo? She had feared that he would distance himself from her, fearful of the damage which could be done to his name. Instead, the opposite had happened. He had volunteered to be her champion. Proud Hugo had forgotten his resentment at her previous refusal, and had offered her marriage again. An unexpected second chance had come her way...

The temptation to give in was very strong. This time she could feel his affection for her warming his words, giving them sincerity. He truly meant what he said. It would be so easy to let Hugo take control of her life, whatever kind of love he felt for her. In other circumstances she might have risked it. But, her situation being what it was, she must not. This time her scruples were not for herself, but for Hugo. How was she to explain this to him without offence?

Tears in her eyes, she faltered, 'Oh Hugo, thank you. I am touched and...and deeply honoured. You can't imagine what your offer means to me. But for your own sake, and for the sake of your family as well, I still can't accept it. I love you all so dearly. How could I let you tie yourself to me? We neither of us know what this business of the bonds will reveal. My...my father's good name is seriously in question and until that is cleared I mustn't think of marrying anyone—least of all you. It is my belief that he was feckless, not dishonest, but what if I am wrong? What if Edmund Staunton turns out to have been a criminal? Please, please don't be offended, but I have to say no. Can you understand? Please say you do.'

Hugo was conscious of a feeling of deep disappointment. But he nodded and even managed a smile. 'If that is your only reason for refusing me, then I think you're wrong. But I do understand.' He took a breath. 'Well then, what shall we do? I think Miss

Staunton must know something of the affair. Shall I go to Dublin to talk to her?'

'Would you?' Hugo's heart lifted when he saw Deborah's face light up in something of the old way.

'Of course. I could do it and be back under a fortnight.'

Deborah's face fell. 'But I don't know where she lives. I know she went to Dublin, but not her address. She has never told me.'

'Probably not very eager to be found, I dare swear. Don't worry—I'll find her. So that's settled then. Now, where are these bonds? I'd like to examine them.'

'In Hester's attic.'

'A good place. In the bureau?'

Deborah nodded. Just one moment before she had been near to complete despair. But now she felt full of life, full of optimism. The situation was not noticeably better. But with Hugo on her side everything was possible.

Chapter Ten

Hugo was as good as his word. Within forty-eight hours he was on his way to Holyhead and thence to Ireland, ostensibly to look for some horses. The rest of the Percevals were slightly surprised that he should choose to go away so soon after his return from Kent, but, as his father said, Hugo was his own master. It was well known that Irish horses were among the best of their kind, and if Hugo could afford them, Sir James would not stop his son and heir from going over to buy what he wanted.

Deborah listened and felt most uncomfortable. But what else could Hugo have said? What possible reason could he give for going all that way just to see Miss Staunton?

Before he left Hugo had looked at the bonds and had asked if Deborah would give him *carte blanche* to deal with them.

'I take it that you would like the affair cleared up as honestly and discreetly as possible?'

'That would be perfect, Hugo. I can't regard the

money as mine, and if you can see a way to return it to the right person without a scandal then I should be very happy. Do whatever you think is necessary. Take the bonds with you if you wish.'

Hugo thought about it for a moment, then said, 'I think not—but I think I'll find a better place for them. There's no knowing when my mother might take it into her head to order Hester's attic to be cleared. She was talking of something of the sort only the other day. The bonds would really be safer somewhere else for the moment. Leave it to me. What about Dodds?'

'Once the bonds are given back there isn't much he can do. I have the impression that he would like publicity as little as I would.'

'There's one thing I should like your absolute word on, Deborah.' Hugo took her hand as he spoke and looked at her very seriously.

'What is that?'

'You must never go out alone. Never! Not even to see Sammy. Dodds will almost certainly be back, and he will be desperate to talk to you again, especially as the date on which they fall due approaches. He might even do worse than that. I've told my parents and Uncle William that there are some undesirable characters about. They will see to it that none of you go out unescorted. But I know you. Will you promise not to give your protectors the slip?'

Hugo looked so worried. And he had done—was doing—so much for her! The least she could do was to give him her word. Deborah gave it.

Hugo gave a sigh of relief. 'Thank you!' He smiled. 'Are you going to wish me a safe journey?'

'Of course,' said Deborah. She stood on tiptoe and kissed him on the cheek. 'Come back as quickly as you can,' she said softly.

Hugo's arm went round her. He tilted her face up again and kissed her back, this time on the lips. When he released her Deborah couldn't move away. She stared at him, her eyes enormous in her pale face. With an exclamation Hugo pulled her to him and kissed her again, this time with passion, holding her up against him so tightly that her feet left the ground. He cradled her, feeling the slender lines of her body through her thin summer clothing, and excitement ran between them like a trail of fire as Hugo kissed her yet again. Then he took her by the arms and set her carefully away from him.

'You're...you're so tiny,' he said unsteadily. 'I could crush you with one hand. Please take care, Deborah! I...I'm not sure what I would do if anything happened to you while I was away.'

'It won't. I promise to be careful. Oh Hugo, I do so hope that things can be cleared up!'

'So do I,' said Hugo. 'And once it is, we shall have our own reckoning, Deborah Staunton!'

As soon as he arrived in Dublin Hugo called on a friend from his Cambridge days, who was now a professor of law at Trinity College. He was made very welcome and invited to stay there while he was in Dublin. They discussed horses among other things while the manservant established Miss Staunton's address. To his surprise she was living in a moderately respectable street near the centre. But, unlike his

Cambridge friend, Miss Staunton was not particularly pleased to see him.

'You'd better sit down,' she said ungraciously. Hugo looked around him.

'A pleasant room,' he said. 'And well furnished. Did you buy some of it with your niece's money?'

Miss Staunton flushed an unbecoming red. 'How dare you, sir! Whatever do you mean?'

'Wrong way round, Miss Staunton! You should have asked me first what I meant. And then, after I had explained, you could have pretended outrage. But you needn't be afraid. I'm not here to talk over your past…indiscretions. Your niece is happy enough with what she now has, without worrying over the money she was deprived of by you. Your reputation is safe— as long as I get what I need from you. It's future family skeletons I want to avoid, not to stir up past ones.'

Miss Staunton looked uneasy. 'What might those be?' she asked cautiously.

'Well, unless we are all very lucky, it's something that no one could disregard, not even the most forgiving victim. Ten thousand pounds is too big a sum to overlook.'

'Ten thou…ten thousand pounds! Oh, the devil! The scheming, conniving devil!'

'Are you referring to your brother, or to Mr Harry Dodds?'

'Harry Dodds, of course! Eddy was reckless, but he wasn't dishonest. Not in his own eyes, at least. But Dodds didn't tell me it was anything like as much as that.' She had spoken without thought. Now she suddenly became aware of Hugo again. 'How…how much do you know about this?'

'I'll be honest with you—a rare virtue among some of your acquaintances, I suspect. We have the bonds. You needn't look at me like that—I don't have them with me. They are in a safe place until we find out what is to be done with them.'

'My brother didn't do anything wrong! That money belongs to us!' she said defiantly.

'So why the secrecy? Why the intervention of Mr Dodds? Perhaps you would like to read Dodds's letter.' He handed over the note Deborah had found in the secret drawer. 'Perhaps what it says there will explain why I don't altogether believe that this business is as innocent as you claim. Not at the moment.'

Miss Staunton was silent. Then she said sullenly, 'If my great-grandfather had been given what was due to him, Eddy wouldn't have needed to take anything.'

Hugo's heart sank. It sounded as if Deborah's father had indeed been involved personally in the theft, and, if that were the case, it would be very difficult indeed to cover it up. His relief was considerable when Miss Staunton went on, 'Not that Eddy actually took part. Harry Dodds got them for him.'

'What happened?'

'Dodds was an old drinking companion of my brother's. A disreputable one. It was after the Ingleshams had finally cast out poor Frances, and Eddy could no longer hope for anything from her side of the family. One night he was drowning his sorrows with Dodds and airing his grievances about the

Stauntons... Do you know the other branch of our family, Mr Perceval?'

'No. Should I?'

'Perhaps not. They haven't spent much time in England recently. Lord Staunton is quite old.'

'Lord Staunton?'

'He is a distant cousin of my father. But...' Miss Staunton paused, then said bitterly, 'There are the rich Stauntons and the poor Stauntons. His lordship is one of the rich Stauntons, and he's made himself even richer. But one of his estates belonged by right to *our* branch of the family—the poor Stauntons.'

'How did that come about?'

'The old story. Several generations ago the youngest son quarrelled with his father and was thrown out. He should have inherited his mother's estate, but though other bequests were paid to his two other brothers, my great-grandfather wasn't given the Linlow estate. That went to the eldest son, my great-uncle, along with the title and all the lands that went with that. Eddy became obsessed about this estate, which he regarded as having rightfully belonged to his great-grandfather, and so down the line to him. And when the present Lord Staunton sold it—for a very handsome sum, incidentally—he was furious. Apparently he poured all this out to Dodds, and Dodds persuaded him to take his revenge. Using Eddy's knowledge of the family procedures, they worked out a confidence trick, by means of which Dodds would get his hands on the money paid for the estate.'

'What was Dodds to get out of it all? I don't suppose he was prepared to do it for nothing—he was taking the risk.'

'Naturally he drove a bargain. He was to have half the proceeds. You can imagine what a blow it was to the two of them when they discovered that the money had been converted into bonds which would take five years to mature.'

'So the bonds are rightfully the property of the present Lord Staunton?'

'Legally, perhaps, yes. I'm not sure whether they are rightfully his.'

'Miss Staunton,' said Hugo briskly. 'Whatever your family history, whatever Edmund Staunton may have believed, those bonds were stolen. I am surprised the thief has not been pursued with more vigour—I can only suppose your cousin was waiting to pounce when someone tried to cash them in a few weeks' time. Where does Lord Staunton live?'

'No! You're not going to tell him…?'

'What I say will depend on your cousin. Where does he live? If you cannot or will not tell me I can easily find it out. I have friends in Dublin.'

In the end Miss Staunton told him that her cousin lived in Dublin's most fashionable quarter—he had a house in Merrion Square.

Hugo lost no time in sending a note to Lord Staunton requesting the favour of an interview. To his surprise, for his friend had told him that the old man was something of a recluse, he was invited to dine at Merrion Square the very next day. The house was one of a beautiful terrace on the best side of the square, and inside it was furnished with taste and luxury. This indeed was a rich branch of the Stauntons!

He was led into a study, where he found Lord Staunton just rising, rather stiffly, to greet him.

'Perceval? I'm pleased to meet you. Take a seat. I hope you don't mind if we talk before we dine. I don't like discussing business matters over food. Something to drink? Sherry wine or a glass of Irish whiskey?'

Once they had settled down in comfortable arm-chairs with their glasses, Hugo expressed his thanks that Lord Staunton had agreed to see him.

'I was curious. The only connection between us that I can think of is Edmund Staunton's little daughter. Deborah, isn't it? I believe she is a ward of your aunt, the Lady Elizabeth Perceval.'

Hugo was surprised and said so.

'I keep abreast, I keep abreast, sir. Perhaps you are not aware, but I let the side down some years ago and went into banking. From the fuss my more consciously aristocratic relatives made you would have thought I had sold out to the French. Trade! They all blenched at the thought. But I've never regretted it. It has made me a rich man, richer than any of them. And it has made my life much more interesting! The banking world thrives on news and gossip, and its networks are worldwide. You'd be surprised what comes to my ears, here in Dublin. In fact, I could make a good guess as to why you're here.'

Hugo's face was expressionless. 'Really?' he said.

Lord Staunton eyed him with a slight smile on his lips. 'If I mention, very discreetly, the word "bonds"?'

Hugo's expression remained unchanged but his mind was racing. Lord Staunton's question revealed several interesting items. The first was that to connect Hugo's visit with Deborah Staunton, and Deborah to the bonds, the bank's intelligence system must be first-rate! Second, and perhaps most important, before connecting Deborah with the bonds Lord Staunton must have had a good idea who had been behind their disappearance in the first place. The third was that Lord Staunton was as reluctant as Hugo himself to make the matter public. He said at last, 'May I ask, sir, what your attitude is to these bonds?'

'I have every confidence in your integrity, of course, but I'd like to know a little more of your interest in them before I tell you.'

'I...I have no direct involvement with the matter. I am acting on behalf of your cousin, Deborah Staunton.'

Lord Staunton's face hardened. 'A reward for their return, perhaps? Is that what Miss Staunton wants?'

Hugo stood up. His voice was icy as he said, 'In view of your age I can hardly call you out, Lord Staunton. But allow me to tell you that you have just insulted a girl whose sole desire is to return anything which might have been...inadvertently removed from your coffers as quickly and as completely as possible. Moreover, I object very strongly to your assumption that I would act in such a matter if it were not so.'

'Sit down, sit down. Forgive me. I should have known better, but in my business we quickly become cynical. I apologise. Sit down. Please?' He waited until Hugo had seated himself then he said, '"Inadvertently'', eh? It's a good word, but not the right one. Harry Dodds knew very well what he was doing.'

'Harry Dodds?' Hugo's voice was neutral, but he was thinking that the bank's intelligence system was even better than he had credited.

'Aye.' The old man leaned forward. 'Let us stop fencing with each other, Mr Perceval! Harry Dodds got together with my cousin Edmund and together they conspired to steal ten thousand pounds from me. Only the fact that the bonds could not be converted for five years prevented Edmund from getting his hands on the cash. Is that frank enough?'

'Then if you knew all this, why the devil haven't you acted before now?'

'I should have thought it was obvious. I haven't lost the ten thousand yet. The money is only irrevocably lost to me when the bonds are cashed by someone else! And though there's never been any love lost between the two Staunton branches, I have no desire to have my family's name dragged through the criminal courts. But I assure you, since Edmund's death Harry Dodds was never out of my sight for long. The moment he tried to do anything with those bonds he would have been snapped up before he knew it. I know, for example, that he left them in Edmund Staunton's care while he ''disappeared'' for a while. And I know he has recently twice visited Abbot Quincey. But what I don't know is what exactly happened to the bonds after Edmund Staunton's death. Any more, I suspect, than Harry Dodds does. But I think that perhaps you know. And that you are here to put matters right.'

'You're perfectly correct, sir. They are in a safe place in Abbot Quincey. And now that I know where they belong, you shall have them as soon as I can arrange for a messenger to deliver them. Shall I send them to you here, or do you have an agent in London?'

'It will be safer, I think, if they are collected from you by one of the bank's own messengers. They are used to looking after large sums of money in transit. It will take me a little time to arrange, but they will be collected before the end of October, Mr Perceval. I would be obliged to you if you would arrange a suitable day with my London agent.'

Hugo smiled inwardly at this evidence of a banker's caution. Lord Staunton might have every confidence in Hugo Perceval's integrity, but he would make sure the bonds were in his bank's possession before the date on which they could be cashed! But he readily agreed to this suggestion. The sooner responsibility for the bonds was in the hands of their owner the better. Lord Staunton then said with an urbane smile, 'Shall we go into the dining-room?'

The meal was excellent, and conversation between the two men flowed easily. But afterwards, when they were once again in the study with glasses of a very fine port in their hands, Lord Staunton reopened the subject of the bonds.

'Have you been told something of our family history, Mr Perceval?'

'Miss Staunton was kind enough to give me some background before I came here, yes.'

'Then you possibly agree with Edmund Staunton that he had some justification for stealing the money?'

'No, of course not. And without knowing the details, I cannot even be sure that his grievance was just.'

'Oh, it was! I've been looking it all up. It's perfectly true that Aileen Linlow's estate should have gone to her youngest son, another, earlier, Edmund. As it was, my grandfather benefited from the family quarrel which deprived both the old and the young Edmund Stauntons of their proper inheritance. Deborah Staunton's father was a fool. If he had approached me I am sure we could have come to a better arrangement than his conspiracy with Harry Dodds to defraud me. But his branch of the Stauntons always preferred reckless adventure to the humdrum necessity of making a respectable living. Aristocratic pride gone mad.' He paused. Then he said, 'I've had good reports of his daughter, however, and I'd like to put matters right. I take it that you are empowered to represent Miss Deborah Staunton fully? Would she accept the bonds as a gift? Take your time to consider.'

This was a magnificently generous offer. Hugo was somewhat overcome. 'Why should you wish to do something like that?' he asked. 'I don't have to remind you that there is no sane reason why you should.'

Lord Staunton smiled at him. 'I am impressed that Deborah Staunton has tried to return the bonds so promptly, especially as she is almost totally dependent on the generosity of her aunt, the Lady Elizabeth. My wife is dead, and I have no children to survive me. I have made more money than I could possibly spend in four lifetimes. After taking out what I intend to leave to Miss Deborah, there will be more than enough left to satisfy the next Lord Staunton and all the rest of the family. Have I said enough to convince you?'

Hugo nodded. 'But though I'm sorry to disappoint you, I am almost sure that your cousin would not wish to take this money. She has no legal right to it, and, in view of its history, would feel uncomfortable about accepting it. If you wish, I will consult her personally about it. I am sure I will be proved right, however.'

Lord Staunton smiled again. 'I had expected no less. Now I have a second suggestion. How would it be if I left her the sum of ten thousand pounds in my will? In that way I would have no need to consult either of you. Would that do?'

'If you genuinely feel that the original Edmund Staunton was done an injustice then that would seem to be an extremely satisfactory solution. You are very kind.'

'I'll see my lawyers tomorrow. And I'll leave the sister a little, as well. She doesn't deserve anything, but this is not the time to be ungenerous.'

Now that he seemed to have done what he had set out to do, Lord Staunton sat back looking very tired. 'I hope to see you again, Mr Perceval. Perhaps you could persuade Deborah to visit me, too. You could bring her when you are married.' When Hugo stiffened he said with a smile, 'Am I presuming too much? It would seem I am. But from what I hear, she would make any man a wonderful wife.' He put his head back and closed his eyes. 'You will forgive me if I don't get up. I am not as strong as I would wish. Goodbye, Mr Perceval.'

Hugo bowed and took his leave. As he reached the door Lord Staunton said, 'Don't leave it too long before you bring your wife to visit me—I may not be here.'

Hugo's Cambridge friend gave him the direction of an excellent horse-breeder, and here they found a pair of bays which were a good match with Hugo's present carriage horses. The arrangements for their shipping and accommodation were speedily accomplished and, very satisfied with everything he had achieved in Dublin, Hugo left for England the next day. He would have been back in Abbot Quincey well before the fortnight was up, but storms in the Irish Sea delayed the packet boat. As it was he arrived two weeks to the day after he had set out.

Meanwhile, in Abbot Quincey, Deborah, unaware of Hugo's success, spent the time in a state of perpetual worry. She worried about Hugo's safety, she worried about the outcome of his talk with her aunt, she worried about the bonds, and she worried about her future relationship with Hugo. His latest proposal was very different from his first, and infinitely more tempting. If…if he succeeded in sorting out her father's part in the theft of the bonds to her satisfaction, then he might well repeat his offer. And she was not sure she would have the strength this time to refuse him. Hugo cared for her. Not as deeply, not as passionately, as she cared for him, but perhaps it was enough. Moreover, Hugo was not like her father. He would never treat her with the bored indifference her father had shown her mother, she was sure. And, most convincingly of all, during Hugo's absence at Robina's wedding she had been taught a lesson. The pain she had experienced at the thought that he might have found someone else, at the realisation that, once Hugo was married, she could never be as close to him again, had been almost too hard to bear. Perhaps beggars shouldn't even try to be choosers. Hugo was offering her a great deal—his affection, his protection, a place in his life at Abbot Quincey among people she loved... Perhaps it would be wiser to settle for all that, rather than to cry vainly, and in loneliness, for the moon.

Harry Dodds, meanwhile, was having a very frustrating time. He had been relieved to find the house in Maids Moreton still empty, but changed his mind when after hours spent searching every nook and cranny he was forced to come to the conclusion that he had been wasting his efforts. An attempt to examine the bits of furniture which had been sent to a secondhand dealer's warehouse in Buckingham had ended in a brush with the dealer's assistant and an overnight spell in the town jail. By that time urgent business in London had interrupted his searches, and, once there, he had only narrowly escaped the attentions of his creditors. He was forced to go to ground for more than a week—he had little desire to spend months in Marshalsea.

By this time he knew he would have to visit Edmund Staunton's sister in Ireland again. She must know more than she had admitted, and he intended to find out what it was. But when he was able to leave London at last, his lack of resources made the journey to Holyhead slow and most uncomfortable. Here he met the crowning piece of his misfortunes. Storms in the Irish Sea—the very same ones which were delaying Hugo's return—prevented him from sailing straight away.

When he finally reached Miss Staunton's house in Dublin he was in no mood to persuade or cajole.

'You'd better tell me where those bonds are kept,' he snarled. 'I've never willingly hurt a woman before, but I don't mind starting with you! I'd have had those bonds in my possession weeks ago if you hadn't played games with me. *Where are they?*'

Miss Staunton was nervous and it showed. 'I didn't play any games! They were where I told you. I never saw them, but Eddy was quite clear. He was dying, but he knew what he was saying. "They're in the box," he said. "In the drawer."'

'I've taken the only box I could find to pieces, you witch,' said Mr Dodds, drawing closer. He took hold of her by the arms and gave her a shake. 'Nothing in it but some recipes. Recipes! I have a recipe for drabs like you, believe me. And it isn't one for soft soap!'

'I swear— Wait a moment! What did you say?

Recipes?' said Miss Staunton, rubbing her arm. 'What box was this?'

'Just as you described. Wood, patterned, the size you said—don't try your tricks on me! It was the box you told me to look for. It was there, just as you said, in that Vicarage. Silver name plate and all. *"Elizabeth"*.'

'Elizabeth!' Miss Staunton looked at him with contempt. 'My sister-in-law's name was Frances, you fool! And she kept letters in her box, not recipes. You stole her sister Elizabeth's box. The one which belonged to Frances must still be there in the Vicarage. You stole the wrong one!'

Mr Dodds looked dumbfounded. 'What? All that work…? All that running about in Maids Moreton, the jail in Buckingham… Why the hell didn't you tell me about the name?'

'I couldn't do it all for you. How was I to know that you would be such a dolt? Everyone knows that the Vicar is married to Lady *Elizabeth*! You'd better try again. By the way, how much did you say the bonds are worth?'

'I'm not giving you Eddy's half. I've had too much trouble. You'll have to make do with a quarter.'

'How much will that be?'

'Two hundred and fifty pounds.'

Miss Staunton regarded him in silence. Harry Dodds was a thief and a lying cheat. She would have done much better not to have had anything to do with him. Two hundred and fifty pounds! He had a nerve trying to fob her off with such a paltry sum! On the other hand, if she told him that she knew the bonds were worth ten thousand, he would ask her how she had found that out. Would she tell him of her recent visitor? Or should she keep silent? Now that Hugo Perceval was in the picture, the possibility that Harry would be caught was quite great. The less she had to do with him from now on the better.

'The whole thing is too risky,' she said. 'You had your chance and you wasted it. You'd do better to forget all about those bonds.'

'Are you mad?' he shouted. 'I *have* to have that money! I need it if I'm ever to get away and begin again.'

'On less than eight hundred pounds?' she mocked. 'That's not much of a stake.'

He checked himself. 'It's enough,' he said.

Miss Staunton made her decision. Harry could stew in his own juice. She wouldn't tell him anything more, not even that Hugo Perceval had been to see her. 'Well, you can have the lot,' she said. 'I'm happy enough here. Just keep my name out of it if you're caught, that's all.'

Harry Dodds regarded her suspiciously. 'What are you up to now?'

'Nothing. I'm tired of games and I don't like you. I've built up a pleasant life here and I don't want to risk spoiling it. So far all I've done is to tell you where Eddy said the bonds were hidden. That's bad enough, but I haven't done anything criminal.'

'What about your other dishonest activities? What about your little niece's allowance—stolen month after month? Aren't you afraid I'll tell someone about that?'

She shrugged her shoulders. 'Tell anyone you like. Deborah must have known for weeks what I did, and she hasn't taken any action about it. She won't do anything now. It's time you went, Harry. I've done more than I should. I'm not doing any more.'

With this she called the little maidservant and Harry was shown out. He went without further protest. If Eddy's witch of a sister wanted to get out of it he wouldn't pursue the matter. Two hundred and fifty pounds extra wasn't much, but it would always be useful. In fact, he wouldn't mind even fifty of them now! Wearily he started to look for somewhere to sleep. Tomorrow he would set out for Abbot Quincey again. He hoped to God the seas were calmer. He wasn't a good sailor at the best of times.

So it was that when Mr Dodds eventually arrived back in Abbot Quincey, travel-weary and in straitened circumstances, he was totally unprepared for the unpleasant discovery that was waiting for him there.

Chapter Eleven

'What's this about buying horses in Ireland, Hugo?' asked the Dowager as Hugo came into her room. He had arrived back from Ireland the night before and had hardly broken his fast that morning before being summoned to his grandmother's presence.

'What do you mean exactly, ma'am?' Hugo said cautiously. He came over, kissed her cheek, then sat down beside her. 'I'm surprised to find you awake so early in the day—are you well?'

'Of course I am! Just don't ask Gossage, she'll give you a catalogue of my ills, but they're all exaggerated. I don't have to ask how you are—you're looking a touch tired, though you're as handsome as ever. And you needn't try to distract me! I want to know what you've been up to! You went haring off to Ireland the minute you were back from Robina's wedding! You needn't tell me it was to buy horses!'

'But I did buy some horses, ma'am. Two of the finest you would find anywhere. And they were a remarkable bargain. I shall take you to see them when they arrive.'

'Hmph! You won't catch me in the stables—I hear enough bad language from that parrot you've landed me with.'

'I thought he had mended his ways?'

'So did I! So did I! But yesterday he forgot himself. In front of Lady Vernon and that prune-faced daughter of hers, too.'

'Carrie?'

'Aye, Carrie. They were so put to the blush that they didn't know where to look. It was all most annoying! Emily Vernon stammered and stuttered in that silly way of hers, and then she was off. It was most vexing! I had no chance to find out whether Richard Vernon is about to declare himself to Edwina, which is why I invited them in in the first place! It's high time he did, but apart from on the hunting field he always was a slow top! And now I dare swear those women won't come near me again for a good long while—not that I mind that. Very dull company, both of them.' The Dowager absent-mindedly gave the parrot a piece of apple while she brooded. 'Mind you, Deborah Staunton hasn't been much better.'

'I thought you liked her!'

'I do, I do! But something's wrong. The girl has been moping about so much that I haven't had a decent game of piquet for more than a week! Are you to blame?'

'I don't believe so, ma'am. I haven't seen her yet. I got back too late last night, and you sent for me before I could pay a visit to the Vicarage this morning. How is she?'

'I told you! Moping. Not a bit herself.'

'I'll try to see her when I leave you. I think I know what might be the problem.'

The Dowager gave him a piercing look. 'That's why you went, isn't it? To Ireland, I mean. Something to do with that girl?'

'Well, yes. Though I did buy the horses, too.'

'Oh, hang the horses! Who did you see there? That wretch of an aunt? Or her other relatives?'

Hugo regarded his grandmother with affectionate admiration. 'You're not slow, are you, ma'am?'

The Dowager's lips twitched, but she said austerely, 'That's no way to talk to me, my boy! And I'd like to know why you've taken to helping Deborah Staunton—to the extent of spending a fortnight on business of hers when you should have been here looking after your own! What are you at, Hugo? I thought you had given up any idea of marrying the girl? She refused you, didn't she?'

Hugo grinned. 'Twice!'

'This isn't a joking matter,' said the Dowager severely.

'I'm not joking, ma'am. Miss Staunton has done me the honour of refusing me twice over.'

'What the devil were you thinking of, asking her a second time?' snapped the Dowager, whose language under stress was sometimes less than ladylike.

'I was worried about her. She seemed to me to need more protection than I could give her in our present roles.' He looked at his grandparent's outraged expression and added, 'She turned me down much more kindly than the first time. And less convincingly, too.'

'What do you mean—less convincingly? Deborah ain't a coy young miss, expecting to be pressed. If she says no, she means it.'

'Not in this case. At least, I hope not. I begin to think you were absolutely right about Deborah, grandmother. I'd like to have her for my wife—I think we should get on quite well together. And, to be honest, I don't think anyone else would understand her as well as I do. She needs someone to look after her.'

His grandmother examined him in silence. Then she said, 'This is all very noble. What do you get out of it? I seem to remember that the last time we talked of it, you regarded her as a liability.'

'I still do! But somehow or other I've lost the will to look for anyone else. Deborah needs me, and I like her a great deal. In fact, I find her quite…appealing. I think we could make a good match.'

'You think…? Oh! I don't understand the young!' the Dowager said in exasperation. 'When I recommended Deborah to you you wouldn't hear of it. And now, just because the girl turns you down, not once but *twice*, you're suddenly desperate to marry her!'

'No! Not desperate. Never desperate,' Hugo said firmly. 'Desperation is not an emotion I intend to suffer. I am very fond of Deborah Staunton, and when the time is right—and not before—we will come to an agreement, as affectionate friends. I'm not sure I want to risk a third proposal—at least, not until I am *certain* she will accept.'

The Dowager eyed him sardonically. 'It's my opinion that you still have something to learn, Hugo,' she said. 'About yourself, as well as Deborah. But, for what it's worth, I wish you success.'

'Thank you.'

'So what business did you have with Deborah's relatives?'

'That's something I can't yet explain. Not until I've seen Deborah. But I can tell you this much. Though it makes no difference at all to the way I feel about her, it might cause you approve of her even more than you do already.'

'Approve? Whatever makes you think that I would approve of a girl who is mad enough to turn you down twice! What was it?'

But though the Dowager teased him, Hugo refused to tell her anything at all. How could he, when he hadn't yet told Deborah herself of her future inheritance?

When Hugo arrived at the Vicarage it was obvious that Deborah had been expecting him for some time. She came out to meet him, looking pale and tense. Hugo had only time to say quietly, 'Everything is fine. There's nothing for you to worry about.' before the rest of the family trooped out to join them. They dragged him in and insisted on hearing all about his journey. His description of the return crossing in the teeth of a storm on the Irish Sea had the twins looking slightly green themselves, and they only recovered when he went on to tell them of his new horses.

'Hugo! Tell us—what are they like?' demanded Edwina, the horsewoman. 'Bays, you say. How many hands?' When Hugo had told her all about his new acquisitons she said, 'Their breeding seems good. It sounds as if they would match your present pair, too. Are you intending to run a carriage and four?'

'Eventually,' he replied. 'When I replace the curricle I shall probably get something bigger.' Reluctant to discuss his wish for something more suitable as a family conveyance, he went on quickly, 'But you haven't yet told me what *you* have all been doing.'

This diverted them. They were eager to inform him that Mr Langham had spoken to the Reverend William, and that Frederica and the curate were now as good as engaged, though no public announcement was to be made as yet. It would be some time before Mr Langham would be in a position to support a wife. Frederica blushed like a wild rose when Hugo teased her. She had never looked prettier, but Hugo felt not the slightest pang of regret. He wished his cousin all the happiness in the world and turned his attention to Edwina. Here too he was given to understand that matters were proceeding very promisingly. Richard Vernon, it was thought, was merely waiting for his future role in the Stoke Park estate to be decided before declaring himself. The Vernons had always been close friends of the Percevals, and both families would be happy with the connection. Once again Hugo expressed his good wishes without the slightest qualm.

'Now,' he said. 'Now for the really important enquiries. How is my friend Autolycus?'

They all assured him that his friend was very well—you might say bursting with energy. Because of the restriction on their activities outside the house,

Autolycus had not had a really good run for two weeks, and though his temper was unimpaired he had shown one or two signs of boredom. The Vicar's slippers would not be the same again, and Deborah had unfortunately left her best straw hat on a chair in the hall...

'I think he is due for some hard exercise. I'll take him with me on one or two of my rides during the week—that should do it. Meanwhile, would any of you like to take a walk with us through the woods?'

'He's my dog,' said Deborah. 'I'll come with you.'

'I'm sure the twins or Henrietta would be delighted to accompany you,' said Lady Elizabeth calmly, but decisively.

'I'll go, Mama,' said Frederica, giving her sisters a look. Edwina and Henrietta rapidly made their excuses.

And so it was arranged. Hugo waited while the two girls fetched their hats, then they collected an ecstatic Autolycus and took the path to the woods. Autumn was approaching rapidly. The feathery, silver-grey puffs of travellers' joy climbing over the bushes were a reminder of the name that the country folk give it— old man's beard. The roadside was a mass of pale gold seedheads, and scarlet rose hips decorated the hedges. A few of the leaves had already turned—red, gold or brown. But the sky was a brilliant blue and the air, though fresh, still had the warmth of summer. They walked for a short while, but when they drew level with one of the cottages just before the wood Frederica stopped.

'I…I think I'll call on Mrs Crabtree,' she said. 'Perhaps you'd collect me on your way back?'

Hugo gave his cousin a quizzical look and she blushed scarlet. 'Of course,' he said politely. 'We'll see you shortly.' Then as he and Deborah set off again he asked, 'Had you arranged that with Frederica?'

'Of course I had!' said Deborah. 'Well, Hugo, I was naturally dying to know what had happened in Ireland, and with Aunt Elizabeth's notions of propriety it was going to be terribly difficult otherwise to have a talk in private.'

'Did you give Frederica a reason for wanting to talk to me in private? Or does she now think you have designs on me?'

Deborah went as red as her cousin. 'Certainly not!' she said emphatically. 'Frederica knows me too well even to suspect such a thing! And nor should you!'

'Well, you have refused me twice—that ought to indicate something.' He shot her a look, but Deborah had turned her head away. He couldn't see her face. Suppressing a sigh, he went on, 'But that's not what I want to talk about. I met someone in Ireland who would very much like to see you.'

'My aunt?'

'No, your cousin. A distant cousin. He's two generations older than you, but he's very charming.'

Deborah frowned. 'My father sometimes talked of cousins, but he didn't like them much.'

'No, from what I heard, there was never much love lost between the two branches of the family. That was why your father thought he was justified in depriving Lord Staunton of ten thousand pounds.'

'The bonds?' Deborah went white. 'So he did steal them?'

'Not exactly. Dodds did the dirty work on instruction from his partner—your father.'

'But that's the same thing! He's still guilty!'

'Don't get too agitated, Deborah, before you've heard the whole.'

'How can I not be? You say that this Lord Staunton—I take it that's the cousin you're talking about—wants to see me. And then I am informed that my father stole ten thousand pounds from him. I assume you have already told Lord Staunton that the bonds will be returned. So why would he want to see me except to demand something more by way of reparation?'

'Really, you're almost as bad as your father!'

'*What?* I'll have you know, Hugo Perceval, that I have *never* been dishonest in my *life!*'

'Don't be such a fool, Deborah! Of course I know that—I've never met such a transparently honest person as you. Sometimes you're uncomfortably so! No, I meant that it never entered your father's head to credit his cousin with a generous disposition. He— and his sister—assumed that the only way to get what he regarded as rightfully his was to take it without asking. What if I told you that Lord Staunton might possibly have *given* your father the bonds if he had been properly approached?'

'I would find that hard to believe. And why bring the question up, anyway? My father didn't approach him, but stole the money. It doesn't make any difference whether he considered it his or not. He took the

bonds without consent. And that makes him a thief.'
Deborah was near to tears. 'So what can I do to pacify
Lord Staunton?'

'I've promised to take you to see him before very
long. He's an old man, Deborah. And a very rich
one.'

'You think I might wheedle my way into forgiveness? Perhaps even persuade him to let me have the
money, after all? I couldn't do it. Not in a thousand
years!'

'Well, that's a relief!'

Deborah stopped in her tracks. 'I beg your pardon?'

'I took the liberty of refusing just that on your behalf. I'm relieved to find I was right.'

'You mean Lord Staunton *offered* you the money?'

'No, he offered it to you.'

'Oh, you know what I mean! Why would he do a
thing like that?'

'He thinks your father's family were cheated of
their inheritance—years back, long before he or your
father were born. And he wants to put it right.'

'It's too late,' said Deborah sombrely after a moment's thought. 'The damage has been done. You
can't accept something which your own father stole.'

'Staunton is a very wealthy man. He can well afford it.'

'That's not the point. *I* can't afford to take it—I
couldn't clear it with my conscience.'

'That's what I thought you would say. So he's going to do it differently.'

'How? Tell me! I might visit him—in fact, I'd like

to—but I warn you, I won't take any money from him.'

'Would you refuse a legacy?'

Deborah thought about it. 'That would be different, I suppose,' she said slowly.

'It would please him if you would accept it. He has a bit of a conscience, too, you know.'

'Yes,' said Deborah. 'Yes, I would do that. A small legacy would be right.'

'How about ten thousand pounds? No! Wait! Before you explode into protestations, listen to me. Let me tell you why he wants to give you, Edmund Staunton's only descendant, this sum of money.' Hugo went on to tell Deborah the unhappy story of her ancestor's quarrel and how he lost his inheritance. He even told her that her aunt was to receive something as well. Deborah was quiet for a long while. Then she said, 'I suppose it's right. But how I wish my father had spoken to this Lord Staunton! That would have been so much better.'

'I agree. But that's in the past, Deborah. You shouldn't regret what can never now be cured. And surely you're pleased that the whole affair has been so easily resolved?'

'Indeed I am! Together with the promise of a fortune! And I have you to thank for both! Thank you!' Deborah reached up and kissed Hugo on the cheek. Hugo smiled and pressed her hand, but was careful not to respond as he had on the eve of his departure. If he let himself kiss Deborah Staunton, if he was subject once more to the riot of feeling which had overtaken him on that occasion, he would find himself proposing to her yet again! One refusal was bad, a second refusal, however kindly, was worse—but a third? Oh no! For the sake of his own self-respect there had to be another way.

So Deborah and Hugo retraced their steps, picking up Frederica as they passed Mrs Crabtree's cottage. And though Deborah had got the news she wanted, and though Hugo was glad to hear that he had dealt with the situation correctly, they were neither of them completely happy with the afternoon's walk.

Meanwhile, Harry Dodds, cursing and swearing, was trudging to Abbot Quincey from Northampton. The wagoner's dray which had given him his last lift had ended up only a mile beyond the town, and Harry had found it impossible to get another. It was midday, and though the sun no longer had the power of high summer it was sufficiently warm to make walking with a pack on one's back most uncomfortable. The only thing that kept Harry from complete despair was the thought of the fortune which was waiting for him in Deborah Staunton's mother's box. In less than a month the bonds could be cashed and he would be rich.

As he walked he was constructing a plan of action. He didn't believe that Deborah Staunton knew about the bonds he had stolen. She had been completely puzzled by his references to the box and the secret drawer. No, they were probably still tucked away cosily in their little nest, just waiting for Harry Dodds to come and take them for a walk. What if she *had* found them? Harry's natural optimism prevailed. She wouldn't have been able to cash them any more than he had. She would probably have left them where they were, until she could exchange them for a fortune—a nice little dowry for a penniless girl. What a shame she wasn't going to get it! Even if she had moved them he would soon have them out of her—a slip of a thing like that would soon tell him where they were.

He reached the wood where he proposed to hide once more just at the moment when Hugo and Deborah were stopping at Mrs Crabtree's cottage. Their paths did not cross. This was a pity, for they would all have been spared a great deal of trouble if Harry Dodds had been seen before he started to put his various plans into action.

Harry soon took over Sammy Spratton's hut, and spent what was left of the daylight making himself as comfortable as possible. The hut had been a substantial shelter for the woodcutters who had once inhabited the forest. Some of their tools and equipment were still there—indeed, Sammy regularly used them to cut himself branches for firewood, or to repair holes in the roof. While Sammy bobbed up and down at the edge of the clearing uttering incoherent cries of distress, Harry helped himself to the meagre store of food in the hut and used the chains he found thrown at the back to make the door secure against intruders. Then he settled himself down for a good night's sleep.

But over the next few days Harry became increasingly desperate. Every time he approached the Vicarage the place was full of people. The door was,

as ever, invitingly open, but whether by accident or
design the entrance hall was never left empty for more
than a few minutes, and some member of the family
or one of the servants was always near at hand. And
the Percevals never seemed to go out! ...But they
would all go to church on Sunday! That was it! A
Vicar's household would be bound to go to church.
He would go back to his lair and wait for Sunday.
The better the day, the better the deed, they always
said!

There was no difficulty in keeping possession of
Sammy Spratton's hut. The poor wretch was so scared
of other human beings that the moment Harry appeared Sammy simply ran deeper into the undergrowth. But the food was running out—he would
have to forage for provender from the cottages on the
edge of the wood...

An hour later he was walking back along the woodland ride with eggs stolen from one old biddy, bread
from another, and a whole flagon of ale from a third.
This last was a temptation he could not resist, and
when he came to the turn off to Sammy's hut he was
so hot and thirsty that he could wait no longer. He
sat down on a fallen tree-trunk at the side of the path
and took a long, refreshing draught. But his well-
deserved rest was interrupted by the sound of voices
coming towards him. Hastily grabbing his spoils, he
buried himself in a dense patch of undergrowth behind the log and waited for them to pass...

Deborah and Hugo were without Autolycus.
Deborah had been visiting the Dowager when Hugo

had joined them, and that devious lady had asked them once again to visit Mrs Bember together. Since Hugo had, true to his word, given the dog a good run that very morning, they had decided that it was unnecessary to call at the Vicarage. Lady Elizabeth would almost certainly insist that they should be accompanied by a third person and neither, for different reasons, wished for one.

Deborah was finding it almost impossible to be calm. She held her questions until they had seen Mrs Bember and were on their way back to the Vicarage, but then she started. 'When did you say the messenger was due, Hugo? Shouldn't he have come already?'

'Deborah, you ask me this whenever I see you. I've told you—I am not sure!' Because Hugo was feeling uncertain he sounded more irritable than usual. He had been with Deborah several times since his return, not always in company. But she had not once shown him any emotion other than friendly gratitude. If anything, she was more distant with him than she had been for a long time. Since he would have welcomed the slightest sign of a warmer feeling, the smallest indication that she wished to reopen the subject of his proposal, he was feeling the strain. He said, 'Sit down, Deborah!'

'But—'

'It's time we talked. Sit down right here and listen!'

They sat down on the very tree-trunk Harry Dodds had occupied just five minutes before. Deborah stole a look at Hugo's face. He looked annoyed, and she thought she knew why. Hugo had cared enough for her to offer to marry her, when she was poor and in danger of disgrace. And now he was finding that his gallant sacrifice hadn't been necessary, after all. Damage to her family name had been avoided, every-thing had been sorted out most satisfactorily, and she had the promise of a reasonable fortune. It was true she had refused that second offer of his, but she hadn't completely shut the door. Perhaps he was now worried that she wished him to reopen the subject? She said apologetically, 'I know I'm behaving badly, Hugo. I'm just so nervous. I shan't be happy until those wretched bonds are handed over, and we are rid of the whole affair.'

'I have them safe, I assure you,' he said. 'And they will be collected any day now by Lord Staunton's own messenger. Be patient, Deborah!'

'I'll try. It's just all so difficult. I'm not even sure that I ought to accept that legacy either. Though I suppose it would make my future more secure...' She thought wistfully, if only he would say that my future is secure without any fortune. Secure with him! She was disappointed when he merely said coolly, 'In what way?'

Deborah made up her mind. She said brightly, 'Well, you must admit, Hugo, that a girl with ten thousand pounds in prospect is in a much better po-sition to attract a husband. And once my father's mis-demeanours can be forgotten I shan't need your help, nor your protection. You would be free to choose any wife you wanted without having to worry about me.'

There was a long silence after this. Then Hugo jumped up and said angrily, 'And that is what you would wish? To be left to look for a husband for yourself? You're finally refusing me?'

Deborah rose to face him. 'I don't need to. I already have. Twice.'

'Yes, but I thought... Oh, never mind what I thought!' He added coldly, 'If you don't want Aunt Elizabeth to be home before you, we had better go. We haven't brought the dog today, so we have no excuse for lingering. Come!'

With relief Harry heard the two set off, the Staunton girl running to keep up with Perceval. They seemed to be getting matters between them in pretty much of a mess. Even he could tell that the girl hadn't meant half of what she had said. But as for the rest...! Harry could hardly believe his ears. They were going to give his bonds back! After all the trouble he had taken to steal them, too! They must be mad! What was he to do? Once the messenger, whoever he was, came for them his bonds would vanish forever. No, no he couldn't let that happen—they meant too much to him. The bonds must be found before that messenger arrived. But *where were they*?

He woke up the next morning with a bad head and a flagon which was empty. The world seemed to have turned against him. No ideas had resulted from furious thinking the night before. The hut was cold and damp. Even the goat had disappeared.

Hugo was equally depressed. His plan to wait until Deborah fell into his arms of her own volition seemed to have failed. The prospective acquisition of a fortune had apparently turned her head, and Hugo now faced a lonely future. He couldn't stand the thought of marrying anyone else. And the thought of Deborah as the *wife* of anyone else had kept him awake the whole of the previous night. He had got up and walked about the room, striding restlessly to and fro, cursing his idiocy. How blind he had been—how complacent, how foolishly confident he would never fall desperately in love! How unsympathetic he had been to all the others, how scornful—even towards Dungarran, his best friend and present brother-in-law. Well, he was being punished for his arrogance now! He had seldom felt such confusion. He had to restrain a strong impulse to seek Deborah out immediately, now, in the middle of the night, and make her see— by force if necessary—that he was the only man for her. As she was the only woman for him. And if that sounded like the behaviour of an idiot, then that was what he was—a blind, infatuated idiot! Hugo Perceval threw himself down on his bed immersed in gloom and self-reproach. But this did not last long. Hugo was made of sterner stuff than this. As the night wore on he began to take a more positive view. All was not yet lost. As far as he knew, at least there was no one else in Deborah's life. He would make himself as indispensable to her as she was to him. He would…he would even propose to her again! She would come round in the end—she must!

He rode over to the Vicarage the next morning. Deborah was there but surrounded by her cousins, and still rather cool with him. Frederica and the others were discussing a projected visit to some neighbours, and once he had ascertained that Deborah was not going with them, Hugo decided to come back later. He would give the dog a run in the forest first. So, after collecting Autolycus, he rode off along the familiar path, only to come to a halt just at the level of Sammy Spratton's hut. Sammy's goat was wandering about the path, obviously lost. Hugo hesitated, but decided to help one of Deborah's friends, even if she wasn't with him. He would take the goat and tie it to a post or something near Sammy's hut. He dismounted, tethered his horse to a stout tree, and took up the loose end of the animal's rope. Autolycus, willing, but by no means sure of the goat's good will, followed at a distance. Hugo soon found a suitable post quite near the hut, and bent down to attach the rope firmly. Autolycus's bark was too late to save him. He felt a sickening crunch on the back of his head and fell. He was aware of curses and barks, and the fading sound of a dog yelping. Then he knew no more.

Chapter Twelve

Harry Dodds couldn't believe his luck! All night he had been cudgelling his brains to think of a way to find the bonds, and fate had delivered the only man who could tell him right into his hands! But he mustn't waste any time. Mr Hugo Perceval was a big, powerful chap and he must be made helpless while he was in no position to argue! Harry dragged Hugo towards the hut, wincing occasionally at the pain of the wound in his arm caused by that cursed dog. Once inside, he collected the chains which had been left in a heap in the far corner, stood Hugo, not without a struggle, up against the stout post in the centre of the hut which held up the roof, and chained him to it by the arms and legs, pulling the chains tight round the post. Then he stood back and admired his work. He was just in time—Hugo was coming to.

'What the devil…?' Hugo tried to move but found he couldn't. 'What the devil's going on?'

'I hope I'm not hurting you,' said Harry Dodds, as he came into Hugo's line of vision.

Hugo made an effort to focus in the dim light of

the hut. 'It's Dodds! Harry Dodds. So you did come back after all! For the bonds, I take it?'

'My, you're quick! Knocked out cold, and quarter of an hour later you can put two and two together like a scholar. That's right—I want my bonds.'

'Not yours, Dodds—they belong to Lord Staunton. And you're too late. They're already on their way to him.'

'Brave try! But not quite right. You've still got them. Now don't waste my time—where are they, and when is the messenger due?'

'Hidden away where you can't lay your hands on them. And if you think I'll tell you anything at all about the messenger, then you're a fool!' said Hugo with a contemptuous smile. His head was aching quite badly, but his mind was perfectly clear. He moved his limbs surreptitiously checking each one. All sound. Only his head had been damaged, and he'd had many a harder knock in his day. Harry Dodds noticed the slight movement and said, 'Pull as much as you like. I've got you trussed up like a Christmas goose. You won't get free until you've told me what I want to know.'

'Then we both have a long, weary wait ahead of us. Give up, Dodds! You won't get them. What did you do to the dog?'

'I'd have killed the brute if I had got hold of him properly! But lucky for him he backed off in time. Don't pin your hopes on the animal, Perceval. I gave him a taste of my cudgel and he went off, howling like a banshee. He won't be back. Now then, let's be sensible about this. I know that I've missed my chance of stealing them from Deborah Staunton. Once she took them out of that drawer, she was bound to hide them safely away—somewhere where I couldn't lay hands on them. I won't even bother to ask where that is. But I can get them from the messenger, as long as I know when and where he will arrive. It's got to be today or tomorrow. You can tell me that.'

Hugo looked at him in contempt. 'You and the Staunton woman will have to go without! I'm not telling you anything!'

'What Staunton woman?' Harry grinned. 'If you mean the one that lives in Dublin then you're out of date. Miss Staunton has resigned from my little scheme. So I have an even greater incentive to get my hands on the money. The whole lot is for me.'

In spite of his aches and pains Hugo felt a surge of relief at this news. It meant that the Staunton family would be completely in the clear.

Harry Dodds tried again. He said softly, 'Come, Perceval! What does it matter to you who has the money? If I take it from the bank's courier, you won't even be involved. No one would ever know… And that old man in Dublin can well do without it. Be reasonable!'

When Hugo remained silent Harry Dodds said in an injured voice, 'You know, you're making it very difficult! I really don't like hurting people, but, if that's the only way, I can steel myself to do it. Those chains will bite deeper as time goes on.'

'Time isn't on your side. My people will soon come looking for me.'

'Not for two or three hours, they won't. You're out

for a ride, remember? And long before the three hours are up you'll be glad to tell me, I think.'

Hugo closed his eyes. Three hours! He had a vision of Autolycus limping back to the Vicarage, deserted except for Deborah. She would wonder what had happened. Even if she simply thought that Autolycus had run away from him for some reason, she would be anxious. She would expect him back, and when he didn't come… What would she do? It wouldn't occur to her that it would be dangerous to come in search of him. Would she be sensible for once and call out the men? How he hoped she would! But past experience would suggest that Deborah Staunton would hurtle towards disaster with all the inevitability of a runaway horse. He would have to compromise.

'What would you do if I did tell you?' he asked slowly.

Harry looked at him suspiciously. 'This is a bit sudden, isn't it?'

'You don't leave me much choice.'

'I'd let you go, of course.'

Hugo gave him a twisted smile. 'You can't expect me to believe that. You couldn't possibly risk my alerting the courier of his danger. No, Dodds, I think you would either kill me outright, or leave me somewhere where I couldn't be found.'

'I've never killed anyone before. I'm not a murderer. You're right that I wouldn't let you go. But I'd leave you where you would be found—eventually. So—what about it?'

Hugo's worst fears were very nearly fully justified. Deborah had found Autolycus cowering outside the stable door, and when she examined him she saw that his back leg was damaged. What had happened? She tended him, then sat beside him waiting for Hugo. He would tell her how Autolycus had come to be injured. He was bound to come back quite soon in search of the dog... Half an hour passed and Hugo still hadn't appeared. Deborah began to get anxious. What if Hugo himself had had an accident? If he had been thrown, both he and Autolycus could have been hurt at the same time!

Once this thought had occurred to her Deborah hardly hesitated. If Hugo were lying unconscious somewhere on the woodland path she must go to his aid immediately! The groom was out with the family, the handyman out in the fields. Nanny Humble was the only servant she could find, and she wasted several precious minutes explaining to her nurse what she wanted.

'But Miss Deborah—'

'Don't argue, Nanny!' Deborah said sharply. 'Find one of the men and give him my message. I can't afford to wait for an escort—I must go straight away. But send someone after me. Do you understand?'

Deborah hardly waited for Nanny Humble's reluctant nod before she had snatched up a blanket and some linen and was haring off towards the wood.

She soon came across Hugo's horse, perfectly sound in wind and limb and chomping peacefully at the grass. He had been tethered quite normally to a tree just by the path to Sammy Spratton's cottage. Where was Hugo?

She made her way cautiously along the path. The

grasses had been flattened quite recently—Hugo must be along here. Then she heard Hugo's voice and stopped.

'No, Dodds, I think you would either kill me outright,' he said. 'Or leave me somewhere where I couldn't be found.'

Harry Dodds! He had come back as she had feared. Deborah grew cold as he said, 'I've never killed anyone before. I'm not a murderer. You're right that I wouldn't let you go. But I'd leave you where you would be found—eventually. So—what about it?'

Deborah wondered desperately what she should do. She dared not move for the moment, for there was complete silence in the hut.

Then Harry Dodds said, 'I won't wait much longer.' A chain rattled, and Hugo gave a grunt. 'And there's worse to follow,' Dodds went on. 'So get on with it.'

Deborah crept towards the window and peeped in. What she saw appalled her. Blood had dried in an ugly streak down Hugo's face, which was deathly white. His eyes were closed, and Deborah saw that he was cruelly chained to the centre post. Dodds had obviously just given the chains a tweak which must have caused Hugo agony. What was she to *do*?

The decision was taken out of her hands. Sammy Spratton came up behind her with none of the caution she had exercised. Dodds heard him, whirled round and was out of the hut before Deborah could take a step. Sammy fled and she was left alone with the enemy. Deborah stamped and fought and scratched, but in the end Dodds was able to drag her into the hut and display her to Hugo.

Harry could not have been better pleased. 'Look what I have here!' he crowed. 'The perfect lever. I'll admit I was at a bit of a loss, Perceval. If you had held out, I'm not sure what I would have done. But now…' He had been busy tying Deborah's hands behind her back. 'Now you'll tell me everything I want to know! Or your fancy piece won't be so fancy any more.'

Hugo twisted frantically, but the chains were too strong. Harry jeered at him and, holding Deborah with one hand, he put his other at the neck of her dress. 'You do understand what I could do, don't you?' Deborah's hands were tied, but her feet were still free. She kicked Harry Dodds hard.

'You won't find it that easy,' she yelled.

It was the wrong thing to do. Dodds gave a roar of pain and smacked Deborah so roughly that her head jerked back and she went limp.

Hugo was filled with black rage, such as he had never before experienced. Beside himself with fury, he strained at the chains, and though they didn't yield, the post to which they were attached did. It groaned and broke in half, and Hugo was released. He leapt forward, and had his hands round his adversary's throat before the man had had time to breathe. Harry Dodds would have died on the spot, but a cry from Deborah saved him.

'Hugo! Look!' Deborah was pointing upwards. But it was too late. Another groan, followed by sharp cracking noises, then the whole roof structure caved in and descended on the three in the hut. They were surrounded by clouds of choking dust, twigs, small branches, and finally the large beams which had been the main supports collapsed and fell too. When Hugo staggered to his feet, he could not at first see anything. Then as the dust cleared he became aware of two figures lying on the ground.

He knelt down beside the slighter of the two figures. Deborah was lying half buried in debris, her face and arms scratched and bleeding. But far more ominous was the huge abrasion on her temple. One of the main beams lay nearby. It had obviously struck her as it fell.

'Deborah! Deborah!' Hugo frantically chafed her hands, but there was no response. For a moment he was paralysed with fright. Deborah couldn't be dead, she mustn't be! He loved her, he couldn't live without her! With his bare hands he cleared away the mass of rubble which covered her, ignoring his own painful injuries. Deborah remained quite still. He would have lifted her, breathed life into her, but he dared not. With such an injury, the less she was moved the better. He must wait till help came and she could be taken to the Hall. Hugo tore off his coat and spread it over Deborah's body, praying that help would come soon. He dared not leave her long enough to fetch it himself. Water! He could fetch some water! Scrambling over the ruins, he hurried to the little stream outside and soaked his cravat. He almost gave way when he saw the blanket and linen Deborah had brought with her. *She* had come because she thought *he* was injured! But he rallied and put the blanket on top of his coat, and carefully placed the clean linen under her head. Then he gently wiped the smears of blood from her face. After a minute he was overjoyed to mark a faint pulse in the side of her throat. She was alive!

He could hear someone approaching and stood up shouting desperately. When they saw Hugo covered in blood and dirt the men rushed towards him eager to rescue him. But Hugo fended them off, swearing at them like a madman, shouting at them to go carefully. The sight of Deborah, lying so still, shocked them into instant obedience. Two of the men were put to clearing a wider path to the main ride, while the third was ordered to take Hugo's horse and ride to the Hall to tell them there what had happened and to fetch transport. Hugo meanwhile sat by Deborah, bathing her face, watching avidly for the least sign of returning consciousness. There was none.

When the cart came they made a rough stretcher using the blanket and branches and carried her out to it, Hugo watching them like a hawk, shouting his orders, all the while indifferent to his own acute discomfort. The journey to the Hall was agonising. Lady Perceval had lined the cart with cushions and they went very slowly but every bump increased Hugo's tense anxiety. By the time they reached the Hall he was strung up like a bowstring.

Lowell had fetched the doctor and they and Lady Perceval were waiting in the courtyard when the cart arrived.

'Hugo!' exclaimed Lady Perceval as her son staggered out of the cart. 'I didn't realise you were hurt as well!'

'I'm not, Mama,' he said pushing her to one side. 'Where's the doctor? He has to see to her straight away.'

'I'm here, Mr Perceval. But you should really have your own hurts seen to—'

'Damn it, do as I say,' roared Hugo.

After a moment's shock the doctor said stiffly, 'Very well. It's better not to move Miss Staunton until I've checked her over. Then she should be taken to a comfortable bedchamber where I could do a more detailed examination.' He moved to the cart and examined Deborah briefly, while Hugo paced round the courtyard like a tiger. He was an awesome sight. His face was still covered in dirt and blood, his hair was wild, he was wearing neither coat not cravat—though some kind soul had flung a blanket round his shoulders. When she was not looking anxiously at the doctor's activities his mother regarded him in amazement. He looked more like a tribesman from Outer Mongolia than the fastidious young sprig of fashion she had known for so long.

'Well?' he demanded as the doctor straightened up.

'I don't think there's any serious damage to Miss Staunton. Nothing to worry about.'

'Nothing to worry about?' Hugo shouted. 'Nothing to worry about? She's been out of her wits for over an hour and you say there's *nothing to worry about*? What sort of a quack are you?'

The doctor had known the Percevals for a long time and this offensive attack by a young man who had always been the soul of courtesy shocked him to the core. He took a deep breath and said that Mr Perceval was clearly not himself. He would suggest that he should be allowed to recover quietly...

Lady Perceval had already sent a message to the housekeeper to prepare a bed for Deborah. Now she stepped forward and took one of Hugo's hands in hers. 'Hugo, my dear,' she said. 'I am sure the doctor will do all he can. Why don't you have a rest? Perhaps a bath first?'

'Mama, I *can't*,' Hugo replied. 'Not till I know what is happening to Deborah!' He saw that the men were lifting the stretcher off the cart. 'What do you think you're doing?' he shouted, striding over to take charge. 'Handle her more carefully—she's not a bale of hay, you know!'

'Hugo, why are you making such a noise? I wish you would stop. My head is aching badly enough already.'

Hugo turned towards the head of the stretcher. Deborah's eyes were open and she was frowning at him. He went to her. 'Deborah! Oh, my darling! My darling girl! Thank God! I've been so worried!'

Her frown disappeared and she smiled. 'No need. Go and get your own hurts seen to.' She put out her hand and he seized it, kissing it passionately.

'Oh God, Deborah... I thought...' His voice wavered and he went even paler.

Lady Perceval signed to the men to carry the stretcher into the house. She went over to her son. 'Hugo, do as Deborah says. You can see she is going to be all right.'

'She is, isn't she? Oh, Mama...' And Hugo Perceval, a young man who had always scorned displays of any excess of feeling, fainted for the first time in his life.

The third victim of the disaster in Sammy's hut had not been so fortunate. The farmhand left behind after Deborah and Hugo had been rescued found Harry Dodds lying where he had fallen. Like Deborah, he had been struck on the head with the beam, but in his case the blow had been fatal. Lacking any evidence of a close relative, he was duly buried in Abbot Quincey churchyard—an act of charity and forgiveness on the part of Lady Elizabeth.

In spite of the fears which caused Hugo to haunt the vicinity of her bedroom whenever the doctor was due, Deborah made a steady recovery with no relapses. In a few days she was able to join the Dowager in the peace and comfort of her apartment, or in the afternoon to sit in the garden under the cedar, enjoying the late Indian summer. The family took turns in keeping her company. They were all eager to do so. It was as if they wanted to reassure themselves that she really was safe and well. They all loved Deborah, but perhaps they had only realised how much when they had been in danger of losing her. No one teased Hugo about his behaviour in the courtyard, not even Lowell. They were all too awed at the depth of feeling it had revealed. Not one of them would have suspected that he was capable of such a public display of raw emotion.

At last Deborah was pronounced to be fit, and the family was prepared to leave her occasionally to her own company. There was even talk of her return to the Vicarage.

'So, Hugo,' said the Dowager as they sat over a glass of sherry wine. 'So you had better get on with it. Once Deborah is back with Elizabeth it won't be so easy as it is here to get her to yourself.'

'Easy! Ma'am, you don't know what it's like here! I never get *near* Deborah, let alone having her to myself! And what do you mean by "getting on with it"?'

The Dowager snorted. 'Asking her to marry you, of course! That's what you want, ain't it? It's the only thing that would excuse your extraordinary behaviour in the courtyard. I hear you ranted like a madman.'

Hugo flushed. 'I was injured myself, ma'am!' he protested. 'I can't explain otherwise why I was so...so...'

'Beside yourself? Out of your mind? Were you perhaps...desperate, Hugo?' She gave him a sly look.

He acknowledged her sally. 'You have every reason to crow over me, ma'am.'

'Of course I have! When was it you swore that desperation was not an emotion you intended to suffer? Last week?'

'That was before...'

The Dowager took pity on him. 'You needn't explain, my boy. I told you that you needed to learn something about yourself, and now you have. You love Deborah Staunton.'

'More than my life, ma'am.'

Hugo's grandmother smiled in satisfaction. 'Just as it should be. And I'll swear she is as besotted about you. So what are you going to do?'

'Deborah fired up at me the first time I proposed because I told her that you had advised me to marry her. If you'll forgive me, I think that this time I'll make up my own mind what to do. But I promise that you'll be the first to hear the result.'

Hugo finally got Deborah to himself that very afternoon. She was sitting under the cedar tree, gazing at the view, with Autolycus at her side. Hugo joined her.

'It's so beautiful here,' she said. 'I ought to be doing all sorts of useful things, but I just sit here enjoying the colours, and the air, and the shapes of the land.' She turned to him. 'How are you, Hugo? I think your injuries were much worse than mine, but I've had all the sympathy, and you've had all the work. I hear that you and Aunt Elizabeth arranged between you for Harry Dodds to be buried, and that you've seen Lord Staunton's agent and handed over the bonds. Thank you.'

Hugo glanced at the house. His grandmother had obviously been busy. It was not by accident that Deborah had been left alone. There seemed to be a surprising number of heads bobbing about at the windows. He said with an amused smile, 'Are you and Autolycus up to a walk, Deborah?'

'Why, yes! Where shall we go?'

'Anywhere out of sight of those windows!'

Deborah followed the direction of his eyes and blushed scarlet. 'Shall we…shall we go the old way?'

'You're not afraid? No bad memories?'

'No. I'd…I'd like to.'

They walked over the lawn and crossed into the path which took them to the woods. The trees were a blaze of scarlet and gold, and there was a scent of woodsmoke in the air. Autumn had arrived.

Now the moment had come Hugo was at a loss. He loved this delicate creature beside him so much. He couldn't bear the thought that she might not, after all, love him. She had refused him twice before. But what he had felt then was nothing compared with the devastation he would feel if she refused him now. How could he possibly risk it? On the other hand, if he never asked her again, how the devil could he make her his wife? He glanced at her. She was looking at him with a faint, questioning smile in her eyes. Her hair, as usual, was falling down her back, her hat was the same tattered straw she had been wearing all those weeks ago. He had never seen anything more desirable. Her very presence was intoxicating. Putting an arm round her, he said, 'Deborah… Deborah, I…'

'Yes, Hugo?' she asked.

Dammit, why couldn't he say the words? Her dark blue eyes were pools in which a man could drown… With an exclamation Hugo Perceval snatched his love to him and kissed her with passion. Then he held her away from him.

'I'm damned if I'm going to ask you a third time!' he said decisively. 'Deborah Staunton, you are going to marry me, whether you want to or not, do you hear?'

'But I do want to, Hugo dear,' she said, laughing up at him. 'I want to very much, my darling, beloved, tongue-tied Hugo!' She threw her arms round his neck and they kissed again. The kiss began with tenderness, then melted into passion. It went on… When Autolycus decided that things had gone quite far enough he barked, amiably, but quite firmly, and they separated in some confusion.

As they went back to the Hall to tell an expectant family their news, Deborah said gaily, 'You see, Hugo, all our worries are now over.'

Hugo grinned down at her. 'Yours might be, my dear, my only love. I rather think that mine are only just beginning. But don't worry—I can deal with them. Just think of all the practice I've had!'

* * * * *

The Missing Marchioness
by
Paula Marshall

Paula Marshall, married with three children, has had a varied life. She began her career in a large library and ended it as a senior academic in charge of history in a Polytechnic. She has travelled widely, has been a swimming coach and has appeared on *University Challenge* and *Mastermind*. She has always wanted to write and likes her novels to be full of adventure and humour.

Chapter One

Autumn 1812

'Ho hum,' said Marcus, Lord Angmering, in his usually bluffly cheerful manner. 'Marriage, it's all a nonsense! Don't know why anyone goes in for it! Everything is much simpler with an accommodating ladybird who doesn't interfere with your life outside the one she shares with you.'

'What about an heir for the title?' drawled his new acquaintance, Jack, who claimed to be a distant relative of the vast Perceval family. 'Only possible within the law—and that means marriage.'

'Good God,' said Marcus, still in his teasing mode, 'with two younger brothers waiting to grow up there can be no problem there, so why should *I* marry? Let other men acquire a leg shackle—I prefer to be free.'

He didn't add that the lack of success of most

marriages didn't exactly offer much encouragement to a fellow to get hitched. So far as he was concerned, all that went without saying. It was only when he was half-foxed, as he was at the present moment, that he indulged in such mad bursts of honesty.

Not that he often drank too much, far from it, but he and his friends had been celebrating a marriage, that of a fellow member of their set, Nick Cameron, to his clever beauty, Athene Filmer.

'Everyone's getting hitched these days, never a season like it,' Marcus continued, taking another great gulp of port, a drink he usually avoided. 'And now there's m'sister getting turned off at Christmas, and you'd think that it was a coronation we were preparing for, what with all the fuss it's creating. Can't think why everyone's so enthusiastic about it all, it must be catching. Well, it's not going to catch me.'

'Care to bet on it?' drawled Jack.

'Why not? Easy pickings if I do.'

'Very well. Waiter,' Jack bellowed at a passing flunkey, 'bring me pen, paper and ink, if you would—and quickly, before my friend here changes his mind.'

'No chance of that,' proclaimed Marcus, looking down his long nose at him. Damn the fellow for thinking that he would change his mind every time the wind blew in another direction! He didn't know

Marcus Cleeve very well if he believed any such thing.

His tormentor was still grinning knowingly at him, as though he had a private glimpse of the future which no one else shared, when the harassed waiter arrived with his order.

'Now,' said Jack, dipping the quill in the ink pot, his grin widening as he did so, 'the only question is, how much? Five hundred guineas? To bet that you'll not marry before a year from now? The money to be handed over to me if you do?'

Marcus was not so over-set that he contemplated the possibility of throwing five hundred guineas down the drain, even if he were bound and determined to live and die a bachelor. Who knew what might happen? He wouldn't put it past his father suddenly to make his future inheritance conditional on his marrying an heiress. In fact he had half-hinted at that already, muttering something to the effect of 'It's time you settled down, Marcus. Marriage tends to steady a man.'

'Oh, I think I'm steady enough without it,' he had returned lightly, not wanting to start a discussion on the matter which might end in an argument.

So: 'A fellow isn't made of money,' he pronounced as gravely as drink would allow him to— he was to think dismally the following morning that it was only the excessive amount of alcohol he had swallowed which had caused him to throw his money about so carelessly. All in all it was a pity he hadn't fallen unconscious under the table before he had begun to brag about his fortunate state.

'It's not,' he added solemnly, 'as though I am usually a gambling man.'

'Time you began then,' announced Jack, who was one, with all the good cheer he could summon. 'Don't play the skinflint, Angmering, we all know that your pa made a fortune in India.'

'True, but I'm not my father. Make it two hundred and fifty, and leave it at that.'

He couldn't refuse to gamble out of hand—that would not be the act of a gentleman, to say nothing of a nobleman.

'Three hundred,' offered Jack hopefully. For some reason which he couldn't really have articulated, he thought that a fellow who was shouting the odds about the joys of the bachelor state so loudly might really be in grave danger of relinquishing it.

'Two hundred and fifty—or nothing,' said Marcus stubbornly, 'or else the wager's off.'

'Very well.'

Jack scrawled down the details of the bet, signed his name, and swung the paper round for Marcus to sign it, too, before handing it on to the others present who drunkenly scribbled their names as witnesses to it.

'That's that, then. Who's for the Coal Hole now?'

'Not I,' said Marcus, who had had enough of Jack for one night. 'Couldn't walk there,' and he laid his head on the littered table and began to sleep—or appeared to at any rate.

It wasn't totally make-believe to cut the evening short, for an hour later the waiter who had fetched the writing materials woke him up, helped him to the door, and called a cab to drive him home. The word was perhaps an exaggeration—it was merely the house in Berkeley Square, his father's home in London—a place which he rarely visited and where he was always unsure of his welcome.

Once there he fell into bed and didn't rise until noon, when his valet woke him to remind him that he had promised to drive his sister, Sophia, to Hyde Park later that afternoon. They had arranged to meet the Duke of Sharnbrook, her betrothed, who was escorting an elderly aunt there in order to meet his fiancé and her brother for the first time.

His valet brought him breakfast in bed and a salver with a glass and a decanter on it: the decanter was full of the hair of the dog which had bit him. Marcus drank the port, grimacing, but that and the food seemed to settle his stomach. He might yet live!

Must remind myself not to go drinking again, he told himself severely. Look where it got Sywell, dead as a doornail and ugly with it!

Feeling much better, he decided to go downstairs and greet the day. He doubted whether his father would be about, and Sophia would surely soon be readying herself to see Sharnbrook. It would be a treat to have the house to himself, read the *Morning Post,* ring for coffee, yawn a bit and perhaps doze. He deserved a little holiday, and some peace, after setting his father's northern estates in order after the previous land agent had neglected them.

Except that when he reached the entrance hall at the bottom of the grand staircase there stood, apparently waiting for him, the most bewitching little filly he had ever seen. She had lightly curling hair of that shade of gold called guinea, which had overtones of red in it, like the metal mined in Guinea itself. Her face was *piquante* to say the least, with an impudent little nose and a mouth so sweet and kissable that Marcus was tempted, there and then, to kiss it.

She was a pocket Venus, too, the type of female which he always preferred, and was dressed with the kind of supreme simplicity which he always associated with the best of taste. Her pale green walking-dress, with its delicate lemon trim, set off her bluey-green eyes and her dashing hair. Why did one always think of hair that colour as dashing? Bluey-green eyes, too, were dashing, were they not?

A female servant stood behind her, carrying band-boxes. Other boxes were being brought in by a footman wearing a livery which he did not recognise. They appeared to be waiting, and none of them had seen him descending the stairs.

A guest, perhaps? Although, to his knowledge, none had been mentioned as arriving.

Overcome, and ever gallant, Marcus spoke.

'May I be of assistance, madame?'

His little Venus swung round and saw him at last. All brawny six feet of him.

'Sir? You have the advantage of me.'

Her voice was pretty, too, with an accent in it which he recognised as French. There was something about her charming face which was oddly familiar. It was as though he had seen her somewhere before, and yet he could have sworn that she must be a total stranger. He would surely have remembered such an exquisite creature.

He bowed, 'I am Marcus Angmering, at your service. The Earl's heir, as you doubtless know. And you have the advantage of me, madame. Has the butler not announced you? You ought not to be kept waiting here.'

'Very kind of you,' she murmured, 'but do not trouble yourself. The butler has just left to inform Lady Sophia and her mama that I have arrived. I am Madame Félice, the *modiste* who has the honour of dressing Lady Sophia for her wedding, and of providing her with a suitable trousseau for her honeymoon.'

Well, that explained the bandboxes, the footman and the French accent—most *modistes* of note being French. It was many years since he had been so attracted to a woman on first seeing her, and if Madame's creations matched her appearance, then Sophia was indeed fortunate in having engaged her.

What to say next? He couldn't let her walk away and out of his life without making some effort to cultivate her acquaintance further—which pompous statement, translated into simple English, really meant without him having the opportunity, at some time in the future, to persuade her to be his mistress. In even simpler words—to have her in his bed.

Marcus had read of what the French called '*coups de foudre*': that is, of being so struck by a woman on first sight that one had an instant determination to make her yours at any cost. He had always laughed at the mere notion, had prided himself on his dispassionate approach to life and love, and now, here he was in this damned uncomfortable situation.

One moment he was walking downstairs, fancy free, and before he had reached the ground a pair of fine eyes and a beautiful face had reduced him to gibbering inanity—no, had struck him dumb. The only explanation for his odd behaviour was that he had been continent for far too long. Living in the wilds of Northumberland, reserving his energies to improve his father's estates, must have taken its toll on him.

He was saved from coming out with some piece of nonsense which would have only served to convince Madame of what a numbskull he was by the arrival of Cardew, the butler, and two footmen: the latter there to carry Madame's excess bandboxes. There were enough, he would have thought, to have dressed five future brides, rather than one.

'This way, Madame Félice,' said the butler, who was now leading Madame and her retinue upstairs, passing by Marcus, who had descended to the entrance hall himself, with a 'By your leave, m'lord.'

Marcus nodded distractedly at him and at Madame, who offered him a brief bow in passing. He watched her, like a lust-struck gaby he thought afterwards, until the turn of the stairs took her out of his sight.

Madame Félice, which was not her real name, did not turn to look after the man who had examined her with such interest. She was used to being the subject of bold stares from men of all ages and every class. She had known that the man descending the stairs was Marcus Cleeve, Lord Angmering, the Earl of Yardley's son and heir. She had seen him recently in Hyde Park when she had ridden there with only a groom as an attendant.

She had recognised him immediately, despite the many years which had elapsed since they had last met when she had been a girl walking in the grounds of Steepwood Abbey. It was plain from his manner that he had not recognised her—which was not surprising, given how much she had changed. Besides, her assumed French accent alone must have been enough to have put him off the scent of her, as it were.

Given that most men of the Ton regarded a *modiste* as fair game, a cross between an actress or a

barque of frailty as the saying went, it was not surprising that they thought of her as prey—or that she
conducted herself as prey would, by defending herself from them in every way she could.

Oh, she knew that look in Marcus Angmering's
eyes, she had seen it so often. The look which told
her how much he was attracted—and which also
told her that he thought she should be flattered by
his attentions. She might be wronging him by thinking this, but she was sure that she was not. Life had
taught her many hard lessons, and this was one
which she would ignore at her peril.

For the present, she must forget him, and must
concentrate instead on the business which had
brought her to Cleeve House. All the same, she
could not help wondering what Marcus Angmering
would think if he were aware of her true name and
history and what ties—even if distant ones—bound
them together. How would he look at her then?

What would he say if he knew that Madame
Félice had once been known as Louise Hanslope,
who had married the late, unlamented Marquis of
Sywell, and had then run away from him to arrive
in London as a French *modiste,* society's latest fashionable dressmaker?

More to the point, what would he say if he also
discovered that her true name had not been Louise
Hanslope either? That she was, instead, the daughter
of his father's long-dead second or third cousin—
she could never remember which—and ought, more

properly, to be addressed as either the Honourable Louise Cleeve, or as the Marchioness of Sywell—if she ever had the means, the opportunity and the desire of proving these remarkable facts.

If everyone had their rights she, too, would be expecting to be married to someone of her own station. In the normal course of events she would have been employing a *modiste* herself to design her trousseau, rather than be designing them for other, more fortunate women. She could not stifle an irreverent giggle at the thought of how Marcus would have reacted had she addressed him as cousin!

Stop that, Louise told herself sternly, things are as they are, and that being so I must concentrate on presenting her wardrobe to my cousin Sophia in my present incarnation of Madame Félice, society's favourite dressmaker.

'Beautiful, quite beautiful,' said Marissa, Lady Yardley, a little later, walking around her daughter, who had been carefully eased into the elegant cream wedding-dress which had been contained in one of the boxes which Marcus had seen in the hall, and who was now admiring herself before a long mirror.

'It is exactly what we wished, Sophia and I: a dress which is perfect in its simplicity. It looks even better than it did in the sketch which you showed to us when we visited your workrooms. If the rest of the trousseau is equally *comme il faut,* then we shall not regret having asked you to design it. Is not that so, Sophia?'

'Yes, Mama, but I am not at all surprised how lovely it is after seeing the beautiful clothes which Madame made for Nick Cameron's bride. The nicest thing of all is that they are so different from Athene's, because Madame has designed them to suit me rather than some imaginary perfect being in a fashion plate. I would have looked quite wrong in Athene's trousseau, as she would have looked wrong in mine, given our quite different appearance and colouring.'

'True,' said her mother. 'Madame is to be congratulated. I am looking forward to seeing Sharnbrook's face when you arrive in church.'

'Most kind of you,' said Louise, bowing her head, and accepting the compliments as gracefully as she could. 'But, m'lady, both your daughter and Miss Athene had the great good fortune to possess faces and figures which are a privilege to dress. My difficulties arise when I have to transform those who are not so lucky.'

They were standing in Sophia's bedroom, surrounded by gowns already made up, and bolts of cloth to inspect for those garments which were still to be created. As well as gowns Madame Félice was responsible for Sophia's nightwear and underwear. She had brought along samples of these as well as some pieces of outerwear, principally a long coat and a jacket like a hussar's for wearing on a cool day, which she felt sure that Sophia would also require.

When Lady Yardley had visited her workrooms Félice, or Louise as she always thought of herself, had almost decided to refuse her invitation to dress Sophia, on the excuse that she already had more work in hand than she could usefully cope with. The strain of entering a house which she might have called home, of meeting relatives who had no notion of her true identity, was almost too much for her.

And then, looking beyond Lady Yardley into a long mirror where she, too, stood reflected, she had told herself fiercely: Nothing to that. I have always stared life straight in the eye, I have never run away from anything—other than that monster Sywell—and I shall not run away from this.

Besides, who knows what might happen?

Now that she was in the Yardleys' home there was even a certain strange spice in knowing who she was, and that the assembled Cleeves were quite unaware of the cuckoo who had entered their nest. Except, of course, that she was not a cuckoo, but was as much of an honest bird as they were!

Nothing of this showed. She was discretion itself as she knelt before Sophia, pinning up her dress a little to show her pretty ankles, adding an extra discreet tuck here and there, suggesting that Lady Sophia ought to wear as little jewellery as possible.

'Yes,' nodded Lady Yardley. 'I was most impressed by the turn-out which you created for the

Tenison child's marriage. I was informed that you had vetoed her mama's wish that she should be hung about with geegaws. I, too, wish Sophia's innocence to be emphasised, not only by her white gown, but also by a lack of old-fashioned family heirlooms, bracelets, bangles and brooches. They can always be worn later when the first bloom of youth has gone.'

'Indeed,' said Louise, rising gracefully, and in the doing showing her own pretty ankles—attributes which Marcus would have admired had he been present. 'Very well put, m'lady, if I may say so.'

Careful, she warned herself, don't overdo grovelling humility. Dignified gratitude would be a better line.

This internal conversation with herself had become a habit for Louise from childhood onwards. She had had so few friends besides Athene Filmer, now Athene Cameron, that to ease her loneliness she had revived the imaginary companion of her lonely childhood, who might argue with her, but would never desert her.

Finally, everything else having been inspected and approved, Lady Yardley was measured for her new wedding outfit, something tactfully discreet as befitted the mother of the bride. Louise had already decided that it was a pleasure to dress Lady Sophia and her mama; they were not only considerate clients, but her taste and theirs coincided exactly.

Lady Yardley might not have been a beauty in

her youth, but her face had character and she had worn well, and was more attractive in middle age than many who had been called pretty when they had been girls. Louise had sometimes wondered what Lord Yardley's first wife had been like. The idle gossip which had come her way had suggested that the marriage had not been a happy one: the same idle gossip, however, credited the Earl's second marriage as having been much more successful than his first.

These were not, however, matters which she could discuss with her clients, but her interest in them was natural, considering that they were, after all, her relatives, even if that interesting fact was never to be revealed. She wondered if she would see Marcus again before she left the house. He was not a conventionally handsome man—unlike his father—but there was a suppressed power about him which Louise found interesting.

After all, what did handsomeness matter? Sywell had been a handsome man in his youth, although in his old age no one could have guessed that.

Louise did not ask herself why she might hope to see Marcus again—particularly as since her unhappy marriage to Sywell she had tended to avoid men. The one man in her life had been such a monster that it was not surprising that she had sworn never to have anything more to do with them.

Which made it all the more surprising that Marcus Angmering had made such an impression on her.

* * *

Marcus found that, contrary to his expectations, his father had not, as he usually did, left the house that morning either to go to his club or—more rarely—to visit Parliament.

He entered the library in search of the *Morning Post* to find that the Earl was there before him. Marcus could not help noticing that his father seemed frail these days. There was a transparency about him which made him appear older than his years. Nevertheless he looked up eagerly when he saw his eldest son enter.

It had been a source of unhappiness to the Earl that there had always been constraint between them: a constraint born out of his failed marriage with Marcus's mother. It had been a great relief to him that Marcus and his second wife had dealt well together. Marcus respected her because she made his father—and his household—happy. She genuinely liked Marcus, admiring in him the ruthless honesty with which he approached life.

'Ah, Angmering, I had hoped to see you,' his father began. 'There are a number of matters which I wish to discuss with you. Not business ones— I have inspected the documents and accounts which you have brought from the north, together with your report of the changes you have made to the running of the estates there. I am more than satisfied with what you have done. I should have got rid of Sansom long ago—advancing years had marred his judgement. I have nothing but admiration for what you have accomplished.

'No, what I wish to speak to you about is something more personal. I sincerely hope that you will not take amiss what I have to say to you. I know only too well how much you value your freedom, and how much the notion of marriage fails to attract you. I must, however, ask you again to consider making a suitable marriage—not only to provide yourself and the estates with an heir, but because I would wish you to find for yourself the happiness which I share with my dear Marissa. I would not like this matter to come between us, but I feel it incumbent upon me to raise it with you.'

Marcus knew how difficult his father must have found it to talk of his desire to see him married by the careful way in which he was speaking, quite unlike his usually bluff and, somewhat impulsive, straightforward manner.

He owed it to him to answer him reasonably. Of late, and particularly since he had reorganised the northern estate so satisfactorily, the stiffness which had lain between them had eased a little. Consequently Marcus's answer was as diplomatic as he could make it.

'You know, father, that I would prefer not to marry, and I believe that my wish not to do so has been reinforced by the knowledge that you now have not one, but two, other sons. Better than that, it is plain that both of them are shaping to be worthy possible inheritors of the title—'

His father interrupted him impatiently. 'That may be so, but fate can be unkind, Marcus. Of recent years I have seen families which appeared to be as well supplied with male heirs as ours lose them all to accident, or sickness, whereupon some unknown appears who has been trained to nothing and who consequently respects neither his new possessions nor his title.

'I would not wish to deprive either Edmund or Edward of the possibility of them—or one of their sons—inheriting, but I would like the bulwark of a son from you. I wish this all the more particularly since you have grown into such a responsible and sensible fellow. No, I would wish you to marry and soon. I know that I cannot compel you—but I would ask you to bring your undoubted common-sense to bear on this matter. I cannot ask fairer than that.'

Marcus bowed his head.

'Very well, sir. I will do as you wish and think about marriage. So far, I have met no one with whom I would wish to spend the rest of my life. Whatever the truth of your marriage to my mother, that to dear Marissa has been a great success, and if I could meet anyone half as worthy…' he stopped and shrugged, spreading his hands before continuing '…but so far, I have not. Were I to do so I should not hesitate to follow your wise example. I cannot say more.'

The Earl's pleasure at this conciliatory speech was manifest. He could only hope that Marcus meant what he had said.

'Excellent,' he said, 'and now I trust that you will find it possible to remain in London until we all visit Northampton to celebrate Sophia's marriage. Sharnbrook has been most obliging about the matter. I can only hope that this wretched business of Sywell's murder will not cast too great a shadow over it. I understand from a friend at the Home Office that nothing further has come to light which might give us some notion as to who was responsible. The trouble is, I understand, that there are so many who might have wished him dead, and no real evidence to suggest who, among the many, it might have been.'

Marcus frowned. He knew that some of the *on dits* which had flown around after Sywell's brutal murder had suggested that his father might be the culprit, but he could not believe that to be true. He had hoped that the real criminal might have been found, so that the *on dits* would be silent at last. Sywell's existence had been like a dark cloud hanging over the Cleeve family, and his strange, and savage, death had only served to enlarge that cloud, not disperse it.

'Two things puzzle me,' he said. 'One is that the Marchioness, his young wife, should have disappeared so completely, and the other is that the authorities should spend so much time and energy trying to discover who killed him. Given the dreadful nature of the man, his own wretched life and the misery which he caused to so many others—including you, sir—one can only wonder why they don't see his death as a merciful release for society, and all his many victims.'

'Oh,' replied the Earl, 'in these sad times when revolution and violent dissent are all around us, those who rule us do not like to think that the death of an aristocrat, even one as hateful as Sywell was, should go unpunished. As for his missing wife, I believe that they now accept that he did away with her, and that further search for her as a possible murderess is time-wasting and pointless. Besides, his death seems to have been very much a man's way of killing, not a woman's.'

Marcus shrugged his shoulders. 'I suppose that there is some truth in both your suppositions. As for his wife, until a body is found, anyone's guess about her fate is as good as everyone else's.'

'True. But since the Abbey and its remaining grounds have reverted to me, after Burneck confessed that not only was my cousin deprived of them by a foul trick, but that Sywell murdered him into the bargain, I have felt very unhappy over the fact that, if she still lives, she has been left a pauper. I would have liked to do something for her. It seems that Sywell led her the devil of a life—which is not surprising, seeing what a brute he always was.'

Later Marcus was to remember this conversation

about Sywell's missing wife and to smile a little
ruefully at it. At the time he had little more to say
about the Marquis and his affairs, but took the opportunity to discuss with his father some further al-
terations to the running of his estates before leaving
to go downstairs and try to find out whether his
blonde Venus had left. If she hadn't, he might contrive to find some way of speaking to her again.

From the bustle coming up the stairs it seemed
that Madame Félice had not yet left but was on the
point of doing so. Bandboxes, hatboxes and bolts of
cloth were being carried out of the entrance hall to
her carriage. She was standing to one side, super-
vising the operation as briskly as though she were
Wellington on the field of battle.

Splendid! He must think of something convincing
enough to detain her for a few moments without that
something looking too obviously contrived. Fortune,
however, was with him. Two footmen had just lifted
out Madame Félice's remaining luggage, leaving her
in the hall with her small bag, when the door was
flung open and his two half-brothers shot noisily in,
wrestling with one another, their protesting tutor following close behind them.

In their puppy-like play they failed to see
Madame Félice, and one flailing arm caught her and
knocked her against the wall. Marcus jumped down
the two remaining steps, caught one boy by the ear
and the other by the wrist before the tutor could
either separate or reprimand them.

'Enough of that,' said Marcus grimly. 'On your knees, lads, and apologise to Madame.'

'Only if you let go of us, Mark Anthony,' exclaimed the larger of the pair. 'We were only funning and had no notion anyone was here.'

'Well, you do now. Both together and quick about it.'

'Sorry, and all that,' said the second boy cheekily on his way down to his knees, earning himself a cuff from Marcus for his easy impudence.

Louise, meanwhile, had moved away from the wall: the blow had been a light one, and the arrival of Marcus like an avenging angel was a source of amusement to her rather than relief. She knew all about boys of this age—the forewoman of the French emigré dressmaker to whom she had once been apprenticed had had three of her own. Louise had even joined them in some of their romps before she had turned from a hoyden of a girl into a young lady who realised that such romps might become dangerous.

'These,' said Marcus when both lads were on their knees before her, begging her pardon in soulful voices, 'are the Two Neds, Edward and Edmund... Like the Saxon kings after whom they are named, they have never learned to control their behaviour.'

'Mama says we're getting too old for you to call us that,' said the somewhat larger boy, Edward, who was the older of the twins by two minutes.

'True,' said Marcus, mimicking his father's favourite phrase. 'And I'm too old for you to call me Mark Anthony.'

'You are only our brother, but you discipline us as strongly as though you were our uncle,' continued Edward, still defiant.

'Oh, come on, Ned One,' said Edmund—he was always the peacemaker. 'He always stands up for us—you know he does.'

He appealed to the tutor, who had remained silent once Marcus took charge. 'And we shouldn't have been larking our way into the entrance hall, should we, Mr Wright?'

'Indeed not, Ned Two. I mean Edmund.'

'Well, seeing that there's no harm done, and that I've accepted your apologies in the spirit in which they were given,' said Louise briskly, amused by what she could plainly see was the friendly rapport which existed between Marcus and his half-brothers, 'you will allow me to leave unimpeded.'

'Only,' said Marcus gallantly, offering her his arm, 'if you will allow me to escort you to your carriage.'

What could she say to that, but 'Thank you, m'lord.' Anything else would have been churlish.

'Excellent. This way, then,' and he manoeuvred her out to where her carriage, piled high with her bandboxes and other paraphernalia, was waiting.

Once outside, though, when she lifted her small hand from his arm he took it gently into his large one, saying, 'I hope that all went well with m'sister's trousseau, madame.'

Why was she so breathless? Why was he so overwhelming? She had even faced Sywell down, so why should one admittedly large, but extremely civilised, nobleman have this peculiar effect on her?

She wanted to snatch her hand away, but reason said go slowly, lest she say, or do, more than she should. She could not believe how cool her voice sounded when she finally spoke.

'Very well, m'lord. Both your sister and her mama were very easy to please, since our tastes coincided.'

'Excellent,' Marcus said again. Something seemed to be depriving him of sensible speech but what could he say to detain her which would not sound as though he were trying to coerce her into meeting him again? Which was, of course, what he wanted to do!

'I believe that your premises are in Bond Street.'

His eyes on her were now admiring, no doubt of that. It was, perhaps, fortunate, Louise thought, that her horses suddenly grew impatient.

'It is time that I left,' she said slowly. 'I have further engagements this afternoon.'

Marcus could not help himself. 'With your husband, I suppose.'

Well, at last, here was something to which she could give a straight answer.

'No, I am not married. I am a widow,' she added.

Perhaps that would deter him from pursuing her further, since that was obviously what he wished to do.

'Not recently, I hope,' he said.

Marcus thought that for sheer banality this conversation took some beating.

Louise thought so, too. *What in the world is wrong with us?*

'Not quite,' she replied—and *what kind of an answer was that?*

Marcus released her hand, but not before kissing it.

'You will allow me to assist you into the carriage.'

Her hand out of his, Louise felt that some sustaining presence had vanished. It was an odd feeling for her, for she had grown used to being self-sufficient. The presence reappeared when he helped her up, and disappeared again when he let go of her.

She was aware, although she made no effort to look back at him, that he watched her until her carriage was out of sight. Something told her that it might not be long before she saw him again—and that something was right.

The question was, could she afford to know him?—however much she might want to. Anonymity had been her protector since the day when she had fled Steepwood Abbey, to find safety far from her tormentor, and from anyone who might remember poor little Louise Hanslope.

Marcus watched her carriage go, his mind in a

whirl. Like Louise, he could not believe the strength of his reaction to someone whom he had only just met. He must see her again, he must.

But how?

Chapter Two

'**K**now anything about a pretty little *modiste*, Madame Félice by name, do you, Gronow, old fellow?'

Marcus thought that Captain Gronow knew everything that there was to know about everybody, and he was not far wrong. It was fortunate that he, too, had been in Hyde Park that afternoon, and he had ridden over to him to pick his brains about Madame.

'Society's favourite dressmaker, has her place in Bond Street, eh? I can't say that I actually know anything—only *on dits* and suppositions which might, or might not, be true. Would that do?'

'Anything would do—better than knowing nothing at all.'

Gronow pondered a moment. He didn't ask Marcus why he wished to be informed about Madame, he thought that he knew.

'Well, she appeared out of nowhere some time

ago and was immediately able to afford not only to buy the Bond Street shop but also have it done over completely. So, the argument runs, she must have a rich backer—either here, or in Paris, since she's supposed to be French. I say supposed, because no one is sure of that, either. But who can the rich backer be, eh? No one has ever seen her with a man. She sometimes rides here in the late afternoon, but she acknowledges no one—and no one acknowledges her. A mystery, eh, what, wouldn't you say? The ladies say that she's very much a lady. Perfect manners, never presumes, unless it's to correct, very gently, provincial nobodies like the Tenison woman, Adrian Kinloch's mother-in-law—whose taste certainly needed correcting, I'm told.'

'A paragon, then,' remarked Marcus somewhat dryly. It was a little discouraging to learn that either his beauty was virtuous or that someone, rich, powerful and discreet, ran her. On the other hand, discretion of the sort which Madame was evidently practising was always to be commended.

'Lives over the shop, does she?'

'Well, even that's unknown. That ass Sandiman apparently came the heavy with her one day at her salon, and the story goes that she gave him a bloody nose for his impudence—which could argue virtue—or the appearance of it.'

Marcus was fascinated. 'She's so tiny, how in the world did she tap his claret?'

'With a poker, apparently. Poor fool wasn't ex-

pecting it, it's said. She led him on for a bit and
then, when he was least expecting it, planted him a
facer as good as the Game Chicken could have
done—except that he don't use a poker! I'd look out
if I were you, Angmering, if you've any notion of
furthering your own acquaintance with her. Don't
want your looks ruined for nothing!'

'Well, thanks for the warning, Gronow. Always
best to know what might by lying in wait for you,
eh?'

'All's fair in love and war, they say.'

'And no real notion of who might be running her?
If anyone? Could the money she spent to set up her
business have been some sort of a final pay-off for
her, do you think?'

'No idea, old fellow, none at all. If I hear anything
I'll be sure to let you know.'

A mystery woman indeed then, Madame Félice.
And strong-minded, too. One might have guessed at
her possessing a fiery temper with hair that colour—
and such a determined little chin: he particularly admired the chin.

Marcus rode back to where his sister sat, talking
to Sharnbrook—and there was a fellow worth knowing. He had to commend Sophia for her common-
sense and good judgement in bringing him to heel.

Now, if he could only persuade Madame—if she
were free that was—that he, Marcus, would be as
good a bet as any to set up house with, then he could
be as happy as Sophia without the shackles of mar-

riage to trouble him. All that remained necessary for him was to find some means of promoting his friendship with her, and that was going to be difficult.

In the normal course of events there were a thousand ways in which he could contrive to meet a woman. If she were in society there was the park, or the ballrooms of mutual friends, or he could make a polite afternoon call. Likewise if she were in the demi-monde there were any number of recognised haunts where she might be found.

But Madame Félice was different. She belonged to neither one or the other of these two groups. She had her own legitimate business, and possibly also a circle of friends—but these would certainly not be the friends of Marcus, Lord Angmering, a member of high society, of the ton. Not that he associated much with the ton himself.

Come to think of it, he had become, except for his brief visits to London, a bit of a solitary. So he would have to devise some ploy, some trick, to further his acquaintance with Madame—which would itself serve to add a little spice to a life which he freely acknowledged had lately been rather dull.

So the afternoon found him sauntering along Bond Street trying to look innocent, although the good Lord alone could explain why he should, seeing that he was bent on seducing a woman who, for all he knew, was truly innocent. Except that in the world which Marcus inhabited, women in occupa-

tions like Madame's were rarely so. Gronow had
hesitated to pass any judgement on her which was,
in itself, remarkable, but that proved nothing.

In his musings he had finally reached Madame's
salon with its little bow-window, a large hat on a
cream-coloured shawl chastely displayed inside it—
an indication of Madame's character? He sincerely
hoped not.

Now to go in—but what to say? He could scarcely
ask her to make him a pretty little *toilette*. On the
other hand, what about a shirt? Would it be beyond
Madame's talents to design a shirt for him? He
could always claim that his present tailor was not
sufficiently up to scratch for a man who hoped to
make a good show at his sister's wedding.

Yes, that was it.

It wasn't a very convincing notion but it would
have to do.

Marcus pushed the shop door open and walked
in.

Louise had had a trying day. Her forewoman had
contracted a light fever, and had consequently been
unable to come in to work: her best cutter had
thrown a fit of the tantrums on being asked to create
something which she did not care for, so that Louise
had been compelled to do it herself to prove that the
design was not only feasible, but beautiful. This had
finally brought obedience from the cutter, but having

been proved wrong she had sulked for the rest of the day.

Now, to cap everything, the assistant who manned the shop counter had come in all of a fluster.

'Madame, there's a man outside who says he wants you to make him a shirt. I told him that you only design for ladies, but he won't take no for an answer, won't go away, and demands to speak to you.'

'Does he, indeed? Does this man possess a name?'

'Oh, I'm sure he does, but he hasn't given it.'

Louise heaved a great sigh. Whatever next would turn up to ruin her day?

'Very well, Charlotte. Remain here while I go and dispose of him.'

A man wanting her to make him a shirt! Whoever had heard of such a thing—and whoever could he be?

She walked determinedly into the shop—to stare at Marcus.

As seemed always to be the case, the mere sight of him was sufficient to deprive her of all common-sense.

'Oh, it's you,' she said foolishly. And then, to recover herself a little, 'I might have guessed.'

He smiled at her and, yes, he really did look rather splendid today—even more so than when she had first met him. Not that he was in the least bit conventionally handsome, his face was too strong for that—and his answer to her was almost what she would have expected from him.

'Might you, indeed? Am I so eccentric?' he asked her, his expression comically quizzical.

'To want me to make you a shirt, yes. Surely you must have an excellent tailor.'

'Quite so, but I wished to further my acquaintance with you, and this was the only way I could think of doing so, seeing that we are unlikely to meet socially, and I haven't the slightest idea where you live—other than it might be over your salon. As a matter of interest could you possibly make me—or create, I believe is the ladies' word—a shirt which would past muster in the best houses?'

Louise began to laugh. His expression was so charmingly impudent when he came out with this piece of flim-flam that it quite undid her determination to be severe with him. She would let him down as lightly as possible.

'Now I know that you are funning. I suppose that I might be able to do what you have just suggested—but are you really informing me that this whole light-minded conversation with me and my assistant was solely for the purpose of getting to know me better? And, if so, to what end, m'lord? I cannot believe it to be an honest one, given the difference in our rank.'

Now this was plain speaking, was it not? And he should surely not have expected anything else from her, not with hair that colour, and with her determined little chin. He would match it with plain speaking of his own.

'*You* cannot know, madame, what an extraordinary effect you have had on me. Or perhaps you can, because I find it difficult to believe that you have never attracted a man's instant admiration before.'

Nor could he know, thought Louise a trifle sadly, that her experience of the ways of men, other than those of her late, brutal husband, was non-existent. She had barely spoken to anyone of the opposite sex since she had fled Steepwood Abbey. Which was, of course, why she had no notion whether it was usual for her to feel as she did every time she met him, which was a kind of wild exhilaration which seemed to take over her whole being.

She had told herself after escaping from her prison that she would never have anything more to do with a sex which could spawn such monsters as Sywell, and here she was bandying words with one of them, and experiencing these strong frissons of excitement while she did so. What frightened her was the thought that if she were to encourage him she might find that he was no better than Sywell— or that he might even be worse.

Could she trust him?

Perhaps when he looked at her as though—

As though, what? She didn't like to think.

'Come, m'lord,' she said, and her voice was sad, all her recent light banter missing from it, 'you must know as well as I that your intentions to me cannot be honourable. A great gulf lies between us.'

Marcus bowed his head. He was not going to deny that. What he could do was reassure her that he would always treat her kindly, would never exploit her in the way in which many men exploited their mistresses, whether they were members of the ton, or of the *demi-monde,* that curious half-world in the shadows which lay between high society, respectable middle classes and the honest poor.

'In terms of the society in which we live—' and goodness, how pompous that sounded! '—you may be right, but as between the fact that I am a man and you are a woman who attracts me strongly that gulf cannot exist. In other words we are Adam and Eve, not Lord Adam and Miss Eve.'

Marcus could hardly credit what he had just said—it was so totally unlike his normal mode of speech—although to be fair he was being his usual downright, honest self with her, and no one could ever accuse *him* of being devious. Except, he thought ruefully, when he was pretending that he had entered her salon in order to have a shirt made— and if that wasn't being devious, what was?

Louise must have been thinking so too, for she primmed her mouth a little comically, and said, 'You will, however, agree, m'lord, that we have come a long way from the days when Adam and Eve walked the earth—and one thing is certain about Adam, he didn't require a shirt to be made for him when he was in Paradise!'

'True,' said Marcus, bowing, and taking the opportunity to grasp her hand and plant a kiss on the palm of it for good measure. 'But I am sure that you grasp the point which I was trying to make. I would like to see more of you, Madame Félice, much more, and the only problem about that is how I can manage to do so when we do not move in the same circles.' The smile he gave her on coming out with this was a meaningful one.

'My problem, m'lord,' said Louise repressively, 'is that I do not move in any circles at all. My life is a quiet one, and I would prefer it to remain that way.'

'But think of the fun we could have,' urged Marcus, still retaining her hand in his, 'if you agreed to relax your principles a little, only a little. One thing you may be sure of, and that is that my word is known to be my bond and I would take good care never to betray or hurt you in any way.'

'Except,' said Louise hardily, 'in the most fundamental way of all. For one thing is quite certain— any arrangement which you might wish to come to with me would not include marriage. I am not of the class of women whom m'lord Angmering, the Earl of Yardley's heir, is likely to marry.'

'Ah, but,' said Marcus, kissing her hand again— it was encouraging to note that she was not attempting to remove it from his grasp—'m'lord

Angmering, the Earl of Yardley's heir, does not wish to marry anyone of any order of women at all—either high or low—and he does not choose his *belles amies* lightly.'

Why was she continuing to bandy words with him when he had made it quite plain that his intentions towards her were dishonourable? Was it that she liked the cut and thrust of argument? Or was it because, despite all, he attracted her so powerfully that the mere sight of him excited her? Nevertheless she must not allow him to persuade her to behave foolishly, so her answer to him must be a measured one.

'Ah,' she said, sighing a little, 'but you must admit that your *belles amies* are light, else they would not be your *belles amies*. No virtuous woman would agree to such an arrangement. Lowly I may be, but virtuous I intend to remain, even though it might mean that I never marry.'

'What is virtue worth,' asked Marcus, smiling seductively, 'if it prevents us from finding happiness?'

'I would not be happy if I were your mistress, m'lord, and I would deem it a favour if you released my hand. I did not give you permission to take it.'

'Certainly, but not before favouring it with yet another kiss.'

'You are impudent, sir.'

'Always when pursuing beauty,' and he kissed her hand again before slowly releasing it. 'I would not displease you by refusing such a reasonable request.'

'Then pray oblige me by agreeing to another reasonable request from me—that you leave.'

'Without placing an order for a shirt?' he asked her, his face comically sad.

Louise could not help herself. She began to laugh, recovering herself sufficiently to splutter, 'Lord Angmering, you are the outside of enough. Please, take your noble self and your unseemly offer away at once. There, is that enough to persuade you that I am serious in refusing even to consider what you obviously think to be a great honour: that I become your latest barque of frailty?'

'So, your answer is no?'

'No, no, and no again—did you expect anything else, m'lord?'

'I hoped—what did I hope?' Marcus was asking himself that question, not Louise. Faint heart, he thought, never won fair lady, and Marcus Angmering prided himself that his heart was not a faint one.

He leaned forward to look down into her beautiful eyes and tried not to drown in them. 'I must inform you,' he murmured confidentially, 'that I have a most inconvenient habit. I never take no for an answer. No, I think, challenges me more than yes.'

Louise repressed a desire to laugh again. She had hoped that her repeated refusal might persuade him to leave. She had deliberately not mounted a high horse by taking a loud moral line, since he had not attempted to attack her physically in any way, unlike

Sandiman and some others she had heard of. Other than by taking her hand and stroking and kissing it gently, that was.

'Do I understand, m'lord, that you prefer a challenge? If so, let me persuade you that I am not prepared to enter a verbal jousting match with you over whether or not I shall become your current ladybird. Had you offered me marriage my answer might still have been no, seeing that our acquaintance has been so short.'

She ended by pulling out her little fob watch and staring at it before saying, her bright eyes flashing fire, 'I calculate that our two meetings, taken together, have not lasted so much as half an hour—which must constitute some sort of achievement, seeing that it has included one improper proposal and two proper refusals. That being so, and seeing that I have a great deal of work awaiting me, I must, again, ask you to leave—and, nobleman though you are—that you will be gentleman enough to obey me.'

Marcus bowed. 'Splendid, madame. I do believe that between us we could write a Drury Lane farce which would rival Sheridan—were we not both so busy I might suggest a collaboration. That fact alone persuades me to go, bearing in mind that "he who fights and runs away, will live to fight another day!"'

Louise could not resist murmuring back at him as

he bowed his way out, 'Oh, is that what we have been doing, m'lord, fighting?'

He turned towards her before he left and shook a finger at her, 'Address me as Angmering, if you please, not m'lord: I can see that you are not yet ready for Marcus. I shall be back, soon.'

Louise sank on to one of the chairs provided for customers, and put a hand to her hot face.

No, I am not ready for this, or for him, nor will I ever be—I think. I thought that being Sywell's wife would have affected me as cowpox is supposed to affect smallpox, as an inoculation against men— but no such thing. And what is the most surprising fact of all is that he bears no resemblance whatso- ever to the handsome hero whom I used to dream about when I was poor little Louise Hanslope. The hero who would come to rescue me from penury and misery. He's certainly not handsome—but he's something better. He's not a dandy either, simply a strong man who is full of confidence in himself.

But he shall not have me for his doxy unless I truly wish it, and I have no notion what my real feelings for him are—or might be.

But she was lying to herself, and knew it. The physical pull of him was so powerful that now he had gone she found herself shivering, and what did that tell her?

Something which she did not want to know.

Marcus could not truly read his own feelings ei- ther. He had not flattered himself that Madame

Félice would succumb to him immediately, but he had been of the opinion that it might not be too difficult to win her.

He thought that no longer. There was steel there. By her appearance he might have thought her fragile. Fragile! Oh, she might look so, but she was actually as fragile as the Emperor Napoleon or one of his marshals. Send her to Spain, and Wellington would surely win his war there in short order!

On the other hand there was little pleasure in an easy conquest. His campaign to win her into his bed might be long, but it would be entertaining if this afternoon was anything to go by, and the prize he would gain at its end would be well worth winning.

To the victor the spoils—and now to return to his humdrum life again, to visit his old aunt, his mother's sister, who had arrived in London for a short stay and had written to him to say that she particularly wished to see him.

What puzzled him was what she could possibly have to say to him. He remembered meeting her once, years before, and even then, when he was little more than a child, noticing that, unlike his mother, she was no beauty. He had heard that she was married to a Norfolk squire and had had a large family: his cousins, whom, for one reason or another, he had never met.

He discovered that she was still not a beauty, but,

like his stepmother, had a face full of character. Her
pleasure at meeting him was great and unaffected.

'Oh, how much you resemble your father!' she
exclaimed when all the proprieties had been gone
through, and they were seated together and he had
accepted a glass of Madeira and some ratafia biscuits.

'I always admired him, you know, and was sad
when he offered for Danielle, and not me. On the
other hand I was later relieved that he had not done
so, for I should not have liked to go to India, so hot
and nasty, and I could not have had a better husband
than my dear Robert, God bless him.'

Robert Hallowes had died some years earlier and
she had been living at the Dower House on the
Hallowes estate near King's Lynn. She spoke briefly
of her life there, and asked Marcus about his in
Northumberland.

'I suppose you knew of, if you did not mix with,
that dreadful man, Sywell. He was someone to
avoid, you know. His reputation was bad from the
first moment he burst into society, and believe me,
burst was the right word! Your father grew to dislike
him intensely and there were some rumours about
him and Sywell both being interested in another
young woman before he met Danielle and myself in
our first season. Fortunately I was not the sort of
youthful moneyed beauty Sywell was always pursuing.'

She gave a jolly laugh after saying this, and

Marcus could scarcely believe that she was his mother's sister, so unlike was she to her. She took a sip from her glass of Madeira before saying in a more serious voice, 'I think that it is time that I spoke to you about the reason for my asking you to visit me. I have often thought that you ought to be told the truth about your parents' marriage and when I heard from a friend that there had always been some constraint between you and your father, and that they thought it likely that it arose because of their failed marriage, I was more than ever convinced that I had a duty to do so—so here we are.'

She stopped, and now she was so solemn that she was like a different person. 'You must understand that Danielle was a great beauty and it was our parents' hope that she would make a grand marriage. They put a great deal of pressure on her to marry your father, who was known to be the likely Yardley heir, and was then a young man of great promise.

'The trouble was that she had already fallen in love with the heir to the small estate next to ours, and was most reluctant to give him up—except that I think that the notion of becoming Lady Yardley one day attracted her. I regret to say it, but she was always flighty, changed her mind every other day and felt it her duty to attract every young man she met. My parents were eager for her to be married. They thought that it would settle her.

'Alas, once she was married, she became more flighty than ever. She regretted her lost love and made up for it by behaving as wildly as she could without putting herself in danger of society ostracising her. She was very like Lady Caroline Lamb is today: defying all the conventions. The worst thing of all, though, is that her behaviour made your father doubt whether you were truly his son. It was only when, as you reached manhood, your likeness to him became so strong that he could no longer doubt that he was truly your father.'

Marcus gave a great start on hearing this. It explained so much of his father's behaviour to him. He said, and his voice sounded strange to him when he spoke, 'Had he any real reason to believe that she was telling the truth?'

His aunt smiled sadly. 'A little, perhaps, but the pity of it was that Danielle, when they quarrelled, which was often, frequently taunted him with the possibility that he was not your father. It grieves me to say this, but the main reason for the failure of their marriage lay at Danielle's door rather than his. He was, in fact, extremely patient with her. Unfortunately her behaviour resulted in the coolness which lies between you and your father. She was unhappy, made him unhappy and destroyed the affection which should lie between father and son. In all fairness to him—and to you—I thought that you ought to know the truth.

'I understand that his second marriage is a happy one, and that you are fond of your stepmother and she of you—but my poor sister had much to answer for before she died. She had already broken off all ties with our parents and with me—to our great grief.'

Marcus sighed. He thought bitterly of the many years during which he and his father had been estranged. Of late they had come together a little, and now it seemed, if his aunt could be believed—and he thought that she could—that he might be able to heal the breach which misunderstanding had created.

His aunt could see his distress. She said, her voice anxious, 'I hope that I was not wrong to tell you this, but I owed you the truth.'

Marcus leaned forward and kissed her impulsively on the cheek. 'You were not wrong, but right, and I wish that I had known of this before. It must have hurt you to speak so plainly of a sister whom you must once have loved.'

'Yes, you are like your father,' said his aunt. 'Brave and strong-minded. He never once complained to anyone about Danielle's folly, but bore it like a man. He has his reward in Marissa—and, I am sure in you. Now let us talk of other, happier, things. I hope that you will all come to visit me. I should dearly like to see your half-sister and brothers.'

'So you shall,' said Marcus energetically, 'and you shall come to Sophia's wedding, too. After all, you are my aunt and now I owe you a debt of gratitude for telling me the truth.'

All the way home his thoughts ran round and

round his head like animals exercising themselves in a cage. As a child he had always thought that there must be something wrong with him that his father had shown him so little affection. Later, his father's manner had changed a little, and the story his aunt had told him explained why it had. He must try to forget his own resentment and make up for the lost years which lay between them.

Had she seen the last of him? Louise rather doubted it. There was a determination about Marcus Angmering which she found admirable, but which frightened her a little. He had spoken the truth when he had said that there were few places where they might meet, but she had no doubt that one way or another he would contrive to meet her.

She owned a little house in Chelsea to which she retired at the weekend. During the week she lived over the workrooms. She drove her girls hard, but only on five days a week, something almost unknown in the trade, but she had found that they worked better in those five days than those did whose employers demanded longer hours and less kind conditions. She remembered her own harsh youth too well to subject others to it, and it amused her to discover the monetary benefits of a more liberal regime.

Two days after Marcus had visited her she became aware—or thought that she did—that she was being watched. Living with Sywell had given her a sixth sense. Twice she saw the same stranger on the corner when she went out for a stroll in the late afternoon. And could it be simple coincidence that the same stranger appeared on the pavement in front of her Chelsea hideaway, whose address no one, not even her forewoman, knew? They all thought that she lived permanently above the salon.

Had Marcus Angmering had the gall to pay a spy to follow her? She would not put it past him. What could be wrong with her that all the men in her life turned out to be domineering creatures determined to have their own way? Wasn't it enough for her to have had Sywell to endure without another such creature turning up to chase after her?

Or was she seeing enemies around every street corner simply because her past life had made her wary of everyone and everything? She liked to think that, but she could not be sure.

Louise was not mistaken. Marcus had driven straight to the address of the ex-Runner whom he knew his friend Nick Cameron had used to discover what he could about Athene Filmer.

'It's a simple task,' he told the man, whose shrewd face and knowing eyes quickly summed up Marcus as the hard sort of gent who knew what was what—and what he wanted. 'Just find out whether she lives above the shop—or whether she has another home away from it, that's all. And whom she mixes with—if she mixes with anyone, that is,'

Marcus added, remembering that Louise had told him that she didn't move in any circles.

Jackson knew better than to ask m'lord why he wanted to know. He nodded, and promised absolute discretion. 'You may be sure, m'lord, that the job will be done in such a way that she won't know that it's being done at all.'

'Excellent,' said Marcus.

The Earl saw Jackson on his way out. He said, his brows raised a little, 'You have had occasion to employ an ex-Runner, Marcus? They are not always either honest or reliable, but I believe that that man is.'

He did not tell Marcus that Jackson had visited him on behalf of the Home Office over the matter of Sywell's murder, nor did he ask Marcus why he had employed him.

Marcus said quietly, 'My friend Cameron recommended him; he found him honest. I need a confidential matter settled before I leave London.'

The Earl did not ask what the confidential matter was, but began to move away. Marcus said, 'sir, there is something which I wish to say to you and now seems as good a time as any—if you have a moment for me, that is.'

His father turned towards him and said a little heavily, 'I always have time for you these days, Angmering. It is my deepest regret that once I had not. I promise to listen to you and give you my full attention.'

Marcus blinked; it was almost as though his father knew what he was about to say. They moved back into the study. His father did not sit behind his desk, but walked across to sit in a chair by the window. He motioned Marcus to the one opposite.

Now that the moment had come, Marcus found that he was lost for words. Once, when he was younger and rasher, he might have attacked his father with the knowledge of what his aunt had told him, reproached him a little for mistreating him because of what he had thought his mother had done. Now he could only feel pity for a man who had been as much a victim as himself.

'Sir,' he began, 'I met my aunt, my mother's sister, yesterday at her request, not mine. She told me the true story of your marriage, and explained to me why, when I was a child, there was always a strong reserve in your manner to me.'

It was the kindest way he could think of to describe the coldness and lack of interest which his father had shown in him during his childhood. Since the Earl made no immediate answer to him, he ploughed on, finding in himself a diplomacy which he had not known he possessed.

'She also explained why, when I grew up, your manner to me softened a little, and when I look at the portrait of you painted when you were my age now and I look at myself, the strong resemblance between us convinces me, as it must have convinced you, that I am truly your son.'

The expression of pain on his father's face was momentary, but it was there. Marcus felt it incumbent on him to continue. 'My aunt also told me that the fault in your marriage did not lie with you, and that you had shown great patience with my mother's behaviour until the day she passed out of our lives.'

He was silent—and so was his father.

Finally the Earl spoke. 'If I find it difficult for me to answer you, it is because I feel, and have long since felt, shame that I treated an innocent child as harshly as I did. Even if your mother had spoken the truth about your fatherhood I should not have visited her sin upon the head of someone as defenceless as you were then. The constraint which still exists between us comes on my side from my stupidity in allowing a lie to dominate my—and your— life for so long.

'I ask your pardon, and trust that from now on we might become friends. We cannot call back the past and change it, but we can refuse to allow it to poison our lives on the future. My own relief is that my behaviour to you did not harm you—you have turned into the kind of son a father can be proud of. I therefore ask you to forgive me, if you can.'

Marcus leaned forward and said in his straightforward way, 'No forgiveness is needed, sir. Understanding rather, for what my aunt told me made me feel pity for you—and lessened the pity I felt for myself.'

His father rose and put out his hand, saying, 'Let

that serve as an epitaph for the dead past, Angmering, and we will shake on it, if you would. It is fitting that before your sister marries we should come together thus and be able to join in the celebrations as a true father and son at last.'

Marcus rose, too. They stood face to face, the stern father, and the son whose likeness to that father was written on his face, in his voice and in his manner.

'Indeed, sir—and that will be the end of that, I trust.'

His father nodded and they remained silent for a moment, the loud ticking of the clock being the only sound in the room: a fit commentary on the passing of life and time.

Marcus did not have long to wait for his hiring of Jackson to bear fruit; after all—as the man had told him—it was a simple enough task compared with most he was given.

On the following Monday afternoon he arrived in Berkeley Square.

'I think I've found what you want, m'lord. The lady lives over her workrooms in Bond Street during the week. After six o'clock on a Friday she hires a Hackney cab and is driven to a little house in Chelsea not far from the river, where she spends Saturday and Sunday. Sunday she goes to church all respectable like and speaks to no one—other than to shake hands with the Reverend at the end of the service.

'Early on a Monday morning she returns to the shop. She has a couple of servants at her weekend place: a housekeeper and a maid of all work. It seems that she does not mix with her neighbours and during a careful watch she had no visitors other than a lad who delivers milk.'

He paused. 'I have to say that I think she's something of a fly lady, because I suspicioned that she knew that she was being watched. On my first day I perhaps wasn't too careful, since after that every time that she went out she looked around her most busily. I made a few discreet enquiries about her, thinking that they might be useful to you. It seems that she has no gentleman callers, either in Bond Street or in Chelsea. The opinion is that she is lady-like and discreet.'

'Excellent,' said Marcus. 'That is all I need to know. Would you prefer to be paid now?'

'If it suits you, m'lord, yes.'

Feeling a bit of a cur for having Madame Félice watched, Marcus handed him his money on the spot, but he did not feel so much of a cur that he did not glumly regret that he would have to wait until the weekend before he paid her a call!

Saturday morning found him hiring a cab and setting off for Chelsea. Either being a *modiste* paid well, or Madame had a fund of money of her own, for the little house was a jewel of a place, newly appointed and painted. He thought that, apart from the paint, it resembled Madame herself. Whistling gently, he paid off the cabbie and knocked on her elegant front door...

Louise had just finished eating a late breakfast and was drinking a cup of excellent coffee—she always shopped at Jackson's in Piccadilly—when she heard the door knocker and wondered who it could be at this hour.

She did not have long to wait. The little maid came in saying, 'There's a gentleman to see you, mam.'

'A gentleman, Jessie? Did he give his name?'

'No, mam. He said that he thought that you might know who it was? He said that he was in need of a shirt—but, mam, could he really mean that? He was wearing a very fine one.'

'Did he, indeed?' Louise jumped to her feet half-amused, half-scandalised. 'Tell him to go away, at once.'

'Yes, mam.'

Jessie disappeared, only to reappear again a few moments later. 'Oh, mam, he says as how he won't. He says that it's most urgent that he see you, and that he's prepared to wait outside until you're ready to speak to him—and he gave me half a sovereign to tell you that—look!'

Louise, who had sat down, jumped up again. Bribery and corruption of her servant, was it now?

What next would the man get up to? For she had no doubt that it was his lordship of Angmering who had somehow tracked her down.

'Do you want me to give it back to him, mam?' asked her maid anxiously.

'Certainly not, by his behaviour he deserves to lose more than half a sovereign. Tell him that—' Inspiration failed her. Oh, bother the man, what message could she send that would be sure to get rid of him?

'Tell him that if he doesn't go away I shall send for the local constable to remove him,' she came out with at last.

'He won't like that, mam,' said her maid, still anxious.

'I'm sure that he won't, but tell him so all the same.'

Out shot the maid again. Louise picked up her cup and began to drink coffee agitatedly.

This time, though, when the maid reappeared she was trailing in the wake of that haughty aristocrat Marcus Angmering, who was apparently so determined to see her that he would play any trick which his inventive mind could think up.

'I wouldn't wish you to go the trouble of setting the law on me,' he said cheerfully, once the maid had left, 'So I decided to speak to you in person, so that we could settle our difficulties without delay— and pray do not reprimand your maid for letting me in. She found it difficult to deny someone so much larger and stronger than she is.'

Louise stared at him, the coffee cup halfway to her mouth, and to her horror found herself saying, 'What difficulties, sir?' instead of telling him to remove himself from her dining room.

'The difficulties relating to your inability to accept my kind offer of protection.'

She put down her coffee cup with a trembling hand. 'Your impudence, sir, is beyond belief. You force your way into my home, terrorise my servant…'

Marcus interrupted her. 'Oh, scarcely that,' he murmured, his mouth twitching. 'I wouldn't describe giving her half a sovereign as terrorising her.'

'Oh…' Louise gave what could only be called a gasp of exasperation. 'You are no gentleman, sir, you twist every word I say. You know perfectly well what I mean—and there *are* no difficulties about your offer of protection—I refused it in the plainest terms possible.'

'But so quickly,' Marcus protested. 'You didn't even pretend to consider it—which is not the proper way to refuse a business proposition.'

'I never pretend, sir,' and oh, dear what a lie that was, since her whole life, and even her name, was a pretence. 'You have had my answer. Pray allow Jessie to escort you to the door.'

'Without even the offer of a cup of coffee,' he said sadly. 'That's no way to treat a guest, madame.'

'You are not my guest,' she flashed back at him.
'You come here uninvited, force your way in—'

'True,' he said, still sad. 'But how else may I
speak with you, tell me that?'

His smile was so wicked, his eyes mocked at her
so gently, that Louise felt as though she had begun
to melt internally. She had never experienced such
a sensation before. No, he was not handsome, but
he was better than that—he must be to have such an
effect on her. She licked her lips, and saw his expression change when she did so—and wondered
why.

Louise was inexperienced in the arts of love because she had never been subjected to anything
other than the acts of frustrated lust. She had no
notion of what might attract or rouse a man. Marcus,
watching her, was, to his surprise, sure that she was
truly innocent, and that the signs of fear which she
occasionally showed were genuine.

He was suddenly ashamed. He had been teasing
her after the fashion in which he teased Sophia and
the Two Neds, but where that had been innocent and
playful this could be construed as malicious. More
so when he could see her quivering lip and her trembling hand.

'I am sorry,' he said. 'I should not be doing this,
I did not mean to frighten you. I ought to go.' And
he began to turn away from her, to leave by the door
by which the little maid had earlier left.

He was going! She would be alone again. Fearful

though she was, Louise found that she did not want
that. Beyond the fear of him which Marcus had
briefly seen lay something else.

She was so lonely. All her life she had been alone.
The only bright stars in it had been her guardian and
later Athene Filmer and she had lost both of them.
If he left her now, to whom would she speak this
day? To the housekeeper, the little maid and later,
perhaps, tradesmen, shop-girls, and barely them.

'No,' she said, the words almost wrenched from
her, 'don't go. You...I...standing there you tower
over me—pray sit down.'

Now what had caused that, Marcus wondered?
There was even the faintest hint of a smile on her
face, a tremulous one. Was he seeing the first breach
in her defensive wall?

He said, as lightly as he could, 'Oh, I am not so
tall that I could be called a tower, but you are such
a dear little thing that I can see I might appear to
be if not a tower, a turret.' And he pulled out a chair
and sat opposite to her at table.

Yes, he had provoked a proper, if rueful, smile
by his last remark. Emboldened by it, he asked,
rather after the manner of a small boy seeking a
favour, 'Would your kindness extend to offering me
a cup of what smells like excellent coffee? I was so
anxious to meet you again that I skipped breakfast.'

Oh, he was impossible! How in the world had he
managed to persuade her into not only allowing him
to stay, but also to sit there, smiling, as though his

proper place was in this room with her as though they had just risen from bed and were being Darby and Joan together.

What was worse was that she was now getting into the spirit of this disgraceful game he was playing with her. She rose, opened the breakfront cabinet which stood behind her and which contained a fine array of good china, took a cup and saucer from it, and poured him his coffee. She pushed it, the jug of cream and the sugar bowl across the table at him.

'My thanks,' he said, and drank the coffee slowly and appreciatively. He looked at her over the top of the cup, and said, now grave, all his former teasing mode gone, 'You must believe me when I tell you that I am going to these lengths because I need to meet you in order to woo you, and you must know how difficult that is going to be—'

'To woo me?' Louise threw at him again. 'To woo me into accepting a proposal to be your mistress is more commonly known as seduction. Have you no respect for virtue?'

Marcus put down his empty cup. 'We could have a useful debate about what virtue consists of—'

'No, we could not. We both know perfectly well what it is. Your behaviour, sir, is abominable—'

'Unlike the coffee,' he interjected, still grave.

'Oh, yes, you *are* impossible. Since you obviously think of me as fair game, why have I allowed you to remain, why?'

'Because,' he said, fixing her with his eyes, 'I

believe that you are as attracted to me as I am to you—is not that so? Believe me that if I made you my *belle amie* I would treat you with the same love and care as if you were my wife—nay, with more love and care than most of my fellows treat their wives. It is not because of your lesser rank that I do not ask you to marry me, it is because I have no intention of ever marrying. With the exception of one, most marriages seem to me to be shams—and I cannot hope that mine would be different from the common run. Accept my offer, I promise to be faithful to you, and do my best to make you happy.'

What he was saying had the ring of truth in it. For what had her marriage with Sywell been but a ghastly travesty of what marriage ought to be? More, she knew how hollow most marriages were. But, and it was a big but, she had a sense of herself, despite all that she had been compelled to do to save herself, as a woman of honour. If virtue and a desire to be honest were all that were left to her, then she must cling to them.

'I believe you,' she said slowly. 'I deem you to be a man of your word, but it is not enough.'

'There is nothing I could say that would change your mind?'

'I can think of nothing.'

He leaned across the table and took her hand. 'I cannot let you go. I need to meet you again, to try to convince you otherwise—'

She shook her head at him.

'No? Not even to meet you as a friend?' What he said next was wrung from him without warning, spontaneously, he could never previously have imagined himself saying such a thing. 'Félice I am a lonely man, and have been so from childhood. If I promised not to badger you or to follow you—'

'Or to have me followed,' she put in.

Marcus bowed his head. 'Yes, forgive me for that, but I was desperate. If I kept my promise to behave myself, could we meet occasionally? If only to talk.'

'How can I believe that you would not—' she began and then, 'But how could we meet? Either in private or in public?'

'Not in society, that is true, but occasionally I could walk with you, or drive you where we are not known.'

'In secret,' Louise said bitterly, thinking that all her life had been one long secret.

'Not entirely,' he told her. 'If you were willing to be a little devious I could be your cousin who has just discovered your whereabouts after many years.'

'M'lord Angmering's unknown cousin?' queried Louise. Her smile was a strange one.

'By no means. I shall be Mr Marks, and we shall be discreetly friendly—if you will permit, that is. Mr Marks's means will be modest—as well as his style.'

Louise gained the distinct impression that M'lord was enjoying himself. He reminded her of a small boy who had been given a new toy. The fear she had felt for him ebbed away a little.

'I should not be listening to you,' she said. 'But—' and she hesitated.

'But you are,' he returned eagerly. 'Think with what pleasure we can meet—simply to converse, of course.'

'Of course,' said Louise her tone sardonic. 'So long as you remember that, m'lord, we shall do well together.'

'Mr Marks,' he corrected her. 'I am to be Mr Marks—you will find our adventure easier since you will retain your name.'

'So long as I retain my honour,' she said, but she was smiling while she said it.

'I promise that Mr Marks will behave himself rather better than Lord Angmering has done. Now inform me that Mr Marks will be allowed to take Madame Félice for a short drive this afternoon—not in M'lord's curricle, but in the Hackney cab in which he will call on you at two of the clock. Reassure your little maid that when he next calls he will behave like a perfect gentleman. In the meantime you may pour me another cup of coffee.'

'Alas, it has grown cold, but perhaps, later this afternoon, when we return from our drive, you will take tea with me.'

Marcus rose and bowed. 'M'lord Angmering will take leave of you, Madame Félice, until this afternoon—when Mr Marks will call on you.'

I must be mad, thought Louise, trembling a little from she knew not what, to allow him any rope at all, any chance for him to start his nonsense with me again. Why in the world have I given way?

She was not being honest with herself and she knew it. She had given way because she had, for once, allowed her heart to overrule her head. She had done so, however, fully aware of the most supreme irony of all: that Marcus Angmering should pretend to be her cousin when he was, in truth, her cousin—even if only a distant one!

Louise was hugging this delightful thought to herself when she walked into the kitchen where the housekeeper and the little maid were in urgent conversation—about her strange visitor, no doubt. She really had no need to explain herself, but thought that it might be politic to do so if Marcus was going to come a-visiting.

'It turns out,' she said after some discussion of what her dinner might consist of, 'that the gentleman who visited me today is my long-lost cousin.' And that was no lie, was it? 'Mr Marks, who has had the good fortune to discover my whereabouts. He will doubtless be calling again.'

If the two women facing her thought that this was the biggest Banbury tale they had ever heard, they offered her no outward and visible sign of their disbelief.

'So that is why he gave me a half-sovereign!' exclaimed the little maid.

'Probably,' said Louise, gratified that she had extricated herself from yet another difficult situation—and hoping that she would not have to do so again… Up to now her life had seemed to consist of one difficult situation after another, and today's was only the latest. She had to hope that her luck, which had held good so far, would not suddenly desert her.

Chapter Three

Marcus Angmering was thinking that luck was with him. Madame Félice's sudden decision to allow him to visit her was promising, to say the least. There was a determination about her, though, which warned him that she would not lightly surrender to his advances. She had received his first overtures with disdain, even though it was plain that she had been attracted to him.

He arrived back at Berkeley Square after his drive with her where he had behaved himself perfectly, to discover that his father had had an unexpected visitor. It was Jackson, whom he met on the point of leaving the house.

'You were looking for me?' he asked a little puzzled.

'Not exactly,' Jackson said. 'I came to see your father in order to clear up some points relating to the Marquis of Sywell's murder. Now that I have seen you, however, I would be grateful if you would agree to speak to me about it.'

Marcus raised his eyebrows. 'Seeing that I was in Northumberland at the time of his murder, I scarcely imagine that I can have anything to tell you which you would find of the slightest use.'

'Nevertheless,' Jackson persisted, 'it is possible that you are aware of something which means little to you, but which would assist me.'

'In that case,' said Marcus, 'go ahead, although I warn you that you might be wasting your time.'

'Oh, I'm willing to risk that,' Jackson said cheerfully as Marcus ushered him into the drawing-room.

'Now, m'lord,' he began. 'I understand that at times you visited Jaffrey House when the Marquis was living at Steepwood. Did you ever meet him, and more importantly, did you ever, by chance, meet, or have occasion to see, his wife?'

Marcus shook his head. 'I was warned by my father to avoid him as much as possible. True, on the very few occasions on which I visited Jaffrey House I occasionally saw Sywell at a distance. Of his life at Steepwood I knew nothing, except for those rumours of which I am sure you have heard.'

Jackson nodded his head thoughtfully. 'As I expected. But his wife, the young Marchioness, did you ever see her? Have you any notion of what she looked like? The thing is, what I find very strange is that no one confesses to having seen much of her at all. If you could remember anything of which you might have heard of—or seen yourself—it would help me.'

Marcus shook his head again. He could hardly tell Jackson that he hated his rare visits to his father and had kept himself to himself as much as possible on them. He thought that might be the end of the interview but Jackson had yet another question for him.

'I understood from one person to whom I spoke that the Marchioness was reputed to be a great friend of Miss Athene Filmer who married an acquaintance of yours. Miss Filmer has given us a description of her which might fit anyone. Now Miss Filmer appears to have had few friends, and I wondered whether you ever saw her with the Marchioness, either when they were children together—or later.'

'I can't exactly remember,' said Marcus, cudgelling his brains. He tried to recall walking in the woods at Steepwood on his visits there. Something fluttered at the edge of his memory. Yes, when he was only a lad of fourteen he had stayed at Jaffrey House for a brief time, and once, when he had been out walking he had come across a young girl who might have been Athene Filmer. She had had another, smaller, girl with her who had tripped while larking around a pond and had cut her knee.

He had stopped and used his handkerchief to clean and bandage the knee and…she had limped off…the flash of memory ended. Except that there had been something about the child which it was important that he should recall. But all that he could remember was that she had had a pretty voice, and so he told Jackson.

'Fairish hair,' he said slowly. 'It was years ago, well before I went to university, that I saw Athene Filmer in the woods at Steepwood with another little girl who had fairish hair, and striking eyes. I suppose that it's possible that she might have been the child who later became the Marchioness. Miss Filmer did say once that she had known her briefly in youth. I can say, however, that I never saw anyone who might be the Marchioness after her marriage to Sywell, because at that time I rarely visited Steepwood.'

What was it about the child's eyes? And what else had briefly intrigued him? He still couldn't remember—it remained on the edge of his mind.

Jackson nodded. 'Fits,' he said briefly. 'I was told that by several who thought that they might have seen her, but that describes too many young women, don't it? It's not particular in any way. And Miss Filmer you said. It's true she hadn't many friends, but one of them is that woman in Bond Street who makes the Quality's dresses.'

'Madame Félice!' exclaimed Marcus. 'She's Athene's friend! How did she come to know her?'

'Exactly,' said Jackson. 'She, the Filmer woman, I suppose that I ought to call her Cameron now, claims that she knows nothing of where the

Marchioness might be—not that I'm after believing her. She's a fly young woman.'

'True,' said Marcus, smiling. 'But it's a big jump from that to suppose that she knows where Sywell's missing wife went when she disappeared.' All the same he was intrigued, and wondered what Jackson would come out with next.

What the man did was to change tack disconcertingly—a favourite trick of his.

'Of course, you know all about your Pa's feud with Sywell, I suppose.'

'Everyone who met him feuded with Sywell,' said Marcus dryly.

'So I'm told. But the more I learn about him the more I learn about the Yardley connection with him. That duel all those years ago, the one where Sywell shot and killed the then Earl—a rum do, that. Burneck's evidence proved that it was a put-up job. Sywell murdered your distant relative and got Steepwood Abbey through it in consequence—not your Pa. It was lost to the Yardleys, apparently permanently.'

Ah, so Jackson was suggesting a motive for his father murdering Sywell, was he? That since Burneck's evidence of Sywell's villainy came *after* Sywell's death, his father might have disposed of him in an effort to regain the Abbey.

'Now, that cock won't fight,' said Marcus coldly. 'The Abbey is worth very little—quite the contrary. Now that my father has recovered it, as a consequence of the fact that Burneck revealed that Sywell gained it fraudulently and murdered my cousin into the bargain, it's going to take thousands to restore. No one but a fool would have murdered the man simply to get it back again.'

'Aye, and your pa ain't a fool,' agreed Jackson. 'I'll grant you that. A pity we have to run anyone in for topping such a regular out-and-outer as Sywell was—but justice must be done, you know. We can't have people running around killing Marquises and getting away with it.'

'Agreed,' smiled Marcus, 'to your first proposition, but not the second—seeing that the law couldn't top Sywell we should be grateful to the man who did. Gave us all a bad name, didn't he?'

Jackson nodded. 'You might say that. Thank you for your time, m'lord—most helpful.' He turned for the door.

'Think nothing of it,' said Marcus to his back as cheerfully as he could, but happy to see him go. He was a little premature, for Jackson swung round as he pushed the door open, and said, 'Oh, and by the by, if you can remember anything more about what Miss Filmer's friend—who might have been Sywell's lady—looked like, pass the news on to me if you would. You know where to find me. I'd dearly like to question her, so I would.'

Marcus stared at the closed door. Now, what was all that about? And Madame Félice, how did she arrive in the conversation? What's her connection with the Steepwood mystery—other than that she was Athene Filmer's friend? And that was something Jackson didn't see fit to tell me when I engaged him to investigate her.

The clever devil obviously guessed that I knew more about Athene's little friend than I could remember, but for the life of me I cannot recall what so intrigued me all those years ago.

Marcus would not have been surprised to learn that Jackson visited Madame Félice on Monday morning, calling at her salon and telling the girl on the shop counter that he wished to see the Missis. In fact Louise told him so when he called at her Chelsea home early on the following Saturday.

She allowed the little maid to let him in, but fixed him with the most freezing stare when he walked into her pretty drawing-room.

'Well, well, Mr Marks,' she said coldly. 'Did you set that man on me, *again?* Because if you did I shall require yet another apology from you.'

'What man?' asked Marcus deviously, knowing perfectly well to whom she was referring.

'Jackson, and don't pretend that you don't know whereof I speak. I saw him watching this house before you had me followed here, and when he arrived, asking to speak to me about my friendship with Athene, I immediately recognised him. He said that although he was an ex-Bow Street Runner he was engaged in government business and because I was

Athene's friend he needed to ask me about her other friends—in particular the missing Marchioness. He mentioned, in passing, but I am sure that it was deliberate, that he had been speaking to you. Did *you* suggest that he came to me? Because if so, you may leave at once.'

'Word of honour,' said Marcus solemnly, putting up his hand. 'I did engage him to find out where you lived, but I said nothing which might send him here to question you. He asked me if I had ever seen the Marchioness, either when she was a child, or later after she had married Sywell, and I told him that I had not.'

'Can I believe you?' Félice's agitation was plain to see. 'If you didn't, why did he visit me?'

'Because he's questioning everyone who had anything to do with Steepwood and Sywell. He even hinted to me that my father had a good motive for killing him—so you are not the only person on his list of those he wishes to interview.'

No, thought Louise, but I am the only one who is the missing Marchioness! The thought made her shiver.

'Can I believe you?'

Marcus went down on his knees beside her chair, and gently took her hands in his.

'Félice, believe me. It was bad enough for me to face his questioning: he made me feel as guilty as any villain in the Old Bailey dock and I certainly would not have had you subjected to him. He reminds me of one of those dogs who gets the bear they are baiting by the throat and won't let go. I promise you that if I ever have you investigated again, I shall ask your permission before I do so! Will that satisfy you?'

She wanted to believe him. He was so blunt and straightforward—even his naughtinesses when he had been teasing her in the shop about making him a shirt, and again when he had visited her for the first time, were mild in comparison with what she knew of the behaviour of other aristocrats who pursued those below them in rank. If he touched her, it was gently—and so far he had rarely done even that.

'So it was his decision that he came to see me? And his only?'

'Yes, I did not send him. If he comes again, be careful—behind that jovial exterior he is clever in the extreme.'

'So I thought—fortunately I had nothing of importance to tell him.' Oh, what a lie that was! Another! For she certainly had no intention of giving her true identity away to Jackson, of all people.

Marcus smiled. 'That would not please him, I think. He is a thief-taker and criminal-catcher, *par excellence.* He resents not being able to track Sywell's murderer down—even though he might think that Sywell deserved to be murdered. His problem is that so many might have wanted to murder him—including his wife.'

'Let us speak of something different. Shall I ring for coffee?'

'I am forgiven, then?'

'Yes, if you like. I don't think that there was anything to forgive, though.'

'And since it is a fine day, even if it is cold, you will walk down to the river with me and watch it flow by.'

All the same, despite the pleasure of being with her there was the agony of not being able to touch her, for the more he was with Félice as he was now beginning to call her, the more his desire for her grew. Not only because of her pretty face and figure, but because he could talk to her as he had never been able to talk to a woman before.

For all her romantic appearance, she was as delightfully down to earth as he was, and did not hesitate to check and challenge him if she disagreed with him. Her pleasures were simple ones, like his.

There was a man with a barrow selling roast chestnuts on the road by the river. Marcus saw her looking wistfully at them and said, waving what Louise always thought of as his lordly hand, 'You would like some?'

'Only if you joined me,' she shot back, 'which would be an odd thing for m'lord to do, would it not? Eat chestnuts in the street!'

'You forget,' he said. 'I am Mr Marks today, and Mr Marks is allowed to be one of the crowd. He is accompanied by no flunkeys, and has no grand position to keep up, something which pleases him. I do not like consequence, my dear Félice, but I am doomed to endure it. Today I am one among many.'

Louise was silent for a moment before she said, 'I think that you truly mean that, Mr Marks. Do you avoid it when you live on your father's estate in the north?' For he had told her that he rarely visited London and preferred the country.

'As much as possible, but *noblesse* does *oblige,* you know, however little I may wish it. It is my duty, you understand.'

'Sywell never thought that,' exclaimed Louise, without thinking.

'No, I believe not, but he was hardly a man one would take as a model of what a man, never mind a nobleman, ought to be.'

When they reached the Embankment they sat on one of the benches which faced on to the river and enjoyed their chestnuts, warming their hands while they ate them from the paper in which the barrow-boy had placed them.

'Chelsea has many places of interest,' Marcus said, 'including the Royal Hospital for the Pensioners. I understand that one may walk in the grounds. There is little to see at this time of the year—other than the building itself, of course. It re-bukes me a little, you know, for it is filled with soldiers who have given everything for their country, while I have given nothing.'

He said this with such feeling that, again without thinking, Louise placed her gloved hand on his.

'Should you like to have been a soldier?' she asked him.

'Yes, but my father would not permit it. And even though, in those days, we were at odds, I did not feel that I ought to disobey him. I may even have thought that I might please him by agreeing with him, but...' and Marcus shrugged his shoulders.

He was telling her things which he had never told anyone. Short though their acquaintance was, again, sitting by her, he felt more like Darby and Joan than many a couple who had spent years living together did.

'I suppose I ought not to ask you this, but are you still at odds with him?'

'No, we have become reconciled recently, and I think it is a great relief for both of us. Oh, I always respected him, but I could not love him. That, oddly enough, was reserved for my stepmother and her sons and the daughter whose trousseau you are making.'

He laughed a little, and said, 'I was very happy to gain twin brothers. You have met the Two Neds. I must confess that it was I who nicknamed them.'

He must trust her, thought Louise, a little awed, and also a little ashamed because she felt that she could still not totally trust him, to tell her such things about his family life.

'I like that,' she said, smiling up at him, so that

his heart gave a great leap in his chest, so sweet was her expression. 'Do they like their nicknames?'

'Oh, yes. You see they love to tease me for being old and passé, so I tease them back about being young and flighty—not too severely, mind.'

'How fortunate you are,' she could not help exclaiming, 'to have a loving family. It is something which I have always lacked.'

Her face was so sad when she said this, that Marcus wanted to take her in his arms and kiss and comfort her, while saying: You can always have me for a family, but he had made her a promise to do no such thing, so he merely pressed the hand she had absent-mindedly placed on his, instead.

It grew steadily colder. Marcus offered her his arm and they walked slowly back to her home, where she invited him in to drink tea with her: it had become something of a ritual. On the way they were so engrossed in one another that neither of them noticed a curious pair of eyes watching them. Their owner shook his head, but did not follow them.

All the same when next he met Angmering he meant to twit him about what must be his newest conquest: it was the little *modiste,* no less, who had successfully held off every man who had made so much as a bow in her direction. Sandiman was not the only unfortunate who had felt the rough edge of her tongue. One wondered what spell Angmering had cast on her that she could look so trustingly up at him.

Marcus had, as he had promised, behaved himself on their little excursion, though, God knows, he had been hard put to do so! He was equally well-behaved as he drank tea and talked about the clown, Grimaldi, who like Madame Félice he had seen performing at Sadler's Wells.

She was too young, she said, to have been taken to see the precocious Master Betty, who had entertained London for a short time nearly eight years ago, before the notion of seeing a young boy impersonate Shakespearian heroes had palled.

'So,' Marcus exclaimed, 'we have another common love: the theatre. If it were not that we might be seen I should be happy to escort you there one evening. It's a pity we don't live in the middle of the last century when you could have worn a mask without comment—but as it is...' and he grimaced.

Louise thought it a pity, too, but did not say so; she felt it best not to offer Marcus too much of herself. The more she was with him, the more she liked him—she dare not use the word love any more than Marcus did, for to do so might launch them into unknown territory.

'And I may come again next week?' he asked her before he left for home, having taken her hand and kissed the back of it, an apparently innocent action which had both parties asking themselves before they parted what it was about the other which affected them so strongly.

Louise asked herself the most questions about this. She was not so knowing as Marcus was. No man had ever roused her, and her late husband had treated her so roughly that she had no notion of the profound influence which the presence of a member of the opposite sex could have upon her body. Other than revulsion, that was, she had experienced a great deal of that!

Now with Marcus all was different. The day seemed to brighten when she was with him; for him to touch her, even lightly, was to awaken strange sensations whose origin was a mystery to her.

No novel she had ever read had spoken of such things. All was decorous. Men and women might banter with one another, but these other stirrings which were affecting her so strongly were never mentioned. For the first time she could understand why women could be seduced by love, for not only the man, but their body also, was betraying them.

So even though she said, 'Yes, indeed,' to his wish to visit her on the next Saturday, she told herself firmly, once the door shut behind him, to be sure to go carefully with him, for the biggest traitor in her camp of virtue was none other than herself!

Marcus found himself at something of a loose end. Back at his country home there was always something for him to do, some problem to solve, some decision to make, some friends to visit or go riding with.

Here in London, though, the days passed in unchanging idleness. He could see why many of his contemporaries drank, gambled and wenched so much—they had little else to do. There was a limit to the length of time that he could sit and read a book, however improving. If he were compelled to live here permanently, he told himself that he would find something interesting to pursue—set up a laboratory, experiment with velocipedes, or study in detail the theory of scientific farming.

Or he might go in for being a diplomat, like Lord Granville Leveson Gower, which was a bit of a joke seeing how undiplomatic he usually was! Or become an MP. Anything would be better than doing nothing. As it was, since he would shortly be returning to the north where he was both happy and useful, he hadn't the time to start anything new.

Wednesday morning thus saw him decide to visit Gentleman Jackson's gymnasium at 13 Bond Street. This also had the advantage of not being far from Madame Félice's work rooms, which gave him the added bonus of perhaps catching a glimpse of her. He could scarcely wait for the weekend to come round again when he might be with her—but he had given his word of honour not to badger her, so he must try to distract himself with other activities, preferably physical ones.

Jackson's was crowded when he reached there.

Among the men present, some already changed to
spar with one of his bruisers, were Sharnbrook, his
sister's future husband, and Jack Perceval. Jack was
busy towelling himself off. He waved at Marcus
when he saw him, and mouthed something incomprehensible in his direction.

Marcus shrugged and sat down, and waited for
the Gentleman, who was busy, to attend on him.
Jackson was something of a friend, for he respected
Marcus's straightforward approach to life, as well as
his good left hook. He was not one of those who
played at being a bruiser—he worked at it on the
few occasions he was in London.

This sitting about, though, left him a target for
Jack, who accosted him cheerfully while Marcus
was talking to Sharnbrook.

'You're a downy bird, Angmering, and no mistake! How the devil did you get that haughty piece
to eat out of your hand while the rest of us were
trying to persuade her to look in our direction, not
arm in arm it with her down the King's Road and
the Embankment?'

Marcus gave Jack a look which ought to have
slain him at ten paces, but didn't.

'Don't know what you mean, old fellow.'

The words 'old fellow' sounded as though they
were a curse, which Marcus meant them to do. It
was a wretched nuisance that one of the Ton's
greatest gossips should have seen him with Madame

in Chelsea—and what the devil was Jack Perceval doing there, anyway?

Jack put his finger by his nose. 'Oh, damn that for a tale, Angmering. Were you, or were you not, squiring that pretty little filly Madame Félice in Chelsea last weekend—or have you both acquired doubles?' He gave a great bellow of laughter as he ended.

Marcus could feel Sharnbrook's knowing eyes on him. Since his relationship with Madame was an innocent one he was feeling something strange—that, for once, he was an aggrieved party. He was also feeling something else strange, and savage—that he would like to plant a real facer on Jack Perceval's inadequate chin to teach him not to take a virtuous woman's name in vain. Marcus had thought that Jack had become his friend and would thus have the decency to keep quiet about what he had seen. On the other hand, though, he supposed gloomily that the temptation to pass on such a rare piece of gossip was too great for him.

Well, he would make sure that Jack would keep silent, for the thought of the knowing laughter and the hilarity about Madame's supposed fall from grace was too much for him to contemplate.

So, he rose, leaned forward, took hold of the towel which was now round Jack's neck, and using both his hands, tightened it gently, while saying, 'What do I have to do, Perceval, to stop you from jeering in public about a woman who has never behaved in such a manner that you have the right to doubt her virtue—and mine—come to that? What would it take, Perceval?' and he tightened the towel a little further as though he intended to use it as a garrotte.

He had no notion of how savage he looked when coming out with this. His face white, Jack spluttered, 'Come off it, Angmering, I didn't mean anything you know—only the give and take we all go in for, you must know that.'

'No, I don't know it, Perceval, and I'll thank you not to blow smoke on any woman's good name when I'm present. Just tell me you won't do so again, and I'll not twist your head off its shoulders.'

Sharnbrook put a hand on Marcus's arm. 'Steady on, old fellow. Don't threaten to murder poor Jack because he's a bit of an idiot. We all know that, don't we, Jack?'

'Yes, but does *he* know it?'

'He does now,' grinned Sharnbrook. 'Say pretty please, I'll be a good chap in future, and Angmering will let you go, won't you?' and he tightened his grip on Marcus's arm.

Reluctantly Marcus released the stutteringly apologetic Jack, dropping his hands, just as the Gentleman came over, saying in his quiet way, 'Now gentleman, no brawling, please, reserve that for the ring. As for you, Mr Perceval, you should be aware by now that I have a rule that we don't tattle about the fair sex in here. Remember that in future.'

'I didn't mean anything by it,' grumbled Jack, his head bent.

'In that case, sir, if you didn't, best not to say anything, eh?'

On that the Gentleman left them, leading Sharnbrook away. He said quietly to him while he laced the gloves on to the Duke's hands, 'I never thought m'lord Angmering had such a short fuse. He's always struck me as the easy-going kind.'

'Oh, where women are concerned,' returned Sharnbrook, falling into a fighting pose, 'we've all got short fuses. Depend upon it, Angmering is in a bad way—and for the first time, I would hazard. And now, let's to work.'

Unaware that, for the first time, she had become the public target of unkind gossip, Louise was working on Sophia Cleeve's trousseau. She had cut out the wedding gown herself, and was busy basting the skirt together when the girl in the shop came in to tell her that the Bow Street Runner was back, asking to see her again.

'Again!' exclaimed Louise, almost sticking a pin into her hand rather than the pin-cushion, so shocked was she by Jackson's return. She had thought to see the last of him, and didn't relish yet another session of polite verbal fencing.

On the other hand, to refuse to see him might look too particular.

'Tell him he may interview me in my office at the back. I'll go there immediately.'

She had no wish to see the man in public with her girls' curious eyes on her. When Jackson finally walked in she said frostily, 'I do hope that you have a good reason for coming here again, Mr Jackson. My good name will suffer if it becomes known that I am constantly being questioned by a prominent thief-taker.'

'Sorry about that, madame,' said Jackson, not looking sorry at all. 'But I am trying to tie some loose ends up, that's all. It's about your early days at Steepwood. I think we've established that you didn't meet the Marchioness when she was living there with her husband—or did we? I think you also said that you knew Miss Filmer, I mean Mrs Cameron, when you were girls together. Correct me if I am wrong.'

'You are not wrong,' said Louise, still frosty. 'Is that all that you've come to say? If so, you might have saved yourself the visit.'

Jackson pulled a grubby piece of paper out of his pocket and stared at it, before scratching his head, and muttering, 'Ah, yes, that's it. What I didn't ask you was whether *you* met the Marchioness when she was a little girl—Louise Hanslope by name—when you were also Mrs Cameron's playmate. One might suppose that you did. If so, perhaps you could give me a description of her. You see, it's an odd thing, but few people seem to have seen her, and what they remember ain't much.'

'You're asking me if I remember a little girl whom I must have last seen years ago in the hope that it might help you to trace a grown woman? I find that even odder than people not being able to remember a woman whom they have rarely seen. No, I cannot remember meeting her, never mind remembering what she looked like.'

What was beginning to frighten her was that Jackson was starting to ferret out the connection between little Louise Hanslope, the missing Marchioness and Madame Félice. His next question proved that she was right to be troubled.

'Well, there is another possible connection, madame. You see, I recently learned, quite by accident, you understand, that Louise Hanslope left the district when still almost a child, to be apprenticed to a dressmaker. You being in that line of business yourself, I wondered if you had ever come across her?'

Oh, yes, the man was more than a ferret, he was a bloodhound: a bloodhound who was threatening the safe life she had built for herself.

'May I ask where this child was apprenticed, Mr Jackson?'

He inspected his grubby piece of paper again.

'In Northampton, as I understand.'

'Northampton!' Louise began to laugh, something which she found difficult to control, for hysteria was threatening. 'No, I have never met the lady—my apprenticeship was elsewhere. I'm afraid that I cannot be of any assistance to you.'

Jackson stuffed his piece of paper into his pocket. 'Pity, that. I wouldn't have troubled you, if it weren't that I seem to be coming up against a brick wall where the lady is concerned. You must forgive me for bothering you again, but I have to inspect every avenue which might lead me to her.'

'Oh, yes, I do understand that. Will that be all?'

Jackson did not immediately answer her. He made for the door, but before he laid his hand on the knob, he turned and said in an off-hand voice, 'I'm not sure. I hope not to come back to you again, but there is one thing which still puzzles me.'

'Pray what is that, Mr Jackson?' This question was wrung from her, for she did not really want to know the answer since she might not like it. She had become suddenly sure that the man suspected something and was baiting her.

'One of the teachers at Mrs Guarding's school remembered that little Louise was very proficient in French for one so young—that was why I thought that you might—' he paused as though searching for a word, came out triumphantly with '—that you might know her—seeing that you are French yourself. However, seeing that you tell me that you don't, then that cock won't fight, will it? If you'll pardon the expression.'

He still showed no signs of leaving. Louise said, as coolly as she could. 'Will that really be all this

time, Mr Jackson? I am a very busy woman, with
several trousseaus to complete. So far as I am concerned, gossip about the distant past is an unwanted
luxury.'

Jackson's smile for her was that of a tiger contemplating its prey.

'All for today, I think, Madame. Good afternoon
to you, I will see myself out.'

Louise sank down into a chair and put her hot
face into her hands. He knows! Or he suspects, that
I am the Marchioness—but he cannot prove it yet.

When, and if, he can, what then?

Never mind that I can prove that I couldn't have
killed my late, unlamented husband, the scandal
which would follow such an unmasking would be
my ruin.

Chapter Four

'**O**h, dear, Madame,' said Cardew, the Yardleys' butler, 'I regret to have to tell you that m'lady and Lady Sophia are not yet ready for you. They send you their apologies, but they had an unexpected visitor this morning, and are at present enjoying a very late nuncheon. They asked if you would kindly agree to wait for them in the picture gallery, where they have sent you coffee and ratafia biscuits. Your footmen and maid are welcome to eat in the kitchen.'

The butler's expression showed what he thought of visitors who were inconsiderate enough to arrive in the morning, and with exquisite courtesy he led Madame to the picture gallery. This was a grand name for a long corridor lined with family portraits and some dated landscape paintings. Sure enough, there was a low table waiting for her with the promised coffee and biscuits on it.

Louise sat down, drank the coffee, which a watching footman considerately poured for her, and nibbled at the biscuits before deciding to pass the time by inspecting the paintings. She gave a cursory glance at the landscapes, which were conventional in the extreme, before she passed on to examine the portraits of past members of the Cleeve family, which included some going back for more than two hundred years. After all, they were her relatives, and it would be nice to know what they looked like, and if she resembled them in any way.

She had just reached a section devoted to some of their wives when the door at the far end opened and Marcus entered. She was so engrossed in inspecting all her unknown ancestors that she did not hear him...

Marcus had spent the morning discussing his future with his father. It was the first fruits of their reconciliation and the two men were easier with each other than they had ever been.

'I want to continue to live at Jaffrey House,' his father had said. 'It is more my home than the Abbey ever was. On the other hand I am determined to restore the Abbey to its former glory, which will mean a fair amount of restoration and rebuilding. Sywell looted it of the little furniture that was left and consequently the interior looks more like a dog kennel than the ancestral home it ought to be.

'My present secretary and librarian tells me that a curse was put on Steepwoods thousands of years ago, by the pagans who created the Sacred Grove and the rune stone. All those who came after them who failed to worship the stone, but followed false Gods, would be doomed to perpetual unhappiness and ruin. Steepwood's chequered history, he said, seemed to bear out the existence of the curse.

'First the Abbey founded here was dissolved and ruined, and every owner of it, all the way down the centuries, lived a tragic life, including Sywell who met with a terrible end. So I am inclined to agree with him that there was such an unlikely thing as a curse, and that it has persisted right down to the present day. Bearing that in mind, I am going to ask you to think carefully about a proposal which I am about to make to you, for that proposal involves the ownership of the Abbey.

'The local landowner who bought much of the Abbey's lands from Sywell has fallen heavily into debt and has asked me to buy them back, to which I have agreed. They will, however, need a great deal of work done with them before they become profitable again. Since you have made such a good fist of restoring the northern estates I am going to ask you to take on the task of doing the same thing for Steepwood's. At the same time you could begin to renovate the Abbey with a view to making it your permanent residence when I am gone to my last rest.

'Jaffrey House could then be the home of the dowager—but such decisions will, of course, be yours to make in the future, not mine. You need not give me an answer immediately, but I would like one soon. Such an ambitious project will have the merit of making work for the local people, and when it is finished will provide permanent employment for the large staff needed to run it.'

Marcus had stared at his father. 'You are sure that you want to do this, father? One might have thought that after waiting so long to regain the Abbey you would wish to begin its restoration yourself.'

His father had shaken his head. 'I am too old, Angmering. I am over seventy and wish to secure the family's future, by giving you *carte blanche* in this matter, since you have proved how responsible you are over and over again. Think of it as reparation for my neglect of you in the past. It is my hope that you will soon marry and settle yourself and your wife at Steepwood as soon as possible. But I also thought that you ought to know of the curse before you make your decision.'

Marcus's immediate response had been to refuse, and then he thought that, after all, his work in Northumbria was done. He could employ a good agent there to run the reformed and rescued lands. Here he had been thinking that he might need occupation and his father was giving him the opportunity of a lifetime—to restore the neglect of centuries, for previous Earls of Yardley had been careless of the land.

As for the curse, he thought nothing of that. He was a true child of the Enlightenment, which had rejected such medieval notions, and possible fear of it would play no part in his decision-making.

His father had again spoken of him taking a wife, and for the first time Marcus did not reject the notion out of hand. A wife would be a great help when the time came to refurnish the Abbey—otherwise he would be entirely in the hands of the furniture makers, bibelot sellers and upholsterers, would he not? He could imagine Félice running round with bolts of cloth, inspecting carpets and mirrors and... His stepmother had told him that her taste was impeccable.

He became aware that his father was expecting some sort of answer from him. He would give him one, and one which he hoped would prove acceptable.

'I cannot say that you have done other than surprise me,' he said at last. 'A month ago I might have given you a different answer. All I can tell you at the moment is that I am inclined to agree to what you wish, but I would like a few days to think it over. You know me, Father. I need to consider a proposition as grand as this carefully, not rush into it without thought.'

'Agreed, Angmering,' said his father. 'But pray do not take too long before you give me your final answer. I am an old man, and I would like to know that I am leaving a sound ship behind me before I finally hand it on to a new captain.'

They had talked of minor matters before his father

left him to visit Whitehall. Marcus made his way downstairs, where he met Cardew in the Entrance Hall. He had always believed that servants knew more about their masters than their masters thought that they did, and Cardew promptly proceeded to prove him right.

'Ah, m'lord, a word with you,' he said. 'M'lady and Lady Sophia have taken their nuncheon late to-day and have asked the *modiste* who has arrived for a fitting to wait for them in the picture gallery, where I have provided her with coffee and biscuits.'

He paused, looking as though he expected some kind of response.

Marcus said, a trifle impatiently—his mind was full of his recent conversation with his father. 'And, Cardew, and? There must be a point to this.'

'Oh, m'lord, just that I thought that you might like to know that Madame Félice is here.'

'Did you, indeed?' And of course the man was right, but damn everything, how did *he* know that Lord Angmering was greatly taken with the *modiste?* Did the whole world know—and how?

Marcus decided not to try to find out. He said instead, 'Thank you for that useful information, Cardew. Tell me, do you think that Madame might care to make me a shirt?'

He had succeeded in rattling the perfect servant— but not for long. Cardew smiled and said, 'Oh, m'lord, I am sure that you could find that out for yourself,' and walked away, cat-footed.

Well, well, well, why not take the hint and visit Madame—since there were no secrets in the Cleeve household he might as well take this splendid opportunity to be alone with her—quite respectably.

He ran lightly back upstairs, and turned on the first landing towards the door which led to the picture gallery. He pushed it open to see Félice standing about halfway along it, looking up at a portrait of his great-great aunt, Adelaide Cleeve.

She had not heard him arrive, and he remained where he was to study her at leisure. She had her head tipped back and was inspecting the painting with the care with which she did everything. A wall lamp threw a halo of light on her head—and in that moment two things happened.

The first was that he knew that firm little chin— and now he knew where he had seen it before. On a child in the woods at Steepwood who, when he had bandaged her leg, had thrust that same determined chin at him, and had said, 'I am not a coward, boy, even if I am a girl!' A child who had been with Athene Filmer and about whom Jackson had been so recently questioning him.

As if that were not strange enough, the second thing which struck him was bizarre in the extreme. For the living and vibrant woman standing in the corridor and the long dead one whose painted face was hanging on the wall were so alike that they might have been twins.

He could not doubt that Madame Félice was no

Frenchwoman, but was little Louise Hanslope grown up, the Louise Hanslope who had become Sywell's Marchioness—and what would Jackson make of *that?* And what did he, Marcus Cleeve, Lord Angmering, the Earl of Yardley's heir, make of a woman who bore the face and colouring of the Cleeves—and why on earth had he never noticed that before?

He was dumbstruck, until Louise moved and, moving, saw him. He thought that the expression on her face might match that on his own, since it was one of complete and utter disbelief.

They stared at one another. Marcus was the first to move. He said, and his voice sounded hollow in his ears.

'I've seen you before, haven't I? Years ago.'

He had not meant to say any such thing. He was aware that it sounded like an accusation, but he could not help himself, the shock was too great.

Louise genuinely had no notion to what he was referring. All she could think to say was, 'Why? Why do you think that? How could you have seen me?' The expression on his face shocked her. She had wanted to be playful—as she usually was with him, to come out with something like, 'My dear Mr Marks, whatever can you mean?' but the words had stuck in her throat.

Marcus was so surprised that he scarcely knew to which puzzle to address himself. The puzzle of discovering that Madame Félice was almost certainly

Louise Hanslope—and all that that implied—or the other puzzle, that of her likeness to his female ancestor.

'Are you telling me that you do not remember having met me before?' he finally said, aware how inadequate such a lame response was.

'Not to my knowledge,' Louise said. 'Why do you think that we have?'

Something about his expression was beginning to alarm her. The discovery of her likeness to Adelaide Cleeve had not frightened her—but the thought of Marcus's response to it had. His claim that they had met before was a mysterious one, and she needed to know why he had made it. The rapport which had been growing up between them was near to shattering—if it were not shattered already.

'You really do not remember?'

To be fair, he thought, perhaps, she didn't. After all, she must have been very young, and although a young girl might, as she grew older, retain a likeness to the child she had been, a boy was likely to change completely in looks between the age of fourteen and thirty.

'It was at Steepwood,' he said. 'I was out walking and met you there one afternoon when you were still a child. I am not sure how old you were. You were with Athene Filmer, and you tripped and fell, cutting your knee. I used my handkerchief to bind it. I remember I asked you not to cry, and I believe you said something to the effect that you weren't a coward—I can't remember the exact words.'

He saw her face change even as he spoke. Louise's memory of the incident was a faint one, but it was there, waiting to be called into existence by some accident, some trick of fate.

'*You* were that boy? I remember, dimly, something like that happening—but you do not resemble in the least the boy who helped me. I should never have known you, and even now it is only because you have told me of the incident that I can believe it was you. Why are you looking at me like that, m'lord?'

'Mr Marks,' Marcus said, automatically. 'I am Mr Marks to you, remember.'

'Not here,' she said. 'Not now. And something else is troubling you, isn't it?'

'Many things,' he said. 'That you are not French, that, if I am right, you are Louise Hanslope and Sywell's widow, and that you have said nothing to me of this—nor to Jackson, either. Why? Why the secrecy? From what I have heard, and what I know of you, it is most unlikely that any accusation that you murdered Sywell could possibly stand...'

He ran out of breath.

'Well, m'lord,' said Louise, seeing her bittersweet affair with Mr Marks dying before her, 'I'm happy that you are willing to concede that I am no murderess, which I assure you that I am not. But I must say again that something else is troubling you, and I am asking you what that is?'

'You know,' he said—and pointed to the portrait before which they were both now standing. 'It is this—that if you are Louise Hanslope it beggars belief that you have the face of Adelaide Cleeve. How many mysteries are you concealing, Madame Félice—and why?'

'Oh,' Louise said, bitter regret consuming her that he should find out her secrets in this fashion, and furiously aware that he, one day to be the lord of all, who lived out his cushioned life in luxury, should be so ignorant of the hard and difficult lives of the lowly, among whom she had been thrown to live by cruel chance.

'What can such a poor creature as I am do, m'lord, when I face ruin at every turn if my true identity is revealed, but protect myself in the only way I can. If Jackson discovers that I am Louise Hanslope, the missing Marchioness, and makes it known to the world, what price my peace of mind, and the business which I have built up with such care? What would be left to me in order to survive, but to accept your dishonourable offer, and when you grow tired of me, sink down as so many women do, to a short and disgraceful life?'

'No,' said Marcus, trying to take her into his arms. 'Trust me a little—tell me Louise Hanslope's history, and tell me—if you know—why you look like my family, the Cleeves.'

Could she trust him? Must she trust him? It seemed that she had no alternative but to do so. What was she to do for the best?

Louise looked up and saw Mr Marks again. Something she had said had changed him. The look of accusation had left his face, and if she saw only pity there, then that was better than anger, was it not?

'I should speak to you of this, m'lord, and will do so. I will not apologise for what I have done, but I will explain why I have kept my secrets from a harsh world. After that, if you wish you may judge me and leave me, if what I have done disgusts you.

'But we cannot speak of it here, not now. Lady Yardley and Lady Sophia will be with me at any moment, and I have a commission to fulfil. The world's work does not stop because M'lord Angmering needs some answers to his questions. I will take the day off tomorrow—I was thinking of doing so, and Mr Marks may visit me in Chelsea if he will leave Lord Angmering at home.'

Oh, she was a gallant creature, if a devious one, and he would agree to do as she wished, because she was the woman he had hoped to meet and he could not, must not, lose her now.

Louise could not sleep that night. She had managed to go through her dressmaking duties with the Countess and her daughter without betraying the distress which had inevitably followed her unmasking.

She had known that Marcus was clever, but not how clever. Clever enough, once he had recognised her—and that after so many years—to grasp at once who she might be. That it was unlikely—as Jackson must also think—that lonely Athene Filmer had had two young friends, not one, and that that friend must be the lost Marchioness.

The only thing which he had not pursued was why she was so like the Cleeves, and if she were going to tell him the truth about Louise Hanslope and how she came to marry, and then desert, Sywell, she also owed him the duty of telling him the most amazing truth of all—who she really was.

And that would be her biggest problem. The problem which kept her awake that night. For would he believe the truth? Or would he think that she was inventing it to claim a name and a lineage which were not hers. However difficult that might be, though, she must bite the bullet. She could not deceive him further if she were to retain his respect, never mind his love.

She might mock him by calling him Mr Marks, she might hold him off when he wished to make her his mistress, she might deny to him that he meant very much to her, but she could not deny the biggest truth of all: that she loved him.

The kind boy who had bandaged her damaged knee had turned into a strong and kind man—however bluff he was to those around him, his essential goodness shone through. She had no idea of how much Marcus's hard life had made him the sterling man he was, but she knew that man and knew him well.

Despite that she would never be his doxy, his light of love, however much she loved him. For she would be as true to herself as he was to himself, and what would follow from that, only time would tell. Worse than that, who and what she was, and what he would learn of her, might stand in the way of their happiness.

Trust me, he had said, and no one had ever said that to her before.

Consequently, on the following morning, she awaited his arrival in a fever of anticipation. She had thought that he might adhere to the code of conduct which said that the quality did not call in the morning, but, as she ought to have guessed, no such thing. Mr Marks and Marcus, Lord Angmering, made up their own rules.

He had been considerate enough to allow her time to breakfast, but the moment that the French clock on her mantelpiece tinkled out eleven, he was at her door. He was very much Mr Marks, simply dressed, as usual, so as not to attract attention: he might have been a lawyer's clerk, and Louise fleetingly wondered what his valet made of him.

She was not to know that he was his valet's despair. He had once dressed his master in a white satin court suit, and had occasionally kitted him out as a dandy, but was more likely to have to help him into the clothes of a labourer, or a gamekeeper when he was running his father's northern estates.

Louise felt awkward when the little maid showed him in, but she might have guessed that Marcus's manner to her would be unchanged.

His bow was as deep as ever. He accepted the glass of Madeira which she offered him as though this was simply a courtesy call, not a ritual during which Louise would make a full confession to him. He was not yet to know how full and surprising that confession would be, but he would not allow it to change the loving consideration with which he had always treated her until that fatal moment when he had seen her in the picture gallery.

For a moment they sat facing one another, speaking of banalities: the weather, that her session with Sophia and her mother the previous afternoon had been a successful one. Louise thought that Marcus's face was a little shadowed as though he, too, had passed a bad night, but she said nothing of that.

Finally, their conversation ran down. Louise put down her glass, from which she had drunk little, and began, 'M'lord—'

'Mr Marks,' he said. 'Here I am Mr Marks.'

'Very well, Mr Marks. I said that I would tell you the truth about the life of Louise Hanslope whom you have known as Madame Félice, and however much it pains me to relive it, it is my duty to you, and to the truth, to reveal everything. First of all I must tell you that Louise Hanslope is no more my real name than that of Madame Félice Morisot is. If, when I tell you my true name, you wish to leave and to forget that you ever knew me, I shall quite understand. It is a risk which I must take.'

She paused, not knowing how to continue.

Marcus said, gently, 'It is a risk which I must take also. But it is not, I think, a great one.'

'So you say now, not knowing it. When you have heard me out, you may think differently.'

'That's as maybe,' said Marcus gravely. 'But first, tell me your story and allow me to be the best judge of how I react to it.'

'Very well, but before I begin you must understand that some of what I shall be telling you was told to me. John Hanslope was not my father. He was first the bailiff of the Earl of Yardley who lost the Abbey, and then of the Marquis of Sywell who cheated him out of it. Consequently he knew the family well, and in particular Lord Rupert Cleeve, who was, of course, your distant relative. He ought more properly to have been known as Lord Angmering, but for some reason of which I am unaware, preferred not to be.

'It seems that Lord Rupert, to the anger of his father, the Earl, married a French lady, Marie de Ferrers, who was a Catholic. The Earl repudiated him and forbade him the house. He even suggested that since the lady was a Catholic their marriage was not a legal one. Lord Rupert, however, told the bailiff when he left his wife and child—a little girl—

with him, while he looked for a home for them, that
the marriage was legal.

'This is the difficult part of my story, for the little
girl was none other than myself, Louise Cleeve. I
cannot, of course, remember any of this, for I was
only a baby then.'

Marcus gave a short exclamation. Louise, her
eyes wide and troubled, stopped, but he waved her
on.

'John told me later that my father returned and
took us away. He later discovered that he left my
mother in Cheltenham while he went back to France
to recover her inheritance. This was of course, all
taking place after the French Revolution had started.
My father had quarrelled with my grandfather over
that as well. He was at first very sympathetic towards the revolutionaries. Later, when the Terror began he changed his mind. Unfortunately he became
trapped in France and died there, exactly how, no
one knew.

'So Lord Rupert, my father, never returned from
France. John never learned whether he met my
mother's family again—or even whether they had
also died in the Terror as so many aristocrats did.'

'Which, of course,' interjected Marcus, 'means
that if your story is true you are, by rights, the
Honourable Miss Louise Cleeve.'

Louise nodded and continued. 'John heard nothing more from Lord Rupert or his wife, although he
tried to trace them, until he received a letter from

my mother telling him of my father's death in France, and that she was living in great poverty in Cheltenham and was dying. She begged him to help her for the sake of her child, myself. She had not approached the Earl for assistance because she didn't want him to have the care of her Catholic-bred child. She was unaware that he had already died, and that your father, a distant cousin, had inherited the title.

'John immediately drove to Cheltenham and reached us in time to be present at my mother's death.'

Her voice faltered. She swallowed tears, before saying, 'I can just remember her death and John arriving, but only after a jumbled fashion. I have, of course, no memory of my father. Before she died my mother begged John to adopt me, for he too was a Catholic, and also to ensure that, as soon as possible, I took my rightful place in the world. He agreed and took me to Steepwood. Unfortunately my guardian, as John Hanslope became, could find no proof that my father and mother had ever married. He could only assume that they had done so in France, although from something that Lord Rupert had once said to him it seemed that they might have been married in England, after all.

'Lacking proof, the Hanslopes brought me up as their own, since they could find no evidence of my legitimacy and would even have found it difficult to prove that I was an illegitimate child of the Cleeves.

Mrs Hanslope had been a governess in a French family, spoke French well, and taught me the language from infancy. She also gave me an excellent education. I had no notion at this time that I was Louise Cleeve. I assumed that my parents had bequeathed me to my guardian and his wife because my true family was poor. It was only years later that John—my father as I called him then—told me the truth.'

Marcus had said nothing while this remarkable story was unfolded. Louise looked across at him and said, 'It is like a Gothic novel, is it not? Something out of one of Mrs Radcliffe's tales. I can quite understand why my guardian did not wish to subject me to the scandal and unpleasantness of proving my birth when I had no evidence to support it.'

'If this story is true,' murmured Marcus, 'and I can see that you believe it is, I still fail to understand why, when my father returned from India, the Hanslopes did not contact him and inform him of your existence.'

'By the time he returned it was too late. Mrs Hanslope had died, the Marquis of Sywell had taken up permanent residence at the Abbey, and since I had always enjoyed dressmaking John apprenticed me to a French sempstress, an *emigré* who had moved to Northampton where she worked for the nobility and gentry. She thought that I had real talent and wished to recommend me to another French dressmaker in London. Before I could move there,

I returned to the Abbey to visit my guardian who was dying.'

She gave a sad little laugh. 'It seemed that I was doomed to lose everyone I loved. Just before he died I met Lord Sywell. He was not quite the debauched wreck he afterwards became and still possessed some of the charm which I understand was his in youth. He became obsessed with me, and of all things offered me marriage. I refused him at first, but when I told my guardian he urged me to accept him.

'It was then that he first told me that I was Lord Rupert's child but that I had no means of proving that I was a Cleeve or that I was legitimate. He said that by marrying Sywell I could regain my place in society and that if I had a child, the Cleeves would have returned to the Abbey which they had lost. Remember that I was very young and innocent and that I was about to lose the last person in the world who could be called my family. I was shortly to be left quite alone. I shall never know why Sywell did not simply take me by force and make me his mistress—but he was a man of great caprice and perhaps it amused him to marry a bailiff's daughter. By then, of course, no genteel family would have allowed their daughter to marry him.

'So, we were married, and it was the worst thing which I could have done. I will not weary you with the story of my life with him. Suffice it to say that it was one long agony. Fortunately for me I was,

from my wedding day, his wife in name only, which
did not prevent him from tormenting me in other
ways. Only my renewed friendship with Athene
Filmer saved my sanity. Finally, one day, I decided
to run away to try my fortune in London, as my old
mistress had suggested. I shall always wonder why
he married me at all.

'I felt no compunction about robbing Sywell of
both money and jewellery before I left; he owed me
that as compensation for the ill-treatment which I
had endured from him. I used it to set up my business, of which you know. That, Lord Angmering, is
my story, and whether you consider me to be deluded, an impostor, or even the true descendant of
the Cleeves, either legitimate or illegitimate, is your
choice to make, since I have no proof to offer that
any of my sad tale is true—other than that I am
Sywell's widow and John Hanslope's adopted
child.'

Silence fell in the pretty little room. Marcus had
listened to Louise's sad tale first with interest, mixed
up with an element of disbelief, and then with shock
when she had spoken so measuredly of her dreadful
life with Sywell.

'One thing is sure, though,' he said at last. 'You
have the face of the female Cleeves of the elder
branch—of which, if you speak true, and I think that
you do—you are the last twig. The women of my
father's line are different in appearance, which was
why I did not at first recognise you for what you

are. It took the portrait of Lady Adelaide Cleeve to do that.'

Louise gave a half-laugh. 'Legitimate—or illegitimate—who is to know which at this late date?'

'Nevertheless,' said Marcus. 'Nothing has changed between us. Your honesty impresses me. Many in your position would have brazenly claimed legitimacy, but you have laid out the few facts of your past with an impartial clarity which would be applauded in a court of law. Whatever else, it seems that we are quite distant cousins. I can only wish that you were more than a cousin to me.'

Louise's heart gave a great leap. She was not to lose him—as she had thought possible.

'The thing is,' he went on, 'that while I can quite understand your desire to remain anonymous so far as this Sywell business is concerned, I think that your guardian, despite his care of you, did you few favours by not trying harder to establish your legitimacy—or rather by giving up the hunt so soon. He also did you the worst disservice by encouraging your marriage to Sywell.'

'All that may be true in hindsight,' said Louise. 'But now that you know my story, what do you intend to do about it?'

'Well, I shall certainly not broadcast it around London, you may be sure of that,' he told her. 'I don't believe that you murdered Sywell. I am sure that you can prove that you were safely here in London when he was killed. Nor has it changed my opinion of you. On the contrary, I am full of admiration for your resourcefulness, Louise. I hope that I may call you that. Madame Félice has suddenly become a figment, a fairy-tale figure behind which Louise Cleeve—or Hanslope—takes refuge.'

So he did understand. He had not called her Louise Cleeve, the daughter of a man who was properly a Viscount, but she never thought of herself as that. The Honourable Louise Cleeve was someone in a romance as she had earlier said, not the down-to-earth woman who made dresses.

Her eyes filled with tears. 'I am so relieved that you do not think me a liar,' she murmured. 'I would never have told you any of this if you had not seen my resemblance to the portrait in Berkeley Square.'

Marcus rose and came over to where she sat. He went down on one knee beside her, and touched her hand to try to reassure her. The look of pain on her face was affecting him strongly.

'My dear,' he said, lifting her hand and kissing it, although to do so was temptation itself, but only a cur would assail her with his love when she was so greatly distressed, 'my dear, you have been carrying such a monstrous burden for so long that I am amazed at the fortitude with which you have faced life. You have my deepest admiration. Now, I am going to ask you to allow me to do something to help you. I would like to consult Jackson, the ex-Runner, about your past, and ask him to try to find the proofs of your parents' marriage and your own birth. I would charge him to do so in the strictest confidence—which I am sure that he would honour.'

'No, indeed not. I do not wish anyone other than yourself to know this. My secrets must remain secrets.'

'Consider this, my dearest heart. In fairness to my father and myself, we must attempt to discover whether or not you are Louise Cleeve, the daughter of Lord Rupert Cleeve. That you might be makes no difference to the ownership of Steepwood, since the estate, like the title, was entailed on the male line. But you should not only take your rightful place in society, but you ought also to have the dowry which would rightly have been yours.'

'I don't want any of it,' she told him stubbornly. 'I am Louise Hanslope who is also Madame Félice, and that is all I wish to be. Even if this Sywell business were not hanging over me, I should still say the same. I don't want the whole world to gossip over my past.'

'To please me,' he said softly. 'You have suffered a great wrong—through no fault of me and mine, I own, but still a great wrong.'

He lifted himself a little and took her into his arms. The sensation was so sweet that Louise gave a low groan and almost surrendered to the light kisses he was favouring her cheek with until she stopped him by pulling away.

'No, Mr Marks, you are not to do that. It was not in our bargain. We are friends, not lovers.'

'But I want to be your friend and lover more than

ever now that I know that you are my distant cousin Louise. Say that you will allow me to speak to Jackson and permit him try to settle the matter once and for all.'

Louise shook her head. 'Mr Marks would obey me in this. Lord Angmering may do as he pleases. I cannot stop him, although I wish that I could.'

'You break my heart,' he whispered, but he made no attempt to take her in his arms again. She looked so desolate that all he wished to do was comfort her, and so he told her.

'And we both know how that might end,' she said sadly. 'There has been enough loose folly in the Cleeve family, enough members of it not troubling about tomorrow, without our adding to it. My father, and my grandfather between them brought me to this pass. Do not let us make matters worse.'

Marcus had to acknowledge the truth of this.

He bowed his head. He could not agree to what she wished, for he thought that later she might reconsider, when the shock of telling him her sad story had worn off.

So he said nothing, merely sat quietly and companionably at her feet hoping that his mere presence might calm her, and he thought that perhaps it did for he heard her breathing change.

Louise hardly knew herself. One part of her wanted to throw herself into Marcus's arms and forget everything she had ever lived by. In them she knew that she might find peace. But that peace would be temporary, and when the initial joy of her surrender was over she would be back from where she had started with nothing solved—and her honour surrendered.

The other part was thinking that she could not bear to confide in Jackson! The thought was horrible. She had learned early in life to trust no one and she certainly was not prepared to trust a predatory thief-taker. If she was doing him an injustice, then she would rather risk that than expose herself to the cruelly idle gossip which revelation of her true identity—whatever that was—would inevitably create.

She knew Marcus well enough to grasp that if he thought that it was in her interest to involve Jackson then he would not hesitate do so. He was plainly a man who was highly protective of anyone who was friend, family or lover. She would not plead with him, nor try to influence him, or play any of the womanly tricks to bend him to her will which she had seen other women employ.

Instead she finally said, rather drowsily, 'Mr Marks, have you no other duties to attend to?'

He looked up into her lovely face, admiring that firm and pretty chin from below. A chin which rightly told, not only of her strength of will, but also of her relationship with the senior branch of the Cleeves.

'None which is more important to me than caring for the woman I love. All else can wait—except...'

He did not finish and Louise said, a trifle ruefully, 'Except that you might wish to talk to Jackson as soon as possible. I would rather you did not.'

'It is in your interest,' he said simply.

Louise shrugged her shoulders. 'I find it difficult to believe that, after all these years, he could find something which my guardian could not.'

'Your guardian was not England's most experienced thief-taker and tracker-down of what many might think unconsidered trifles, and Jackson is.'

She had no answer to that, other than to change tack completely and ask, 'Would you care to stay and take nuncheon, Mr Marks?'

'With pleasure, Louise, my darling.'

So they ate nuncheon together before Marcus left, privately resolved to see Jackson immediately. It had taken all his strength for him to sit quietly opposite to her, eating and drinking when all the time what he really wanted to do was to take her in his arms and...

He told his body to behave itself and wondered if his love was feeling as calm as she looked. Did she burn for him as he burned for her? Was he overestimating her feelings for him? He hoped not.

What he did not know was that Louise's wish for him not to touch her owed everything to the fact that his mere touch was liable to undo her. Even the reverent kiss which he offered her hand when he left had the most powerful effect on her. If she had ever believed that she was a cold woman whom no man could affect, then meeting Marcus Angmering had taught her otherwise.

Chapter Five

Louise was not mistaken. Marcus had every intention of setting Jackson the task of trying to prove whether or not she was really Louise Cleeve. He made up his mind to visit the man at once, but he did not need to do so. He again entered Cleeve House to find Jackson on the point of leaving.

'You were looking for me?' he asked.

'No, I needed to speak to your pa again, but he is out.'

'Again?' queried Marcus, 'I thought that you were finished with him.'

'Oh, in my line of business we rarely finish with people until a crime is solved, and seeing that the Home Office are still urgent in this matter I must carry out my duty. Your pa's secretary has arranged an appointment for me. Now, what can I do for you, m'lord?—for I can see that your interest in me is most particular.'

Marcus gave a snort of laughter. 'Am I so transparent, or do you own a crystal ball, Jackson?'

'Oh, a man's manner tells many things about him, if one knows how to interpret it,' offered Jackson. 'No magic is needed there, m'lord.'

'Well, there's no denying it, I do wish to speak to you and urgently. But before I do so I must ask you to treat everything I am about to say to you with the utmost confidentiality—otherwise this interview is over.'

'You would wish me to buy a pig in a poke, m'lord? Come, come, that is not a possibility in my line of business.'

'Suppose half of what I am about to tell you would clear up one of your lines of enquiry in the Steepwood mystery, and that the other half has nothing to do with that—or the Home Office for that matter, what then? I am an honest man, Jackson, treat me as one and save yourself much future work.'

Jackson stared at him for some time without speaking before shrugging his shoulders and saying, 'Very well, m'lord—I trust that you are not bamming me because if you are—why then, look out, I say!'

'No bamming,' said Marcus. 'Now, come into the study, and I will tell you an interesting couple of stories.'

Jackson nodded. 'Very well, m'lord, but be short, I am a busy man.'

Marcus, as briefly as he could, began by telling him that Madame Félice had confessed to him that she was indeed Sywell's missing Marchioness, and also that she could prove conclusively from her shop accounts and the day-book her man of all work kept that she could not possibly have murdered her late husband, since she had been working in London at the critical time.

Jackson had fished his piece of paper out and was nodding over it while Marcus spoke. When he had finished, he said, 'Well, m'lord, you have confirmed what I already believed: that Madame *is* Sywell's widow and the friend of that pretty little fox, Miss Athene Filmer as was. They make a good pair. I already have reason to believe that Madame did not kill her husband and, furthermore, did not hire anyone else to do so.'

Marcus stared at him. 'Then, knowing this, why were you continuing to badger her?'

'Oh, dear, m'lord, you're a clever fellow. You ought to know that it's one thing for me to believe something, but until I have proof I have to continue to check and probe before going on to other lines which might lead nowhere because my belief was not correct. You follow me, I'm sure. Yes, we can write the lady off, but I would still wish her to tell me her story, not just have it at second-hand from you. Now, m'lord, what's the other problem you have?'

'Well, that concerns Madame, too,' and Marcus

recounted as plainly as he could the mystery of Louise's birth. 'What I would like you to do for me, if you would, is to try to trace any records which could prove, or disprove, her story.'

Jackson whistled. 'Interesting, m'lord, most interesting. So the guardian, you say—rather, she says—could find nothing at all. What she has told you might explain, if it is the truth, something about her marriage which has always puzzled me.'

He stopped and stared hard at Marcus. 'Think hard, m'lord—you are a man of the world—what is damned odd about the marriage, if you will pardon the expression.'

Marcus had never really thought about Sywell's marriage to the supposed daughter of his bailiff. If so, he might have concluded that it arose from a sort of whim on the part of a man whose judgement was already faulty. He was about to tell Jackson that when something else struck him.

He said slowly, working things out as he spoke, 'Sywell was a damned debauched rogue, and when he married was already impotent—so why did he marry her at all? He may have been a rogue but he wasn't a fool. He always looked after his own interests and be damned to everyone else. One might have spoken of it as softening of the brain, but are you thinking that there was more to it than that?'

'Aye, m'lord. You have just told me that Madame might be a Cleeve, part of the family which Sywell had spent his life destroying. Think, m'lord, think.

Hanslope might have given her secret away without meaning to, to Sywell himself or to his creature and by-blow, Burneck, who kept watch on everything for his master if he is to be believed. So, if the girl is a Cleeve, what a splendid joke it would be to marry her, in order to gloat over having a hold over yet another member of the family. What, too, if he knew of, or had acquired, evidence that would prove her identity? Imagine his delight in tormenting and maltreating her while he hugged that knowledge to him? Oh, yes, that marriage has always puzzled me—and I believe that I may have lighted on a possible explanation of its mystery.'

'It's a bit of a leap in logic,' said Marcus thoughtfully, 'but it jibes with what we know of Sywell.'

'Aye, that it does, and think, there may still be evidence in existence. Oh, yes, m'lord, I'll take on your commission. I've wanted to have another go at Burneck, the man's nearly as big an offence against nature as his late master, that he is. If I do find anything it won't solve Sywell's murder, but I believe I'm getting near to doing that as well.'

'And you will keep what I have told you confidential—about Madame being Sywell's widow?'

'Oh, indeed, she's out of the reckoning now, no need to put the poor lady into the way of more trouble.'

'Indeed,' said Marcus in a heartfelt voice. 'Her life has been one long trouble, it is time that she had some happiness in it, some relief from perpetual worry. Once she has told you her story, and you are happy with it, I would like you to inform her, if you would, that you will keep her secret and will not need to trouble her again.'

'Very well, m'lord. Leave matters to me.'

'Thank you,' said Marcus, shaking him by the hand but wondering wryly what Louise was going to think of him for having spoken to Jackson after all—even if the result was going to be that she was no longer suspected of having murdered Sywell. Perhaps she would forgive him when he told her that Jackson had agreed to try to trace the evidence that would bring her out of the shadows.

The only trouble was that if she were a Cleeve then his continual offers to make her his mistress must have seemed a gross insult to her, and he could scarcely continue to chase after that hare. On the other hand, and Marcus gave a slow grin at the mere idea: Why not make her my wife? After all, even before I knew that she was a Cleeve I was toying with the notion of offering for her.

I should lose my bet with Jack and look a boastful fool into the bargain—but what of that: I should be uniting the two branches of the family and gaining myself a nonpareil as well. Few women could have survived such a childhood and on top of that have managed to make themselves a tidy little fortune as well.

Yes, as soon as all this is safely behind us I shall make an offer for her, and settle down at last. The prospect so entranced him that walking upstairs he allowed the Two Neds to halloo by him without even noticing that they were there.

'Speak to Jackson again?' exclaimed Louise. 'But why? You have told him everything about me which concerns him.'

'He has his duty to do,' explained Marcus. 'What I told him was hearsay—yours will be direct evidence of which he can take due note.'

'And he will make nothing public, you say—no tattling to anyone of who Madame Félice really is.'

'He agreed to that, but my darling, you do realise that if he proves beyond a doubt that you are legally my cousin Rupert's daughter, that will inevitably have to be made known if you are to resume your true name.'

Louise shuddered. 'Will this never be over? I feel that I am walking through my life looking over my shoulder at what has gone before. I want, I need, a present and a future. I scarcely know what my true name is.'

They were on their way to Chelsea's autumn fair, not a venue where they might expect to meet anyone who knew them. Marcus was wearing his clerk's outfit and Louise looked like her little maid on an outing and did not resemble in the slightest that elegant *modiste,* Madame Félice. She was wearing a simple blue and white print dress, stout black shoes, a plain straw bonnet with a blue band, and an anonymous light shawl, for London and its outlying districts were experiencing an Indian summer, and the sun was hot upon them.

'I don't give a farthing for what your true name is,' Marcus declared. 'You are my dear Louise and that is quite enough for me.'

'But I do,' fretted Louise. 'After all, you have no need to worry about such things. You are Marcus Angmering, heir to that Lord of All, the Earl of Yardley, so you can afford to dismiss such matters as trifling. I, on the other hand, have no notion of whether I am legitimate or illegitimate, and I should dearly like to know which state I might claim to be. Even to be sure that I am neither a Cleeve nor legitimate would be better than not knowing whether I am fish, flesh, fowl or good red herring.'

Marcus gave a shout of laughter. 'All my favourite foods, my darling, so even less reason for you to worry. Now smile, we are on our way to enjoy ourselves and forget tomorrow. I have the notion that you have never had much enjoyment in your life and I intend to see that you have a plentiful supply of it in the future.'

This did bring a smile to her face. 'I'm sorry for being grumpy,' she said. 'And I suppose that, so long as he keeps to his promise to be confidential, you were right to speak to Jackson. I am being ungrateful, am I not?'

'Understandable under the circumstances,' said Marcus cheerfully. 'Now, seeing that we have reached the fair, why don't I pay for you to visit one of the fortune-tellers? She, or he—there are some hes—might solve all your problems in a trice. Which do you prefer, crystal balls, palm readings or tarot cards? I am sure that they are all on offer.'

'Well,' said Louise dryly, 'it might be as useful as anything which Jackson could find after all this time, so yes to that—so long as you agree to play Find the Lady. In view of our circumstances, rather apt, don't you think, Mr Marks?'

'Excellent,' Marcus replied, 'but don't expect me to win at cards—I have had such good luck in finding my particular lady—and you know the old saying, lucky at cards, unlucky in love, and I suppose that works in reverse at well.'

His reward was the first heartfelt laugh he had ever heard from Louise, and into the bargain she did what other young girls were doing with their swains—she slipped her hand into the crook of his arm.

The idea of Marcus being a swain amused her, and so she told him.

'Hmm,' he said thoughtfully. 'I always thought that swains were rustic creatures with a straw in their mouths, not lawyers' clerks on holiday. I believe that we are known as pen-pushers.'

This earned him another laugh and Marcus began to think that things were really looking up if his darling could enjoy herself and forget her cares. It turned out that Louise had never been to a fair before, and Marcus had certainly not attended one in his character as Mr Marks. He liked the idea of being a nobody on holiday among other nobodies, but he was honest enough to admit to himself that he would probably not like being one for life. This profound thought served to increase his admiration of Louise's feat in transforming herself from nothing into a person of consequence.

What made Louise happy was that no one stared at them, nor remarked upon them at all. She did not have to remember who she was, but simply enjoyed herself, her delicate arm tucked into Marcus's strong one. He insisted on buying her a toffee-apple, to which she only agreed when he promised to buy himself oysters from the next booth they came to—and eat them in the street.

'And I'll have a toffee-apple as well, to keep you company,' he announced magnanimously, and Marcus, Lord Angmering, known for his strict adherence to all the proprieties, walked along chewing away at an apple on a stick, between the booths which offered everything from a captive mermaid in a tank, to fairings ranging from ribbons and cockades to cheap china busts of the King and the Prince Regent, to representations of nymphs and shepherds. He could not have done anything more calculated to win his beloved's heart.

Next Louise bought him a cockade to wear in his shabby hat, and, in return he stumped up for a bunch of blue ribbons—'to bind up your bonny fair hair,' he half-sang to her, altering the words of the old ballad to fit Louise's red-tinged golden locks when he handed them over. Singing in the street—even if so low that only she might hear—what next would he do? wondered Louise, who, like Marcus, had never enjoyed herself so much for years.

What next, indeed? Next turned out to be the fortune-teller. This one offered everything from crystal balls to tarot cards—'You pays your money and you takes your choice,' was painted in crude words across the front of a canvas tent.

'I'll pay,' announced Marcus, to be met with, 'No, I will,' from Louise and they had a friendly wrangle in the entrance to the booth, to the delight of the small girl who was collecting entrance money.

Inside was dark and somewhat smelly. The smell came from a few candles burning in the gloom. The fortune-teller was a gypsy woman, rather elderly, with a face like a witch in a painting which hung in the corridor at Cleeve House in London.

She stared at the pair of them and said in a deep voice, 'You've paid for one only, so I take it that it's the lady who wishes to know her future.'

'Yes,' said Louise, staring at the crystal ball on the table between her and the gypsy woman. Beside the ball rested several packs of tarot cards, a bowl of clear water, and something which looked like a magician's wand.

'And which do you choose, m'lady?'

Louise said, to Marcus's amusement, for, all unknowingly, she had assumed Madame Félice's haughty tones, 'Why do you address me as m'lady?'

The woman leaned forward and said 'Come, come, you are m'lady, are you not? Do you think to deceive me by wearing the clothes of a servant?'

Louise, flabbergasted, stared back at her, and then, in a most unladylike manner, jerked her thumb at Marcus, and her manners having deserted her completely, asked, 'And him? What about him?'

Without turning her head to look at him the woman smiled and said softly, 'Why, he's an even bigger fraud than you are. Is this a prank you are engaged in? A prank designed to trick me, so that you might go home to boast to the quality of how you unmasked the gypsy fortune-teller? If so, you must do better than this.'

Marcus, who had been listening to her, his face a picture—although what sort of picture he might have found it difficult to say—now spoke.

'You are right, madame—and yet you are also wrong. Unriddle me that.'

She looked straight at him for the first time. 'Oh, my fine gentleman who has never worked in an office in his life, do you hope to trick *me* with such a question.'

She put her hands over her eyes before dropping them and saying, 'I am right that you are quality, so why are you dressed as though you are not? Is it possible that you have put on your false clothes to deceive the world rather than me? That you entered my tent on a whim and not by design?'

'Oh, bravo,' said Marcus softly. 'And now let me unriddle *you* a little. I am dressed as a clerk, but I betray nothing of what a true clerk is. My cuffs are neither frayed nor ink-stained, my poor stock is clean and new, and has not been laundered so many times that it is frayed. My hands betray none of the signs that I spend the day with a quill pen in them. My nails are clean and my writing finger is uncallused.

'Shall I go on? Or shall I inform you how you know that I am a gentleman and that my companion is not a servant. Oh, I forgot our manner... Everything you have told us so far is the result of careful observation, there is nothing magic about it.'

The gypsy woman did something strange. She threw back her head and began to laugh. 'Oh, you are a rare one, you are. Everyone who meets you tends to underestimate you. They think that because you are straightforward you are not clever—and cunning—tell me how I know *that* simply by looking at you?

Marcus shook his head. 'No, no, you have not only looked at me, you have heard me speak. Now, scry for my companion—I believe that is the phrase—and tell me of her future, something which you could not guess simply by looking at us and speaking to us. I am willing to pay you to use all of the tools of your trade, if that is what you call it.'

'Oh, I like you, m'lord, as I believe you to be. I wish I had met you when I was as young and pretty as your lady is, we could have had a rare time together. Does she know how lucky she is going to be when she shares your bed?'

Louise blushed, and, adopting her Madame Félice voice again, for it was pointless trying to pretend to be her own servant, said, 'I came here to have my fortune told, pray tell it.'

'You're a fair match for him, I see,' said the woman. 'Give me your hand, dearie, we'll begin with that.'

Louise laid her hand palm up on the table. The woman peered hard at it saying, 'Ah, yes, you are a lady, but not yet a lady. I cannot tell from this what your future might be, for it is strange, but not as strange as your past. Your hand tells me of that and little more—which is passing wonderful. Should you wish to learn your future then I must look in the crystal—do you wish to learn your future, lady? Many do not.'

'Yes,' said Louise swiftly, before she could change her mind. 'I am tired of contemplating my past—I would learn of my future if possible.'

'Then keep your hand in mine, for you have a power which few possess: and that is to prevent anyone from truly knowing you if you are minded not to allow them to. That is why your hand is closed to me. Open your heart to me, lady, and I may be able to help you.'

Louise nodded agreement and tried to reveal herself to the woman before her. The gypsy muttered some words before looking deep into the crystal.

Suddenly, however, she threw Louise's hand from her with a guttural cry, exclaiming, 'No, your past is so powerful that it insists on being known. Blood, lady, you are surrounded by blood—but none of it is yours, nor have you shed it. All those whom you most dearly loved were taken from you. Your father you never knew, he died in blood not long after you were born. You had a husband who was no husband—I cannot see him—I only know that blood surrounds him, too.'

She cried out again, before adding, 'Let me rest a moment, for you have tired me greatly. I think that I can see that you have a future, and a long one, but it is dim.'

Marcus's mouth twitched. He had been trying not to smile at what he thought was a fine old piece of pantomime, until the gypsy spoke of Louise's husband who was no husband, and of the blood which surrounded both him and her. He saw that his love's face had grown pale and for a moment thought of taking her away from someone whom he had earlier decided was a charlatan and trickster—but now he did not know what she was.

Except that Louise made no effort to rise, or to leave—and the decision must be hers, after all. The gypsy was stirring again. She had begun to mutter words in a language which neither Marcus, nor Louise, knew.

'I have broken the spell which binds you,' she said, reverting to her accented English. 'It was laid on you and yours long ago—and it is on him, too,' she added, pointing at Marcus. 'It curses you both because what you inherited was sacred and was stolen from those who raised it and false gods put in its place. Now, I will look again in my crystal in order to discover whether, having banished it, I may read your destiny more plainly.'

She took Louise's hand again, and this time recited a form of words, again in that strange language, before she looked deep into the ball before her.

'Yes,' she exclaimed, 'there is something there, it is still dim, but I can read a little of what the magic is trying to tell me. Alas, it is not clear, it is still vague and distant so that I have nothing detailed to tell you. All I can say is that you will gain your heart's desire. What you have been looking for all of your life you will also surely find, although I cannot plainly see what that is. It involves a name and a great house—a strange house—and there your joint destinies lie. More, I cannot tell you. Your will is strong, lady, and I needed to subdue it to see even the little I have.'

She relinquished Louise's hand and lay back in her intricately carved chair panting as though she had run a race.

'Oh, I am so tired. To break the spell which binds you both was a feat almost beyond my endurance.

'This spell,' asked Marcus, intrigued even though he still thought that the old woman was making this whole farrago up—and even though she had spoken truly of some parts of Louise's past. 'This spell, Madame, to what does it relate?'

'All I can tell you is that there is a Grove which was called Sacred which was despoiled long ago, and they who live in and own it will suffer from a curse placed upon them by the original owners, a curse which will ruin their lives so that they will rarely know happiness. Far away from it, some might find contentment. More than that I cannot say—other than that I have lifted it from you and your lady, so that you may live long and happy lives.'

Both Marcus and Louise were thinking of Steepwood's Sacred Grove, and of the ruined lives of all those who had ever owned the Abbey and the grounds in which the grove was situated. It was not until his father had left England—and the grove—behind that he had found happiness in India.

He half-began to ask the gypsy whether she could lift the curse altogether, but true child of the Age of Reason that he was, he found himself inwardly laughing at such an absurd notion.

Yet the old woman had said so much that was true.

Louise had begun to stir. She had been shocked

by what the gypsy had told her. She said, her voice low, for she was still distressed by what she had both seen and heard. 'You said that I would be happy, and that I would find that for which I have always wished. Can I believe you?'

The old woman's smile was weary. 'I can only tell you what I saw—and hope that you and your man will find in the future the happiness which you seek. Time alone will prove me right or wrong, but I believe that the crystal told me true.'

She looked Marcus straight in the eye, saying, 'You do not trust me, young sir, because you are limited by your cleverness. You only believe in what you can see, hear and touch, not in the something more than that which lies around us and which we can only dimly understand, if at all.'

Marcus rose and bowed to her, and acknowledged what she had just said. He spoke without mockery, quoting from Shakespeare's play, *Hamlet*. 'There are more things in Heaven and Earth, Horatio, than are dreamed of in your philosophy.'

'Exactly so, young fellow. Leave me now. I may scry no more this afternoon. You brought a strong and evil power in with you, and that power has gone, but it was heavy work for me to rid you of it, heavy work.'

They were outside again, blinking in the orange sunlight of an early October afternoon. Louise said, her voice faltering a little, 'Are we to believe all that, Mr Marks?'

Marcus turned around and slipped an arm around her shoulders. For the first time since he had met her she looked frail and wan. He gave her a reassuring hug, careless of passing watchers. After all, a young clerk might hug his sweetheart in the street, might he not? The constraints which bound Marcus Cleeve did not obtain here.

'I don't know,' he said. 'I thought her a fraud at first, but later...I find later difficult to explain. All that talk about blood, and then the Sacred Grove and the curse of which we both know...'

'Exactly,' said Louise, echoing the gypsy's last words to them. 'How could she know of that? And the Abbey—the strange building she called it, and so it is being religious house and home combined. You must admit that was frightening. I agreed with you when you told her that she could guess that we were not working people because to an observant eye everything about us betrays our true station—but the rest—how did she know that?'

'Louise,' Marcus said gravely. 'Try not to think too much about what she told you. Or, if you must, believe what she said at the end.'

'About our future happiness?'

'Yes, you were speaking of the future earlier this afternoon. Try to believe that she spoke truly. Look, I do believe that the roses are already returning to your cheeks, my dear Miss Louise. Keep them there and I promise to eat oysters again if you will eat jellied eels! How is that for a great concession on my part?'

'Dear Mr Marks,' said Louise, who after the strangeness of their recent experience had forgotten that she was supposed to be holding Marcus off, not encouraging him. 'Dear Mr Marks, how kind you are. Yes, I will eat jellied eels though I have never done so before and hope that they will not make me feel sick!'

Nor did they. Eating from their paper screws full of fishy delicacies Marcus and his love found it possible to forget past and future, and enjoy the mindless present which was Chelsea Fair.

'Blasted Northamptonshire, and bloody Steepwood,' grumbled Jackson aloud. 'It would be raining again.'

He had come hot-foot from London, which he considered to be the only civilised place in the Kingdom, and was bound for the cottage in Steep Ride where Solomon Burneck now lodged.

It would be a pleasure to upset the surly bastard once more. It quite made this whole tedious business worthwhile.

The cottage was at the end of a muddy lane leading off an equally muddy by-way. Jackson watched from a distance until he saw the landlady leave—he wanted no witnesses to what he was about to do. Burneck himself opened the door and made a disagreeable face at him.

'What, you again!'

Almost the same words as Marcus Angmering had used, but the tone was very different.

'That's right,' Jackson said, 'regular bad penny, aren't I? Let me in, will you, this rain's damned wet.'

'Why should I?' asked Burneck. 'You've no right…'

'This is my right,' said Jackson, 'and a damned useful one it is, too.' And he put a hard and horny hand on Burneck's chest and pushed him into the cottage's small front room.

'Hey, damn that,' spluttered Burneck. 'I haven't invited you in and an Englishman's home is his castle.'

'Number one,' said Jackson. 'This isn't your home, you're only a lodger, and number two, it's not a castle, so I can do as I please. Is the Missis in?'

'Yes,' lied Burneck.

'Now there's a lying tale to begin with,' grinned Jackson, 'for I saw her leave with her shopping basket not five minutes ago.'

'She'll be back any moment.' Burneck sounded desperate.

'If she does, and I doubt it, I'll tell her that you're gallows-meat I'm hauling off to the County gaol. So now you can take me upstairs and we can have a cosy little chat.'

'What for? You know that I had nothing to do

with my pa's death. Why should I kill him? I've lost room and board and my position in life.'

Jackson began to laugh.

'Your position in life! What's that? The place where you're beneath everyone's feet and consideration?'

He slammed the door behind him, saying, 'Now, you piece of low-life filth, tell me all that you know about the Marchioness, Miss Louise Hanslope as was. I've a burning curiosity about the lady, seeing that Sywell chose to marry her when he was a ripe piece of spoiled beef.'

'His choice, not mine,' grumbled Burneck. 'Can't imagine what you want to know about her for.'

'Well, I'm after wondering why Sywell married her at all—his bailiff's adopted daughter, wasn't she? Now, what I want you to tell me is who she was before Hanslope adopted her.'

'And how the devil should I know that? I've no idea.'

Jackson grabbed him by the collar. 'Why is it that I don't believe you? Tell me the truth, damn you. Tell me all about the child Hanslope brought here out of nowhere, and tell me why your master, who always had an eye for the main chance, married her. What main chance was he thinking of when he did such an odd thing? Knowing Sywell's reputation, there must have been something in it for him.'

Burneck began to shake his head. 'I don't know…'

Jackson took him by the throat this time and breathed ale fumes into his victim's purpling face.

'Keep mum, you lying wretch, and I'll run you in for Sywell's murder, that I will.'

'You wouldn't do that. You know that I didn't do it,' Burneck croaked desperately.

'Wouldn't I just! My masters want this business ended and don't care how it's done. I could end it tomorrow by fitting you up as the murderer. You'd do as well as another. Save yourself by telling me about Sywell and the girl. Otherwise...'

Burneck began to babble at him, his eyes wild. 'Let me go, then. If I have your word that you'll leave me alone if I talk, I'll tell you everything. After all, what's to lose, if I do? They're all dead but the girl.'

'Exactly—now talk. And I want the truth, the whole truth and nothing but the truth or you'll be in the dock at the Old Bailey.'

'It was when Johnny Hanslope came to my pa and said that his sister was dying and he had to go to Cheltenham to see her safely buried and to bring her little girl back with him. M'lord said he could go, grudging-like, and when Johnny had gone to make ready for the journey I told M'lord that to my certain knowledge he had no sister, and what was he doing pretending that he had one and going all the way to Cheltenham to rescue her?

'M'lord always loved a puzzle and he liked to know everything about those who worked for him.

Knowledge was power, he always told me. He gave a great laugh and said, ''Follow Johnny there and find out what he's up to. Perhaps it's nothing but an old mistress of his and her by-blow, but we might as well know. Don't let him twig you're after him, though.'''

'Just like that, eh?' queried Jackson, who was beginning to be intrigued by this tale and was also amused by the way Sywell alternated between being Pa and M'lord to his bastard son.

'Aye, he was bored, you know. So I ups and follows Johnny to Cheltenham, and true enough there was a dying woman and a little girl. I took rooms at the local inn and made a few discreet enquiries. What really interested me was that the dying woman was a Frenchie. What was Johnny Hanslope doing with a Frenchwoman? She had a funny name, too.

'So, I watched the house and one morning Johnny came out with the kid and walked over to a neighbour who I'd been told was giving him and the girl dinner. After a short time he walked back into the village. So I entered the house by the back way, and searched it. Upstairs I found the Frenchwoman lying on the bed—quite dead, but still warm. I suppose that he'd gone to fetch the laying-out nurse.'

Burneck stopped and offered Jackson a knowing grin: from not wanting to tell his story he now seemed to be enjoying doing so—a phenomenon which Jackson had often seen.

'The thing was—and I can tell you it really

knocked me flying—that I knew her. I'd seen her
years before when Lord Rupert Cleeve had secretly
visited Johnny Hanslope. How she had arrived in
Cheltenham with their child was a mystery. There
had been a rumour that Lord Rupert had married a
Frenchwoman—some said that he'd only pretended
to marry her—whatever the truth, here she was,
dead, and Johnny Hanslope had her kid.

'It occurred to me that she might be carrying
proof of her marriage, if there had been a marriage—and the child's birth, and that my pa would
be pleased as punch if I stole them for him so that
Johnny couldn't take the child to Lord Yardley.
Besides, to bastardise one of the Cleeves would be
the sort of caper he'd like, anyways.'

'Aye, and the idea pleased you, too, didn't it,
Burneck, didn't it?'

'If you say so. So I searched her belongings—
there weren't many—and found her marriage certif-
icate and the record of the kid's birth as well as her
diary. I took them and scarpered. I was right about
M'lord—he laughed fit to bust, he did, and hung on
to them. Johnny never even knew I'd been there. Pa
often had a good laugh about it when he was drunk,
and when the kid grew up and became a beauty he
laughed even harder when he married her, though
he was past everything by then, poor devil.'

Devil certainly, but hardly poor—who could pity
Sywell, thought Jackson grimly. What he said was,

'Why have you stopped? What happened to the papers when Sywell was murdered and went to Hell?'

Burneck put his finger by his nose. 'Aye, well, I knew where he kept his secrets. Them as was sent to solve his murder went through the Abbey and never found his hiding-places, but if they'd done so they'd have found nothing, because I'd been there before them.' He laughed hard at his own cleverness.

'So *you* have them now?' asked Jackson. 'First you steal them for Sywell, and then for yourself. What did you propose to do with them?'

'Knowledge is power, they might come in useful some day.' And this time he offered Jackson a wink.

'Not to you, they won't,' said Jackson, grinning again, 'for if you don't hand them over to me I'll haul you before the nearest beak for theft—because that wasn't all you lifted from Sywell, was it?'

'Oh, I knew you'd cheat me,' howled Burneck. 'Never trust a Runner, I should have known better.'

'Dear, dear,' said Jackson. 'Give me the legal papers and the diary and you can keep the rest, by the look of them they're not worth much.'

'Only things to remind me of my poor pa—you can have the papers—I'll fetch them for you.'

'Big of you,' said Jackson, 'seeing that I would have taken them from you without your kind assistance. I want to look at your other booty, too, in case there is anything there that will help me solve your poor, dear pa's murder. I'm sure you'd want that.'

Burneck gave up. He pointed to a battered trunk in the corner of the room, and handed Jackson its key. 'At the bottom,' he almost groaned, 'inside a Bible my pa once gave me.'

'Sywell gave you a Bible,' exclaimed the entranced Jackson, throwing out grubby clothing and a couple of tarnished silver candlesticks in order to find it. Sure enough, there were the papers and the diary which told the truth of Louise's birth, but the Bible interested him, too. It was an old one, the King James version bound in scuffed and battered leather, and had an inscription in the front: Philip Cleeve, his book, it said, 1642.

'A bit of Sywell's loot,' said Jackson, putting the papers back inside it. 'I think Lord Yardley might like his property back.'

'No!' Burneck shrieked. 'It's all I have left of me dad!'

'Who stole it from its owner. Console yourself with your happy memories of the dear departed,' said Jackson nastily, 'and be grateful I don't haul you off to Newgate for stealing the rest of the stuff in the trunk, which I would, if it were worth anything.'

He laughed to himself as he walked downstairs to the sound of Burneck's lamentations. Well, at least M'lord Angmering was going to be happy with what he had found and that was all that concerned him.

And now for home. Dear old London, it might smell bad, but it was still better than these dead and alive holes scattered around the Shire counties!

'Marcus,' said his stepmother that same morning, 'I would be grateful for a private word with you, if you could spare a moment.'

'Always ready to spare a moment for you, my dear Marissa,' he said gallantly. He thought that she seemed worried, and he also thought that he could guess what was troubling her.

He was right. Once they had reached her pretty little sitting-room, where they were unlikely to be interrupted, she came to the point at once. Marissa had many practical virtues and was nearly as forthright as Marcus and his father: something which they both valued more than showy good looks, which were often associated with an empty head.

'It's your father, Marcus. He is not well—oh, I mean more than that his advanced years are afflicting him, that is to be expected—but after a fashion which troubles me. I think that he has some deep worry which is preventing him from sleeping and which is ruining his appetite. Have you any notion what can be wrong? More to the point, perhaps, have you noticed any change in his manner recently—or am I imagining things?'

'Dear Marissa,' he said, 'I don't think that you are. I, too, have been perturbed about him recently. To say that he does not seem himself is an understatement. He is very much *not* himself. True, he and I have achieved a *rapprochement* which I once would never have thought possible, but even that does not appear to have made him happy. It has made me so, but not him.'

Marissa nodded thoughtfully. 'True, he told me of it, and I agree with you. I have asked him if there is anything troubling him and he has been unusually brusque in denying any such thing. It occurred to me that it might be something which he did not care to confide to me because I am a woman, or because he does not want to trouble me, so I wonder if I could ask a favour of you...' She paused.

Marcus said, 'You would wish me to speak to him?'

'Oh, if only you would. He's such a punctilious man, you see, and it's passing strange that he's keeping a secret from me. We've always told one another our troubles, and this secrecy is most unlike him. I do know that that ex-Runner who keeps popping up has the power to distress him, but why should that be?'

'You need not worry about him,' Marcus assured her. 'He's been coming to see me rather than father—I've asked him to do an errand for me. On second thoughts, perhaps it's only because I have been refusing to marry that has been distressing him.'

His stepmother shook her head. 'Oh, he's spoken of that to me at length—and by the by, he has my full support. You would make a splendid husband and father.'

'But I'd be pushing the two Neds out of line,' protested Marcus.

'Oh, pooh to that. The dowry I brought with me will give them a good start in life, and when I look at the history of the Earls of Yardley I'm not sure that I would wish the title on either of them. Now, you, Marcus, are a different kettle of fish. You are a strong man, stronger even than your father—and I know that you'd look after my darlings. You look after everyone and everything, don't you? Even that pretty *modiste,* Madame Félice whom you've been meeting secretly!'

Marcus gave a great moan. 'Now how the devil— forgive me, my dear—do you know about that?'

'That tattling fool Jack Perceval has been spreading gossip about seeing you with her in Chelsea. If it weren't that she is a *modiste* I'd say she would make a good Lady Yardley, and encourage you to offer for her, but marrying out of one's class is never a good notion.'

Marcus shook his head. 'I don't really think that whether or not I marry is worrying him so much that he is looking ill. After all, there are always the Two Neds to fall back on—even if you're not too happy about one of them becoming the next Lord Yardley. I promise you that I'll try to winkle out of father what's troubling him, but you know how stubborn he is—if he wants to keep mum he will.'

'Oh, but you're even more stubborn than he is, so my money is on you. Don't let me down, will you?'

What could he say but that he wouldn't, although it was simply one more thing for him to worry about. As for Madame Félice being out of his class—well perhaps Jackson might have the answer to that when he came back from Steepwood. Then he might think about marriage. What was the old saying? 'Better marry than burn!'

Well, he was certainly burning, so marriage, either in or out of his class, was becoming to look more and more attractive.

Chapter Six

Louise could scarcely wait for the weekend to arrive so that she might meet Marcus, no, Mr Marks again. She had visited Berkeley Square once more, to fit out the Countess this time, but he had not been present. Sophia had said something about Marcus having gone to visit an old school friend in Surrey, but he had told her that he hoped to be back in London by Friday at the latest.

One odd thing about the visit was that when she was showing Sophia a new idea for a small crown of silk flowers to wear on her wedding day she had caught Lady Yardley watching her with an odd look on her face.

Now, what could all that be about? Marcus had not told her that Jack Perceval had seen them in Chelsea, for he had not wanted her to worry over-much about the gossip that would inevitably follow. All the same, Louise worried a little about such a close inspection before telling herself sternly not to see a bear behind every bush. On the other hand, she had survived her unhappy start in life by using her intuition, which had frequently told her much about the people around her—often things which they did not want known.

The only time that her intuition had failed her was when she had agreed to marry Sywell. Thinking about Sywell made her remember her late guardian, and that brought her back again to what Jackson might, or might not, be finding when he started his search for her origins.

Which simply served as an excuse to think of Marcus who had hired him. Marcus, whom she now knew that she loved. Oh, if only they could meet more often, and on equal terms! She hated playing out a charade of the Prince and the beggar-maid with him, even though he tried to lighten that aspect of their relationship by calling himself Mr Marks.

Dear Mr Marks! She was still thinking this when she returned to Bond Street to find Lady Leominster and her suite present in full cry. The lady was demanding a new wardrobe and had been unhappy to find Madame absent.

'I hear that you've been visiting the Yardleys,' she carolled. 'Of course, Sharnbrook is biting the bullet at last, is he not? Such a dear girl, Sophia, I hope that you are doing her proud, Madame. Oh, yes, we never thought Sharnbrook would be leg-shackled, and now that he's gone, one supposes Angmering will be the next.'

'Oh, m'lady,' simpered one of her toadies who had been given the lady's reticule to guard. 'Have you not heard? He has bet Jack Perceval that he will not marry during the next year. Of all things he said that…' she crimsoned a little, but her patron, never one to be mealy-mouthed, said forcefully, 'Spit it out, my dear. I'm sure that Madame will not be troubled if you are over-frank—after all, she is French, and we all know what they are like.'

'Well, he said that he preferred having an arrangement, if you take my meaning, since the lady who agreed to one would be less demanding than a wife—or something like that…'

'Spoken like a man,' said the lady, giving Louise a glance which could only be interpreted as meaningful. 'One hears that he has found such a lady—I wonder, who can it be?'

She did not intend to be malicious, merely to enjoy herself and her domination of all around her. Louise took the opportunity to hide her crimsoning face by kneeling down to pin up the gown in which her forewoman had dressed the lady before she had arrived from her visit to the Yardleys. She said, her voice muffled, 'I really have no notion, m'lady. Your guess is as good as mine.'

Far from annoying society's dictator, this amused her. She had been told the night before, in confidence by Jack Perceval that he had reason to believe that Angmering had taken up with that *modiste,*

Madame Félice. Such bare-faced lying was to be admired.

She bent down and hissed sweetly into Louise's ear, 'Oh, I'm sure that you know better than that, m'dear, but I wish you well. Angmering's an admirable fellow but eccentric. Mum's the word, eh?'

Louise straightened up, stood back, and said, 'I don't think that that colour suits you, m'lady, too garish. Would you not prefer another shade? A delicate mauve would be better than purple.'

If a lady could be said to wink, then Lady Leominster did. 'Oh, I defer to you always, Madame, such discretion, and such taste. You may always dress me in future. That wretched woman I have been using has been making me look like a gypsy at a fair.'

Gypsies at fairs reminded Louise of Marcus, Lord Angmering, who made nasty bets with nasty people like Jack Perceval. She would never call him Mr Marks again. Mr Marks would not pursue poor girls in order to ruin them and win his shameless bet. Lord Angmering, on the other hand, was apparently capable of anything. Just wait until he came visiting again this Saturday. To use the kind of language that that supposed high and mighty lady had just been employing: she would give him what for and no mistake!

Saturday had come and Marcus was all impatience. He had arrived back in Berkeley Square early on Friday morning, and late in the afternoon Jackson had arrived, bursting with news. Marcus had heard him out, and could only regret that he had to wait until morning to tell Louise that she was well and truly Louise Cleeve, and possessed the means of proving it.

For some reason, though, when he arrived in Chelsea the little maid showed him into an empty room and told him that Madame was busy and would join him once she was free.

He had never felt so impatient in all his life, and after half an hour had dragged by he rose to his feet and paced the room agitatedly, although it was scarcely big enough to satisfy his urgent demand for action.

Finally the door opened and his beloved entered. Instead of offering him her usual happy greeting, however, she impaled him with a fixed stare, and said coldly, 'Well, m'lord, what is it this time that you come so early?'

'Mr Marks,' he told her smiling, for he half-thought that she must be playing a game with him, her manner to him being so different.

'Mr Marks?' queried Louise. 'Now, who may he be? I do not know him—and I think that you do not, m'lord.'

Marcus could no longer deceive himself. Something had happened which had revived the haughty creature whom he had first met. All the playful banter which had enlivened their recent meetings had quite disappeared. He moved towards her to try to take her hand, but she retreated from him, the hand upraised to repel him.

'What is it?' he asked her. 'What have I done? What has caused you to treat your dear Mr Marks so unkindly? I thought that we had become friends, nay, more than friends.'

'How can you ask such questions?' she told him, her face still frozen, 'when I learn that the *on dit* is that not only have you bet that you will never marry, but that you have also proclaimed that an arrangement with a willing woman would be far better. Almost immediately afterwards I discovered that it is all over London society that you are meeting me secretly. That gossiping gorgon Lady Leominster made it quite plain that she knew that we were doing so, and had the gall to twit me with it.'

What he had feared when Marissa had spoken to him of his meeting Louise had come to pass. Regardless of everything, the moment he had discovered that, he should have gone straight to Bond Street to tell her that their secret was a secret no more. Instead he had stupidly hoped that if he said nothing then it was unlikely that, living outside that society, she would ever find out.

He might have known what gossips many society hostesses were, the Leominster creature being the worst of them. She had probably deliberately let Louise know what was being said in order to mischief-make between them. If so, she had succeeded.

'My dear,' he said, 'I have never lied to you. I told you that I wanted you for my mistress—and that the choice was yours. As for the ton knowing that we are meeting, they did not learn that from me, but from that ineffable nodcock, Jack Perceval. What's more, once you had told me that you did not wish to have a liaison with me I have treated you with as much respect as I would treat my own sister, Sophia—nay, more, for I have always twitted and teased her insufferably, something which I have never done to you. Dear Miss Louise, forgive your cavalier for what he has not done, particularly when he comes to you with such splendid news.'

Louise stared at him. Could she believe him? The trouble was that she knew how unscrupulously the aristocracy and gentry often pursued those well below them in station. She had comforted more than one green young sempstress who had been betrayed by an upper-class lover. They would say anything to gain their ends, and then they would walk away, having deprived their victim of her virtue, or, at the worst, having left her with a bastard child as well as a ruined name.

She had vowed that she would never be such a fool, and until she met Marcus she had never been tempted to be one.

'Am I to believe you?' she asked him, her face softening a little. 'Or are you treating me with such care, such kind consideration, in the hope that one day I shall be foolish enough to give way to you?

Can you honestly deny that that has not been your aim?'

Marcus said, and it pained him to do so. 'You have asked me to be honest, and so I shall be. Yes, in the beginning, after you had first refused me, I had that in mind, but the more I knew you the more it became impossible for me to commit such an act of betrayal. What is more, when I have told you what Jackson has discovered I shall ask you a question which will prove my honesty to you.'

Louise was in a quandary. She dearly wished to know what Jackson had found, and that being so she could not treat the bringer of that news with the contempt and dismissal which she would have done had Marcus come empty-handed. After all, it was he who had spoken to Jackson of her story, and paid him to look for the truth and the proof of it. Even if, at first, she had not wished him to do so, now that he had, and the quest was ended, she must know that truth, for good or ill, and judging by Marcus's manner, it did not seem for ill.

'Very well,' she said, 'because I half-believe you, and because you have done me a great favour you may sit there—' and she pointed at the armchair which he always used '—and you may tell me what Jackson has found.'

All the eagerness which Marcus had felt until Louise had walked into the room came surging back.

'Oh, my dear girl,' he said. 'He has returned with absolute and positive proof that Madame Félice is undoubtedly Louise Cleeve, the grand-daughter of the previous Earl of Yardley. What's more the proof, is so complete and authentic that no one could call it false or forged. With your permission we shall hand it over, once you have inspected it, to the Cleeve family lawyers so that you may return to your proper station in society.'

For the first time in her life Louise thought that she was about to faint.

'Proof? Absolute proof,' she half-whispered, 'after all this time? Where did he find it? My guardian could not. Where was it?'

Marcus told her the story which Jackson had told him, ending with the information that Sywell and Burneck had always known who she was.

At this point Louise, who was recovering herself rapidly, said, 'So *that* was why he married me. Oh, the devil, the wicked devil that he was.'

'Yes,' said Marcus, marvelling again at his love's quick wits. 'So Burneck said. Apparently they thought it a joke, he and Sywell.'

Louise rose to her feet and began to pace the room as Marcus had done earlier. 'A joke! My life was a joke for them! All that suffering, that hard work, that loneliness, not really knowing who I was or who my relatives were, fearing that I was some abandoned bastard. And all the time they thought it was a joke.'

She remembered the long and difficult hours she had spent learning her trade, and although she did not regret them, yet the knowledge that all that tedious time she had had a place in life which had been denied her was almost more than she could bear.

Before their recent difference over his bet and the revelation of their secret meeting, Marcus would have taken her in his arms to comfort her, but under the circumstances he thought that it would be tactless, would be merely mistaken for part of his campaign to overcome her.

He must be patient, for the decision he had already made before Jackson's visit, and after a sleepless night spent pondering on it, meant that in a moment or two he would say something which meant that Louise would never have cause to doubt his honesty again.

Instead, he said, 'Shall I ring for the maid to bring you some tea—or even something stronger?' for her face was so pale and her manner so shocked that he felt that she might need some kind of sustenance.

Louise shook her head and said in a strong voice, 'No, I must not have the vapours like a fool who has never had to face the hardships of life. I am trying to believe that what you are telling me is true. It makes me look at my previous life in a totally new light. My guardian told me when he lay dying that I was Rupert Cleeve's daughter, which gave me a name, but not legitimacy, and now you have given me both, which means that I must apologise for speaking so harshly to you when you arrived.'

'Very understandable of you to feel harsh towards

me after listening to Lady Leominster,' Marcus said, moving a little closer to where she stood, her hand now on the mantelpiece to steady herself. 'I left myself open to such accusations because of my behaviour to you when we first met. Now, if you feel well enough to deal with more revelations I have a very important question to ask you.'

Did she feel well enough to answer an important question? No, but the main rule of Louise's life had been never to admit weakness, or bow to it. So why should she do so now? Besides, what else could he have to say to her which could either shock or surprise her? Louise was afterwards to wonder how naïve she had been to ask herself such a question!

So she turned and shook her head at him. Unknown to her, her colour was returning, and the man who loved her thought that she had never looked more beautiful nor more gallant. He moved even nearer to her, took her hand and said hoarsely, 'My dear, it would please me if you would sit down before I ask my question.'

Louise was still so shocked that she did not refuse him but sat down immediately, to leave him standing before her, straight and tall, looking down at her with the most tender expression on his face.

'My dear Louise,' he said, 'I am about to do something which I have never done before—and hope never to have to do again. I cannot sufficiently express the admiration which I have come to feel for you over the last few weeks, and the reservations which you expressed earlier about my behaviour have only enhanced that admiration, not dimmed it. If that were not enough, I have also come to love you dearly, something which I had never thought to do for any woman before. That being so, pray make me the happiest man in England by agreeing to become my wife.'

Marcus had not thought beforehand of what Louise's reaction to this splendid proposal might be. If he had he would have thought that after it she would fall gratefully and lovingly into his arms.

He had not only brought her a magnificent prize, her true name and her legitimacy, but he had also offered her his heartfelt love, so that when she leaped to her feet and exclaimed, 'Certainly not! I see what this is all about. When I was Madame Félice the *modiste* the only thing that I was fit for was to be your mistress, but, of course, Louise Cleeve, the descendant of Earls, is quite a different thing. *She* must be your wife. If Mr Marks had offered for Madame Félice, without knowing that she was either the Honourable Louise Cleeve, or the Marchioness of Sywell, then *that* would have been a different thing and would have earned him a yes immediately. But as it is, my answer must be a most definite No.'

Marcus was thunderstruck. He did something completely out of character. He fell on his knees before her to plead with her, and took her hand in his—but she rejected it, and threw it from her, her face stony.

'No!' he exclaimed. 'You wrong me. I had already made up my mind to marry you before Jackson discovered your true identity, but I wanted to tell you of it and offer for you at the same time.'

'So you say now,' said Louise, the tears not far away. All her life everything important which had happened to her had turned to dross, and now even Marcus's proposal seemed to be tainted because he had never offered her marriage before he had discovered that she was Louise Cleeve, but only after. 'So you say now.'

Marcus was suddenly desperate. 'Only consider,' he begged of her. 'Ever since we first met we have each been drawn to the other, otherwise you would never have allowed me to become your friend—you would have rejected me immediately. I know that I was attracted to you the moment I saw you. Say yes, my darling, only say yes.'

But she turned her head away from him again, saying, 'I was lonely. You lightened my loneliness, that was all.'

'No.' And now he rose and moved towards her, to try to take again the hand which she had pulled away from him after he had made his proposal, but still she refused him.

It was hopeless—for the moment at least. He remembered the old adage: He who fights and runs away will live to fight another day. He would leave now, not torment her, but he would return, for he could not lose her now, he could not. More than ever he wanted to make her his wife, not only because he loved and desired her, but because he wished her to be the mother of his children.

Even the stoic spirit which she was displaying while refusing him had only served to make him love her the more. Her strength of will, her determination to be true to herself, impressed a man who valued such attributes almost before anything else. Perhaps, when he had gone and she had had time to consider carefully everything which he had told her, she might change her stubborn mind.

After all, she had received so many great shocks recently that it would only be when she had recovered from them that she could contemplate his proposal objectively, and realise that the strength of his passion lay behind it.

If he deluded himself, then so be it—but he must not trouble her now.

He rose to his feet and said as calmly as he could, 'I will leave you to think over all that I have said today, and hope that when you have done so you might feel able to give me a better answer.'

Louise nodded mutely, before saying, 'There is one thing which I must ask you, Lord Angmering, and I hope that of your goodness you will obey me in this. Pray bring me my mother's marriage lines and the other papers which relate to my birth. Do not give them into the keeping of lawyers before I have had time to decide what best I should do now that I know my new station in life. I may, or may not, wish to remain simple Madame Félice, for I shall never call myself the Marchioness of Sywell despite my marriage to him, and I trust that you will allow me to make that decision for myself after— as you say—due consideration. I must also ask you to say nothing to anyone of what Jackson has discovered until I have made that decision.'

'Yes,' he said simply, 'the decision must be yours. I shall see that you receive them. Only remember that you have now acquired a whole new family, who, I am sure, would wish to try to recompense you for the years of hardship which you have endured in obscurity. Their love and friendship awaits you.'

He did not say that he would bring the papers in person, for he did not wish to behave in such a manner that she might think that he was blackmailing her into receiving him when, for the moment, she had rather not.

After he had gone, closing the door carefully behind him, Louise rose and walked to the window to watch Mr Marks walk away. Since their recent friendship she still had great difficulty in thinking of Marcus as Lord Angmering. The man who wore clerk's clothing, ate oysters in the street, and talked to her so simply and cheerfully was quite unlike the few great men she had ever met.

She was not to know that the workers on the

Yardley estates in the north also thought the same
of the man who walked among them wearing country clothing, who had learned how to shoe a horse,
to work in the blacksmith's forge and who had insisted on being taught how to plough a straight fur-
row.

Some had despised him for trying to acquire the
basic knowledge of a working farmer rather than sit
back in his grand house and idly accept the rents
which the land brought him. Some respected him
because he wanted to share in their hard lives a little.
Others, like Louise, were somewhat baffled by him.

But why should she be baffled? Marcus's nature
was a straightforward one. He had told her quite
plainly when she had first met him that he wished
to make her his mistress. He had not wooed her with
fair words, pretending that he was courting her, using that as the means to an end, and that end seduction, betrayal and desertion.

He had treated her more kindly than any other
man she had ever met. She thought of Sywell, of
the brutality which he had inflicted on her, and
which had caused her to run away and hide herself
from him in London—a place he detested and
avoided. There had been other men whom she had
met when she had visited great houses in London in
order to outfit their wives, daughters and sisters.
Men who had not hesitated to accost her and whis-
per their base desires into her ears.

There had even been one who had tricked her into

being alone with him on the pretext that his sister, for whom she was making a wedding dress, had asked that Louise visit her in her drawing-room. She had escaped ravishment only by the merest chance, and her own cunning, but the memory could still make her shiver.

No, Marcus was not like that at all, and his last words to her, that she would be acquiring a family, had struck a chord which vibrated inside her long after he had gone.

She had always been alone. The few people she had known and loved in childhood had, one by one, disappeared. Mrs Hanslope, whom she had called mother, then John, her guardian, and she had lost Athene Filmer when she had left Steepwood to be apprenticed in Northampton.

She had made few friends in London, and knowing and loving Marcus had been to her like manna found in the desert by the starving Israelites. Only her own deep sense of integrity had prevented her from consenting to be his mistress when her mind, as well as her senses, told her to accept him, if only to fill her empty world.

Louise told herself briskly not to repine. She had work to do, decisions to make, and so many different futures had opened before her—who until now, had had none—that she was quite bewildered.

Besides, she was already beginning to regret having sent Marcus away...

Chapter Seven

Marcus arrived back at Berkeley Square determined not to let the afternoon's events overset him. He cursed his own folly in not grasping what Louise's reaction to his delayed proposal of marriage would inevitably be. He was sure that her own common-sense would guide her once the shock of his news had worn off. Her unexpected refusal had only served to increase his determination to make her his wife. Nevertheless he knew that he was doomed to a few uncomfortable days, but he had survived them before.

He met his father in the entrance hall. He immediately thought that Marissa was right to worry about him: he looked old and ill.

Impulsively he said, 'Is it possible that I could have a word with you, sir? If it is convenient, that is,' for he saw his father flinch away from him a little, which disappointed him, since he had thought that they had reached a better understanding of each other since their recent confidential talk.

'Of course, Angmering, let us go to my study. While we are on our way allow me to inform you that I was buttonholed today by some fellow from the Home Office who told me that the enquiry into Sywell's death has been abandoned. Other more urgent problems relative to the state of the country—the Luddite riots in the Midland counties in particular—demand the attention of those who have been pursuing it. It seems that it must remain a mystery which might solve itself in time.'

So Jackson's task was over. He would doubtless be returning to the Midlands, but for a different reason.

'At least they will not be troubling you again, sir,' he offered as his father pointed him to a chair facing his desk.

He sat down and hesitated for a moment, not quite sure how to broach his, and Marissa's, worries to the man opposite to him. He took so long that his father said suddenly, 'Well, what is it, Angmering?'

'It's this, sir. Both Marissa and I fear that something is worrying you so much that you are beginning to look quite ill. She fears that it may be more than your health, and I share those fears. If it is possible for you to confide in me, pray do so. A trouble shared is a trouble halved. If anything is wrong it may ease matters if you speak to me of it.'

'I know,' said his father, turning his face away

from him. 'I cannot speak of it to Marissa, although she has begged me time and again to tell her what is wrong. Is it possible that I can confide in you?'

'That, sir, you must decide. Believe me, my one intent is to serve you as a good son ought, and I fear that of recent years, I have not always been the kind of son in whom you could confide—now that matters have changed perhaps you may be able to do so.'

'True, Angmering, true. For my part I have never given you credit for being the sound fellow that you are; that being so, I feel that I may trust you to hear what I have to say. At the end I would appreciate it if you would give me some notion of what you think I ought to do. It is a long story I have to tell, and not a pretty one. It goes back many years, and I fear that, at the end, you may not wish to know the man who tells it to you.'

Marcus had already heard one story which reached back in time, and now it seemed that he was to hear another. He had helped Louise, and now, strange though it seemed, his father now needed his help and advice as well.

'Until you tell me all, Father,' he said, dropping the impersonal sir, for he thought that his father looked even more ill when he had finished speaking than he had done before, 'I cannot advise you.'

'Before I begin,' his father said, 'I must ask you to treat what I shall tell you in complete confidence. You are to inform no one of it, no one, however much you think that you ought to do so. Without that assurance given to me on your word of honour, I shall say no more.'

Marcus was about to reply without thinking, 'Of course, sir. You must know that my word is my bond,' when he remembered that he had said something similar to Louise—and then he had immediately broken that word solemnly given.

One result of that betrayal—even though it had been done with the best of intentions, had inevitably been to weaken Louise's trust in him, and had probably influenced her subsequent refusal of his offer of marriage.

This time, and always in the future, whatever the cost, he would keep his word. He saw that his father, registering his hesitation, and unaware of what was causing it, had put his head in his hands as though he could no longer bear its weight.

Marcus said, and his voice rang with truth, 'You may depend upon it, father, I shall reveal nothing of whatever you are about to tell me. I will swear an oath before you to that effect if that would reassure you.'

His father lifted his head again, 'No need, no need, Angmering, your word will suffice. After all, I have little time to live, although I hope to survive long enough to see Sophia married at Christmas, and when I am gone—what I shall tell you will fall into the vast pit of the past.

'I must no longer delay. My story begins long ago

in the last century when I was even younger than you are now—when I was plain Thomas Cleeve with apparently no hope of succeeding to the Earldom since the senior and junior branches of the family had separated so long ago. It was the year 1765, and I had met a beautiful and devoutly religious young woman by the name of Sophia Goode and fallen desperately in love with her.'

He smiled a little wryly at Marcus's slight start of surprise. 'I think that you will shortly guess where your half-sister's name came from. It was I who chose it, you see, but I must resume. We were so in love that we decided to marry, since there was nothing to prevent us. Her parents and mine were delighted that we should do so, since love matches are rare in our class.

'We were about to prepare for the wedding when she sent me a letter which destroyed the happy world in which I had been living. She said that she had changed her mind about marrying me and had decided to convert to the Catholic faith. Her one wish now was not to be my bride, but to be the bride of Christ, and to achieve that end she was entering a convent.

'You may judge of the shock I sustained on reading this. I drove to her home to try to persuade her to change her mind, but she had already left and I was never to see her again in this life. I was like a madman when I realised that she had gone for ever. I railed against God and fate, since everything I saw was hateful to me if I could not see and share it with my lost love. I left for India to get away from everything which reminded me of her. After ten years I married your mother, as much from loneliness as anything else—and I was rewarded for my careless folly by the marriage being a disaster.

'Finally she left me for another, and shortly afterwards died. I was never quite sure of the circumstances, nor did I care enough about her to discover them. I was happy to be a free man again, with a son whom I wickedly neglected because he reminded me of her. Then I met Marissa, who has become my guiding star—and yours, too, a little, I think, and have been happier than perhaps I have ever deserved to be. So much time had passed that I began to forget my first love, and enjoy what was left of my life on earth without that shadow hanging over me.

'Alas, early this year I received a package which contained a few small personal possessions and a letter which was addressed to me. It came from someone called Sister Mary Margaret, something which puzzled me until I read it. It told me, among other things, that she was my dear, lost love. The package had been sent to me by the Abbess of her convent because she had recently died, and her last wish had been that I should receive it.

'It was bad enough to learn of her death, but what was even more shocking was what the letter told me. It explained why she had deserted me so suddenly and without warning. She had been deliberately seduced and virtually raped by my friend, Lord George Ormiston, he who later became the Marquis of Sywell. Sywell was then a most attractive and handsome man. He had traded upon her innocence, which had been so great that she had assumed that once having bedded her he would marry her. That would have compelled her to give me up—but, in any case, she no longer wished to marry me after giving way to Sywell.

'She was grossly mistaken in him. Sywell treated the whole business as a joke, jeered at her for expecting marriage, and she was left having betrayed herself, myself, and the religion which she prized, for the love of a wretch who had taken her virginity and had then made a mock of her. She felt that she was so damaged by what had happened that not only could she not marry me, having dishonoured herself, but she must retire from the world altogether.

'You may imagine my feelings after I had read the letter. A past I had thought long dead had sprung from the grave to revive all the misery of my departed youth. On learning of Sywell's wickedness all that I wished for was to be revenged upon the monster who had caused my love to leave the world altogether. I remembered with pain the years of misery I had endured after she had gone. I burned to see him, to reproach him…to do…I knew not what. I forgot my happy life with Marissa in remembering the suffering which Sywell had inflicted on the woman whom I had loved so dearly.

'I went at once to the Abbey to confront him, to reproach him, to make him pay for what he had done to me and to her. You may imagine with what results. Debauched and degenerate, he was a caricature of the man whom he had once been. He mocked me for having lost my love first to him, and then to God. He told me, laughing, ''The bitch wanted it, and it's not my fault that she had a religious fit after I'd bedded her. It seems to me you were well rid of such a silly cow. When all's said and done I did you a favour.''

'I would have killed him there and then, except that his by-blow, Burneck, was always in attendance on him, and stood by, watching him. I made up my mind to finish him off in such a fashion that no one could be suspected—even that vile brute, Burneck. So I swallowed my hate, thanked Sywell for doing me a favour, which made Burneck laugh, and even pretended to do a little business with them.

'That made it possible for me to invite Burneck to Jaffrey House on the night I had decided that I would kill Sywell. There was no moon, and no one would be likely to see me. I contrived some excuse in order to keep him at the house overnight. He slept in the servants' quarters, which meant that suspicion could not fall on him. Unfortunately, what I had not considered was that it might fall on the missing wife, Hanslope's daughter. Later, though, Jackson assured me that there was no way in which she could have committed the crime, seeing that she lived in London and had not the means to pay anyone to kill him for her.

'I dressed myself in gamekeeper's clothes in case anyone saw me in the dark. I took my pistol with me and all the way to the Abbey I thought of killing him without feeling the slightest remorse. I told myself that, for all his many crimes, he deserved to die a hateful death. I was still thinking this when I entered the Abbey and climbed up one of its secret ways so that if by ill chance anyone were about I might not be seen.

'I found Sywell in his bedroom. He was even more disgusting than when I had first confronted him over his debauchery of my love. I could not help remembering what he had been like when we were young men together: he had been a very Adonis. And now he was this wretched, bloated *thing* on the bed. He had been trying to shave his hairy face and his razor and towel lay on a table by the bed.

'He stared at me, and said blearily, "What the hell are you doing here at this time of night, Yardley?"

'"Come to send you to hell," I told him. "The ball I shall kill you with is my present to you from Sophia." I lifted the pistol and pointed it at the *thing*. It wasn't a man any more.

'He slipped out of bed and stood facing me. He

grunted, ''You haven't the guts, Tozzy, to kill your old friend in cold blood.''

'He had used my nickname, the one I had been given at school, and whether it was that, or something else, I don't, and shall never, know. It was as though I'd had a blinding revelation, or else my happy life with Marissa flashed before my eyes, but whatever it was, I knew that I could not kill him, even if he deserved it. I thought of what might happen if the law caught me, and of what that would do to Marissa, to *my* Sophia, and to her marriage already arranged for Christmas, by which time if I had been arrested I should be due to hang.

'It came upon me that he wasn't worth it. That he was already in hell, in a hell of his own making. By his own actions he had destroyed his beauty and addled his brains, while I, one of his victims, had survived to build myself a happy and prosperous life, and raise a loving family.

'That took a long time to say, but no time at all to think. I lowered the pistol and, like a fool, laid it on an occasional table, saying, ''Die in your own ordure, Sywell. I've no wish to put you out of your misery.''

'Oh, I had misjudged him again! He gave a great bellow and sprang at me before I could pick up the pistol. He had snatched his cut-throat razor up and was upon me in an instant, determined to kill me, whatever the ultimate cost to him. But he had misjudged his last victim. Old and feeble though I

was—and am—I was infinitely more powerful than
the *thing* he had become. I caught him by the wrist
and wrenched the razor from his grasp, only to have
him spit in my face and say, ''I told you that you
hadn't the guts to kill me, Tozzy, didn't I?''

'I don't know what came over me then. It was
something like the old berserker rages our Viking
ancestors used to experience. I was suddenly a madman, cutting and thrusting at him until exhaustion
overcame me, and he lay on the floor, dead. This
time *he* was the victim of his last insult. I reeled
away, throwing down the razor and picking up the
pistol which had fallen to the floor. I was covered
in blood myself and had to get away.

'I don't clearly remember what happened next because I was both shocked by what I had done, and
at the same time could feel no remorse for having
done it. After all, if I had not killed him, he would
have killed me. Before I left I took Sywell's great-
coat from where it had been flung on the floor and
carried it away with me.

'When I reached the pool where he and I had
swum as boys I stripped off my outer garments,
which were soaked with his blood, and buried
them—where I have no notion—I was in no condition to trouble about such things. I then washed
myself, put on Sywell's coat to make me at least a
little respectable, and made my way home. I met no
one and reached my bedroom without disturbing

anyone—so far as my valet and staff were concerned they had seen me to bed at the usual time.

'When the uproar about Sywell's murder began they were able to testify, quite truthfully, that they had seen me to my bed at the usual time, and that I was in it early the next morning. Jackson questioned me, but could not shake me. My one worry was that someone innocent might be accused of Sywell's murder—which was not a murder, but self-defence—and I would then have to confess to what I had done. I could not let another go to the gallows in my place.

'Today, as I told you earlier, I learned that the authorities believe that it is not possible either to find, or to convict, anyone of the murder. Unless something further is discovered which might reveal who killed Sywell, the matter will remain forever a mystery. All the obvious suspects, including myself, have unbreakable alibis, so the problem remains on the table, as it were.

'I have lived with this burden of knowledge on me for so long, that, coupled with the illness which my doctors believe will kill me before a year has passed, my life has become not worth living. I tell you of it in case any innocent person should be accused of murder after I am dead and gone. Then, and only then, will you take this paper which I will give you now, and which contains my confession, and hand it to the authorities—I wish no one else to suffer for what I did.'

By now the Earl's face was ashen. There was a glass of water on his desk. He drank it down with a shaking hand and looked into his son's face, which was as white as his own.

Marcus, an expression of enormous pity on his face, said, 'Of course, I will do as you ask, Father. Knowing Sywell's reputation and yours, I believe that what you did, you did in self-defence, but without witnesses you would have difficulty in proving that. More particularly because, by your own confession, you went there intending to kill him. And I quite understand what drove you to that.'

His father said, 'Thank you, Angmering. I think that I went a little mad after reading Sophia's letter. Only when I looked down at what I had done to Sywell did sanity have me in its grip again. I knew, too, that whatever else, my lost Sophia would not have wished me to seek to avenge her. Nothing excuses what I did, nor the lies I have told. I, who have always prided myself on my truthfulness, have had to live with the knowledge of my falsity...'

Marcus rose, and walked round the desk, saying, 'Stop, Father, stop! What's done is done, and besides Sywell, who got what he deserved, the only person to suffer has been yourself. In the end everything against any other suspects fell down because, fortunately, they could prove their own unshakeable innocence. Now that you have confessed, try to find peace again. Rest assured that I shall say and do nothing other than the two things which you have asked of me—silence and the passing of your confession to the authorities, if that proves to be necessary. Now, go to your room and try to rest.'

His father said simply, 'I don't deserve you, Angmering, nor do I deserve Marissa. For a time in my youth I was nearly as profligate as Sywell. Whether Sophia would have steadied me I shall never know. Only her desertion of me achieved that. Oh, God, one always thinks that the past is over and done with, but heaven help me, it returned to destroy me again.'

What could he say which would lessen his father's agony? Nothing, only gently help him to his feet, saying, 'Let me take you upstairs, father, where you may lie down and try to forget the past in sleep. Living or dead, Sywell is not worth tormenting yourself to your own death. Think that he brought his own upon him by his wickedness, and leave it at that.'

His father consented to do what his son wished and, arm in arm, the Earl of Yardley and the son whose worth he had come to value in his old age mounted the stairs together, where Thomas Cleeve, purged by his confession, at last found in sleep the peace which had long been eluding him.

Between his thwarted love for Louise and what his father had told him, Marcus was in a ferment, and that night, having helped his father to rest, was unable to sleep himself.

When at last he did he was haunted in his dreams by the terrible tale which his father had told him. Sywell rose from the dead to haunt him, and Louise was there, too, her face white with misery as it had been when she had told him her sad story.

Except that at the end, the darkness which had surrounded him lifted, and he was at Steepwood, walking in the woods, and Louise was by his side, and when he turned to look at her, her face was rosy, and her eyes were filled with love and happiness. She was carrying a bouquet of winter flowers, and was saying to him, 'There, I wish to go there...'

He tried to speak to her, but in the doing the dream vanished and he was awake in the grey light of early dawn. But the shadow which had hung over him since he had heard his father's confession had lifted, and he was ready to face the day and the future.

Louise was tired of the knowing stares which she was receiving from some of her customers these days. They told her that they had heard the gossip linking her with Marcus. Oh, nothing was said openly, but it was plain that it was going the rounds of society and would continue to do so until some new piece of scandal arose to entertain those whose lives were so dull and empty that only the current tittle-tattle could enliven them.

She had just completed the trying on of the wedding dress of yet another young woman who was to marry at Christmas, and was sitting down alone in her little office for the first time that day, when the girl who kept the shop came in, saying breathlessly, 'Oh, Madame Félice, the gentleman who wanted you to make him a shirt is here again. He said, "Tell Madame that Mr Marks wishes to see her urgently on a matter of business."'

Marcus! It was Marcus, calling on her in Bond Street regardless of who might see him. Whatever could he want? What was urgent? At their last meeting he had seemed to say that he would send her the documents which Jackson had recovered from Burneck—but did his presence here mean that he had changed his mind?

Her assistant, still breathless—and was that just Marcus who made her so, or was it her usual habit and she had never noticed?—said, 'What shall I tell him, mam?'

'Madame Félice, not mam,' said Louise automatically. 'Tell him that I will see him.'

And when she did what would she say then? She had thought long and hard of what she ought to do. Marry Marcus—or not marry him? Make her claim to be Louise Cleeve, the present Earl of Yardley's distant cousin—or not? Try to have her marriage to Sywell annulled—or not? She had thought of that last action after Marcus had left her, since she had no wish to be known as the Marchioness of Sywell. After all, a brief examination by midwives would be enough to confirm her untouched virginity.

Once she had thought that if she could prove who she was then the decisions which would follow would be easy ones. No such thing…

Marcus's entry put an end to these musings. He was dressed in his Mr Marks' clothing and was carrying a despatch case—for her papers presumably. Why was it that when she saw him after a few days away from him he always looked particularly desirable?

Her wayward heart gave a frisky little jump when he came in, and her breathing shortened. She told her body to behave itself, but it wouldn't. The worst thing—or was it the best?—was that he did not even have to touch her to make her feel that her only rightful place was in his arms—a place which she had never really visited.

'Do sit down, Mr Marks,' she said to him as though he were a real lawyer's clerk. 'I take it that you have come to deliver my legal papers to me.'

Oh, the darling! was Marcus's internal response to that. I have only to see her to want to make her mine in the shortest time possible, and I do believe that the minx knows that and is teasing me! That must be a good sign.

'Indeed,' he replied, with an underling's bob of the head which set her smiling, and oh, what a joy to see her looking happy. 'I decided that it would be best to deliver the documents in person. That way I would know that you had received them.'

'Very thoughtful of you,' she returned graciously,

and put out a hand for them after he had extracted them carefully from the case. 'Particularly when I understood at our last meeting that you would not come yourself.'

Marcus smiled, and arranged it so that his hand touched hers at the precise moment of take-over. His reaction to that simple contact was rather like that of one of Signor Galvani's frogs when attached to a battery—all his senses jumped together.

By Louise's expression something similar was happening to her. She was becoming even more breathless than her little assistant. She began to put the papers down, but he said immediately, 'I think that you ought to check them against the list I have made. I have also your mother's diary to give you.' And he lifted that from the case and handed that over, too, again contriving to touch her hand.

This time Louise jumped. His smile broadened, particularly when she opened the book and began to examine it. In the middle of her delight at recovering it—a delight which was in some ways even greater than that which she had felt when he had handed her the proofs of her parents' marriage and her own legitimacy—she felt a tear gather and run down her cheek, to be followed by another.

'Oh, no,' she said, dashing a hand at them, only for Marcus to pass over her desk his large linen handkerchief to help to stem the cascade which followed the preliminary two.

'I'm so sorry,' she said, 'to behave like an errant

watering-pot, particularly when you have made me so happy. But this is the only thing which I have left to me which belonged to my mother, and to have it is bitter-sweet—joy and sorrow combined.'

It was a tribute to Marcus's delicacy—something which few who knew him would have thought that he possessed—that he knew what she meant. He was sorry to see her overset, but at the same time he was pleased that her manner to him was so different from that of their last meeting.

Indeed, it was as though their last meeting, with her rejection of him, had never taken place. One further proof of their new rapprochement, and their meeting of minds, came when Louise had wiped her last tear away and they both said together, 'I have been thinking...'

They looked at one another and both of them laughed, before they both said, together again, 'You first...'

Marcus put his head on one side and adopted what Louise always thought of as his Mr Marks face— one of humble and pleasant enquiry. 'Allow me to say that after our last meeting, which was so full of disharmony, I thought that we would never be able to speak to one another again. This meeting, how- ever, is so full of harmony that—'

He paused, for Louise to say smartly, 'That we can barely speak to one another because we are too busy saying the same thing!'

'Exactly,' said Marcus. 'Why do you think that is?'

'Because,' said Louise, a trifle warily, 'I have been thinking over our situation very carefully and, among other things, I have concluded that I behaved extremely badly to you at our last meeting. You had taken a great deal of trouble to find out something which I have wanted to know all my life, and your only reward was for me to reject you in the rudest fashion possible. After that I wonder why you should ever wish to speak to me again! I decided that when, or rather if, we next met I should try to be as civil as possible to you.'

'Oh, no,' said Marcus, 'do not reproach yourself. You had a great shock and when I began to think matters over I rapidly grasped how tactless I had been to propose marriage to you at such a juncture. You see, my darling, since wearing the lawyers' clerk's clothes I am beginning to talk exactly like one of them. My hurt pride made me short with you, and altogether I made a fine mess of things. But then, I always was a bull at a gate.'

'Dear Mr Marks,' said Louise affectionately, smiling at him through a shimmer of tears, present, but refusing to fall. 'The word you should have used was we. We both made a fine mish-mash of things, did we not? I refuse to allow you to take the blame.'

'By all means, let us agree to share it,' exclaimed Marcus. 'Recently I had a conversation with my father which made me realise how short life is, and how quickly we must grasp happiness to us when we meet it, lest it fly by and be gone forever. I immediately determined that I would come to you as soon as possible and try to mend matters. It does rather seem, though, that we are of like mind, since I take it, from what you have said, that you felt exactly the same as I did.'

'Indeed,' said Louise. 'But I also have to tell you that I have not yet made up my mind what to do about these...' And she waved a hand at the papers. 'There is another matter, too, which troubles me, and that is that I do not wish, ever, to be known as the Marchioness of Sywell, and I would want the marriage to be annulled—if that is possible now that he is dead. I was a fool to agree to marry him, but my guardian was dying when he begged me to accept Sywell. He had been so kind to me that I did not wish to distress him by refusing his last wishes. Nor did I then know how great a monster Sywell was. I wish to be rid of him, once and for all.'

'Well,' said Marcus, 'my advice is that you go to a genuine lawyer, and not the false one I am, and talk to them about the legal implications of your papers and whether or not you may petition for an annulment. I must say that I have no wish to marry the Marchioness of Sywell, even if Louise Cleeve agrees to my proposal. But I see by your expression that you have not made up your mind about that.'

'No.' Louise was restless.

She rose from her chair and walked to a small

side-table which held a jug of water and a pair of matching glasses. More so that she could recover herself a little and decide what she had to say in a manner which would not cause Marcus further hurt, than for any other reason, she said, 'I need a drink of water. Would you care for a glass, too?'

'Yes,' said Marcus, who understood that this delaying tactic meant that Louise was probably about to tell him something which he did not wish to hear. 'Talking is thirsty work, and I am not used to it. The farmers and artisans I deal with on father's northern estates are silent creatures. We converse in monosyllables.'

'And we have scarcely been doing that,' agreed Louise, handing him his glass. 'I hope that you will understand that what I am about to tell you is not my final word. The truth is that I am torn in two. You see, I am building up a fine business here in Bond Street and if I were to marry you then I should have to give it up. The wife of Yardley's heir cannot be a tradeswoman entering the homes of his friends as something little more than a servant when she is engaged on business there. On the other hand—' and she paused to take a sip of her so far neglected drink '—on the other hand I find that I am in love with Yardley's heir and would wish to be his wife. I trust that you see my dilemma.'

She had not yet sat down at her desk again, but stood before him having laid her glass upon it.

Marcus, his face ablaze, rose, and before she

could stop him, took her in his arms. 'You love me! That is all I know—and all I need to know. Oh, my darling heart, I have longed to hear you say these words. I have confessed my love to you, but I had no notion whether or not it was returned. Oh, to hell with words, they are not my *métier,* not my *métier* at all. This I do know—and it is better than any words.' And he began to kiss her passionately, his right hand holding her head, his left around her shoulders, so that his kisses might rove around her face like butterflies softly alighting.

He was, at first, gentle with her, for he knew her to be a virgin, and a virgin who might have been ill-treated by that swine, Sywell. At first she resisted him a little, but then her passion, fuelled by his, grew to the point where they were exchanging kiss for kiss and caress for caress until they were both so aroused that they neither knew nor cared what they were doing on the inevitable path to consummation.

Louise had never before experienced the sensations which were sweeping over her. For the first time she understood the power of the passion which could overwhelm a man and a woman: a passion which was heedless of propriety, of circumstance, of the social differences between them. So fiercely was she affected that her response to him surprised her.

They remained, twined together, lost to the world, until Marcus, the more experienced of the two, broke away from her, gasping, 'Not here, not now, anyone might enter and find us. I must not ruin you when you have not yet accepted my offer of marriage. You will accept it, won't you? Say that you will.'

Louise, her hair dishevelled, her eyes dilated, her lips swollen, and her face rosy from their recent passion, at last managed to offer him a coherent answer.

'I may not do so until I have solved my two conundrums—whether I wish to become Louise Cleeve, or whether I wish to remain Madame Félice. Oh,' she suddenly wailed, 'what shall I do, Marcus?' For since he had taken her in his arms and begun to make love to her, he was no longer either Lord Angmering, or simple Mr Marks, but only Marcus. Marcus who loved her. Marcus whom she now knew that she loved.

'I am being unfair to you,' she ended sadly. 'I know I am.'

'Unfair to both of us,' he whispered, still standing away from her, since he dare not touch her lest they both go up in flames again. 'Do not be long before you make a decision, I beg of you.'

'By Saturday,' she said. 'Visit me again on Saturday—as Lord Angmering this time. I am sick of shams. I have unknowingly lived a lie all my life, and do not wish to tell any more, either knowingly, or unknowingly.'

Marcus nodded agreement, even though the four days which would pass before Saturday arrived would seem an eternity.

It was only after he had gone, with one last agonised look at her, that Louise knew that, when she had told him to call on her as Lord Angmering, she had already—unknowingly—made her decision.

It only remained to inform him of it.

Chapter Eight

On his way home, for he had come to think of Berkeley Square as home, Marcus was accosted by none other than Jackson. If the Runner thought that M'lord was a little oddly dressed, nothing in his manner betrayed it to Marcus. Marcus, for his part, was too busy going over in his mind his recent encounter with Louise to trouble about such trifles as his clothing.

'A word with you, m'lord, if you would allow me the liberty of speaking to you in the street.'

'Certainly,' said Marcus. 'As you see, I am dressed for such an occasion. No one will remark upon us.'

'Quite so, m'lord—or should I call you Mr Marks?'

Marcus could not help laughing. He clapped the Runner on the shoulder, exclaiming, 'Is nothing hidden from you, man? Have you been tracking the man who employed you to track others? If so I can only commend you for your diligence—and your impudence. I cannot decide which is the greater.'

'Quite, so,' said Jackson with a grin. 'The more a thief-taker knows, the better he is at his chosen task. I have been keeping a weather eye on Madame F—which meant keeping one on you when you decided to visit her. Her little maid was very helpful. She told me when I took her to the fair that you were Madame's cousin—which, of course, is true— and a lawyer's clerk, which isn't. Now I no longer need to keep an eye on either of you. I suppose that your pa told you that my masters have decided to end the enquiry into Sywell's murder?'

'He did, indeed. Which leads me to wonder why you should feel a need to speak to me.'

'Well, m'lord, it's like this. One might think one knows who did commit the foul deed—if murdering the likes of Sywell can be called foul—but it's a different matter to prove it in a court of law. Convincing evidence is sadly lacking—all the possible principals having splendid alibis—including your pa, which let him off the hook. To be honest he was my prime suspect; he had a lot to avenge, what with his family losing the Abbey and all—but pinning him down might be difficult. Besides, my masters wouldn't like me to go around accusing belted Earls of murder without proof.'

He stopped and gave Marcus what could only be described as a meaningful leer. 'Now, you're a right sharp fellow—not in the least like most of the nobility and gentry I've had to deal with. Follow the plough and shoe the horse, eh? Now, if you'd not been in Northumbria when the deed was done, you'd have topped my list of suspects, but you had the best alibi of the lot—'

'I didn't know that I either needed one, or had one,' said Marcus with a grin as knowing as Jackson's.

'Aye, but like father, like son, I always say. Now, take your pa. Went to India and made a fortune didn't he? By his own efforts, and not many of the nobs do that. He's a man what does things, what looks after his own. A man I can respect, not a swine like Sywell. So then I ask myself, what's justice? Sure as fate, it ain't the law—or leastways, not always. I'm sure you takes my meaning. So, I tells my masters that, to my regret, I have no proof of who might have topped Sywell. I didn't say, after all I had heard about the swine, that whoever did it should be given a medal—except that he didn't finish the job properly, and do for that slimy devil Burneck as well. Now, *his* alibi interested me the most, particularly when I knew who had arranged it. Enough said, eh?'

'If I knew what you were trying to tell me, Jackson, I might agree with you.'

'Oh, but you do, m'lord, don't you? Now you may both sleep easy—for your different reasons acourse. I wish you well—though by the looks of him your pa ain't long got much longer on this earth.

Let's hope Heaven's law—or justice, call it what
you will, is better than ours. Who's to say?'

He gave Marcus one last bow, sweeping off his
greasy hat with an 'I bid you good day, m'lord,' and
was off, crossing the road, where he was soon lost
to view among the passing crowds.

He knows, thought Marcus dazedly, he knows,
and he has, in his own words, let my father 'off the
hook'. How the devil does he know?

Which was a question Marcus was never able to
answer to his own satisfaction. What he *did* know
was, that for his own reasons, Jackson had spared
his father obloquy and the hangman's noose.

Still another confrontation awaited him when he
entered Cleeve House. His father and stepmother
met him before he had mounted the main staircase
to go to his room to change into something more
fitting for the Earl of Yardley's heir.

They both stared at him. His father said, more
mildly than he would have done a few weeks ago,
'What the devil are you doing in that get-up,
Angmering? Bit early in the day for a masquerade,
isn't it?'

Thinking furiously on his feet, Marcus said cheerfully, 'I've been working with a friend's horse this
morning, and I'm about to change.'

'Really, Angmering? Really?' said the Earl. 'If
that was so, why are you not wearing something
more suitable than a clerk's clothing? I thought you

were one of Lawyer Herriott's men come to badger
me about my will. Which reminds me, I would wish
to speak to you this afternoon about some of the
minor details. You know the major ones so far as
they affect you already.'

'Certainly, father,' Marcus replied, stifling a grin
at his father's cheerful sarcasm about his clothes.
'When I am more suitably in the pink, perhaps, than
I am now. Or would a clerk's clothing be more suitable for examining a clerk's work than appearing
dressed as a member of the dandy set?'

Marissa who had also been smiling at this agreeable exchange of rudenesses, added her own contribution to them. 'My dear Marcus, however finely
you dress you never look remotely like a member
of the dandy set. Everything about you is too down-
to-earth for that.'

'Oh,' said Marcus, pulling a comic face, 'I can
see how much of a disappointment I am to you
both.'

'Indeed, not,' said Marissa, leaning forward to re-
tie his well-worn linen cravat for him. 'I much prefer
your down-to-earth manner to the false and artificial
compliments and dress for which the dandy set are
famous. The only thing is, I would dearly like to
know the reason for your present appearance. I hope
the explanation does you credit, that's all.'

'Very much so, dear Mama.' And Marcus gave
his stepmother a kiss on her cheek. 'When I ulti-

mately tell you the reason for it, you will quite understand and forgive me.'

With that he bounded upstairs to change into clothing more suitable for Yardley's heir. Its only drawback was that it was so much less comfortable than his clerk's humble attire. Nevertheless when he walked into his father's study to discuss the draft of the will which a true lawyer's clerk had left with him, the Earl looked approvingly at him, saying, 'I wish you would always take such care of yourself, Angmering.'

He received in reply another cheerful smile from Marcus, and: 'Exactly what my valet has just said to me, sir. Depend upon it, I will try to follow your joint advice in future.'

Even his father, usually so staid and proper, laughed at that piece of impudence.

'And now,' he said, 'let us get down to work. I informed you the other day of the main thrust of the will so far as it affects you, Marissa and the Neds. I do however, have one problem, and that relates to our cousin Rupert's lost daughter. The estate and its moneys came to me as the next Earl, unencumbered by any dower or provision for his child. I feel, though, that it is my duty to make some kind of reference to her in my will when all the other settlements are finalised.'

Marcus was in a quandary. He wanted to tell his father that Lord Rupert's daughter was no longer lost, and more than that, that he wished to marry her! But he had given his word to Louise to say nothing about her having the power to prove that she was the missing Cleeve daughter until she had decided whether to claim her birthright. Since he had once nearly lost her love because he had broken his word, he was of no mind to do it again—and lose her for good.

He sat silent for a moment before saying, 'I honour you, sir, for wishing to remember her, which was more than her father was able to do. Perhaps you could put in trust a sum large enough to give her a useful income if, by chance, she were ever found. Something in the order of what her father would have left her, had he been spared to return to England.'

'Excellent, Angmering,' said his father energetically. 'I was thinking of something along those lines. I will see to it immediately. Now there are a number of other, more minor matters we must discuss before Marissa summons us to partake of this newfangled notion, tea in the afternoon!'

Marcus nodded and they worked until Cardew threw the door open and announced, 'Tea is served in the blue drawing-room, m'lords.'

If Saturday could not come soon enough for Marcus, Louise was in the same case. One thing which he had said affected her more powerfully every time she thought of it: that she would be gaining a real family, something which she had never possessed before.

Sometimes this thought frightened her. She had already met Lady Yardley and Lady Sophia, and they both seemed to be good and kind—they had always treated her considerately—unlike some other great ladies. But what would they think, and how would they behave when a nobody of a *modiste* entered their lives claiming to be their cousin? How would society and the ton treat her then?

Her reappearance would, of course, create the most intense excitement. Some would not believe that she was Louise Cleeve, even though not only the documents which she possessed, but also her appearance, would give the lie to such doubts. Was it perhaps even possible that Marcus's reputation might be harmed if he married her?

Fortunately at this point her sense of humour, and her common-sense, took over. One thing was sure, Marcus would not give a damn about what others thought of him, or his reputation—so no need to trouble herself about *that*.

Her other worry about ceasing to be Madame Félice was soon put to rest. There was no reason why she should not continue to be the business's patron. She could put in her chief sempstress, a middle-aged woman of great competence and taste, as its manager. If Lord Yardley could run his India business from England then surely, she, when Lady Angmering, could run a business in London from an infinitely shorter distance. She would always be there to offer help and advice—if any were needed.

Thus the last obstacle to her agreeing to accept Marcus's proposal of marriage being out of the way, she would tell him on Saturday that she would accept it—something which she had once thought that she would never do.

But then, she had not realised how deeply she would fall in love with him: she could not visualise a world in which she and Marcus would not live together. The ugly ghost of Sywell, her late husband, was banished into a limbo from which it would never return, and she could only thank God that he had never made her his true wife.

Saturday morning saw her dressed in her most elegant walking-out gown. It was a pale green, to enhance her porcelain complexion and her hair. Cut on classic lines, it cleared the ground so that a pair of dainty black shoes with tiny silver buckles could be seen—as well as a pair of trim ankles. Her bonnet was so small that her hair and face were not hidden by it, and the ribbon which tied it was of the same colour as the dress.

That and her reticule lay beside her on the sofa when the housekeeper—the little maid was out on an errand—came in to inform her: 'A man who calls himself Lord Angmering is at the door and asking to call on you, but, madame, I think that I ought to inform you that he is the man who has been here several times before. He was then calling himself

Mr Marks.' She stopped, but was obviously bursting to go on, so Louise said gently, 'Yes, what is it? Something is troubling you.'

'Oh, madame,' said the woman anxiously, 'I know that you run a business and seem to know what's what, but you are still only a young woman. Do not think me impertinent, and do not know my place, if I tell you that the gentry and nobility often use such tricks in order to deceive and betray women whom they are pursuing. Pray be cautious, I beg of you. He seemed a nice enough young fellow when he called himself Mr Marks, but Lord Angmering—why, he may be quite a different kettle of fish—if you will pardon me for saying so.'

Louise rose and took her by the hand. 'Do not worry, my dear,' she said. 'It is kind of you to warn me, but I have known since I first met him that his true name is Lord Angmering. He called himself Mr Marks so as not to embarrass me, and his visit to me today is an honourable one. Now please go and admit him immediately. He has been kept waiting for so long that he may be thinking that something is wrong.'

'You are not annoyed by my frankness...' the housekeeper began.

'Indeed, not. Now do as I bid.'

If Louise thought that she had dressed herself rather magnificently for Marcus's visit, she found when he entered that he completely outshone her. He was, for once, dressed like a very tulip of fashion. His valet had outdone himself in his delight that M'lord should wish to look like a proper gentleman for once, and so he had told Marcus who had laughed, saying, 'Oh, do I usually look like an improper one, then?'

To have his man answer severely, 'You know perfectly well what I mean, m'lord. I wish that you always took such care. You really do repay for dressing, if I may say so.'

'Oh, indeed you may say so,' replied Marcus. 'But do not think that you are going to get me up like the veriest painted maypole every day. By no means. I prefer to be comfortable. I am sure that I shall not be able to sit down in these breeches.'

'Now you are funning, m'lord,' said his valet. 'I told the tailor that you didn't want them skintight and he nearly had a fit of the vapours at the notion that they might be loose, but I hounded him until he did my bidding. Not that that pleased me any more than it did him.'

'I wish to God you had to wear the damned breeches,' muttered Marcus, but he had to admit when he saw himself in the long glass that, as his man said again before he left, he looked ready to rival all the beaux who decorated London society— and what a pathetic ambition that was!

He got his reward, however, when Louise said to him, 'No wonder that my housekeeper was overset when she saw you. She has spent the last five minutes warning me against such fine gentlemen as you. She agrees wholeheartedly with the old song, "One foot on land, one foot on sea, Men were deceivers ever."'

'So that was why I was kept waiting on the doorstep,' exclaimed Marcus. 'I began to fear that you had changed your mind about receiving me.'

'No, I gave you my word, and I always keep it.' She looked expectantly at him. 'I assured her that your intentions were honourable. I do hope that you have not been deceiving me.'

'Not at all,' Marcus said, bowing low. 'But, for some reason, I do not wish to propose to you here. I have come in a curricle as well as in modish splendour, and I would like to drive you to somewhere romantical—I believe that is the word which ladies use—to make my proposal in the hope that it might soften your hard heart a little.'

He said this because everything about Louise's expression, added to her beautifully elegant toilette, seemed to tell him that he was about to receive a favourable answer. He hoped to God that he was going to be proved right—if only because wearing these damned clothes would not have proved a waste of time.

Or so he told himself, if only to prevent himself from being over-confident of the answer which he expected from her.

'I have never,' Louise told him, her eyes shining, 'been driven in a curricle before.'

'I guessed that, my darling girl, so I thought that

between providing you with a splendid treat, as well as allowing you to admire the River Thames from on high, I might, by doing so, be able to bend you to my wicked will—as your housekeeper might put it—except that, as you already know, my intentions are completely honourable.'

He offered her his hand, smiling and bowing, for he was sure of one thing—that if she were not prepared to accept him, Louise would not have accepted his offer of a drive in his curricle, either.

Outside the house a tiger, clad in gold and black stripes so that he resembled a large wasp, was holding the reins of two chestnuts who, he told Marcus, were rapidly growing impatient.

'Thought you was never coming out,' he grumbled, adding 'm'lord' as an afterthought.

The curricle itself was a gorgeous thing: like the tiger it was also picked out in black and gold.

'Yours?' queried Louise, entranced, when she was finally seated beside him, with the tiger up behind them—she had not associated Marcus with such a frippery thing.

'Alas, no,' he sighed. 'It belongs to a friend of mine, namely my sister's future husband, Sharnbrook, who has lent it to me with the promise that he will call me out for pistols at dawn if I do not return it to him in the same condition it was in when he handed it over. So I must ask you to behave yourself with due decorum at all times. No larking about which might disturb the horses, please, and cause an upset—not even larking of what I believe is called the genteel kind.'

Louise was growing to like it when Marcus teased her. She had never been teased—or flirted with—before. The normal life of most pretty young women had passed her by.

'I promise to behave myself,' she said demurely, 'just so long as you propose to behave yourself.'

'Now as to that,' said Marcus, preparing to negotiate a difficult corner in order to enter King's Road which, as was usual on a Saturday morning was full of traffic. 'The reason I came in the curricle was in order to propose to you in public, because were I to do so in your drawing-room, and were you to accept me, I fear that were we in private I should have a great deal of difficulty in controlling myself once you had done so! You, my darling girl, are temptation personified.'

'Really?' asked Louise. 'Really, Marcus?'

'Yes, really, and if you look at me like that again, we shall have the tiger telling me to behave myself. Tigers are the most dreadful tyrants, are they not, Jarvis?' he called over his shoulder.

'If you say so, m'lord.'

'I do say so.'

They were now running along the road towards Pimlico and Belgravia which ran parallel with the river, and where Louise was a little worried that they might be seen and recognised.

She told Marcus so.

'No need,' he said. 'We shall shortly stop and turn off on to the Embankment—you remember the Embankment?—where Jarvis will dismount and look after the horses and carriage for us. I have brought us a long way round because I wanted you to have the pleasure of the drive before I popped the question, as I believe it is called in lesser circles than ours.'

He gave a little laugh. 'What could be more romantical than proposing to you on the banks of the Thames in the middle of an Indian summer, as the Yankees call this warm autumn weather.'

Marcus is in such high spirits that he must be sure that I am going to accept him, thought Louise. I am, but how can he know that? Of course, what a nodcock I am! He knows me, and that I would not be dressed in the pink of fashion if I were going to refuse him—and here is the Embankment again, and I must think what I am going to say to him.

'This is the bench we sat on before,' said Marcus, after he had handed the curricle over to Jarvis and told him to take a short spin in it. 'You remember the occasion, I am sure. I was Mr Marks but you were still Madame Félice of unknown origin, and now I am Lord Angmering, and you are Louise Cleeve. Do you feel any different, my darling heart?'

'Oh, a little strange,' she said. 'But not much has changed yet. I am not Louise Cleeve, nor will be until the lawyers have settled matters. I went to one the other day, a man called Herriott. I had heard Lady Leominster talking of him. I showed him my documents and told him that Messrs Jackson and Burneck would testify that I was the child named in them who was rescued by John Hanslope all those years ago. I suppose that Mr Burneck will testify,' she added a trifle anxiously. 'So I am afraid that we shall have to wait a little before you can introduce me to your family as Rupert Cleeve's long-lost daughter.'

'Oh, yes,' said Marcus with a knowing grin. 'We can sic Jackson on to Burneck again if he tries to refuse. As for Herriott, he is a proper bulldog of a fellow I am told. You chose well.'

'Yes, but it seems that since Sywell is dead I may not have my marriage annulled because I cannot bring a lawsuit against a dead man. What I can do, he said, is renounce the title and call myself Louise Cleeve when that is settled. For the moment you are sitting beside Louise Hanslope. Apart from my business I shall not call myself Madame Félice again.'

'I don't give a damn what name you use when I sit by you,' said Marcus determinedly, 'since I am now about to ask you to marry me, and if you accept me, which I beg that you will, since I am so lost in love for you that I am beginning to fade away, you shall be Louise Cleeve, Lady Angmering. I can't go on my knees here—you will have to imagine that. Good God! I am beginning to wish that I had not been so virtuous. This would all be a deal easier if we had stayed at your home, and I could have kissed and cuddled you to my heart's content when you did say yes.'

'As I am about to do exactly that,' said Louise putting on an expression of mock severity, 'it is probably just as well that you brought me here, since I don't think that we should have stopped at mere kissing and cuddling—and I have no wish to go to my marriage forsworn, if you take my meaning. As for fading away, I have seldom seen you look more robust!'

'I'm marrying a Puritan, and a truthful one at that,' moaned Marcus extravagantly, 'and even if we are in public I am going to give you a surreptitious kiss.' And he proceeded to do so just as Jarvis brought the curricle back.

'Well done, m'lord,' said Jarvis when Marcus helped Louise back to the curricle. 'I see that you and your lady have not been wasting your time, if I may say so.'

'No, you may not,' said Marcus, but his voice was amused. 'Does Sharnbrook allow you all this familiarity?'

Jarvis sniggered. 'Oh, he's a rare one is His Grace. He likes to know what's what, and we go a long way back, but enough said about that.' And he put his finger by his nose. 'Home again, is it?'

'Back to my lady's,' said Marcus. 'We are about to celebrate our recent betrothal by drinking a decorous dish of tea. Then you may return the curricle to your master and I will call a Hackney cab to take me home again.'

'I thought that you dared not be alone with me,' Louise twitted him when Jarvis had disappeared down the road.

'Oh, that was before, but this is after. I will try to behave myself, but I cannot guarantee that I will. Cry no, if I exceed myself, and I promise to obey you.'

'Which puts the responsibility back on to me,' sighed Louise. 'What a fine marriage we are going to have, if this is how we begin!'

'Except that we are not yet married,' Marcus pointed out as they walked into the hall.

'True, now let me order nuncheon for two and at least try to be good while we eat that.'

'Am I to understand, then,' said Marcus, offering her a wicked look, 'that after nuncheon licence may reign supreme? I will be sure to remember that when afterwards arrives.'

Oh, what a wicked tongue he had! Louise had never enjoyed herself so much before. Her early life had been a hard one, with little fun and laughter in it, but Marcus was rapidly remedying that sad situation. She had never thought that love could be so happy.

Even while they were eating their nuncheon, served by a housekeeper delighted by the news that they were to be married and that her mistress was not to be the prey of an unscrupulous nobleman,

Marcus kept up a running fire of light-hearted raillery.

And afterwards? Why, afterwards he made gentle love to her, beginning to teach her its grammar, and nobly, at some pain to himself, refraining from taking her too far along the path towards their passion's final consummation. His reward was her flushed, joyful face, and after he had awakened her slumbering senses, her co-operation with him in the early games of love rapidly grew and blossomed.

At last, he disengaged himself gently from her and whispered hoarsely, 'You have not cried no, but I must. I would have a virgin bride, even if I do not deserve one, since my life has been as careless as that of most young men of title. I would not mock the wedding ceremony by anticipating it with you, and I believe you feel the same.'

Louise offered him dazed eyes. 'I had not understood how easily one might find one's self breaking the conventions which bind us. I have always wondered how girls could allow themselves to be seduced—but now I know. Had you chosen to go on making love to me, I could not have resisted you, so sweet and powerful are the feelings which are overcoming me. Are they overcoming you?'

'Of course,' Marcus said, privately cursing his errant body which was finding consummation rejected a painful experience. 'Which is why I stopped. Now we must order ourselves a little and make some plans for the future. I believe that you have agreed that you will declare yourself a Cleeve to my family, as soon as the lawyers have acted. Once that has happened we may tell my father and the others that we are betrothed. My sister, Sophia, as you know, is being married at Christmas. I would have preferred an earlier wedding, but I think that it would give my father and Marissa a great deal of pleasure if we were to be married at the same time. Unless, of course, your memories of Steepwood are too painful for you to agree to that.'

Louise shook her head. 'Not all my memories are painful. I remember some happy times with Athene, and I would wish for her, and her husband, to be present. It will be a strange experience for me to make my own wedding dress—and not someone else's!'

'So that is settled,' said Marcus, 'and now I must leave you, lest temptation strike again. When your legitimacy is settled we shall be able to meet more easily, and on equal terms—and I cannot wait for that day.'

'Nor I,' said Louise, and after he had gone she sat and dreamed of a time when she and Marcus would not be parted, and when she would have a family of her own, a settled place in the world, and a name which was not an assumed one.

Marcus's father had intended to stay only a short time in London, but his physician had persuaded him that he should not return to the country, where medical help for his condition would not be adequate.

'Wait until we are sure that we can do nothing more for you,' he had said. 'It is possible that my diagnosis may be wrong, and if so, you may need other treatment—again of a kind you would not easily find in the Midlands.'

'If I am going to die fairly soon I would prefer to do so at Jaffrey House,' grumbled the Earl. 'London is not my favourite place on earth—it's too smelly and too dirty.'

'Nevertheless,' the man persisted. 'It will not be for long, I promise you.'

Marissa had backed him, and even Marcus when consulted had said of his father's medical adviser in his own forthright way, 'Why buy a dog and bark yourself, sir?'

'You seem uncommon cheerful these days,' his father had replied, but he had taken his son's advice.

The Earl was dozing in his study some weeks after Marcus had proposed to Louise when his son came in—looking dashed happy as usual. He had to hope that he wasn't smoking opium like some other damned fools the Earl knew. The biggest damned fool was, of course, himself, since the physician had prescribed it to ease the occasional strong pain he had begun to feel.

'Sir,' Marcus said, 'I wish to talk to you about matters of some importance. I am of the opinion that you will be both relieved, and astonished, when I have finished.'

'Eh, what's that?' said the Earl, recovering himself slowly from sleep. 'Something about your coming management of the Abbey?'

'In a sense,' Marcus said. He wanted his father to be happy, because every day he seemed to grow more transparent, more wraith-like. His illness was beginning to consume him. 'It is about two things. One is my marriage, and the other is the lady whom I intend to marry.'

'Marry!' exclaimed the Earl. 'Have you come to your senses at last? If so, I shall be ready to die happy, knowing that everything will be in competent hands, and the continuance of the line will be ensured.'

'Well, as to that only time will tell,' grinned Marcus, 'and we still have the Two Neds to fall back on. However, I not only intend to marry, but the lady has agreed that the ceremony should be celebrated at Christmas at the same time as that for Sharnbrook and Sophia—if they are agreeable, that is.'

'But will not your bride's family wish to see her married from her home?'

'Well, as to that, sir, that is the second matter of which I wish to speak. I believe that she will, after a strange fashion, be married from her home. You see, my intended bride is none other than the missing daughter of Lord Rupert Cleeve, whom Jackson and myself, acting in company, have discovered. She is also the missing widow of the late Marquis of Sywell who was supposed to be the daughter of John Hanslope, his bailiff, and was always known as Louise Hanslope.

'She has proved her identity and her legitimacy beyond a doubt, and the lawyers are satisfied that her claim is a true one. An examination by midwives has also shown her to be virgin. I had to persuade her to reveal her identity, because she originally wished to remain private and anonymous, and not cause you all distress by making such a claim. But I have convinced her that she owes a duty to herself, and to our family, to reveal her true identity. I now have her permission to speak to you of this. I must also tell you that Marissa and Sophia already know her.'

Marcus paused, for now here came the difficult part of his explanation. His father's face was a picture of bewilderment when he had said that his stepmother and half-sister knew his proposed bride.

His father filled the pause by saying, 'You mean that I do not know the lady, but they do, but how can that be?'

'Because—' and Marcus bit the bullet '—she is now known as Madame Félice, the *modiste* who is making Sophia's wedding dress and trousseau.'

'And you are marrying her—a—dressmaker! How in the world did you ever come to know her?'

'That, sir, is a long story, and not to be told now,'

said Marcus firmly. 'But she is the woman I love and whom I intend to marry. I believe that you, too, will come to love her when you meet her. I wish to bring her here as soon as possible so that I may introduce her to her family as our cousin and my future wife.'

'Well, well, Angmering,' said his father. 'I suppose that you know what you are doing, you usually do. But I do hope that the lady will not wish to continue being a dressmaker after you marry her! Sywell's widow, you say? Now that is an astonishing turn-up, you must admit.'

And that, thought Marcus with an inward grin, was rather how he might have expected his father to react to what must have seemed to him, amazing news.

What he said was, 'Sywell's victim, say rather. His victim in every way, as I will shortly tell you.' And he informed his father in detail of what Jackson had discovered from Burneck.

When he had finished his father said grimly, 'More than ever I cannot regret having disposed of such a monster—other than that I might have brought dishonour on to the family if what I had done had become known. Poor child, to think that she was living the hard life of a dressmaker's apprentice and later of Sywell's victim when, if I had known of her existence, I should have been happy to take her into my home and treat her as one of my immediate family.'

Now if only my father will tell her *that,* thought
Marcus, returning to his room, all will be well and
my darling will have no regrets about declaring herself a Cleeve.

'Do I look well?' Louise asked her forewoman,
who was fitting her into a charmingly simple pale-
blue afternoon frock designed to give off an impression of youthful innocence. Marcus was due to
arrive at any moment to drive her to Berkeley
Square to meet her new family.

'I am sure,' he had said, 'that you have no need
to worry about your reception, you will find the
warmest of welcomes waiting for you.'

He had already told Marissa and Sophia of her
and they had both spoken of their new relative with
all the kindness and consideration which he had expected of them. But it is all very well for him,
thought Louise, for he is not the stranger who is, of
all people, Sywell's widow. Never mind that I shall
not acknowledge his existence, since I have formally
renounced my title, but that does not alter the facts
of the matter.

She was still feeling awkward, although her forewoman had assured her that she looked most *comme
il faut* and fit to be presented at court when, with
Marcus by her side, she was formally ushered by
Cardew into Cleeve House's splendid drawing-
room, where all the Earl's family were assembled.
For once the Two Neds were behaving themselves,

sitting demurely side by side on a sofa almost too dainty for their growing bodies.

They, together with the Earl, rose, and bowed deeply when Cardew bellowed, 'M'lord, Viscount Angmering and Miss Louise Cleeve.'

Louise blushed and looked towards Marissa and Sophia, who also rose, and offered her smaller bows. The moment they were over Marissa walked over to Louise to take her into her arms, after kissing her cheek, and murmuring into her ear, 'Oh, my dear, if only we had known of your existence we could have done so much for you. But now that you are to marry Marcus we must concentrate on making you both as happy as sandboys.'

She could not have said or done anything more calculated to put Louise at her ease. Marcus gave his stepmother a surreptitious smile: he might have known that she would turn up trumps, and Sophia, too, who said, smiling, 'I do hope that this does not mean that you will not be able to continue making my trousseau!'

'Not at all,' said Louise, 'for it is almost finished, leaving me plenty of time to make my own. They will be my swansong, you understand. In future my forewoman will run the business for me, and I shall provide any capital necessary to develop it further.'

'Excellent, my dear,' said Marissa, giving another approving smile. 'I must compliment you, Marcus, on marrying a lady with so much sound common-sense. The Yardley estates will have two splendid nonpareils running it and its future will be assured.'

The Earl, who had watched his wife and daughter take over Louise's welcome into her new family, now walked forward, saying, 'I had meant to offer you a more formal welcome, my dear, but as usual, I have been forestalled by my women! Rest assured that my pleasure on seeing you in your rightful place is as great as theirs.'

He had spent two mornings with his own, and Louise's, lawyers, examining papers and speaking to Jackson about his interview with Burneck. But it was not until the Earl actually saw Louise for the first time that any doubts about her true identity flew away.

'You are the exact image of one of my Cleeve cousins, Adelaide by name,' he said. 'You have her very look. If I had seen you on one of your previous visits when you came to fit Sophia I would have thought I was seeing a ghost—for Adelaide died in childbirth when little more than a child herself, and so she has always remained young for me.'

He did not add that he had had a *tendre* for her when he had been little older than the two Neds, but her father, who had been a great stock-breeder and improver of his sheep and cattle, had thought it unwise that cousins should marry, and they had been kept apart until she had been married off to a neighbouring squire.

Louise stared at him with great eyes and then,

before she could stop herself, she began to cry, gently and quietly. Marissa put an arm around her and said, 'Child, do not be distressed or overset. You must know how happy we are that Marcus is to marry you, and that you are restored to us.'

'I am not crying because I am sad or overset,' Louise said, through her slow tears. 'But because I am happy. No one, I do assure you, has ever said so many kind things to me in such a short time as you have done. No one has ever welcomed me so warmly. Indeed, apart from my dear friend Athene no one has ever welcomed me at all. You will think me a regular watering-pot, but believe me, I have seldom cried in the past, and hope not to do so in the future.'

She turned to Marcus and said, 'You will all think me most ungrateful for returning your kindnesses with tears.'

'No,' he said, thinking that she looked more beautiful than ever, with her eyes shining and her soft mouth quivering. 'It is most understandable. We all know that you have met with very little kindness while you were still Louise Hanslope and then Madame Félice. We will say nothing of Sywell, for he deserves nothing.'

Louise smiled through her tears at this blunt statement, so typical of Marcus. 'After that,' she said, 'I must contrive not to disgrace myself.'

'Tea!' exclaimed Marissa. 'That is what we need—and time for Louise to become used to us.

We have not even had the grace to introduce her to my Two Neds, who have been behaving in the most unusual fashion ever since you were announced. They are being so good and quiet that I fear that they may be sickening for something.'

'Pooh to that,' said Ned One cheerfully. 'It is because our tutor has been given the afternoon off so that we may join you in meeting cousin Louise. We seem to have very few relatives, so it is rather jolly to discover a new one—particularly when she is so pretty. Mark Anthony must be congratulated on his taste, as well as on his enterprise in discovering our lost cousin.'

'Oh,' said Louise, winning the two boys' hearts immediately, 'I can see that, whatever else, this particular Ned is well on his way to becoming a diplomat. Is the quiet one a diplomat, too?'

'Certainly not,' exclaimed Ned Two. 'I leave that to my senior. I wish to be a soldier, only Marcus tells me that once we have beaten the French there may not be any more wars for some time. That does not change my mind. To be a soldier and not worry about getting killed would add to the fun of wearing a uniform, not detract from it. Later on, Cousin Louise, I should like to show you my collection of toy soldiers—if Marcus can spare you, that is.'

'I should be delighted,' she told him truthfully, happy to be treated as one of the family. She had known few boys, but she could judge immediately that the Two Neds were splendid specimens of young manhood. It was already obvious that when they had gained a few more years both boys were going to be heartbreakers, whatever else they might become.

She listened with some amusement to their mother telling them both, with mock severity, to stop being frivolous, but Louise had experienced so little of such light-heartedness in her hard life that she welcomed it.

Tea, when it came, was a jolly meal, and after it the Earl asked her and Marcus to join him for some private conversation about the future.

'Angmering tells me,' he said, 'that you will be giving up your business in London and, once married, will make your home at the Abbey, when it has been improved to your taste and it is fit to live in. I have talked to my wife and we would both be most happy for you to form part of our household in Northamptonshire until you marry at Christmas—if that is what you would wish. After that I propose that, since Marcus will essentially take over the role of my retiring agent, you will live in his house until the Abbey is ready for you. After my death Jaffrey House would make a splendid residence for the Dowager Lady Yardley and the Two Neds. Such arrangements, are of course, subject to your approval.'

What could she say? With Marcus smiling happily at her, and the Earl so welcoming in his kindness, to refuse would be impossible even if she had wished to do so.

'I hardly know how to thank you,' she told him. 'Of course, I will do as you suggest—when I have wound everything up in London, that is.'

'Excellent,' said the Earl. 'Marissa is already planning your wedding, and that you should be married from the Cleeve household, as befits a member of the Cleeve family, can only add to our pleasure.'

And so it was settled. Later Marcus took Louise into the garden at the back of the house, and they had a few private moments to share their pleasure in one another's company.

'The trouble is,' groaned Marcus, after they had exchanged some hurried embraces away from the overlooking windows, 'that it is going to be deuced hard for me not to ravish you before Christmas. You grow more bewitching by the day—which shows what happiness and contentment can do to a person, I suppose—but I hardly like to tell you what it is doing to my contentment, to say nothing of my will-power.'

'So you don't mind losing your bet with Jack Perceval?' asked Louise, who was having some difficulties of her own in remaining as chaste as she ought before marriage.

'Not at all,' said Marcus. 'I had rather lose it, and gain you, than win it and not have you. I would wish that you would stand still for a moment, I have a mind to kiss you again.'

'Except that I think that we really ought to go indoors again. Your parents will be wondering what we are finding to do out of doors on a chill Autumn afternoon.'

'No, they won't,' said Marcus, with a meaningful grin. 'They will know perfectly well what we are doing—but you are right, if only because I am growing more desperate to ravish you by the minute, and much though I think that you might enjoy it, the back garden of Cleeve House is scarcely the most romantical or sensible place, to engage in such goings on.'

Reluctantly they drew apart, both wishing that Christmas—and marriage—would soon arrive, after which they could pleasure themselves to their heart's content. For the moment they would have to be happy in the knowledge that Louise, after her hard journey through life, had at last reached harbour with the man she loved—and who loved her.

Epilogue

Christmas Eve, 1812

'Oh, mam, I mean m'lady, you look like a fairy princess in that dress, indeed you do!'

Louise smiled down at her little maid, who had been translated from being her general help in Chelsea to being her personal maid since she had left London in mid-November to come and live at Jaffrey House before she married Marcus alongside Sophia and her handsome Duke. They had decided on leaving London once Louise's true identity became known, not only to society but also the Radical press.

Her sudden reappearance had, indeed, stunned society and produced enough *on dits* about her to last a lifetime. The last thing anyone wanted was that idle sensation-seekers would fill the church. Instead, the ceremony itself was to be held in the small private chapel at Jaffrey House before the bride's and groom's immediate families. Their friends and more distant relatives would attend a reception in the Great Hall. The Earl's staff and many of the faithful villagers from round about would be having a party in the kitchen after the reception was over and dancing had begun.

The only worry that Marissa and Marcus had was whether the Earl, who was daily failing, would have the strength to cope with such a demanding event.

'Nonsense!' he had exclaimed when Marissa had, cautiously, broached the subject with him. 'I would be a poor thing if I could not stand up at my children's weddings, particularly when I have spent the last ten years begging Marcus to marry.'

And so it was settled.

Rather than employ someone new to be her lady's maid, Louise had taken Mary Smith with her to Jaffrey House. Marissa's maid had instructed her in her new duties and Mary was rapidly losing her timidity and beginning to acquit herself with honour. She was already walking out with one of the footmen—and wedding bells seemed imminent.

'It's the most beautiful thing you've ever designed,' she said, adding diplomatically, 'after Lady Sophia's gown, of course.'

Louise thought that there was not a pin to choose between the two dresses. She said, a little shyly, for she was finding it difficult to believe that her time in exile was behind her and that she was really going to marry Marcus today, 'I hope that m'lord will agree with you when he sees it.'

'Oh, I'm sure he will. I don't suppose you know that Lady Yardley was very strict with him this morning. He wished to come and see you in your finery before the service, but she told him that on no account was he to do any such thing. It was bad luck, she said, and you had had enough of that already to last a lifetime. He wasn't best pleased, I can tell you, but M'lady said that seeing you were going to spend the rest of your days together, a few hours apart shouldn't be too heart-breaking for him.'

Now, wasn't that just like Marcus! The one thing she liked best about him was his positive forthrightness—so unlike her first husband's cunning evasion about everything. You always knew where you were with Marcus, whereas Sywell—and she really ought to stop thinking about him on this happy day—but for a moment she had remembered the dreadful nature of her first wedding, with Burneck standing at Sywell's shoulder and grinning away at them.

He had been invited to the party in the kitchen, Marcus had decreed, because he had turned up trumps in the end and had told the lawyers everything—even more than Jackson had wrenched out of him—so that her right to be called Louise Cleeve had been established beyond a doubt. Louise wasn't sure that she wanted him there, but Marcus's kindness was something else which she valued, so she had not argued with him.

Jaffrey House was crammed with guests: a large number from outside the county had been staying at some of the better inns, or with local landowners who had been invited to the joint weddings. Athene and Nick Cameron, together with Athene's mother, who had recently married the Duke of Inglesham, her first, and only love, had taken over the Filmers' old home. The Duke had had it renovated and improved in double quick time as an occasional refuge for him and his Duchess when London society became too much for them.

'Who would ever have believed that we should be here, having celebrated my wedding and being about to celebrate yours?' Athene had whispered to Louise when the Ingleshams and Camerons had called at Jaffrey House, the day before the wedding.

'Do you remember the many times we walked in the woods and talked about our prospects in life and our possible futures? You said to me on the last occasion on which we met before you ran away from Sywell, "I have no future—and no past, either," and now look at you! Louise Cleeve, long deprived of her inheritance, restored to it, and about to marry one of the nicest men in society—after my Nick, of course. It's better than a play, is it not? And as for my mama, words fail me, which, as you know, they rarely do.' And she looked across to where the Duchess, a smile on her pretty face, was talking eagerly to Marissa about her new and happy life. 'But she deserves all the happiness she can get.

I was always troubled that because she was so good and gentle she would remain lost in a country village for ever. It only goes to show that we never know what the next day may bring.'

'Which is fortunate,' said Louise in her quiet way. 'Because the next day is not always happy.'

'Oh, but tomorrow will be, that I do know,' said Athene in her forthright way—she was nearly as forthright as Marcus, thought Louise, amused and enlivened as she always was by her best friend.

'A double wedding cannot be other than a triumph. Inglesham says that everyone in London is furious at being deprived of the opportunity to be present, but commends your common-sense for depriving them! Nick, of course, agrees with him. By the by, have the Kinlochs been invited?'

'Invited,' said Louise, 'but they are unable to be present. Emma is breeding, is having a poor time of it and her Mama and Papa have gone to Scotland to visit her for Christmas, so they will be absent, too.'

'And thank goodness for that,' exclaimed Athene. 'But poor Emma, to have her mama inflicted on her at such a time—although Nick tells me that since she married Kinloch Mrs T's manner towards her daughter is greatly changed, and so it is to be hoped.'

'And what has Nick been saying that you quote him?' asked Athene's husband, who had come up to where they sat side by side on the sofa.

'Oh, Nick, there you are. I was telling Louise that

Mrs Tenison no longer bullies Emma so much now that she is married to a peer of the realm.'

'True,' said Nick, and the three of them, Louise remembered, chatted together about this and that— 'Because,' said Athene, 'you will have little time to spend on us when you are busy tomorrow entertaining the hordes who I understand have been invited.'

Now she gazed at the clock, and realised that she would shortly be no longer plain Louise Hanslope but fancy Louise Cleeve who was about to marry her Prince Charming. And what a comic name that was for forthright Marcus Cleeve! But it suited him because he had rescued her, and made sure that she did not have to run away before midnight, but would be waiting for him to marry her without the intervention of fairy godmothers. Nor did she have any ugly sisters nor a wicked stepmother either.

Only Marissa, who was Marcus's stepmother, and she was proving to be the mother whom she had never had. On cue, as if she had read her mind, Marissa entered, to help Mary put the final touches to Louise's toilette.

'Oh, you look ravishing,' she exclaimed, handing her a spray of Christmas roses, white chrysanthemums, winter jasmine and green Christmas ferns, tied round with a wide cream sash ending in a giant bow. 'And here is your bouquet. The gardeners collected the flowers from the hothouse for you and Sophia this morning, and my maid and I prepared them for you both.'

Impulsively Louise leaned forward and kissed her benefactress on the cheek. 'You have been so good to me,' she murmured, the tears not far away. 'I did not know such kindness existed.'

Marissa smiled at her. 'This is no time for repining,' she said. 'Marcus and Sharnbrook are already making their way to the chapel, and you must be ready to join them in a few moments, and do exactly what you did at yesterday's rehearsal. Remember that afterwards you and Sophia and your bride and groom will enter the drawing-room on either side of the Earl and will be led in by Cardew, who will announce you.'

'I know I am being silly,' Louise said, 'but how is it that it all seemed so easy yesterday, but today I am all of a quiver?'

'Oh, wedding day nervous fits are commonplace,' said Marissa, smiling again. 'I was supposed to be beyond such megrims, but when I married Marcus's father I was barely able to walk down the aisle. That—and the Earl's frail health—persuaded me that a small private ceremony at Jaffrey House might be the best thing for us all. To be married among friendly surroundings takes much of the apprehension away—at least I hope it will for you.'

It had certainly taken it away from Sophia, who was on her highest ropes, but Louise found the whole business so dazzlingly exciting that the ceremony, and the reception afterwards, passed in a dream.

Was it she who walked towards Marcus, Sharnbrook, and the waiting parson? Or was it someone else? She remembered that Marcus had never looked so handsome, that the Parson had smiled at her, that she managed to say all her lines in the right order, and if her voice had sounded strange to her, it seemed to have appeared quite normal to everyone else.

Marcus had kissed her at the end, whispering, 'Welcome, Lady Angmering, to your new title.' After that she and Marcus, Sophia and Sharnbrook walked ahead of the Earl and Countess and the rest into the Great Hall, where the other guests were waiting for them. The hall had been decorated with boughs of holly and ivy to celebrate Christmas as well as the weddings of the house of Cleeve.

A long table, piled high with food, had been laid at one end of it—the whole arrangement being rather like those in exclusive gaming hells, was Marcus's private joke to Sharnbrook. Chairs and little tables had been distributed around the walls so that the guests might have somewhere reasonably comfortable to sit.

Everyone clapped when they entered, and after the formalities were over, conversation became general, and friends who had not seen each other for many months found one another after the newly-weds had received them, and rapidly began to exchange news and views.

'I had so hoped to meet Beatrice and Harry

Ravensden,' exclaimed Lavender Brabant. 'I know that they were invited, but I gather that like Lewis's wife, Caroline, Beatrice is also breeding, and the journey here would have been too much for her.'

'Oh,' said Athene, 'they are very much in the fashion, for she is not the only one. I am beginning to think that there must be something in the air of Northamptonshire to produce such an army of babies! Jack and Olivia Denning are also unable to be present for the same reason, but I gather that there are others here who have been more fortunate, since their condition has allowed them to travel.'

'And you, Athene?' asked Lavender, her eyes alight with mischief. 'Are you one of that number?'

Athene offered her a sphinx-like smile. 'At this present moment, my dear, all that I can say is, perhaps, but I am hopeful. And you? I hear that I must congratulate you on being delivered of a book. A Flora, I believe, most apt. I shall boast about you when I go north. It is not everyone who knows an author.'

Lavender's pleasure was apparent. 'You are very kind,' she said. 'But I fear it is only a modest offering—not at all like something written by the Author of Waverley.'

'But much more useful,' returned Athene, 'only you must not tell Nick so! Being a true Scot, he is sure that no one can compare with a writer who comes from Caledonia. I need not ask if you are happy,' she added, before moving on. 'Both you and

Barnabas look like the man who lost a halfpenny and found a half-crown! I hope to speak with him before we leave. At present he is being cornered by Dungarran. They are probably having a jolly coze about Newton and numbers!'

On the contrary, as Lavender later discovered, Barnabas had been quizzing Dungarran about the marriage state. 'I gather,' he had just said to him, 'that you and Hester are the Romeo and Juliet of Steepwood. How are you faring now that you are married? Do you talk about mathematics all day and everyday—or only on Sundays when the Parson's sermon has been dull?'

'Not all the time,' returned Dungarran with a straight face, before reducing the crowd about him to happy laughter by saying, 'But I do have to tell you that addition having been completed we are now multiplying.'

Barnabas was, for once, a little slow in grasping the joke, but on doing so said with a grin, 'Oh, I suppose that you mean Hester is expecting. Congratulations and all that.'

'Accepted,' said Dungarran with a bow, 'and I gather that you, too, are to be felicitated, you lucky dog. It is not everyone who acquires a vast inheritance—but I suppose that you deserve it more than most. Looking around me, I would hazard a guess that most of our friends and relations have much to be pleased about.'

'Yes,' said Barnabas. 'The odd thing is that most

of our good luck seems to have occurred since Sywell's demise, but we'd better not dwell on that.'

'No, indeed,' agreed Dungarran. 'I understand that the Home Office has given up the search for his murderer, on the grounds that they are desperately short of staff, and that rather more important crimes need to be solved. After all, Sywell was no great loss.'

'True,' replied Barnabas. 'I must say that I am relieved to have heard the last of that business. So long as that shadow was hanging over us, no one connected with the wretch could be truly happy today.'

They were not the only persons present who touched briefly on Sywell's murder, but no one was tactless enough to mention it to Louise, or any of the Yardleys.

Louise, indeed, looking around her, Marcus's comforting presence by her side, many of her friends and acquaintances enjoying themselves before her, was starting her new life by banishing her old one to the shades.

Marissa whispered in her ear, 'You look even more radiant than you did this morning, and your deportment during the wedding ceremony was all that was perfect. You see how foolish your fears of the morning were.'

So she had not disgraced herself as she had feared, and now she could enjoy herself. Hugo Perceval was coming towards her, his wife,

Deborah, by his side, looking as radiant as Louise was beginning to feel. She must be sure to congratulate them prettily when they had congratulated her.

Alas! On their way towards her Deborah half-turned to acknowledge a friend she had just seen, and in the doing she collided with a footman carrying a trayful of glasses of champagne to the long table. Glasses and champagne cascaded to the carpet, but by great good fortune many of the glasses remained unbroken, so that the champagne missed drenching most of the surrounding guests.

Deborah looked at Hugo in dismay. He grinned, 'Things are improving, my love. Usually I am your victim, but I seem to have escaped unscathed this time.'

'Oh, Hugo, I never mean any of it to happen, you know that.' She sighed. 'It's very sad. I haven't had an accident for ages.'

'No, indeed. Not since you drove us into the duckpond shortly after our wedding,' he agreed, smiling down at her.

'What an unhandsome thing to say! That wasn't my fault,' she began indignantly. Then, with a characteristic change of mood, she said gloomily, 'What a liability I am. I don't know why you put up with me.'

Hugo laughed and raised her hand to his lips. 'Deborah, you are the delight of my life, and I adore you. I wouldn't change you for the world.'

He led her to where the Duke and Duchess of

Inglesham sat with Athene Cameron and her husband Nick in an octagonal recess away from the main noise in the room, but where they could see everything which happened. They were busily engaged in enjoying the good food and wine which the Yardleys had provided in such quantity.

Hugo said, 'Sit here, Deborah, my darling, and talk to Athene while I collect some food and wine for us. She is sure to make you laugh.'

'Now that,' said Athene, with mock severity, 'is a statement certain to doom me to conversation of such absolute dullness that all it will result in will be heavy yawning—but do fetch Deborah something nice. We can all eat, drink and be merry together.' And she pulled forward a chair for the embarrassed Deborah.

'Oh, you cannot imagine how...' Deborah began to Athene, who gave a jolly laugh in reply, saying, 'Oh, yes, I can. I tripped over my overlong court dress when I was presented to the Prince Regent. Imagine my consternation and the expression of all the flunkeys present when I ended up in a position suitable for someone who wished to kiss his feet. Now that is true embarrassment.'

'Are you funning me, to make me feel better,' asked Deborah doubtfully.

'Indeed not. That is all perfectly true, is it not, Nick?'

'Yes,' nodded Nick. 'The only person present not overset was the Regent himself, who said, ''The spectacle of a pretty woman prostrate before one is a sight to delight Princes is it not?'' And then he offered her his hand to enable her to rise. More than that, her popularity was ensured when she did so without apology and offered him a grand curtsey before moving on.'

Hugo returned with 'enough fodder to feed a regiment', as he informed them cheerfully, to find his wife chattering animatedly away, all her hesitant and apologetic manner quite gone.

Of course, as Nick and the Duchess well knew, the whole Prince Regent farrago was a total myth designed by kind Athene, and adroitly supported by her husband, to put poor Deborah at ease, and in that it certainly succeeded. Louise, meanwhile, might have lost Deborah and Hugo to talk to, but she had gained Dungarran and Hester, who were invited by the Earl to join them at the separate table before the empty hearth where the main wedding party was about to be served.

Once seated, Dungarran leaned over towards Marcus, saying cheerfully, 'I was never so surprised in my life as when I received an invitation to your wedding, Angmering. Some fellow named Jack Perceval who claims to be a distant relative of mine—with what justice I don't know—said that he had a bet with you that you would not be married before the year was out. He took you on—and here you are—well and truly hitched. Was there any truth in his claim or was it just a silly *on dit?*'

Marcus, with one rueful eye on Louise, said, 'Yes, indeed, and willy-nilly I paid Perceval his winnings when I lost my bet. Not that it was a major sum, mind you, but even if it had been, once I met my wife, I knew I was going to have to cough up. What's money compared with winning a peerless woman?'

'What indeed! But I have to inform you that, charming and clever though your wife is, she is not peerless so long as my Hester is in the running for such a title.'

'To say nothing of my Sophia,' quipped Sharnbrook, breaching etiquette by kissing his bride on her cheek. 'If there are any peerless stakes being run she is sure to be a prime candidate!'

'There speak three happily married men,' said the Earl, who had been listening to what his son had got up to with some amusement. 'I thought that you never gambled, Angmering, but now I know differently.'

'Ah, well, sir,' said Marcus with a grin. 'I only did so that night because I was half-cut and miserable—unusual states for me, you will agree.'

'That is true,' admitted his father. At which point Ned Two leaned forward and said, 'I thought that you never got drunk, Marcus. What a horrid bad example you do set to the pair of us, eh, Ned One? I shan't listen to another of your lectures about *our* bad behaviour after hearing that.'

'Now, boys,' said their mother. 'You are not to

be impertinent towards your brother on his wedding day.'

Ned One, from his position down the table, said, 'Does that mean that we can be impertinent towards him on all other days, Mama?'

'Oh, I can see that we have a future logic-chopping lawyer here,' said Dungarran, laughing. 'A Lord Chief Justice, no less.'

Ned One shook his head vigorously, 'Indeed not, sir. Marcus told us that you are a noted mathematician, and that is what I intend to be when I leave Oxford. Perhaps you could give me some advice on the matter, after luncheon is over.'

'Well, if I can't,' said Dungarran, raising his glass in Ned One's direction, 'then Hester will. I am the more pedantic of the pair of us, and she is the more original—a regular female Pascal.'

Hester, thus called on, engaged in mock reproof of her husband. 'Now Dungarran,' she said. 'Behave yourself. You make me sound fearsome, but no matter, I shall be only too happy to help Ned with his maths.'

This lively and light exchange set the tone for the table's conversation. Louise, who was already dazed by the mere fact of being married, was quite overcome by the cheerful banter which went on around her. She had never before been a member of a happy family party, and so she whispered into Marcus's ear.

'Are they always like this?' she ended.

'Usually,' said Marcus. 'But particularly so today, when they can see how happy Sophia and I are.'

'Truly,' said Louise, who could scarcely believe that she had finally arrived in what seemed to her an earthly paradise. Oh, she was not foolish enough to believe that there would be no unforeseen pitfalls in her future life, but to someone who had always been ignored, exploited, overlooked and neglected they would be as nothing compared with what she had experienced in the past.

Toasts were exchanged, and she soon began to understand that if she were not to end up under the table she must only take a sip of her wine at each tribute which was offered to her. The noise in the room grew—and that, too, was a new experience for her.

Marcus saw that she was becoming not so much weary as bewildered by all that was going on around her. When the syllabub at the end of the meal was served, he whispered to her, 'After we have eaten our dessert, we must rise and tour the room making our formal farewells to our guests. Then the musicians will enter once the remains of our meal are cleared away and you and I, Sharnbrook and Sophia will lead the first dance before leaving. The celebrations will go on long after our departure.'

Secretly Louise was relieved to hear this. She was enjoying herself, but she wanted to be alone with Marcus as soon as possible—and she knew that Sophia felt the same about being with Sharnbrook.

They were not leaving Jaffrey House, but would retire to a suite of rooms there, while she and Marcus would drive to the land agent's house near the Abbey. It had been made ready for them to live in until the Abbey had been repaired, redecorated and provided with new furniture, all fit for the heir to an Earldom to enjoy.

Touring the room was a happy event, though. Everyone was smiling, everyone seemed to be as happy as they were. Athene said to her, her voice low, 'I can only wish you as fortunate as I am with Nick. I like your Marcus. He seems a sterling fellow and everything which you deserve in life.'

'Oh, he is,' said Louise fervently. 'And I am so happy for you, too.'

The last persons to whom they said farewell were the Earl and Marissa. If the Earl looked even more frail than usual, his pleasure at seeing his son happily married was so evident that it overshadowed their fears for him. Marissa, of course, wished them all the best, and the Two Neds were as irrepressibly naughty as usual.

After that the newly-weds visited the kitchens where the servants were busy laying out their own banquet, and the butler led the toasting to their future happiness.

Once they were in the entrance hall with the doors open while they waited for their chaise to be brought round, Louise, her bouquet in her hand, was astonished to see that it was still daylight, and said so.

'Which,' returned Marcus, 'is not surprising, seeing that it is only two thirty on a fine, if cold, December afternoon. I must say,' he added, 'that I am glad to be alone with you at last. My face has grown quite stiff from smiling at people and making small talk. Not my thing at all.'

'Nor mine, either,' agreed Louise, 'which is ungrateful of me, I know, since everyone seemed genuinely happy to see us married.'

'Particularly my father,' said Marcus. 'He thought that I would remain a bachelor, turning in due time into one of those old men who sit in London clubs grumbling that everything is going to the dogs!'

Their chaise finally arrived on the gravel sweep, and before they were helped into it, Louise turned to Marcus and said, 'I trust that you have not forgotten to inform the coachman of our first destination.'

'No, I made quite sure that he will not take us straight home. I see that you still have your bouquet with you.'

'Yes. Sophia threw hers into the room before we left, and it was caught by one of Dungarran's sisters.'

Marcus laughed and kissed her before they set off, saying, 'I assume that she's yet another mathematician in that family, since Ned One was so taken by her that he could not stop talking to her. By the by, when we stop will you be warm enough in what you are wearing, or shall I help you into your pelisse before we leave the chaise?'

'Please,' said Louise, and then lay back, silent, watching Marcus, still scarcely able to believe that she was actually married to him.

'The only thing which I ask of you,' he said, leaning forward to take her hand in his, and looking deep into her eyes, 'is that we do not take too long over your mission, since I have been in a truly wretched state ever since the Parson pronounced us man and wife. If I don't get you into bed with me soon I'm fearful that I shall need a doctor to minister to me before we get there.'

'Oh, I think that I can provide you with all the necessary ministrations when we do arrive there,' said Louise naughtily.

'Hope deferred maketh the heart sick,' quoted Marcus mournfully.

'On the contrary,' returned Louise, 'the old adage has it that "Desires are nourished by delays."'

They both laughed together, and Marcus remarked, 'It is fortunate that most proverbs and old sayings contradict one another, thus providing us with a contest which neither of us can win.'

'And, seeing that it is our wedding day, that is a most excellent thing,' was Louise's answer to that.

They were still laughing when the coach stopped at the edge of the wood in which the Sacred Grove stood. Louise took off her pretty white kid slippers and exchanged them for a pair of stout shoes which they had brought with them. The shoes which Marcus had worn to be married in were stout enough for him to walk on the path through the wood. The day was moving towards its close, the sun was riding behind a cloud and the dark wood lay before them.

'Fortunate it is,' she said to Marcus, after the footman helped them down, 'that it is a fine day, even if a little gloomy now.'

'Our first walk as a married pair,' said Marcus. 'Take my arm, Lady Angmering.'

'Willingly, Lord Angmering,' she replied, and they strolled along the path towards the heart of the wood, passing from light into dark as the trees clustered nearer and nearer together. They fell silent, for there seemed something almost mystic about their journey which compelled a holy quiet. Finally they reached the Grove and the rune stone which stood in its centre.

'There,' said Louise, as she had done in Marcus's dream. 'I wish to go there,' and she pointed to the stone.

Facing it was an iron bench, placed there by some long-gone Earl of Yardley. Marcus had brought a blanket with him, which he spread on its seat before they sat down.

After they had remained silent for a short time, he asked her, 'Now, Lady Angmering, tell me why you wished to come here and why you have brought your bouquet with you.'

'Because...because Athene and I often visited the Grove and tried to imagine what the people were like who carved the runes on the stone and called it Sacred. We both knew of the legend: that the pagans who built it cursed all those who might come after and who would not worship the stone as they ought. The curse said that the new owners of it would not prosper—and who is to say that the curse was not effective? Think only of the Dissolution of the Monasteries, the ruin of the Abbey, and after that the unhappy lives of the Cleeves, Earls of Yardley, who took over Steepwood, until they lost the Abbey to Sywell—and then remember how horrible his end was. Now we shall inherit them both: the land and the curse.

'The gypsy fortune teller told us that she had lifted the curse on us, so perhaps we shall be safe, but I wish to see it lifted for everyone who comes after us. I don't like to think of our descendants inheriting unhappiness and ruin, and so I want the curse to end once and for all. That is why I asked you to bring me here today, and why I brought my bouquet. I want to lay it before the rune stone, and tell it, and its attendant spirit, that we honour the men who erected it, and the women who lived with them. That being so, we beg them of their mercy to lift the curse, so that the Cleeves, and those who might come after them, may live and die as ordinary people, not as those doomed. Do you think me foolish, Marcus?' she ended.

'No, my dear,' he said, 'never foolish. Besides, it cannot hurt to try to exorcise the curse. Lay your flowers before it, and say your prayer.'

Louise rose. She knelt before the stone, regardless of what it might do to her finery, and placed the bouquet between herself and the side of the stone with the runes carved on it.

'Accept this offering of my wedding bouquet,' she said. 'We honour those who made you, and beg most humbly that since we also honour the spirit of the stone, you lift the curse not only from us, but from our children. We beg you to send us a sign that you have accepted my offering so that we may not see them, or their children's children doomed to unhappiness.'

She put her hands together as if in prayer, and knelt there for a little time before beginning to rise.

Even as she did so, the sun broke through and a ray of the purest light, the first of the day, streamed out to illuminate the stone and the bouquet which lay before it.

'A sign,' Louise breathed. 'A very sign.'

She turned towards Marcus, holding out her hands to him. He took them, then swept her into his arms to kiss her on the lips, not with the passion which he was later to display, but with reverence.

'Sign or not,' he said, 'I commend you for what you have done. And now, Lady Angmering, let us go home and bless our marriage in the time-honoured way.'

'Yes,' she said, and they walked towards their waiting coach, and to the happy future which lay before them, their children, and their children's children.

*   *   *   *   *

The Steepwood Scandals *may be over,*
but July 2007 sees the launch of an exciting
new Historical continuity:

The Medieval Lords & Ladies Collection

Don't miss the first thrilling and romantic volume,

Conquest Brides.

A young woman disappears.
A husband is suspected of murder.
Stirring times for all the neighbourhood in

THE STEEPWOOD
Scandals

Volume 1 – November 2006
Lord Ravensden's Marriage by Anne Herries
An Innocent Miss by Elizabeth Bailey

Volume 2 – December 2006
The Reluctant Bride by Meg Alexander
A Companion of Quality by Nicola Cornick

Volume 3 – January 2007
A Most Improper Proposal by Gail Whitiker
A Noble Man by Anne Ashley

Volume 4 – February 2007
An Unreasonable Match by Sylvia Andrew
An Unconventional Duenna by Paula Marshall

A young woman disappears.
A husband is suspected of murder.
Stirring times for all the neighbourhood in

THE STEEPWOOD

Scandals

Volume 5 – March 2007
Counterfeit Earl by Anne Herries
The Captain's Return by Elizabeth Bailey

Volume 6 – April 2007
The Guardian's Dilemma by Gail Whitiker
Lord Exmouth's Intentions by Anne Ashley

Volume 7 – May 2007
Mr Rushford's Honour by Meg Alexander
An Unlikely Suitor by Nicola Cornick

Volume 8 – June 2007
An Inescapable Match by Sylvia Andrew
The Missing Marchioness by Paula Marshall

Medieval
LORDS & LADIES
COLLECTION

When courageous knights risked all to win the hand of their lady!

Volume 1: Conquest Brides – July 2007
Gentle Conqueror by Julia Byrne
Madselin's Choice by Elizabeth Henshall

Volume 2: Blackmail & Betrayal – August 2007
A Knight in Waiting by Juliet Landon
Betrayed Hearts by Elizabeth Henshall

Volume 3: War of the Roses – September 2007
Loyal Hearts by Sarah Westleigh
The Traitor's Daughter by Joanna Makepeace

6 volumes in all to collect!

Medieval LORDS & LADIES

COLLECTION

VOLUME ONE
CONQUEST BRIDES
*Two tales of love and chivalry
in a time of war*

Gentle Conqueror by Julia Byrne

Lisette knew there was little she could do to resist
her Norman overlord – but she was determined to try.
Her delicate beauty belied her strength of character,
and her refusal to yield won Alain of Raverre's respect.
Now the courageous Norman knight would have
to battle for Lisette's heart!

Madselin's Choice by Elizabeth Henshall

Travelling through war-torn England, she needed a
protector. To her horror, the haughty Lady Madselin
was escorted by an arrogant, rebellious Saxon!
Edwin Elwardson's bravery and strength soon
captivated her. Yet could Madselin defy her
Norman upbringing and follow her true desire?

Available 6th July 2007

...International affairs, seduction and passion guaranteed

Volume 1 – July 2007
The Future King's Pregnant Mistress by Penny Jordan

Volume 2 – August 2007
Surgeon Prince, Ordinary Wife by Melanie Milburne

Volume 3 – September 2007
Bought by the Billionaire Prince by Carol Marinelli

Volume 4 – October 2007
The Tycoon's Princess Bride by Natasha Oakley

8 volumes in all to collect!

THE ROYAL HOUSE OF NIROLI

...International affairs, seduction and passion guaranteed

VOLUME ONE

The Future King's Pregnant Mistress
by Penny Jordan

As the King ails and calls for his heir, it's time for playboy prince Marco to claim his rightful place...on the throne of Niroli!

Marco Fierezza: Niroli's playboy prince, he's used to everyone obeying his every command... especially the women he beds!

Emily Woodford loves Marco, but she knows she's not marriage material for a future king. It's devastating when Marco summons her to Niroli as his mistress to continue their discreet affair.

But what will this king-in-waiting do when he discovers his mistress is pregnant...?

Available 6th July 2007

The Regency
LORDS & LADIES
COLLECTION

Two glittering Regency
love affairs in every book

MILLS & BOON

www.millsandboon.co.uk

The *Regency*

LORDS & LADIES
COLLECTION

Two glittering Regency
love affairs in every book

MILLS & BOON

www.millsandboon.co.uk